Margot Radcliffe  now, but surrenders years, so it's hard to Regardless of locat side while she write make readers laugh heroines who aren't afraid to take what they want, and confident heroes who are up to a challenge. She loves creating complicated, modern love stories. She can be found @margotradcliffe on Twitter and @margot_radcliffe on Instagram.

Regina Kyle knew she was destined to be an author when she won a writing contest at age ten, with a touching tale about a squirrel and a nut pie. By day, she writes dry legal briefs. At night, she writes steamy romance with heart and humour. She is a two-time winner of the Booksellers' Best Award. A lover of all things theatrical, Regina lives in Connecticut with her husband, daughter and two melodramatic cats. When she's not writing she's most likely singing, reading, cooking or watching bad reality television.

SINFULLY YOURS

MARGOT RADCLIFFE

DIRTY SECRETS

REGINA KYLE

MILLS & BOON

First Published in Great Britain 2020
by Mills & Boon, an imprint of HarperCollins*Publishers*
1 London Bridge Street, London, SE1 9GF

Sinfully Yours © 2020 Terra Rogerson

Dirty Secrets © 2020 Denise Smoker

ISBN: 978-0-263-27768-5

MIX
Paper from
responsible sources
FSC® C007454

This book is produced from independently certified FSC™ paper
to ensure responsible forest management.
For more information visit www.harpercollins.co.uk/green.

Printed and bound in Spain
by CPI, Barcelona

SINFULLY YOURS

MARGOT RADCLIFFE

MILLS & BOON

To Christina and Potter,
for reading literally anything!

CHAPTER ONE

LAURA EDWARDS LOVED CHRISTMAS. Not just because she rivaled Mariah Carey as the queen of Christmas either, though that was very true, but because standing in the lobby of the hotel she'd been hired to transform into a winter wonderland made the foster-care past that always seemed to haunt her seem far behind. A time so faded from her memory that it was almost as if it hadn't happened at all, which was just what she'd always wanted.

"Could you move the silver garland up a little farther?" Laura asked her assistant Maisey before she stepped forward to the massive twenty-foot tree and fixed the glittery beaded strands herself.

Maisey gave her a wry side-eye which Laura had received an inordinate number of since this particular hotel job began nine months ago. It might be possible that Laura's level of micromanaging had skyrocketed since landing the lucrative #goals job for the exclusive WW hotel chain, but it would be worth it in the end. This client was going to catapult her business to the next level of success, her name synonymous with event decorating in every major city in the country. Since she'd moved to New York five years ago, she'd been building her business, taking any and all jobs she could, but this was the break that would take her from boutique business to industry go-to.

Once out of design school she'd started a staging business for Realtors and from there slowly built a company that designed window displays for department stores across the country. She'd competed against the biggest designers in the city to get the WW Hotels contract and she wasn't going to let even a small, seemingly meaningless detail like garland placement go overlooked.

"It already looked perfect," Maisey grumbled as Laura stepped away from the tree, "so how does it look better now that you've adjusted it?"

Laura laughed, still considering whether or not to relocate one of the shimmery crystal snowflakes to a less congested area of the tree. "You have an eye too, Maisey, that's why I hired you."

Maisey shook her head, still looking the tall evergreen up and down, all the silver-and-gold decorations sparkling like jewels beneath the multitude of crystal chandeliers. "No," Maisey disagreed, "I can help you carry out a vision, but I couldn't have dreamed this up in a million years."

Laura slung her arm over her assistant's shoulders, pulling her in for an encouraging squeeze. "You'll be doing this same thing in no time, I promise. Look at the kind of stuff you were doing when you first came to me and what you're creating now—we're all constantly learning."

Maisey shook her head, clearly not accepting the logic and compliment. Laura took her mentorship of Maisey very seriously and was prepared to settle into another meaningful life lesson that her young assistant would surely hang on and treasure forever when Maisey's attention was pulled away.

Her blue eyes went wide as she gripped, not especially lightly, Laura's hand. "Oh, my god, I think that's him," Maisey whispered furiously, nearly out of breath with excitement.

"Who?" Laura asked, leaning in closer to Maisey to hear her better, but also because her assistant was literally pulling on her arm which, because Maisey was much shorter than Laura, was causing Laura to hunch over as if she were playing an impromptu game of reverse limbo sans the stick and catchy tunes, and well, bending backward.

"Will Walker, our boss," Maisey managed above a deep, yet silent gasp of excitement. "He's headed this way."

Laura's stomach dropped basically all the way down onto her feet at the mention of Will Walker. The research she'd done on him while preparing for the job had produced photos of a man she'd known once upon a time in a life she'd spent a lot of time forgetting. But the intervening years and the fact that his name was different had made her unsure if she had the right person. More significantly, there was also the note that she'd left with his secretary that had gone unanswered and the countless letters and emails she'd sent him during the fifteen years since they'd seen each other that had always been returned.

That her old friend might be mere feet away from her now sent her pulse thundering in her veins like a marching-band drum line. As soon as he approached, her body instinctively knew it was him, the best friend she'd ever had in her life. And for a variety of reasons, but mostly because she'd *had* to abandon him to a shitty life with a foster family from hell without so much as a goodbye mere days before Christmas, she felt like she might vomit right onto the gleaming black onyx floor of his hotel.

"Do you like this tree?" a male voice asked. His voice was much deeper than it'd been when they were kids, but it was familiar all the same. The drawn-out vowel sounds and clipped consonants they'd grown up with in New Jersey were still apparent. Her own accent had softened years ago, mostly by design, to distance herself from a past she had hoped to outrun.

Maisey nearly broke Laura's fingers before letting go of her hand completely, as if just now realizing that holding her boss's hand in public was strange. But Laura had more pressing problems than Maisey being self-conscious. Mainly that she was about to come face-to-face with her first love, her first real friend and the first person in her life after the deaths of her parents who she'd ever considered family.

She struggled to breathe as he gazed up at the work of art she was privately referring to as Quirky Christmas because of its tongue-in-cheek play on luxury. WW Hotels were considered a playground for the rich and famous, so she'd found carved-crystal slides and platinum seesaws, sneakily nestling them alongside the hand-painted glass ornaments.

"I do like it, yes," she finally answered, keeping her eyes focused on the tree as her chest tightened with fear and dread. Did he not know who she was or had he actually gotten the note she'd left him and finally come to see her? "Do you?"

Her heart stopped for a beat as she waited for his answer because considering that she now knew who he was, it would be awful if he hated her work. She'd always hoped that he'd be proud of who she'd become.

"I don't know," he answered, tone gruff. "People keep telling me it's inspired, but fuck if I know what that means. It looks like just another Christmas tree to me. An expensive one, but a Christmas tree nonetheless."

Laura could see Maisey's mouth open to come to her defense, but Laura squeezed her hand to silence her.

When Maisey appeared to get the message, Laura peered at the tree again trying to see it from a man's perspective, but it was impossible. All she saw were the months of hard work, planning and curation glittering like so much fairy dust under his modern black minimalist light fixtures.

"Well, it has a certain whimsical charm mixed with a modern flair that is in sync with the reputation of these hotels," she told him, as if she were one of his hotel guests instead of the person who created *just another Christmas tree*. As if she weren't melting from the inside out, terrified of revealing herself and receiving a blank stare of nonrecognition on his face, or worse, the contempt she knew she deserved for deserting him.

It didn't help her peace of mind, either, that the electrical current she felt at being in close proximity to him was plucking her nerve endings up like a dog who heard his owner's key in the front door. As hundreds of hotel guests rushed by them, Laura was experiencing every available human emotion within the course of five minutes.

On top of everything else, she'd been hoping for a better first meeting with her technical boss. Maybe one that included effusive accolades and shocked expressions of speechless wonder, but she'd deal with it. It was what she did, after all. That was her superpower. She dealt with whatever steaming pile of crap life threw at her, starting from the death of her parents at age four to the endless line of negligent foster parents all the way up to the one who nearly hit her. It just so happened that the reason she'd made it out of that life alive was due nearly entirely to the man standing beside her.

"Whimsical charm," Will repeated, mulling the term over. "I guess anything would be lost on me since I hate Christmas."

Maisey audibly gasped, the thought simply too much for her to bear.

"That's a long season to dislike," Laura pointed out.

"The fucking longest," he muttered, the irritated statement uttered in his deep, gravelly voice so like the Will she remembered as a kid. He hadn't minced words then either.

When she couldn't stand not knowing her fate, she finally turned to face him but saw that he was already facing her. His dark brows were knitted and the muscles of his neatly squared-off jaw were ticking as he put the pieces together.

And when their eyes met, she knew they both knew.

"Laura?" he asked at the same time she said, "Will?"

It was as if someone had dropped her insides out of a thousand-story building without a parachute when she slowly locked gazes with the boy she'd thought she'd lost forever. The one up until this moment, she'd thought hated her and deliberately didn't want her in his life.

The moment stretched, loaded with unresolved history, neither one of them knowing what to say.

"I thought it was you in all the Page Six photos," she finally blurted. "But you look so different from when we were kids and you changed your name so I couldn't be sure. Then you didn't return the note I left with your assistant, so I figured I had the wrong guy after all."

"Wow," Will said, running a hand through his too-long black hair as he stared at her. "I can't believe it's really you. Shit, that you're even alive, I—" His words trailed off as dark brown eyes roamed her face, taking in all the changes the years had made. She was still young, but she certainly wasn't sixteen anymore like she'd been the last time they'd seen each other. When he met her eyes again, the tormented look in them was gone. Then he said, "Of course, if I'd gotten your note I would have gotten back to you. My assistant has strict instructions about what to push through to me."

His response brought some relief that maybe he didn't completely hate her, but all she could manage was, "I like the new name."

Finally, he spoke. "Yeah, I figured my parents hadn't done anything for me, so why should I do anything for them by keeping the name going?"

The callback to their childhood returned her to the grimy old apartment building and crappy foster parents who didn't even care enough to buy food for her let alone put it on a table. It was no longer painful for her to think about those days; that work had been done in the years of therapy that followed, but seeing Will reminded her of how far she'd come. Of how far he'd come.

"Understood," she said, fighting against throwing herself into his arms for the hug she so desperately wanted. To finally confirm that he was her friend, that he didn't hate her was heady. "I, uh, changed my name too."

He held her eyes as his hands slid into the pockets of the ripped jeans that still must have cost a fortune. He wasn't a typical hotelier, more comfortable in leather jackets and jeans than Wall Street suits and the effect wasn't insignificant. The worn leather conformed to his wide shoulders and made him look a touch dangerous while his ripped black jeans molded to muscular legs probably honed on the back of a motorcycle. He'd always looked like a brawler even as a teenager just trying to get by in their lousy neighborhood, but now the young boy she'd known was a man who was more likely to deliver a single cut to an assailant's neck than use his fists.

His gaze flicked to Maisey, who seemed to drift away from them, realizing the import of the reunion. She imagined that pointed look of his sent many of his own employees scurrying away, as well. He had a presence.

"You look just the same, Laura," he finally said.

"But you look different," Laura smiled, trying to act normal. "You're all grown up."

Their eyes held and Laura felt a weird nostalgia for those days even though they'd been her worst ones on record. Will had been her bright light, her only friend for so many awful, harrowing years where the only thing she had to look forward to was turning eighteen and getting out on her own even though that most certainly meant an aimless and harder life on the streets.

"I missed you," she blurted, saying the stupidest thing possible but unable to regret it. It was the truth. "When I left, that is."

A corner of his wide mouth kicked up just like it always had when her mouth was faster than her head, which in those days had been often. "You too, Laura. But then I wasn't the one who left without a word."

A vise clamped around her heart, just like it had that day and a lot of the days after when she thought of Will. For five years, they'd been the best of friends. Will had gotten her food when she'd been hungry, forged signatures on papers for school when her foster parents had been too drunk or high to do it themselves, stolen her clothes when she'd outgrown the others, kept her safe from the thousands of threats that had visited a child. And she'd left him without so much as a goodbye.

"I wanted to leave you a note, but child protective services came to school to get me. There wasn't time for anything but grabbing my stuff." It wasn't exactly the entire truth, but enough of it.

He nodded like he'd suspected as much. "Yeah, John and Nancy, upstanding citizens that they were, got caught with drugs and were carted off to jail when I got home that day. I figured someone had come to take you back to the center."

Laura shook her head, skin crawling at the memory of her awful foster parents who vacillated between neglectful and downright mean. That day when child services came to get her hadn't been easy because it meant abandoning Will, but she'd done the right thing. When she tried to find him at school to say goodbye, he hadn't been in any of his typical hangouts and when she'd tried to leave a note for him in his room she'd found the window of his bedroom, the way they normally met up with each other, locked. Fast forward to the unanswered emails and returned letters and this was like some kind of fantasy where she got to right her past wrongs and also look at an insanely attractive man as she repented.

Getting herself under control, she explained, "I got placed with a family way out in the suburbs, nearly to Pennsylvania."

"Ah," he said, absorbing the information of where she'd been all these years. "Good one?"

"The best," she confirmed. "I'm heading home tomorrow for the holiday."

That wry, half smile again. "Good, Laura. You deserved it."

"You did, too, Will."

He shrugged as if it didn't matter, but she knew it did and her heart broke all over again for how she'd left him. She had so many questions to ask and while the lobby of his hotel didn't seem like the right place, she had to know.

"Did you—" she started to ask about what happened to him after she left, but he interrupted her with, "So that's why you like a whimsical Christmas, huh? Because you got your own Christmas present that year. Out of the shithouse and into a home of your own." He gestured to the tree. "Does this live up to your fantasies?"

She knew a deflection when she saw one, but allowed it. "Well, since I'm the one who designed it, I should hope so."

He did a double take then and she had a moment of satisfaction at surprising him. "You're Dream Designs?"

"That's me."

His eyes grazed hers again and she felt that tingle of electricity she'd begun to feel as soon as she hit fourteen. She'd loved him fiercely, like a brother when they'd first met and she'd been twelve but it had changed as she'd gotten older. And now he was looking at her like he knew what she looked like without clothes on and she liked it very much.

"Will," she started, because she needed to thank him. For so many things really, but mostly for just being her friend and keeping her alive. "I've wondered about you all these years. I wish—"

"You did a good job," he interrupted again, clearly not interested in talking about the past. "Everyone loves the lobby. You've given me the most talked about holiday display in the city. Not an easy feat."

The compliment had her beaming inside, but she didn't like that he wouldn't let her talk about the past. More than anything else in her life, she regretted not being able to tell him just how much he'd meant to her. How much he still meant. She had a ton of friends now, but none as important or as good or as dear as he'd been to her.

Her childhood nightmare had ended when she'd been adopted by the family she left him for, but it'd taken her a long time to accept that she was worth their regard, that she was worth loving at all. The vague memory of her real parents had faded by the time she knew Will, but he'd made her feel that way too, safe and loved, and she wanted him to know, hoped that she'd been that for him, as well.

She locked her eyes on his, hoping to telegraph just what she was feeling even though he wouldn't let her say the words. "Thank you. I appreciate that. Christmas jobs are my favorite and this was a special one for me, so that means a lot." She wanted to say that she'd created it for him, so in some weird way she could give him the Christmas he deserved.

Will nodded as if his compliment was no big deal, and then he suddenly pulled his phone from his pocket, his face scowling at the screen. Within seconds his scrolling grew choppy and his face agitated, which made her anxious because she was about to miss her chance to reconnect with him.

After several more moments, his eyebrows edged together as regret colored his dark eyes. "I have a thing I need to do right now, but can I take you to dinner later?"

"Of course," she chirped, sounding like someone who never left the house and was jumping at the chance, but she didn't care. There was so much she needed him to know.

He gave a quick, decisive nod before sliding his phone back into his pants. "Good, I'll be in touch with the details."

And then he was striding off into the crowded lobby of his hotel, leaving her to wonder just how the boy who'd eaten by stealing them food from the corner store was now a billionaire hotelier.

That was one mystery, at least, she hoped to finally solve.

CHAPTER TWO

As Will had promised, his assistant texted Laura within an hour of their meeting in the lobby with details about dinner, including the time, place, dress code and the type of car that would be arriving to pick her up. Everything was taken care of, but by the time she showed up at the restaurant, a celebrated diner not far from her brownstone, her nerves were in the stratosphere.

This afternoon's meeting had opened up a door to her past that she liked to keep firmly closed, and the rest of the day she'd been lost in it. Will's appearance had her reliving those years of fighting girls who picked on her, of hiding from her volatile foster father who always seemed on the verge of hitting someone, of the overwhelming loneliness and sense of worthlessness that defined her childhood.

In the blink of an eye, she'd gone from a happy four-year-old to a foster kid shuffled from the home of one family who didn't really want her to another, most of them doing it for the nominal income they were awarded by the government and not any real interest in her welfare. It'd been difficult and she didn't like revisiting it because it undermined the hard-earned self-worth she'd built over the years. It had taken many years of constant reassurance from her parents that she was worthy of love, and despite her unfortunate track record of leaving guys before they could leave her, she'd mostly accepted it.

Through it all, Will had been there and she'd never been able to properly thank him. Until she'd met him she'd had no hope back then that her life would get better. After three other unsuccessful foster homes and the group home, life had felt unbearably bleak. But from the day she arrived in their Newark suburb and found that he was her neighbor, he taught her that there might be something better out there for her.

Will had always been plotting. He'd had a plan for when he got out of foster care—he was going to get a construction job, make enough money to buy a house in the suburbs and have three children. He was going to have the life that was taken from them both. They'd walk the neighborhoods looking at nice houses with happy families inside and he'd proclaim that one day he'd have the best house on the block. All of it had seemed like some magical pipe dream of his that would never happen.

But Will had made it happen. At least the money part.

The driver stopped at the curb and helped her out of the town car and into the chilly December. The air was icy as it sliced into her lungs with each inhalation. It was just days before Christmas and she'd be leaving the city tomorrow to drive back to her hometown for the holidays, but the clean smell of snow had already arrived. The wind cut through her wool coat as she quickly headed into the restaurant, thankful for the rush of heat as she entered.

Handing over her coat and scarf to the hostess to check, she was directed to a booth in the far corner of the restaurant. She'd never been to Maxine's before, but it was a semi-gritty New York institution where celebrities were even known to pop up on occasion.

When Will spotted her, he rose from the brown leather booth. Dressed in black jeans and a black cashmere sweater with a different black leather jacket on, he looked like a barely caged animal, alert and ready to attack anyone who might challenge him. His smoky gaze traveled over her from top to bottom, her skin tingling where his eyes touched. The blatant perusal reminded her that things were different now in the present. They weren't children anymore and hadn't been for a long time. His reputation with women alone was more than enough proof of that as well as the very adult way her own body responded to his.

"You look stunning," he told her.

"Thank you," she told him, proud that she'd worked her way up to a point where she could spend a little extra on a dress for a date. The red sheath with a flirty ruffle at the knee-length hem and wrists wasn't going to get her photographed for Page Six like him, but it was tailored to show off her curves as well as being festive for the Christmas season that she was all-in on. "You, as well."

He did a one-shoulder shrug as he helped her into the booth. "My uniform is generally black on black. Makes shopping and dressing simple."

"Efficient," she agreed, though she doubted he was doing his own shopping at this point. Some bright-eyed buyer was probably plucking out the most expensive black pieces and having them delivered straight to his closet.

Taking his seat across from her, his brown eyes roamed over her face again, as if he was making sure again that it was actually her. But she felt it in all her nerve endings, the warm intimacy of his attention, taking her back to how she'd felt when she'd had a crush on him as a kid, how she'd count the minutes until he appeared at her window to hang out.

"I still can't believe you're here," he said, holding her eyes. "It's been fifteen years since I saw you. This afternoon when I stopped at the tree, I thought I was just looking at a girl with the same color hair as yours, but I never thought it would actually *be* you."

That little tell, that he'd remembered her hair color sent a little thrill through her. She had meant something to him, after all. To finally shut the door on that uncertainty was a relief.

Laura shook her head, about to tell him as much

when the waiter came over with waters and the wine list.

Will ordered a decadent cabernet and met her eyes.

"Thank you for inviting me tonight," she told him. "You know, I looked for you on social media over the years, but you never popped up, which since you changed your name explains that. I always thought you'd do well, but I would have never dreamed that you owned the WW Hotels."

He gave a wry laugh, his eyes crinkling at the corners in a way that straightened her spine; a swarthy dimple just visible under his stubble appeared, as well. Time was working for him, and apparently, for her too. "No, I don't suppose anybody who knew me then would ever make that connection."

"Considering our past, we should have entirely different lives," she agreed. She'd worked through her past in therapy, but her guilt over Will was completely separate. After the first couple of years she'd started feeling like a fairly well-adjusted person, learning to accept the happiness she'd found, which had been a lot more work than she'd thought. She wondered if Will had done the same, if he was able to truly appreciate how far he'd come.

She held up her glass. "But here we are, having dinner together at one of the best restaurants in the most exciting city in the world."

"Here we are, indeed," Will echoed, his eyes locking with her.

The delicate glass clinked and they each drank the chalky red wine. Heat shimmered between them in a way that it might have when they were kids if their lives hadn't been so screwed up. Whatever the case, she definitely felt it now, the connection stretching between them like an invisible electric current. All her secret teenage dreams about him finally coming to life, the yearning, the angst, the certainty that he was the love of her life.

"So are you going to tell me how you built your hotels?" she asked, so curious about his life.

Will leaned back into the booth, staring into his wine with a faraway look on his face. "I got out of that building when you left," he revealed, running a hand across the rough shadow of a beard. "I couldn't stand it anymore so I bailed. I hung out with some older kids in an abandoned squatters apartment for a couple of months until I graduated high school, worked while I went to community college, then got a scholarship to finish up undergrad at Fordham. I majored in business there and started out at a hotel in the city, then basically worked my way up. I saved my money, met some investors who saw that I was hungry and was willing to work hard, came up with a novel concept, took some reckless chances that paid off, and in a nutshell, here we are."

She laughed at his ultra-abbreviated rags-to-riches story and his eyes darkened with interest as he watched her. Unlike when they were kids, he wasn't trying to hide that he was attracted to her. "You make it sound so easy," she told him, taking a drink of water to cool herself down, "but I know it wasn't."

He snorted, refilling her glass now that it was below the halfway mark. Pinpricks of pleasure that he was still looking after her spread over her skin. He was a powerful and important man now, but he'd just gone out of his way to care for her. It gave her hope and felt like the hug she'd needed from him earlier. "No, those first years after I left the old foster parents were hell. I mostly slept in burned-out houses and couch-surfed when I needed to. But I knew I was working toward something and that kept me going. What about you? How'd you get to be, as my employees call you, queen of Christmas?"

She smiled at the accurate label. Christmas was definitely her niche. "Well, first, I actually got my grades up enough after I got to the new family to get into design school. My grades, as you know, had been crap. But then same as you, I apprenticed, but eventually found that I loved Christmas most of all, kind of concentrated on that and here I am," she informed, giving him a smile. "Thank you, by the way, for hiring me. And all joking aside, I do hope you like the lobby."

He paused, his drink in hand, to look directly at her in a way that sent shivers of awareness down her spine, darkly serious and direct. "Even though I hate Christmas, I thought it was excellent work before I knew you'd created it, and now I'm blown away. You definitely have a talent."

A smile pushed at her lips because he looked like a tough guy on the outside but just like when they were young, he still had a kind word for her. He'd built her up when she was down more times than she could count.

"That's nice of you to say," she told him, feeling her cheeks heat.

"It's not nice," he told her, setting his glass down as his eyes held hers and she grew edgy. "It's just the truth."

Two tuxedo-clad waiters appeared with enormous round trays heavily laden with multiple plates of food for far more than two people. "I ordered food already, by the way," he informed unnecessarily.

When she met his eyes he just shrugged. It was high-handed of him to order without her, but it was clear that she was living in his world now and he was a man who ordered when and what he wanted now.

Trying to distract herself from staring at him as she wanted to do, to drink him in and soak him up after all of these years even though she knew he'd hate it. She peered at the famous steak au poivre and pork chops and mountains of homemade pasta. It all looked divine and there was so much she wanted to say to him but as she watched him shrug off his leather jacket to eat, the sweater underneath clinging to the breadth of his shoulders and chest, she got a little distracted.

Sliding her eyes away and back to the mountain

of food so he wouldn't catch her staring, she joked, "I suppose I'll be able to find something edible."

He raised an amused eyebrow as she plucked out a plate of the steak and dove in. Choosing the steak as well, he began eating too, silence descending for a moment as she willed herself not to watch the sculpted planes of his jaw shift as he chewed.

After a few minutes Will met her eyes, his gaze once again direct and dark with intent. "It's probably none of my business, but that's never stopped me before. Are you seeing anyone?"

Her legs clenched together as a shiver of lust took over her body, but she managed to shake her head in the negative. "No. Not presently seeing anyone." She'd seen a lot of guys over the years, but all of her relationships seemed to have a sell-by date.

"I guess it's my lucky day," Will murmured, the blunt statement making her stomach tilt with excitement that she wasn't in this alone. That he felt the same pull to her as they'd had back then, that she still felt. "I had a major thing for you when we were kids, but you probably knew that."

"I did not," she said, grinning stupidly. She'd thought her romantic teenage daydreams were all one-sided. Hearing that they weren't and that he wanted to revisit their relationship was stunning; heat and hope and excitement flooded her.

"To say I had a crush on you would be an understatement," she admitted, a corner of her mouth curving in wry amusement. "I'm pretty sure I was hopelessly in love with you, but knew you thought of me like a kid sister."

His eyes drifted down to the cleavage she'd dusted with a touch of shimmer; it wasn't that he was doing it on purpose, just that his eyes were drawn there, because after he realized what he was doing, his eyes snapped back to hers, apologetic. Then he came back to the conversation. "Maybe in the beginning when you first came to the building, but once we both hit high school I definitely did not think of you as a sister," he said, his voice deepening just a touch at the end, the edge rippling across her skin like a call to action.

She felt the look, the words, *him* at her center and itched to follow through on the flirt. To take all those girlhood fantasies and live them in present time in all the Technicolor and dirty detail his current repu-tation promised.

"Do you ever wonder what it might have been like if I had stayed?" she asked. "I was all packed up and ready to leave with you that day, you know. We would have been braving the city on our own together."

Just like that, with no warning, his eyes went flat. Just dead, the heat vanishing in an instant.

"I guess at least we would have been together," he said flippantly, breaking eye contact to continue slicing his steak.

The barb hit home because, of course, yes, at least they would have been together. Meaning that he wasn't over the fact that she'd left him on his own. An awkward silence descended upon them, with her wishing that the guilt pressing on her chest again would give her just a moment's rest. Because he'd been a boy she'd left, but now in the present he was a man she'd hurt and it was killing her. The only person in her life to show her kindness and she'd abused it again somehow.

"I really hope after this dinner we can be friends again," she offered, the sentiment weak and awkward after the cold front he'd erected. She cleared her throat and tried again. "What I mean is that I would like to see you again."

He looked up; those same eyes that had been so focused on her throughout the meal now barely noticed she was there. "This has been a nice night, Laura," he replied, his tone mild, but noncommittal. "It's been good to see you again."

Just that. *It's been good to see you again.* A platitude without any hope of a returned sentiment that he'd like to be friends or continue the acquaintance. He bit into another piece of steak and then another as if she hadn't opened her heart to him. Things had been going so well and then he'd brought down his wall so hard it appeared she was permanently left out in the cold.

She ate the rest of her meal, slightly numb. She couldn't believe that she'd blown it again, and her worst fear—that he hadn't forgiven her for leaving him all alone—had been confirmed. The despair

and guilt that she'd fought to bury in the intervening years rolled over her in waves so huge she was
drowning.

Then his cell went off and he wiped his mouth
with the maroon cloth napkin. "I'm really sorry about
this, Laura," he said, meeting her eyes, but all business now, "but I need to go. Finish your meal, everything is paid for and my car will take you home."

With no more than a cursory peck on the forehead
and a wave he was gone.

Her long-lost friend was apparently going to remain a stranger.

CHAPTER THREE

LAURA STARED HELPLESSLY at the curly-haired front desk receptionist at the WW Hotel, her anxiety climbing by legendary degrees.

"You're sure you don't have anything available?" she pleaded. "I literally have nowhere else to go."

It wasn't strictly the truth because she could go back to her apartment, but Maisey's entire family was there visiting at present. Since Laura's original plan was to be well ensconced in her parents' home in Tewksbury baking gingerbread cookies for her nieces and nephews and watching Christmas movies in warm fuzzy socks by now, she'd offered her apartment up for Maisey's family to use for the holiday. She hadn't planned on having to find an open hotel room in New York City during Christmas. She might as well be looking for the real Santa Claus.

Carrie, her favorite of the receptionists while she'd been working on the hotel lobby, looked pained as her forehead wrinkled. The poor young woman was probably looking at a completely booked schedule pretending there might be a possibility just to make her happy.

"It's okay," Laura said, just able to hold back her sigh of frustration. She'd thought maybe they'd let her stay in one of the permanently open rooms hotels saved for royalty or something, since she'd worked for them, but she wasn't going to put Carrie in a weird position by asking outright. "I'll figure something out. Maybe I'll go buy an air mattress and sleep in Maisey's apartment with her three cats that I'm dangerously allergic to."

Carrie looked stricken and started scrolling furiously. "I'm so sorry," she gulped, worrying her hot-pink lip. "But there's just nothing. This week has literally been booked for months. People really like seeing the tree and stuff." This last was said with a sardonic and commiserating look as if to say that it was a little bit Laura's fault that there were no rooms available for her.

"I appreciate you trying," Laura told her, ignoring the perpetual holiday gift of irony. "It was wishful thinking on my part that you guys would have any openings."

She should have known by how stiff Carrie's body language had become, but she'd been too focused on her own misery to notice that Will, who apparently didn't want to be her friend again, had appeared next to her.

"Openings for what?" he asked, that raspy voice straightening her spine. Had he just taken a shot of warm whiskey or did he gargle rocks? Or maybe he just frequently destroyed the hopes of old friends to get that sexy gravel.

She deliberately refused to look at him, ignoring the electricity that was zapping between them like a broken telephone wire on an asphalt road. Even his bad attitude hadn't put a damper on that, unfortunately.

"I was hoping to book a room," she explained.

From the corner of her eye, she saw his hands slide into the pockets of another pair of dark jeans. "We've been booked for the season for quite some time."

"So I've been told."

"I thought you'd be well on your way home to spend the holiday with your family by now."

"There's a blizzard coming in, according to the latest weather forecast. I waited too long to get out of the city."

"What's wrong with your own place in the city?" he asked, regarding her.

"My assistant's family is staying there. I told them months ago that it was theirs for the week."

And she wanted them to stay and be a family together on Christmas with Maisey whom she loved and wanted to help out where she could.

He didn't answer right away and she grew irritated. If he didn't want to know her, then, fine, he didn't have to. Her feelings might be hurt, but she knew from experience that was survivable. She'd left him before when he'd been a nice person, the second time around shouldn't be nearly so bad. No crying over a letter he'd never read or constantly looking out the back window of the state employee's car as she drove away, hoping for just one more glimpse of him to cherish forever.

"Right, well, I have some other hotels to check," she said, clearing the throat that was clogged. "Merry Christmas."

Then she rolled her bag away, calculating just how much allergy medication she'd need to purchase to make it through a week on Maisey's studio apartment floor.

"You could stay with me, you know," she heard his rough voice soft but firm from behind her. "I have the penthouse which has several extra bedrooms."

Stopping in her tracks, Laura wasn't ready to turn around, but it also made her realize that she hadn't actually looked at his face this entire time.

"I couldn't impose," she told him, turning halfway around. "I'm sure you have Christmas plans."

He waited until she finally met his eyes, dark and unreadable, before speaking again.

"You wouldn't be imposing," he said, locking their gazes together as his eyes grew darker, more intense. "It's the least I can do for a friend."

She didn't even have time to tell her stupid heart not to flutter at his words, it just up and did it without listening to any reason whatsoever. Ridiculous. But she'd thought after their dinner that she'd blown it and despite his going all stoic on her last night all she really wanted to do was apologize.

"If you're sure," she finally managed, "I would really appreciate it."

"Of course," he said, his tone turning brisk as he pulled out his phone. "I'm out to a meeting right now, but I'll text you the door code." So saying, her phone beeped with a message. "Make yourself at home."

Then he nodded to Carrie. "Can you send someone up with the usual?"

Carrie nodded so fast Laura thought her head might fly off her shoulders. "Yes, sir."

And then before Laura could say another word because her mind had stalled on whatever "the usual" was, Will was halfway to the front doors. She probably wasn't the only woman who Will had in his penthouse, which she shouldn't find deflating, but definitely did.

Laura looked to Carrie who was currently on the phone relating orders to whatever employee was on the other end. When she hung up, she gave Laura instructions on what elevator buttons—Will had his own—to press to get to the penthouse. Once she was inside said elevator she felt like she was in an alternate superswanky universe, which only continued when the doors opened into a jaw-dropping penthouse. She was so in awe that the doors nearly closed again with her still standing inside because she was frozen to the spot.

The penthouse was breathtaking. Floor-to-ceiling

windows at least thirty feet high spanned three sides of his living area, overlooking Midtown Manhattan from forty floors up, the view absolutely breathtaking. Low-slung black leather furniture nestled near a fireplace while ivory marble end tables anchored the space. The open kitchen was more black—onyx countertops with rich mahogany cabinetry and formidable stainless steel Wolf appliances.

A glaring omission, however, was that the entire place was devoid not only of any sign of Will, but most notably, Christmas. Not a single twinkle light, ceramic snowman, pine garland, beribboned wreath or even a tree in sight. Laura thought of her parents' house, every inch as if a Christmas store exploded in their home and each item placed with care and tradition. It was her favorite time of the year for so many reasons, but mostly because of how warm being home felt. And now she was probably going to be stuck here in this huge penthouse, which was absolutely stunning obviously, but so different from how she'd imagined spending Christmas.

And damn it, she wanted some gingerbread cookies and hot cocoa by a fire, by God. It wasn't too much to ask for of a Christmas, what she thought of as *her* holiday, because she'd made a career of making it as special for others as it was for her.

Following the rest of Carrie's instructions, she entered a long hallway and opened the first door on the left. The windows were far smaller and the ceiling a normal height, which was better for her, but like the rest of the place, it very much felt like a hotel room. All the amenities but lacking any real warmth or comfort.

Laura unpacked her suitcases into the spacious closet and dressers, thinking with some measure of positivity that she could get more clothes from her apartment now that she was staying in the city. But then was depressed again as her other luggage was brought up, namely the suitcase that contained all the gifts she wasn't going to get to give out on Christmas morning.

She put that entire suitcase in the closet and tried to forget the fact that she was spending Christmas with a virtual stranger, and a taciturn one at that. Imagining the life Will had described to her last night, of basically drifting, she supposed he had some right to that, but she hoped this would be their opportunity to clear the air and put the past where it should be—in the past. And not only because she wanted something different in the present.

But after two hours of waiting for Will to return while flipping through his immense cable package, and learning that "the usual" was just a care package with designer toiletries and an assortment of expensive nutrition bars, her anxiety was growing. Her eyes kept drifting to the mantel above the fireplace and the glaringly empty corner of his apartment absolutely begging for a Christmas tree.

And within a matter of minutes she was bundled up in her coat again and heading back into the streets, her purpose now clear.

She had a chance to smooth over whatever she'd done last night to make him mad and also make up a little for the past. She could finally give Will Walker the Christmas he'd deserved when she'd left him.

Will hated Christmas for probably the same reasons Laura loved it. From his time in the group home to horrible foster homes, Christmas had been the biggest reminder that his life was a steaming pile of shit. Until he'd met Laura Harris, which was what her name had been back then before her permanent foster parents must have legally adopted her.

The Christmas she'd left had been his hardest one in memory. They'd been planning on breaking out together; he'd been planning on getting out anyway the day of high school graduation, but then they ran out of time. She couldn't have stayed with that coked-out, abusive asshole of a foster father another day and Will knew he had to get her out for her own safety. It would have been scary, but he had money saved and they had each other and he'd been determined to make it work. He would have made it work because their lives would have depended on it. For her, he'd been willing to risk everything.

But then Laura had left without a word. And he'd been alone. Again.

God, how he'd hated being alone back then, which was ironic considering how much he loved being by himself now. He'd been against the grindstone working his way toward the dream of a hotel for so long: schmoozing every potential investor he met with a money clip and platinum card, scraping up money to attend every hotel-management conference available and meeting anyone along the way who could be of use to him from extraordinary housekeeping managers to lauded CEOs, and finally working one-hundred-hour weeks. And none of it had been alone. Especially not now living in a busy hotel that he owned.

Some days he'd give away a million bucks to not have to see a single human being. But it'd been no surprise when he'd offered his place to Laura for Christmas. Even now he couldn't imagine not protecting her. She'd been the only girl who had genuinely ever broken his heart. When he'd still had one to break, that is. Relationships were something he had absolutely no time for since he wasn't exactly a talk-about-his-feelings type of guy.

Sex was about the only thing he let into his life. And his attraction to Laura was palpable even when they were in high school. He'd been interested in her then, but he'd known her since she was twelve. It would have been the height of awful behavior to go from being her big brother figure to some asshole trying to date her.

She was still the most beautiful woman he'd ever seen. He'd thought that when they were kids and nothing had changed. Her adorable light brown freckles still scattered across the bridge of her nose even though her new sophisticated style was light-years away from the dingy hoodies and scuffed sneakers of their adolescence. But that radiance she'd always had was still there in spades and coupled with a sexuality that virtually oozed from her with every move she made.

Where she'd been stick straight and starved for food before, now her curves had filled out and were made for a man's hands, her lips soft and plump along with cheeks that were always rosy. Blondes, brunettes, blue hair, he'd really never had a preference for women before, but he'd purposely stayed away from strawberry blondes because they reminded him of her, always. No one had hair like that, not that exact shade that turned rose gold in the right light or looked blond in the shadows. It was why he'd stopped to talk to a woman in his lobby who reminded him of her. He'd never actually expected it to be the girl he'd thought he'd seen a million times over the years. Especially during this time of the year when she was always on his mind, that to find her again was truly something.

What he hadn't expected to return was the anger. She'd clearly never felt the same way about him as he had about her back then or else she never would have left. He'd taught her over and over the signs of government workers, had designated hiding places for when one showed up in the apartment building or at school. Because as deplorable as their foster parents were, the group home was even worse. The sadness there was enough to break any spirit. But Laura hadn't taken any of their usual precautions and chosen to leave him. It was that simple. She had a choice and it hadn't been him.

It was fine, obviously. He was a grown man and that part of his life was so far behind him it often seemed like it hadn't even happened at all, but then she'd shown up in his hotel looking so painfully lovely and the relief just that she'd been *okay*, something that often plagued him over the years, had been enough to bring him to his knees.

During dinner when she'd swept it all away as if she hadn't had a choice but to go with the social worker, like it hadn't been that big of a deal, it'd pissed him off. And yeah, he'd been a dick, but Christ, he'd been so goddamned worried about her. For weeks he'd looked all over the neighborhood for her even though his gut had known the truth. Her friendship had meant something to him and besides a few guys from college, she was the closest thing to a best friend he'd had before or since.

So when the elevator doors opened to his penthouse and the first thing he saw was a fifteen foot pine tree already strung with enough lights to make his entire hotel seem to onlookers as if it was on fire, he tried not to immediately toss her off his balcony.

"Um, what happened here?"

Laura popped up from behind his kitchen island, a red bow in her hair and a glittery Christmas apron tied around her waist, looking so insanely happy while simultaneously fuckable that he had to stop himself from reaching for her.

It was then he realized that something was actually *baking* in his home. A place where he'd barely turned on a stove burner to boil water. In fact, he was pretty sure he hadn't even done that because what did he ever need to boil water for? Nothing. He ordered in literally everything. He lived in his own hotel for just that reason.

Laura's cheeks colored and he figured that the look on his face was probably scary. He'd been told he had Resting Dick Face on numerous occasions and he was also a little enraged at the moment. He'd given her a place to stay against his better judgment and she'd vomited Christmas all over it. Bushy strands of pine garland studded with red velvet bows and more twinkle lights were strung across his mantel above the fireplace, in which there was a roaring fire. Little tchotchkes she'd probably bought from street vendors crowded his end tables, his dining table had been effectively tablescaped, a term his employees were endlessly telling him was extremely important, with tapered lights and shiny plates and embroidered placemats. It barely looked like his place anymore.

"I'm making some cookies," she said, holding up a hand covered with an oven mitt that had a chubby cartoon penguin on it, that frankly, was egregiously jolly. Where the hell had she even gotten all of it? He'd been gone for all of five hours and she'd shopped and decorated within that window of time. She was, in fact, just as hard of a worker as he was.

"You're making cookies," he repeated, still shell-shocked.

Her delicate eyebrows rose. "Yes, some gingerbread now, but I got the ingredients for all the standards, like sugar cookies, peanut-butter blossoms, linzer cookies, snickerdoodles, thumbprints, shortbread. You know, just the basics."

Taking a small spatula, she started removing uniform gingerbread men onto a grated metal rack.

"That's a lot of cookies just for the basics," he pointed out, his mouth watering of its own volition even though he certainly wanted to hate those cookies.

Laura shrugged. "It's not that many really and I'll give them away to people."

"If you're not going to eat them, why do it at all?"

"It's what you do on Christmas," she said simply, as if this explained everything. As if spending too much money to do an excessive amount of work for something you weren't actually going to use made any sense whatsoever. But then he'd never actually celebrated Christmas so what did he know?

"Well, can I get my staff to take down all this stuff? I'm not exactly a decorations kind of guy."

He knew it was an asshole thing to say and it was only emphasized by the stricken light that came into her generally cheerful brown eyes. He didn't want to put that look on her face, but it was clear he had some unresolved issues he needed to figure out. Which was what he'd planned to do after their dinner, but instead of having time to sort through the dregs of his past, she was now his roommate.

"Never mind," he heard himself saying. "I'll just be in my room."

"You don't like it?" she asked just as he turned around to go. By being near her, he was hurting her feelings or trying to figure out how to get her into bed and neither of those things was a good choice so it was best that he just stay away.

"I'm not really a Christmas person." An understatement, since he could barely think of a thing he loathed more.

"You've mentioned that," she said, then met his eyes, an endless well of determination apparent in their depths. "But I can change that."

An unexpected laugh escaped him, the sound rusty even to his own ears. "Give it your best, Laura, but I wouldn't hold your breath."

A light eyebrow raised and she held up a gingerbread man. "Eat this."

"I'm really watching my carbs."

She snorted and held the cookie out to him and his empty stomach growled. He wanted that fucking cookie more than he wanted to tear down all these ridiculously merry decorations.

With a mock glare, he took the cookie from her, stuffed the warm, spicy confection into his mouth and tried not to sigh in pleasure as it tickled his tongue and warmed his stomach. He'd always had a weakness for sweets, considering it was rarely something he'd been able to have as a kid. Sure, he'd stolen his fair share of candy from the gas station close to their house because they'd had to eat, but a fresh-out-of-the-oven cookie, well, that was something you couldn't steal.

At her grin, he knew his face was giving away more than he wanted. "It's okay," he told her. "For a cookie."

Laura rolled her eyes and it reminded him of how she'd been when they were kids. A tough girl who made a career of rolling her eyes was now giving him that same attitude as a woman and it was a surefire way to make his dick hard.

"I know you love it," she said, hands on her hips, making even that silly penguin mitt look bossy.

A corner of his mouth quirked as he stole another cookie from the rack. "I'm hungry."

That got her full-on smiling and his dick started to pulse, but still he hesitated on pulling the trigger. Had she been another woman he would have already gone in, but he didn't know how to play this one. Laura wasn't just another person he slept with and he wasn't sure about the consequences of that with her.

"If you really don't like the decorations, I can take them down," she said, interrupting his salacious thoughts, "but I'm just missing being home for the holidays and I thought this would cheer me up."

"Well, I would never take away anything that made you happy, Laura." He meant it to sound sardonic, but it had come out as earnest and he knew it was because he did still care for her. Once upon a time he'd have done anything to make her happy.

"Thank you," she said. "And this place is amazing, by the way. You really did it, Will. If I haven't said it before now, I'm really proud of you."

Something inside his chest grew suspiciously warm, and not just from the gingerbread, as the words echoed in his head.

"You too, Laura," he got out, his voice gruff. Clearing his throat, he continued so he didn't look like a complete idiot, "Since you're busy baking, would you like me to order some food for dinner?"

Laura shook her head. "I already made it. Pot roast is in the slow cooker."

He nearly fainted. Pot roast was one of his favorites and one of those meals you just didn't have as a single person who didn't cook.

"I have a slow cooker?"

"Of course not, I borrowed it from the kitchen."

He blinked then pulled out a leather chair from the island and sat as she stirred a bowl of bright white icing he assumed was going to be used to decorate the cookies.

"Of course you did," he said, watching her as she

carefully filled a plastic bag with the icing. "Would you like help?"

Laura's brown eyes met his. "No, because I have way more planned for you tonight and before I'm finished you're going to be a lover of Christmas."

He could hardly wait.

CHAPTER FOUR

LAURA DIDN'T LIE; Will would give her that. She did, indeed, love Christmas. And for a moment he almost enjoyed the fact that he got to eat her gingerbread cookies while he watched her zip around the tree she'd bought putting an entire array of decorations on it. He'd poured himself a glass of bourbon and sat down to pass an evening with her.

But as he got deeper into the holiday spirit she was thrusting upon him, he realized he'd let this farce go on long enough. He needed to set some boundaries for what this relationship was and stick to them, not waffle around it like he'd done the night of their dinner. He'd attempted to cut things off between them before they began and now here he was standing in his apartment that could not be described as any other way than aggressively bedecked. He was sending out mixed signals and he didn't want to lead her on because he didn't do relationships and cozy nights at home.

"Was this your entire plan for the evening?" he asked.

"Pretty much," she explained as she hung a red glass ornament for the third time on a different limb. "Most people I know in the city have gone home for the holidays."

"Mmm-hmm," he said, knowing he should help her decorate, but not ready to succumb to the chummy mood she was intent on creating.

Because honestly, he was having a rough time remembering to keep his hands off her despite the wholesomeness of his current state of affairs and his best intentions. Gone was the sexy apron from before in the kitchen and now her fitted forest green sweater was cinched in all the right places to show off a figure that was melting his resolve and good judgment.

"Do you have any plans for Christmas?" she asked, oblivious to his pervy train of thought.

He watched snowflakes fall outside, the white puffs disintegrating into water as they hit the glass of his windows. The roads were covered and probably impassable anywhere outside the city; she'd been smart to not risk the drive into a blizzard. Just like that, his memories tumbled in, of both of them without coats in the snow, running from the bus to their lousy apartment building for just a modicum of heat. He remembered her as a scared twelve-year-old girl who cried when she hadn't received a Christmas present that year so he'd stolen a couple of candy bars and drawn a picture of her to make life just a little less unbearable. It hadn't been enough then, though, and he'd tried every day since to make sure he never had to see someone be that sad again.

"I don't do anything for Christmas," he finally said, not for the reason that he actually wanted to answer the question since he knew what kind of reaction he'd get, but because the silence had stretched too long and his douchebag routine was wearing thin as the memory of her as a kid came flooding back. Other memories, too, always returned this time of year, which were another reason he didn't celebrate it. The Christmases he'd spent with his mom before she left him at the group home when things had gotten too hard were always just a wayward thought away, ready to collapse all the hard work he'd done to be a high-functioning human being. "I'm usually working."

Laura's shoulders slumped and mountains of pity welled in her eyes, as he'd predicted. "That is the saddest thing I've ever heard, Will."

When she started blinking rapidly he knew he'd really done it. "I can't say I've given it much thought. It's usually a good day to get work done without any interruptions."

She'd gotten herself under control, the blinking back of the tears portion of the evening hopefully behind them. However, she was still staring at him like he was a lost puppy off the street. He'd be damned if anyone had ever looked at him that way. In his adult life, people had either been afraid of him, respectful of him, stayed clear of him, but never had anyone looked at him and what he'd built and supposed that he was anything other than the self-assured grouchy billionaire he presented to the world.

"I wish we'd found each other sooner."

So did he.

But then he actually had thought about finding her over the years. It would have been easy enough for a person like him who had virtually unlimited resources, but he hadn't. The thought of her had been too painful and after a while, he'd mostly just wanted to forget the past and move on with his business, a project he'd eschewed nearly all his scant personal relationships to build. And he'd succeeded, so he supposed it had all been worth it in the end. He'd never have to worry about not being able to afford a coat again, would never worry about being so cold that he lit scraps of paper on fire in a trash can to stay warm. Never fucking again.

"Yeah, well, I've been okay on my own, but I appreciate that."

Their eyes met again and for not the first time they stood between the past and the present, time forgotten and irrelevant as they both tried to sort out what exactly they were to each other now. For his own part, he was fine to be friends, but the more she moved, talked and laughed, and honestly, just breathed, the more he remembered how much he'd wanted her as a teenager too.

So yeah, it was time to end this little cozy evening.

"Would you like to go with me to a party for a

magazine tonight? I need to speak to some people who can get some movement on city permits so I can start building WW East."

Laura eyed him and his unexpected audible on this evening's plans speculatively before asking, "So fancy dress?"

"Yeah, you have something?"

"I have dresses, but they're in my apartment."

As they watched the snow fall down outside, the balcony already covered with inches of it, the problem was clear.

"We're not The Plaza, but I've got designer boutiques downstairs," he said, pulling out his wallet and handing her a credit card. "It's on me."

Laura stared at it, her eyebrows crashing together. "I don't want your money, Will."

Without another word, he put the wallet back into his pocket. "Can you be ready in an hour?"

"Of course," she said, already on her way to the elevator to buy her own dress at his stores.

But she was ready within the hour and they made it to the restaurant, the few blocks to the event taking nearly a half hour to traverse in the snow. Will hated every fucking minute of it, but his mission of getting out of his apartment had been accomplished even if it just meant that they were stuck in an overheated room with a bunch of rich blowhards.

Nursing his second whiskey, he asked Laura when she came back to his side, "Was James Hess flirting with you?"

She paused, her holiday cocktail halfway to her mouth. He thought it was a peppermint martini, but somehow it annoyed him how into Christmas she was. To him, it seemed like a constant celebration of their separation.

"What?" she asked, taken aback by the invasive question.

"The guy you were talking to earlier, James Hess, he's a real estate developer."

"Oh, so he's the jerk responsible for turning New York City into a chain store paradise?"

Will snorted at the familiar refrain. "Everybody hates progress."

Laura rolled her eyes.

"Just be careful with him, okay?" Will warned. "He's a major player and there have been whispers about his predilections."

"You think I can't defend myself if I wanted to?" she asked him with a raised eyebrow. "Even though I learned how to fight from one of the best teachers?"

He caught her eyes. "I was a dumb kid."

"You might have been a kid but you were never dumb, and a knee to the balls is a skill I've used a couple of times over the years."

A bolt of fury swept through him at the thought of her being in danger. He'd never forget her face that night her foster dad nearly hit her. Never. That she'd been in that same kind of position again left him feeling just as enraged as he'd felt then.

She must have read something on his face because she began to backtrack. "Nothing like that. Nothing ever was as awful as him—I promise," she assured, which aided in returning his blood pressure to a somewhat normal rate.

"Good."

She plucked out a bacon-wrapped shrimp from a passing tray and plopped it into her mouth as he watched mesmerized while she chewed, like some hopeless schoolboy.

"I hope you're not planning on charging me for coming to this event, are you?" he asked as she grabbed a mini quiche from another passing tray. She was obviously nervous around him and he was truly enjoying it. "Your services are not exactly cheap."

Still chewing, Laura rolled her eyes. "And here I thought you were enjoying yourself and getting into the Christmas spirit. I mean, we're at a lovely Christmas party and you're just over there thinking your old friend is angling for more money. Frankly, I'm shocked and insulted."

He laughed and dug in, liked teasing her again. "Can you blame me? I ran through your itemized bill the other day and I had no idea you could, one, buy glitter in bulk, and two, that it cost so damned much."

She swatted him playfully in the arm, a completely innocuous move but one he felt in his gut. This was what he'd missed for so long, the familiarity, the easiness of being with someone who knew him.

She cleared her throat, obviously seeing something of his thoughts in his eyes. "Glitter is a holiday essential. You can't put a price on it, Will."

"You certainly did," he snorted. "Over ten thousand dollars, in fact."

She stuffed another canapé in her mouth, a caviar-topped blini this time eaten without regard to the luxury. Yeah, he was getting to her just like he had at the first dinner before she'd mentioned leaving and he'd shut things down. At some point, he'd need to deal with that, but for right now, the present was far more appealing, her painted coral lips closing delicately over the little pancake, her pink tongue darting out to catch a bit of sour cream from her lips.

"Ten thousand dollars is dirt cheap for magic." She shrugged. "You're welcome."

He bit the inside of his lip to keep from smiling and shook his head. "Well, I apologize that my gratitude was previously unforthcoming. Thank you, Laura," he said, wanting to keep her off-balance. "For the magic."

He watched as she tried to figure out if he was being serious or not, if she understood how much he'd wanted to give her magic back then, when a group of people parted the crowd, pressing her into him until they were nearly chest to chest.

When she realized just how close they were, her eyes slowly combed up his body and he felt her gaze in every cell. Her breasts were a hairbreadth away from his chest and he knew he should step back, that just standing here like an idiot was on the verge of creepy, but he was glued to the spot and she wasn't moving either.

Their eyes finally met and he didn't miss the dark desire in her brown depths, the lids hooding as her rosy tongue flicked out to lick her lips. It wasn't a calculated move, just reflex because what was simmering between them was undeniable.

So he took a step back, not leaning into the moment because it was too soon. There'd be a time when it wasn't too soon. He hadn't decided what the future would be, but if they were going to go to bed together he wanted her to be so pent up with lust that there was no mistake that they wanted each other and they weren't just conveniently hooking up because they were essentially snowed in together and stuck.

"Sorry," he said, his voice gruffer than he'd meant, but her light citrus scent was still in his nose. "I didn't know you were so close."

Her knowing look called him a liar, but she didn't push it. Instead, she straightened her dress, stretching the fabric more tightly over a pair of perfect breasts, perfect for the palm of his hand, perfect because they were hers.

Christ, a couple of cookies, a Christmas tree and a party and he was losing his goddamn mind.

Laura was on the brink of flipping out. Bake cookies, she'd thought, that'll be a nice, innocuous activity to do with an old friend as the world shut down around them.

Instead, the look on his face when he'd eaten those gingerbread men had her clothing almost literally in flames. They might as well be ash on the floor because his eyes darkening in pleasure, so obviously against his will, was off-the-charts hot. And his eyes as he watched her under thick lashes when she'd come out of her room in the long glittery silver gown that hugged every curve she had, the heat, the intent in them. She felt it everywhere.

Now there was no mistaking what he wanted and she looked at him the same way. All evening she couldn't get enough of watching him, the long, defined muscles of his arms, the black suit jacket tightening against his hard abs as he moved.

And that moment when their lips had been so close, so extremely close and yet so far away.

She almost wished he'd done it, just kissed her right then so they could get it over with because the anticipation was killing her. She'd essentially been waiting over fifteen years to kiss him; it was an expert study in masochism.

"Food is good," she blurted, finally able to get words out as he moved away from her, taking them to a slightly empty corner. The reality, though, was that there was no privacy whatsoever in the small event room where the party was held. That was the thing about New York City; nothing was especially spacious.

"I haven't noticed. I was saving room for what you cooked," he said, and in a way that broke her heart, the same way he'd looked when he'd tasted her cookies. She hated that Will had been on his own for so long, hated that she hadn't been able to be there with him. But she'd make up for it now because there was no way he was getting out of her life at this point. Mister Didn't-Need-Friends was her friend whether he liked it or not. Physical relationship or not, they were friends.

"Don't you find your penthouse a little impersonal?" she asked, ready to leave the party since he'd already greased the wheels he'd needed to grease. "Why don't you have a regular home somewhere? It's not like you can't afford one."

She thought of her own meticulously curated brownstone that Maisey's family was currently enjoying and bit back a sigh.

Will shrugged. "I don't need much to be happy and finding an apartment takes too much time. Even if I delegate responsibility I'll still have to waste time going to look at places. And besides, I like the penthouse. All my meals and the housekeeping are free. That's a lot of smart savings."

Laura laughed at the last. "You don't care about money."

"Not necessarily true. I have enough money because I care very much about it. We both know that no matter how much we make, you never miss the feeling that you could be back out on the street at any moment."

Laura did know that feeling, which was why, like

him, her ambition was always pushing her forward. Or people assumed it was ambition, but it was really fear. Fear that she'd never truly let go of the scared girl she'd been, scrounging for food from local restaurants, swiping the weird-looking discarded fruits and vegetables from grocery store storage rooms.

"Yeah," she said, her voice subdued as she met his eyes. "I do. But you can't live in the penthouse forever," she pointed out.

Will shrugged. "No. I own some property in Connecticut and California, same in the Hamptons. One of these days I'll hopefully spend some time there. Do you have a place in the city?"

"A duplex in a brownstone in the West Village." It'd taken so much work to get it, but it felt amazing to call it hers. The first real home that was totally her own.

"Good investment," Will said, impressed. He was starting to hover over her as she took a sip of her martini. In fact, she'd noticed him inching closer to her ever since they'd been nearly smooshed together, as if he hadn't wanted to truly be *not* near her.

"What are you doing?" she asked, taking a step backward.

"Getting closer to you," he told her, no prevaricating. It was so Will.

"Do you not have enough room?" she asked, knowing it was stupid, but they were in public and she wanted to rip his clothes off. Certainly some measure of restraint needed to be exercised.

She started backing away from him, but he grabbed her arm to still her progress. "I think the problem is there's too much room."

Unable to not do it, she looked down at his large hand on her pale, freckled arm and tried to get her libido in check. When his hand slid away, she didn't meet his eyes, just took a step closer to him.

However, she still tried to keep things casual.

"So admit one thing you like about Christmas so I don't think you're dead inside."

Will gave her a side-eye as an older couple squeezed past them on their way to the buffet. "I am dead inside, Laura."

She knew it was said in jest, but she couldn't help but wonder if it was a little true. For him to have the life he had growing up and to become so successful, he'd had to give up a lot and she suspected personal relationships were at the top of the list. He'd looked after her, but who had ever looked after Will Walker? She should have been that person.

"You are not," she told him, grabbing his hand on her arm and giving it a squeeze.

He raised an eyebrow and took his hand back, considering her. "So you can cook, bake, decorate, run a business, manage my entire staff? You have really turned into a one-woman enterprise, haven't you?"

Laura smiled, her heart warm because this was the Will she remembered, always lifting her up when she'd wanted to stop trying, stop believing. He was the one she turned to in those moments where any-thing seemed better than the life they were living and she so desperately wanted to give that back to him.

"A compliment from the famously tight-lipped Will Walker," she acknowledged with a grin. "Now that's a Christmas miracle."

Their eyes locked, heat gathering again between them like it had done earlier. It was another long look fraught with tension and considering as they both sized the other up trying to figure out where they stood.

So when the martini glass disappeared from her hand and his warm body leaned into hers, she wasn't surprised. But the moment stretched as they both considered the consequences of their actions. For her own part, Laura didn't see a downside to a physical relationship with Will except that things could never be casual between them and to a man like Will, who clearly didn't do any type of personal relationship, that might be a problem.

But any higher reasoning stalled out when his lips met hers, strong and firm and in charge. Time tilted, her breath simply quit and her entire body went limp. They'd barely touched and she was already unsteady on her feet. His taste, like whiskey and something deeper and more complex that was all Will tanta-lized her tongue, drawing her deeper into lust and fascination with him.

And just as she was leaning in for more, ready to abandon herself to it, he was gone.

"That was too soon," he muttered, backing away from her into the crowded restaurant. "I'm sorry I overstepped."

"It's okay," she told him, her voice mortifyingly breathy. "Consider it another Christmas present from me to you."

CHAPTER FIVE

Do not think about the kiss was the mantra Laura had needed to adopt the next day when, in fact, the only thing she could think about was kissing Will. Spent the entire night alone in her bed behind a door she'd locked specifically so she wouldn't go to his room, and had subsequently still spent every sleepless hour talking herself out of just saying the hell with it and going straight for him.

Which was why, on a surprisingly bright and sunny Christmas Eve when Will emerged from the hallway looking devastating with his too-long dark hair pushed back from his forehead, giving him a carelessly rakish appearance, Laura felt like resistance was futile.

She'd imagined spending Christmas Eve by his fire making more cookies and watching Christmas movies, but Will had insisted that they go out again. And while it wasn't what she'd envisioned, she agreed that their proximity to each other was dangerous. Just being around him and smelling him, like leather and Will, was akin to some kind of modern willpower-trust exercise. The time they spent together alone was just her counting down the seconds she could last without touching him. And frankly, each minute she lasted was a miracle. To be presented with physical evidence, namely his face and whole person, of that kiss all day would be a nightmare. For crying out loud, his lips were just always *right there*. Just out in the world for anyone to see, as if something so lewd shouldn't be unlawful.

So that was why they were going to get the hell out of this hotel again. And why she'd squeezed herself into a green sweater dress and heeled leather boots to be the woman on his arm like she'd been last night. Today they were going to a charity brunch for a children's hospital at the Four Seasons, a hotel that he'd disparaged several times in the last hour, to hobnob with more of the city's rich and famous. The minimum donation for a plate was ten thousand dollars, which meant it was an event for the elitest of the elite.

"You could save a good chunk of money if you just went by yourself," she pointed out as she met Will in front of the elevator's doors.

He raised an eyebrow at her. "I normally buy two and sometimes three plates at these things so I don't have to talk to whatever jerk they seat me next to."

"Wow," Laura remarked, eyeing him as he put on his overcoat, covering up and yet accentuating his broad shoulders. "I didn't realize just how deep your disdain for other people was."

He gave her a knowing look. "Give me a break. You've already met some of these people—you get it. They just don't miss a chance to talk about themselves or all the great things they do with the family money they inherited. I fucking hate it—I don't know why my money isn't enough."

Laura raised an eyebrow even though he was echoing her own thoughts. "I'll remind you that you're the one who chose this activity. I wanted to drink wine, get a pedicure in your hotel spa and watch Christmas movies."

Will rolled his eyes. "Yeah, I'm not really a Christmas movie kind of guy. And if I have to go, it's only fair that you go too since I'm giving you a place to stay. Plus, you were an excellent buffer yesterday so that I don't have to speak to these people. Also, not for nothing, Laura, you should be networking, as well. They're idiots, but these are the people who have enough money to afford even your outrageously priced services."

She laughed at his repeated posturing about her fees. It made her feel like they were friends again and she loved it. "I already got a few contacts," she informed, her insides warming as she remembered him talking up her lobby design at the party last night. He couldn't help himself from looking after her. "And don't worry, I will continue to be the best buffer you've ever seen," she promised.

The elevator door dinged open and Will gestured for her to precede him into it. A concession to the fact that it was a brunch event, a tailored black blazer and black button-down replaced Will's usual leather jacket, but he didn't look any more civilized than usual even with the expensive black cashmere over-coat on top of it.

Fate was a cruel, cruel player because while Laura would gladly sleep with Will and be adult about it the next day, she knew it would be a mistake. He hadn't even wanted to be friends with her in the be-ginning so chances were slim that he'd ever want to be something more. In fact, she doubted that if she hadn't shown up in his hotel practically homeless that she ever would have heard from him again. And the idea of going from his best friend to being one of his transient women literally chilled her to the bone.

So they couldn't sleep together.

And it was fine.

She'd maybe just need to push a dresser in front of her door or something to keep from sneaking to his room in the middle of the night. Or something larger like a piano. Or the bed. Probably all of the above would just barely work.

When the elevator doors opened into a garage, he led her to the black town car that was waiting and held out a hand to help her in. She would have ap-preciated the polite gesture, too, if even the touch of his leather-gloved hand wasn't fraught with anticipa-tion. She reluctantly took it, but she could still feel the strength in his thick fingers, the wide palm of his hand—all of it Will Walker, her very own former hero who'd grown up to look like an actor who played one on television and who just happened to kiss like a god.

She let go of his hand too quickly and bounced into the back seat rather inelegantly.

Will met her eyes, his gaze loaded. "This is going to be a long day, isn't it?"

Laura just sighed, not exactly sure it was good to acknowledge their sexual attraction so openly, but feeling comfortable because it was Will. "Yep, pretty much."

"Well, here we go then, Sugar Plum Fairy," he said as the car lurched from the curb, "let's get this over with so I can get back to my liquor cabinet."

Arriving at the brunch, they picked their way through the crowd in the Four Seasons, a hotel that was known for its traditional elegance. Marble columns extended from floor to towering ceiling while gold embellishments gleamed from the walls and massive crimson poinsettias the size of small trees graced every surface. He led them back to The Garden restaurant where the live trees that grew straight up through the floor from the ground were decorated with twinkle lights and glittering white ornaments. Heavy crystal vases as tall as toddlers with abundant white-and-red roses blooming out from the top in overflowing sprays anchored each round table. All of it was old New York City with a touch of the new, which was the thing that defined New York in the first place. The bones might stay the same, but the rest of the city was moving forward at light speed.

The brunch was still a crush even with the record-breaking snowfall from yesterday. Will went into the fray first, in command of himself but not stopping to talk to anyone even though several people called his name.

When he finally stopped at the bar, he ordered a beer for himself while she ordered one of their featured holiday cocktails after the bartender rattled off a litany of complicated ingredients. Will met her eyes, his expression sardonic at the lengthy and arguably pretentious drink description. She loved it, though, and just as she was about to ask the bartender for the recipe so she could make it for her family when she was finally able to escape the city, Will complained, "This is already awful."

She shot him a glance as she sipped the delicious minty concoction. "Uh-huh."

Will moved her aside as a large rolling cart with an ice sculpture of a Christmas tree came up behind her and nearly clipped her in the legs.

"Aren't you having just so much fun?" he mocked in a high voice. "Maybe next we'll be accosted by a group of Wall Street guys trying to sell me Bitcoin. Though it would still be better than the ice skating you originally suggested."

She couldn't help it, she laughed, shaking her head at his nonsense. Being around people really rattled him, but she always knew the real source of the problem was that they were both on edge.

"I think we should have given ice skating a chance," she said. "You seem to hate socializing so much that I can't imagine you liking anything less than this."

"Right."

"What?" she pressed. "We never got to do something like ice skating when we were kids."

"Thank god," he muttered, taking a long swig of his beer.

She grinned at his bad attitude. "For all you know, you might have even found a new hobby."

"Oh, yeah," he said, rolling his eyes. "I can really see myself diving into ice culture."

"You keep this up," she laughed, "and I might start snorting in front of all these fancy people."

Will grinned and held out a hand. "Come on. Let's go find our seats and pray for it to be over."

"Is there a scenario in which I can leave you here and go home instead?" After all, the overarching point was to be away from each other.

Raising an eyebrow, Will regarded her. "The Laura Harris I knew was never a quitter."

Laura started at the use of her old last name, the one she'd used for most of her life before her final foster parents had legally adopted her. She remembered the reckless girl she'd been before she had anything to lose, how brave she'd had to be because there'd been no other choice. The reminder had her wanting to be a good friend to Will and stay to make sure he had a good time.

She took a step forward to grab his outstretched hand and the rough, bare skin had her sucking in a breath. Dusty old visions of him sprang into her mind, shirtless in the summer when they'd sneaked into the public pool, but he'd been scrawnier then, obviously. His warmth against her was heady, the breadth of his shoulders making her feel swallowed up in his protection somehow. The thoughts were probably just left-over hero worship, but it felt so good to be near him, to feel him again.

"You want another round?" he asked, giving her hand a slow squeeze before letting it go, trailing his fingers and then his thumb slowly over her bare palm and down her middle finger. "Or have you had too much to drink already? You're looking a little flushed."

Shaken, her body fully awake, instead of answering she simply walked toward table three, which was the number the registrant at the entrance had given them, sat down, and struck up a conversation with the first person she saw. Anyone was better than talking to and touching Will.

"As always, taunting you worked wonders," Will observed, joining her at the table after she'd finished a conversation with a handsome but boring tech investor.

Her head swiveled over to him and she asked, "What is that supposed to mean?"

"You don't remember anything about back then, do you? I could get you to do anything as long as I made you think you couldn't do it."

She stared at him, snippets of memories coming back to her, of him challenging her, but then being her biggest cheerleader. He'd been a really lovely friend all around but maybe she had blocked a lot of that time out for self-preservation. She was surprised to hear that he hadn't locked it away as well, considering he wasn't exactly sharing personal information right and left.

"I remember," she finally said, watching him fold into the seat beside her, his proximity sending SOS alerts to all her erogenous zones and knocking her out of the past. "It's just hard to really go back there."

Will nodded in understanding. "You were the best part of it, though."

Her drink paused halfway to her lips, she met his eyes. "You too."

In that moment, she couldn't have pulled her eyes away from his for all the money in the world. It felt like they were the only two people in the restaurant despite the urbane roar of the guests echoing off the marble walls.

"I wanted you so much back then," he murmured, his fingers finding a strand of her hair as he draped his arm on the back of her chair.

Ripples of pleasure drifted up from her tingling feet to her damp palms. "I didn't know."

A corner of his mouth quirked. "Yeah, you did," he murmured. "Just like you know now."

"I thought we were here to have a nice brunch," she replied gamely, trying to power through it. "You know, to eat omelettes with hydroponic veggies and imported French cheese and stuff." God, she was hopeless. Her desire was eradicating all her common sense.

The universe was on her side because the meal was served then. Waiters in tuxes and white gloves appeared with a parade of artfully decorated small plates. To further ignore Will's attempts to lure her into ill-conceived flirting, she made small talk with her neighbor, a friendly middle-aged man who seemed almost as uncomfortable and out of place as she felt.

Meanwhile, Will's hand found her knee, her back, her inner thigh until she was slowly sinking into a sea of desire and probably would have stripped on the table in front of society's best for him if he'd asked, she was so mindless.

"I know what you're doing," he murmured darkly in her ear after fifteen minutes of her studiously ignoring his maddening "accidental" touches.

She swatted him away and heard his deep chuckle as she resumed her conversation with her tablemate. Will could wait all day because they just couldn't do what he wanted. No matter how desperately she wanted to. She needed him in her life too much, never wanted to let him go again, and she just couldn't risk all that for sex. What was sure to be mind-blowing sex aside, it still wasn't worth it.

After Roger, said tablemate, told a joke that wasn't actually funny, but that she laughed at anyway because it was polite, Will ran a finger down her spine, leaning close so only she could hear him. "You're being a scaredy-cat again, Laura."

She put a hand on his arm to somehow prove she wasn't, but it was such a mistake because she felt the strength and sinew beneath the fabric of his coat. Their eyes met and there was just no point in denying anything.

"Let's get out of here," he urged, as the plates were cleared. He took her hand and met her eyes, prepared to lead them to the exit, saying pointedly, "Don't chicken out again."

They made it to the front doors and once they were back onto Sixth Avenue, Laura met his eyes. "I didn't think that was so bad."

He just rolled his eyes and started off down the sidewalk, his boots grinding into the snow. "If I had to listen to that man flirt with you any more, I was going to start throwing punches."

"Aren't we waiting for your car?" she asked, the cold slithering up her legs underneath her skirt and through her sheer tights.

"It's easier to walk," he declared, not waiting for her to follow him, just setting off in the direction of the WW. It wasn't that far of a walk, just a couple of blocks on Sixth Avenue down to the cross street of Thirty-Eighth Street where his hotel was, but she was in heeled boots and so she stayed put. He was halfway down the street before he realized she wasn't following him.

"What's the matter?" he called, his dark overcoat fanning out behind him as he swiveled to face her.

"I'm not walking on the ice and snow in heels," she returned, tapping on her phone for a car service.

He returned to her, his brows knitted with agitation, and pointed to a black town car in a line of town cars waiting at the curb. "Let's go."

"Were you going to inform your driver you weren't using him?" she asked once they were in the car.

"My assistant would have taken care of it."

It seemed the height of rudeness to her to not just tell the driver to go back to the hotel without him, but did remind her that while they'd both traveled leaps and bounds from where they'd started in life, he was leading a very different one from hers. As this brunch and last night's party illustrated, his world was incredibly rarified and she didn't know the rules.

Once they were back in the hotel, she practically had to run to keep up with his hurried pace. His little touches during brunch had made him just as crazy as they'd made her.

"Are you mad at me or something?" she asked, trying to normalize what was happening between them. Bring it back to safer ground, give both of them an out.

His eyes snapped to hers, intensity pulsing in the brown depths. "Let's cut the bullshit, Laura," he said, his voice low and measured. "Last night we kissed and it was good. I know it was good, you know it was good. Off-the-charts good before you chastise my superlatives. You've been looking at me like you want me all fucking day, so I apologize if I haven't made clear what's wrong. I want you in my bed. So let's just stop pretending that we can ignore our attraction to each other while you're living in my house for Christ's sake because we clearly can't."

Laura took a deep breath because she felt his words like lightning bolts to her senses. Loved that he could be so blunt with his desire for her, his honesty and Will-ness catching her in the gut. Thank God she'd found him again, this person who'd known her at her worst and still wanted her.

The black elevator doors opened up to his penthouse. She'd left the tree lights on, which made the evening feel surreal but also a little magical, even without thousands of dollars of glitter. Here they were, long-lost friends who found each other at Christmas. It didn't happen to just anyone. Especially not to the two of them who were used to being the unlucky ones.

Facing him in the living area, she met his eyes which had not moved from hers since his speech. "I'm not trying to deny our attraction, but I think we both know that having sex isn't a great idea."

Twin eyebrows shot up. "We do? Because from

where I'm standing I'm having a hell of a time figuring out why it's a bad idea."

"We have history, Will. A lot of it," she reminded meaningfully, before continuing, "and I'm not a casual relationship type of person and you seem to be."

She waited for his expression to change, but when it didn't she tried again. "If we have sex it could never be just about the sex. There are already feelings involved and they could be hurt." *Her* feelings which were already there, unchanged from when they were kids.

Will's gaze still held hers, penetrating and considering. "I like the odds."

"You don't think you're in danger of falling in love with me?" she grinned, attempting to lighten the mood and maybe sidestep this epic land mine.

"I don't care if I am," he shot back, sending her own heart thumping wildly inside her chest. It felt like when they were young and about to do something incredibly dumb but fun anyway. He was daring her again to do the risky thing and she knew he was doing it to get what he wanted and wasn't thinking at all about the consequences, but that little part of her that thought he actually was considering them was what got her. He'd already played out all the scenarios in his head, because Will planned for the future in his sleep; it was what you did when it was all you had. The fact that he knew exactly what could happen between them and was ballsy enough to do it anyway. That was what was enticing her to play the game too.

"You've never had your heart broken," she challenged. "It won't be easy if this ends badly."

His ruler-straight jaw gave a single twitch, his eyes giving nothing away. "I never said my heart hadn't been broken before."

Laura opened her mouth, wanting to ask more questions. Outside his wall of windows, the lights of New York City flickered on as dusk fell on Christmas Eve, illuminating the purple sky beyond them. Who could ever break Will Walker's heart? He was always the toughest kid she knew.

"Another kiss," he proposed, testing her resolve. "If we don't want to continue, we won't."

It was a sucker's bet because there was no way she wouldn't want it to continue and he knew it.

But fuck it, she always was a sucker for Will.

So she pulled him into her, taking charge of her own destiny. He moved forward too, their eyes locked as he slowly tugged off her blue cashmere scarf and dropped it to the floor before lowering his lips to hers.

Just like last night, the soft but firm press of his lips immediately set her body on fire. Hell with the future when the present was so damned good. His big hands threaded through her hair, taking all the time they hadn't last night when they'd discovered each other by accident. She grew instantly too hot in her coat now that they were inside and when she began going for the zipper his other hand stayed her and he took over himself.

"I'd be an awful host if I made you undress yourself," he murmured, his voice lower than normal, intimate in a way she'd never been privy to.

She held her breath as she watched him unbutton the etched silver buttons of her peacoat and throw the garment on the back of the couch. When she reached for him to return the favor, he beat her to it, shrugging out of his black overcoat and letting the expensive cashmere drop to the floor, revealing a black button-down shirt that looked luxurious and dangerous all at once. She liked that he wasn't some suit-wearing entrepreneur with glossed wing tips and classy cufflinks; what she was seeing was a Will she could have imagined him being when they were kids. Honest, real and irreverent, a man who did exactly what he wanted and to hell with the rest.

It became even more clear when he unbuttoned his shirt.

He pulled her back into his arms and met her lips again. She hadn't been prepared for the searing heat of his bare skin as her fingers found his chest and she sucked in an embarrassingly loud breath, but he ignored it, a corner of his mouth lifting almost imperceptibly. His abs weren't cut like models or athletes, but they were hard and outlined, the scruff of hair on his chest soft against the pads of her fingers.

With a sigh, she fell into the kiss then, giving over to what she wanted. She loved it when he went deeper, exploring her mouth, their tongues tasting and touching and teasing. They took frantic breaths before meeting each other again, she tugged on his tongue, he pulled at her bottom lip causing her to whimper with need. When he gave her more like she wanted, her fingernails drove into the skin of his back and she gave up.

Her heart might not be strong enough to take him on, but the rest of her body was up to the challenge.

"You're right," she said, pulling back to meet him squarely in the eyes. "Just a kiss is not enough."

CHAPTER SIX

WILL'S BODY HAD been hyperaware of Laura's all day, her warmth, her smile with those silly dimples that he should find ridiculous, but instead adored. She'd hated them as a teenager because they'd made her look soft at a time when they'd truly needed to be tough to survive, but now here they were right in the lap of luxury and he wanted to lick and caress and worship those dimples for the soft place to land that they were.

She was his soft place to land. Always the memory of her had sustained him over the years. He had the capacity to feel, to care; he knew that on some level, but he hadn't been willing to make the effort. He was man enough to admit now that her leaving had left emotional scars on his heart so deep he hadn't even had the guts to examine them. More than even his mom leaving because that at least he understood. But now, holding Laura, he knew. He'd loved her so much that her leaving without a word had nearly broken him; he could admit it, see it and maybe let it go.

The anger he'd held on to was dissipating; it'd left him when he'd seen her baking cookies in his kitchen. The first rule of their childhood had been to take every opportunity as it came. He'd been the one to teach her that and she'd followed his instructions to the letter; he couldn't fault her for it. Wouldn't do that to a friend.

But as she kissed him, her entire body locked against his as her hands slid through his hair to control the kiss and to elicit more of a response from him, he realized that he *had* been holding on to it, using it to keep his distance from the only person who'd ever meant anything to him in his life. That was a mistake.

So he brought her closer against him, his veins burning like a brush fire under his skin, catching the rest of his body aflame without any rhyme, reason or direction until he was completely overwhelmed by her and what it meant that they were finally together in the way he'd always wanted.

His hands traveled down her back, taking her rear end into his hands. She'd filled out from the starved, bony kid she'd been and he liked it, liked the curves, loved the breadth of her ass in his hands. Lifting her up into his arms, he headed to the bedroom. For once, the two of them were going to do things in comfort together, not in the space of hurried or stolen moments in between the rest of their shitty lives.

Her squeak of surprise had him smiling against her lips as he nipped at them, pausing in his route to the bedroom to lean her up against a wall, her long legs tightening around his back, which got him painfully rigid. She seized the opportunity and dove in, their mouths crushing against each other, begging for more, more contact, more connection. He wanted it all, felt himself coming alive under her touch. Really letting himself be inside an experience instead of just standing outside it like usual. She'd always been his; it had been predestined, and now it was time to claim her.

He slowly unzipped her dress and let it fall to her hips so that they were skin to skin, burning each other as they stood locked together against the wall. Her breasts, the tips hard and budding beneath the silk fabric of her black bra, absolutely unmanned him. He stared, trying to work out just how many times he'd wondered what she'd looked like with her shirt off, feeling dirty at the times when her breasts accidentally brushed against him. In his wildest dreams, he never could have imagined that this was the scenario in which he'd finally see Laura naked for the first time—in a luxury penthouse high above the world and her in a silk bra that cost more than a month's rent of their foster parents' crummy apartments.

Pulling down the black strap, his breath stopped in his chest, the moment so surreal that he was caught between the past and the present, wanting to care and protect her but always wanting to completely wreck her like he felt. He pulled down the straps with reverence and slowly unhooked the gold metal front clasp, watching the fabric fall away to reveal the most perfect pair of breasts he'd ever seen.

Feeling the moment in his knees, he met her eyes, not caring how he must look, crazed by lust and stunned by the wonder that they were finally together after all this time. The destiny of it, the rightness, made him feel strangely comfortable in a way he rarely felt with women. This wasn't transactional; he didn't have to worry about sending enough signals that it was sex-only for tonight or that they wouldn't be hearing from him again, and he didn't have to worry about paying them enough money to ensure that they wouldn't try to show up at one of his hotels to embarrass him.

His entire life from childhood to now had been solely about work, relentless and all-consuming work, but Laura was pleasure. Divine, lazy pleasure and he was going to steep himself in it for as long as humanly possible.

"You're incredible," he told her before lowering his lips to her breast, he dropped reverential kisses along the delicate crest, drifted down to the lower curve, lifted it up slightly to press one to her abdomen, loving how warm her skin was there compared to her hands and arms, cold from being exposed to the freezing outdoors.

Finally, he took a dark peach nipple into his mouth, sucking gently at first, then his tongue gliding over the puckered velvet of her skin before exerting more pressure, her nipple braced against the roof of his mouth as he sucked her. Her soft murmurs of pleasure echoed in the empty hallway and his blood heated to an ungodly degree. Lifting her from the wall, he let her nipple fall from his mouth with an audible pop, loving how her breasts jiggled against his chest as he walked them into his room. The eighteen-year-old kid in him was positively gleeful at seeing it.

He set her down on the floor first so he could make quick work of her dress, his hands quivering as he pulled down her matching black silk underwear. He'd seen a lot of women's underthings in his day, from lacy scraps of nothing, to hip-huggers, cotton, silk, polyester, cutesy designs, but nothing prepared him for Laura. Because no one had ever measured up to the girl he'd cherished back then. He should have known Laura was a purist at heart, that despite all her glittery and new fancy digs, at the heart of her was the no-nonsense rough-around-the-edges girl she'd always been. Her plain black underwear was the sexiest thing he'd ever seen.

He contemplated what his next move might be because he needed to make this unforgettable for her. She wasn't getting out of his bedroom without him knowing that he was the best she'd ever had. Because already, just by being her, this moment had already topped his charts.

Angling her back onto the bed, they stretched out onto the thousand-thread-count white duvet cover.

Kissing her again, he ran a hand through her hair, the cool strands slipping through his fingers lighting up every nerve ending in his body. He wanted to eat her alive, drive her crazy until she didn't know her name, the year, what planet they were on, literally nothing.

"Tell me what you want, Laura," he asked, biting down on her earlobe, a little too hard because he barely had a handle on himself. He'd never felt this way about a woman and it should have been sending warning alarms through his head, but he didn't care.

Her breathing was heavy, the rise and fall of her chest pronounced as she battled her own lust. "You," she choked out when he ran a hand over her ass and gave it a gentle squeeze.

He reached over and grabbed a feather from his nightstand because he wanted to surprise her, make her so insane that she'd never forget tonight. Regardless of what happened when the snow melted and normal life resumed, she wasn't ever going to forget about him again. Not outside the bedroom and certainly not in it. He drew the soft feathers over the hard, wet nipple he'd just nursed with his mouth, watching as her entire body pebbled over with goose bumps. Provoking her was like a drug he wanted to overdose on.

Flipping her over, ignoring her halfhearted mumble of protest, he planted his knees on either side of her legs, running first a finger down her spine, but then the hard tip of the quill. Her breathing audible, he ran the soft feathers over her entire back, down the sensitive backs of her arms, the exposed sides of her breasts, the smooth expanse of her legs, then back up to drift over the very heart of her. Smiling as she twitched under his ministrations, he did the same pass over her body again only this time swishing it lightly back and forth, the motion repetitive and hypnotic. The weight of Will against her back, the soft brush of the feathers against her skin was like heaven.

He dropped a soft kiss on the small of her back that had her rolling her hips up. She heard him chuckle as he drew a thumb down the seam of her ass, teasing, testing as she whimpered.

Then he pulled her hips up until she was secure on her knees and she opened her mouth to remind him to use a condom, but he had something else in mind entirely. Fingers opened her up, spreading her to the air and she thought she might actually collapse from need. She wanted him closer and got her wish when he ran a finger from her front to her back, spreading her moisture and teasing.

She bucked up, wanting him to get on with it, to put a condom on and get to work, but he was willful. Pulled her open again and his mouth settled fully on her sex, his tongue sliding into her, rolling and licking; he grunted lightly as he fucked her thoroughly, her whole body growing heavy with longing.

Taking the slippery bud into his mouth, Laura cried out as his teeth bit, her limbs shaking as she got closer to climax. He took her there, his rough, thick fingers plunging inside her as he sucked her clit rhythmically; it was hypnotic and slow as he drew out the sensations, but she'd need it faster if she was actually going to come. Moving her hips against him to hurry the process, she received an open-handed swat on her ass and his hands gripping her hips to hold her still.

"This is how I play," he murmured, removing his face from between her legs completely.

She looked back to see what he was doing and saw that he had his own rigid length in his hand, stroking slowly as his eyes locked on her pussy, open and pulsing for him. Watching him, the way his fingers, glistening from her own wetness, closed around his thickness, another wave of heat washed over her. Survival seemed unlikely and she took matters into her own hands, reaching down to her clit to get her own self off just as he was, but seeing her, a hand still on himself, he reared back and stopped her. It'd been so long since he'd given a fuck about anyone that part of him felt like it was waking up again after a hibernation.

He brushed another soft kiss to her bottom and she lifted herself up, encouraging him to keep touching her, but he moved away again leaving her in the cold.

"Do you want to come, Laura?" he taunted, his voice low and rumbling in the darkness.

"Yes," she choked, watching a drop of his own

come form on the tip of him, her eyes riveted as his locked on hers as he drew the moisture around the rounded head.

"I'm not going to let you until you beg for it," he told her, a glint in his eye that told her this was the game. To torture her until she could no longer take it. And she was close to not being able to take anymore, but she felt like she'd been waiting a lifetime to be in Will's bed and that she was going to accept the challenge.

Regardless, she levered up until they were both sitting on their heels in front of each other and she reached out and took him in her hand, covering his own. Together, she guided him down his length, her wetness still on his fingers slick as they went. She leaned down to take him in her mouth and she was surprised that he let her, but he just grunted as she pulled his hand away and licked over his leaking tip. Then she took all of him into her mouth and that was when he backed away from her, tipping her onto her back so she was sprawled before him.

The feather appeared in his hand again, tracing the path of her arms, breasts, abdomen and legs, sliding slowly over the sensitized crease of her, dragging the wetness up her stomach before he licked it clean. Her hips bucked without her even realizing it, seeking more contact, seeking him inside her finally. He dipped a thumb to her clit, a quick nuzzle that ramped her up and then he was gone again, swishing the feather lightly over her skin. It was enough to drive her insane. Every nerve ending, every brain cell in her body, every follicle on her skin was waiting, begging for him to take her but he was content to play.

She should have known this about Will. Everything he did was under his control. He operated an empire, had guided them as kids, had protected her, all because that's who he was. He was a master of his own universe and she'd just happened to be a part of it tonight so she let her head fall back into the heavenly soft pillows and enjoy. Her mind eventually went blank, the only focus on the predictable brush of the feathers on her skin, running figure eight patterns over her abdomen.

Every so often he would add a thumb to bring her to the brink of orgasm again, until she was panting for him, whimpering for him to continue.

"I am begging," she finally said as his finger slowly slid over her engorged center, her voice choked and hoarse with unspent desire. "Please, I need it."

But he wasn't convinced and repeated the entire circuit, only this time, he rolled her to the side and ran the softness down the vulnerable undersides of her arms and ticklish sides, but she wasn't laughing; too keyed up from the delayed orgasm, she barely had an awareness of time anymore; her entire world was centered on his touch.

Finally, the feather disappeared and she heard a drawer open and the crinkle of foil.

"Thank God," she sighed. Rolling her again,

he took her from the front, their eyes locked as he slowly slid into her. Words would have been frivolous to say, but she felt them bubbling up in her throat as he stretched her, found the place inside her that had been waiting for him for so long. She always thought he'd be her first, fantasized about it, but nothing would have ever prepared her for this, her body's total surrender. She was his; he had to draw her legs up himself and put them around his back, pulling him farther into her because she was so gone. Eventually, her body took over, lunging upward to him as he plunged into her hot wetness, the sound of their bodies coming together cutting hungrily through the quiet room.

He wasn't easy, the strength of him pistoning in and out of her was like bolts of lightning, hitting the perfect spot each time, but leaving her body shocked with sensation.

When it arrived, her climax hit her like an avalanche burying her in pleasure; deep, drugging blankets of happiness fell over her body, obliterating any other thoughts or feelings. It had never been like this.

But he wasn't finished, his hands threading through hers and pinning them to the bed as he moved hungrily against her, grinding into her clit, effortlessly sending her over the edge again. Her inner muscles clamped down on him, keeping him inside her, gripping and he gave a final push in, groaning with the effort as his body shuddered under his own release.

Laura's eyes closed, her head unmoving on the pillow; her hand reached up to brush a hunk of dark, sweaty hair from his eye.

"I think I'm dead," she managed, her voice low and wry.

His forehead hit hers as his breathing slowed. "I'll get you the prettiest coffin I can find."

She huffed out a laugh as he rolled off her, depositing the condom quickly into the trash before joining her in bed again. She found herself in his crook, his nose in her hair.

"It wasn't too much?" he asked.

She shook her head. "It was perfect," she told him, wrapping an arm around his rigid abdomen.

Her body was literally falling into a sex coma from which she wasn't sure she needed to wake. It was the best she'd ever felt and it was all because of Will, not just what he'd done, but who he was.

"I'm going to make you so many more cookies," she promised, her voice sounding groggy even to her own ears.

The last thing she remembered was his soft kiss to her forehead before sleep overtook her.

CHAPTER SEVEN

LAURA WOKE UP in Will's dark and quiet bedroom, still in a hazy state of disbelief over what they'd done, the absolute wonder of it. She expected some kind of regret or self-consciousness to interrupt an otherwise lovely Christmas Eve evening, but she only felt good about what they'd done. It was probably the height of foolishness because her heart was in a very precarious position, but it didn't matter.

"You literally kicked me straight in the gut at least two times," a sleep-scratched voice accused from the other side of the bed. "I think I'm bruised."

Laura cleared her throat, mildly embarrassed. "Yeah, I'm not a great sleeper," she admitted. "Sorry about that."

A warm arm pulled her back against his chest and she didn't bother to fight it as his lips came to greet hers. "You don't have to apologize. I'll just make sure my face is uphill from your legs next time."

Then he kissed her again, lazy and long, her body falling back into deep relaxation even as tendrils of lust curled in her veins.

"Can I order room service for dinner or do you have something planned?" he asked, drawing lazy circles on her shoulders.

"Planned," she said, having gotten all the ingredients for her traditional Christmas Eve dinner previously before Operation: Give Will a Christmas had been basically thwarted by his insistence on dragging her to society events.

He gave her another quick kiss. "I don't hate you in my bed," he said, almost thoughtfully, as if he was just considering it.

"Good to know," she said, the thought of just how many other women he'd had in this bed popping up in her thoughts like a sneaky fox poised to steal the goodness of the day. She'd heard the stories about Will and the women he dated, and couldn't help but wonder if she'd eventually become, just that, another story.

He ran a possessive hand over her hair, gripping the ends just slightly before letting go of it to head to the bathroom, bold and bare-ass naked.

Taking a minute to enjoy the show, she watched until he closed the door. With a sigh, she got herself up and headed to her own room to shower and change clothes. She pulled out a pair of pajamas with little reindeers on them that she'd bought for her family's annual silly Christmas photo and padded out to the kitchen to start dinner.

Within minutes of chopping up an onion for the marinara sauce that would go in the lasagna, Will appeared from the hallway looking sexy and slightly rumpled in a pair of gray sweats and a faded black thermal. He flipped on the fireplace and the orange flames immediately came to life behind the grate. Just like last night it was extremely cozy and considering what they'd just done, Laura was already feeling anxious. Worried because not only did she want to do it all over again, but because she couldn't imagine wanting to not do it. Ever. Which was a problem when something had an expiration date.

"Smells good already," he told her, coming to stand behind her at the stove, his body as hot as the flame in front of her. "What's on the menu?" His nose nudged her hair aside and lips gently touched her neck and it felt like the same kind of care and consideration she'd always yearned for from him.

Holding back a sigh of sublime contentment, she answered, "Lasagna. Nothing fancy, but it's tradition."

His hand slid down her arm and away, lighting a match and then stepping away from the fire. On purpose, she knew now, to drive her crazy. She missed his touch already. He was dangerously addictive and she had to be careful because this was an anomaly and as soon as the snow and her houseguests were gone, so probably was this.

He made a low sound in his throat that she felt in the middle of her thighs. "Lasagna is one of my favorite meals. Need any help?"

She pointed to the plastic cartons and cheese on the counter. "You can mix together the filling if you want."

"Just dump all this stuff in a bowl?"

She nodded and he got to work after pausing to turn on some Christmas music, something he'd refused to let her listen to yesterday.

"Thanks," she said, suddenly feeling unsure of herself. After chopping up a carrot, her secret ingredient, she poured a can of tomatoes and tomato sauce into the pot and let it all come to a simmer.

Watching him stir the cheese, egg and parsley mixture, she started grinning. "Do you think our teenage selves could have ever imagined us doing that?" she asked, nodding to indicate what they'd done in his bedroom.

He looked at her out of the corner of his eye. "Um, as I mentioned before, that's about all my teenage self imagined doing with you, so, yeah."

Her eyebrows rose. "You never gave any indication that I was anything other than a sister to you."

He hit her with a speculative look, his eyebrow raised in doubt. "I really don't know how you would have been so clueless, but I did have all those thoughts. Trust me."

"You should have said something. We were friends—it would have been okay to be honest." And maybe she would have stayed with him if she'd known and he wouldn't have been so alone and cut off like he was now.

He was silent for a moment. "You were my best friend, yeah."

That statement and his tone sucker punched her in

the gut. For him to make the differentiation of best friends versus just friends in a casual conversation meant that she'd been extremely important to him.

"And I definitely wanted to have sex with you too," he threw in when she would have pressed.

She laughed. "Well, you hid it well."

The only sound in the room was the wooden spoon softly clicking against the white ceramic bowl as Will stirred his cheese mixture. She took a moment to watch through the windows as a blanket of snow fell down, effectively shutting the rest of the world out.

The water for the noodles was boiling so she started putting a couple of them in at a time while ladling sauce into the pan so she could layer all of the ingredients.

She was thankful to have something to do because she was still feeling awkward. Wanting to talk more about what they'd done and what it meant. Usually after one-night stands she left the scene; she didn't stay around and make lasagna while pretending it wasn't the biggest holiday of the year. It also didn't help that he was staring at her, his eyes zeroed in and following every movement and action as if he was trying to memorize it.

"I should have told you how pretty you were," he said, stalling her, her chest thumping wildly at the compliment. Will had never been one for words, but when he delivered them, they meant something.

Ladle full of sauce in the air, she met his eyes,

knowing her own gaze was probably embarrassingly vulnerable. "What?"

His eyes were dark. "It was just one of the tons of things I regretted not telling you after you left."

A pang of emotion so deep hit at a raw spot in her chest that nearly leveled her. She still remembered having to leave him. It had killed her, the silent sobbing in the back of the caseworker's gold Dodge Neon, the interior worn but clean. She'd choked back the tears then because they would have ruined her. But once she was out of the city, in the safety of the hotel room they were staying at before the formal transfer to her new foster family, the tears had come and hadn't stopped until morning.

She hadn't had a choice. It was either escape with him to survive on their own with not even a high school diploma between them or a shot at the family she'd always wanted. She'd done what she'd thought was best, but none of that meant she hadn't been devastated to lose him.

"Thank you, Will," she managed through the lump her throat. "And I always thought you were handsome, then and now."

A dark, winged eyebrow rose over his eye and one side of his mouth crooked. "Handsome?"

"Yeah," she confirmed, raising her own eyebrows in question, glad for the return to levity.

He made a kind of grunting noise, but didn't say anything.

"What is wrong with being handsome?" she pressed, hiding her own smile.

"It's a word used to describe little boys in suits."

She rolled her eyes and started placing a third of the noodles over the sauce. "Give me a break."

She could feel his eyes on her as she worked, but he didn't say anything so she glared at him. "You can't be seriously mad about it."

"Not mad, but I just think you should be accurate is all."

Snorting, she wiped her hands on a paper towel, having gotten some sauce on them. "Just say you want another compliment, Will, and I'll give you one."

He gave her a bland look as if to say she was being the irrational one.

"You were a good-looking teenager," she told him, giving him what he wanted anyway because she wanted him to have it, wanted to make him feel as good as he made her. Just wanted to see him smile, possibly, if that was a thing he ever did. "But as an adult you are devastatingly hot, Will."

Hooded eyes met hers. His voice low and gravely as usual, he teased, "Was that so hard?"

She shrugged. "Nope, but I'm sure you've heard it before."

"Not from you, though," he pointed out, handing her another noodle.

"We just got out of bed together—I would think how I felt about your appearance was pretty clear."

"Would it help if I said that as a teenager you were adorable, but as a woman you're extraordinary?"

"Okay, what's going on here with these compliments?" Laura demanded, waving a wooden spoon at him as her insides went gooey. "Who are you and what have you done with Will Walker the man who cursed every waking being today at brunch?"

Their eyes met, his tongue stuck in the side of his mouth. "I'm the same guy you always knew. I just don't have to hide the fact that I want you anymore. But I do want you to tell me why you're brushing it off and making a joke of it? Because I don't say a lot of nice things nowadays, so when I do trust me to mean it."

"I didn't mean to do that," she apologized. "They do mean a lot to me."

He gave her a nod of acknowledgment. "Same for me."

Her mind drifted, wanting to find the right thing to say. To right the past with Will so they had a chance of moving on. So that she had an opportunity to be in his life permanently. It'd taken so long after she'd moved in with her family that she could even believe she was worthy of good things. The warmth, the camaraderie, the bone-deep sense of belonging she'd yearned for all given to her one day out of the blue had felt too good to be true. If she'd never found her parents, Laura just didn't know how unhappy she would be now, never having known unconditional love and support.

But she'd found Will on Christmas over a decade and a half later and it was her duty to help him find that kind of peace and acceptance, as well.

"Do you ever think you'll want a family?" she asked, spooning small dollops of the cheese mixture onto the noodles.

"Nah," he told her, not even thinking about it. "I'm not a dad."

"That wasn't the question I asked," she clarified.

"It wasn't?" he asked, genuinely confused.

"The question wasn't whether or not you'd be a good dad, which you would be. If anyone knows that, it's me. You always made sure we had food and protected me when I needed it. If that's not the basics of parenting, I don't know what is. But regardless, the question was if you want a family?"

He met her eyes, an eyebrow lifted at her insistence. "Then no, I don't want a family."

She waved her spoon to encompass his vast penthouse fit for someone transient. "So you just want to live here in this hotel penthouse forever? You don't want to settle into an actual home where some faceless person hasn't touched and made sure your toilet paper is shaped into a diamond point before you use it?"

His eyes lighted with sardonic humor, but he otherwise ignored her toilet-paper comment. "I have other hotels—I thought about living there, as well."

"You know what I mean," she insisted. "This is a lonely life here."

His entire body stiffened and she felt the tension suddenly grow in the room, and regretted overstepping. She'd pushed too hard at the sensitive bits.

"Yeah, well, I worked damn hard for this lonely life, so if it's okay with you I think I'll enjoy it the way I want to."

Yep, totally whiffed. Good job, Edwards, way to make him feel like a complete loser because he didn't have a bowl of potpourri and a wreath on his door. Projecting much? But her dream had always been to make a home and family, to give her children the security and warmth she'd been deprived of for so long, and she couldn't imagine a future without that. But now that she'd found Will again, she also couldn't imagine a future without him.

"I'm sorry, Will, that's not what I meant," she said, laying a hand on his thick forearm, thankful that she could at least touch him now. "I just mean that maybe someday you'll want to find someone and make a home, that's all. I'm so proud of everything you've done. More than proud. I'm astonished, impressed, in awe, and yet, not at all surprised because to me you were always a star."

Their eyes met and he was clearly still annoyed, but her honesty had taken the sting off her insinuation.

"I just hate thinking of you alone," she continued in clarification. "You deserve someone special in your life."

He held her eyes, his expression serious as the moment stretched.

But then he shook his head and looked away and they busied themselves with the task of putting the rest of the lasagna together. She noticed the deft way he took over placing the hot noodles for her, not even flinching as he took them straight from the pot of boiling water and arranged them in the pan as if he'd been doing it his entire life.

The silence grew tense and his body was so close to hers that she could smell the remnants of their afternoon in bed on him and it came flooding back to her in all its racy detail, simmering heat dancing along her skin. She'd never felt this kind of insistent ache and need for someone before, but it made sense that it would happen with Will.

After finally sliding the lasagna into the hot oven, she leaned against the kitchen island, meeting his eyes.

"Do you want to take your pants off now or would you like me to do it?"

Both his eyebrows shot up in surprise, but a little smile tugged at the corners of his mouth.

"I'd love for you to do it."

"Your wish is my command," she teased. She pushed away from the counter and stopped in front of him, running a hand down his chest, the fabric of his thermal soft under her fingers. "I'd like to return the favor from earlier."

"I'm not standing in your way," he told her still not touching her.

Laura hooked her fingers into the waistband of his

gray joggers, and pushed them down his lean hips, but was still holding his eyes.

When she finally looked down she saw that he wasn't wearing any underwear, and his thick cock sprang out, already semihard.

"Italian food really does it for you, huh?"

"Nah," he shook his head, refusing to play, "you."

A thrill of power went through the circuit of her veins like hot oil, her entire body heating from the inside out from his words. He was just so sexy, his mouth opened just slightly as he regarded her, his eyes focused, clear and hooded the tiniest bit, the dark pools intent on her.

His pants fell to the wood floor with a soft whoosh and she reached out a hand, almost afraid to touch him without the heat and urgency of their first time. That had been a temporary stay of sanity, an anomaly, something they could chalk up to combustible passion out of their control, but standing before him now was a different thing entirely. She was about to touch him and that would be a choice made with a clear head, with deliberation and thought.

In some weird way, she still felt like she needed to atone for leaving him all alone, and all alone on Christmas to boot. A vision of the messy-haired boy who tried so hard to care for her rose up in her head and her entire chest clutched with the guilt she'd so long ago put away in a box, never to be examined. But there was no choice now, so she sank to her knees in front of him.

"I'm sorry," she told him, laying her head on his upper thigh, breathing him in like he was oxygen, life-giving and necessary. And maybe he was becoming that for her. Maybe he always was that. The only person who knew her when. There was something powerful in that. She didn't like remembering the girl she'd been, but that scrappy, foul-mouthed teenager was a fighter and that was something Laura had never left behind. And she should have fought harder to find Will, she understood that now, looking around at how empty his life was and acknowledging her own ineptitude at opening up in relationships.

His long fingers threaded through her hair. "Don't apologize to me, Laura."

She shook her head, unable to stop the tears from forming behind her eyes. Blinking furiously, she wouldn't let them fall, but the agony of all of it was swarming her, of how much he'd meant to her then and how much he already meant to her now. How much time they'd been lost to each other.

"Don't tell me what to do," she commanded, kissing a line of soft kisses across the ridged sections of his abdomen. Her tongue darted out, tasting the salty skin, the smooth, warm expanse and drowning in the blissful intimacy. It'd been a long time since she'd wanted to give someone a blow job, but when her hand wrapped around Will's cock, fully hard now after her exploration, she could feast on him for days.

Her hand crept down, exerting pressure when she felt like it, but otherwise content to feel him, to show him with tenderness and desire that she wanted him like no other. She wanted to know him, every piece of skin, every strand of hair she considered under her purview. Then maybe she could scale his walls and make him believe in his future, one that wasn't simply buying more hotels and living alone in them. Or maybe that was what she was afraid her life would be if she didn't slow down and let someone else in for real. All her relationships ended before they'd really begun because she was looking for someone who would stick, who she wanted to build a family with and no one was ever special enough to fit the bill.

But this, giving Will pleasure, making him happy, that she could do. What she desperately needed to do to atone.

Drawing a thumb down the underside of his pulsing vein, excitement poured through her and she adjusted her legs wider to ease the friction. Her tongue followed the same line of her finger, tasting and testing as he remained rigid and seemingly unaffected by her. When she came to the top of him, her other hand traveled farther back as she took the head of him into her mouth and sucked gently, reverently. Her finger found that sensitive skin just beyond his balls and rubbed gently as she ran her tongue over his tip tasting the salty drop of him.

She took more of the rigid length, driving him deeper into her mouth inch by delicious inch. When she got to the bottom, he finally touched her, tilting up her chin so he could see her eyes. He held her there, the moment stretching, taut with meaning and lust and the complications that came with being the two of them. Unlike other men, he didn't try to nudge her. When she swallowed, his eyes closed, opening again with a fire and pure heat in them, sending chills up her spine. He wasn't sexy, he was sensuous, his rough-hewn body wound tight as a drum. She wanted his fingers in her hair, guiding her like she was used to, but he just held her chin there until eventually she moved with him, the erotic control of it thrilling.

He still followed her pace and when she accepted that he wanted her eyes on his, she sped up, her tongue flying over the velvet skin of his cock, feeling his cum mix with her own saliva, reveling in just how much she liked this. She was in control, totally and absolutely, of Will Walker, the man who owned the very structure they were standing in. The man who had built an empire on dreams and determination alone, his jaw clenched and fists white at his sides as he took his pleasure.

But he didn't make noise, didn't show her that he was enjoying it, their eyes locked as she slid him in and out of her mouth, her hand coming to grip the root of him. Taking a moment to swirl her tongue around the smooth bulbous head, a small sigh of pleasure escaped her throat as she took him all the way in again. In response, he caressed a hand down her hair, cupping her chin again, his thumb coming to rest on the corner of her lips as she worked him over.

She hummed again as she tasted and applied pressure to him, not caring if it lasted forever. She loved having him under her spell.

The only inkling she got that he was close to exploding was that he broke their eye contact to twist his head to the side, the stiff columns of muscles in this neck straining with his own pleasure as he grunted out his release.

She took all of him, satisfied that she'd pleased him, satisfied that she'd atoned just a little bit.

He helped her stand, drawing her into his arms, his hand lazily caressing her back.

I'm sorry, she wanted to say again, knowing it was the exact wrong thing to say, but not being able to think of anything else. She was looking for absolution and it wasn't fair to him to provide it if he was still hurting. Which, looking around at his life, he was. Just like part of her always would, thinking that she didn't deserve the kind of happiness other people took for granted.

He drew back, his eyes boring into hers. "You're really good at that, but just so we're clear, Laura, I don't ever want a pity fuck. You get me?"

She nodded, but it only made her feel worse. Because while that hadn't been what this was for her, she did need forgiveness from him. And she knew there was no way she was ever leaving this penthouse until she got it.

CHAPTER EIGHT

WILL COULDN'T REMEMBER how he'd spent any of his previous Christmas Eves, but he assumed that he'd been alone. And honestly, that had been just fine. But eating lasagna in front of the television with Laura was a new level of good that he hadn't experienced yet.

Hell, he couldn't remember the last time he'd had a home-cooked meal period, let alone a friend he wanted to share it with. In fact, he'd never truly had a home, which made the whole meal thing kind of impossible. His mom had tried her best, but she'd been an addict. He'd known even as a ten-year-old boy that something wasn't right. Having been let down by every adult in his life, *jaded* didn't even begin to describe how little faith and trust Will put into other people.

That was, until a scared twelve-year-old Laura had moved in next door and reminded him that some people were worth going out on a limb for. Now that he thought about it, the food she'd cooked tonight had been made in his hotel, which meant that it was as close to that home-cooked meal he'd coveted as a kid. Plus, he had the girl he'd once loved by his side, which made definitely made it his best Christmas Eve in memory. Add in the blow job she'd given him earlier and he was feeling as jolly as Santa Claus himself..

"Why are you staring at me?" Laura asked, fork full of cheesy lasagna poised to enter her mouth.

"The entire left side of your face is covered with sauce," he lied.

She rolled her eyes, not falling for his dumb jokes. She never had really, which was why he'd liked her. Laura was never gullible, always quick and sharp, but still always the first to laugh. He'd missed that on his own. He'd missed a lot of things on his own if he was being honest with himself, which he usually was. He didn't have time for anything else. He knew he was too scarred from his childhood for a relationship, would never expect someone to understand how it felt to feel worthless for so long and know that the entire world agreed. He had a lot of money now and things were different, but he didn't expect any woman to stick around in a relationship he didn't know how to have.

He reached down, discreetly dragging a finger through the red sauce on his plate before wiping it on the side of her face. Brown eyes bulging, she stared at him in utter shock. "Did you just wipe sauce on my face?"

"Yeah," he confirmed. "You should thank me—I almost chose the butter."

Holding his eyes as she wiped her face off, her expression tight with incredulity, he couldn't help but grin. Christ, it'd been a long damn time since he'd just had fun.

"Are you twelve?" she asked, tossing the napkin on the wide glass coffee table.

"Maybe," he told her. "By the way, this lasagna might be the best thing I've ever eaten. Thank you very much for making it."

She let out an exaggerated huff of irritation that had him smiling again, biting the inside of his mouth to stop himself from laughing. He'd always loved to goad her, to tease and prod until they were in a fake fight and she'd shove or push him, which had always been what he'd wanted. For her to touch him in any way. He'd been a crafty kid and was now even a craftier adult.

"You know, I'm not going to keep falling for this thing where you're kind of a jerk and then you say something super lovely. Can't you just be nice to me without the rest?"

"Tomatoes have lots of antioxidants," he told her. "I was doing you a favor. Getting rid of all those free radicals that dull the skin. What's nicer than that?"

Her face screwed up into a comical confused state, lips twisting and eyes narrowing. "What the hell are you even talking about?"

He shrugged. "A man has to take care of his skin. I've learned things."

She tried to flick him in the shoulder, a move he definitely remembered from their youth. So he caught her finger before she could actually inflict any pain on him. "Hey, I'm serious. I really appreciate you making the lasagna, the goofy tree, everything. You didn't have to do any of it, but it means a lot that you did."

Her eyes got soft then and the hand he held in his grew slack as he released it, but she leaned forward to give him a soft kiss on the cheek. "You're welcome. I'm happy to cook for you and thank you for letting me. It's my Christmas tradition, so it's nice to have it even if I can't be home."

"No need to thank me," he told her, picking up the remote for the television. "I'll give you the choice of movie to show you with actions my immense gratitude."

She took the remote from his hand, looking at him speculatively. "You're really laying it on thick, aren't you? I'm not going down on you again tonight if that's what you're angling for."

He laughed, his chest vibrating with mirth. "Well, while I'd love that, I understand you have your limits."

"You're cracked," she muttered, flipping on the television.

"Do you remember the Christmas that we had to borrow the neighbor's car get to the mall and see a movie? We snuck into three different ones because we didn't have any money?"

She snorted. "Yes, and we lifted snacks from the 7-Eleven first and I nearly got caught by that mean old cashier who hated me so much because I knocked over the chip stand that one time and he never forgave me."

"Well, in his defense, you knocked down the chips to distract him while I smuggled half of the cookie shelf out," Will pointed out dryly.

Laura laughed, the dimples appearing in her pale cheeks, warming him from the inside out. "How dare you take his side!"

"I would never," he told her, holding her gaze as they both grinned. "If I recall, we nearly got thrown out of the movies because of those contraband snacks in the first place."

She nodded. "Yeah, they were jerks. But we managed to get through all three movies."

"And never got caught taking the car either."

Laura sighed, forking off another piece of messy lasagna. "I'm glad we didn't have to go into professional crime together, but we were clearly naturals."

He laughed. "Yeah, I put my life of crime behind me as soon as I possibly could. Nothing on my rap sheet after I turned eighteen. That stuff stays with you."

"Probably for the best, but we could have been like Bonnie and Clyde, you know," she teased, glancing over at him, eyes twinkling with mischief.

"Who knows what adventures we could have gotten up to?"

"We would have gotten ourselves an adventure in jail," he said, his chest clenching involuntarily even as he joked around. Because no matter how crappy it might have been, he had wanted it to be just the two of them back then. He'd had a plan to get them to a better life, would have taken care of her then, too, just like he'd taken care of himself. That she hadn't needed him was fine, but opening just a small door to the past was dredging a whole bunch of other shit up too. Like the devastation of being left again without a word, just like his mom, just like the foster parents who barely paid him any attention. At least his mom had promised him that she'd be right back. Laura hadn't even bothered to lie before she'd left him.

"You were too smart for jail," she argued around a bite of noodles.

He shrugged. "Maybe." That she'd had so much faith in him felt confusing; why had she left then? If she'd known he'd take care of them. "I'm just mostly glad I don't have to do that stuff anymore."

Shoveling the lasagna into his mouth, he pushed back the surge of unwelcome emotions. Laura had deserved to find a secure home, not be subjected to the dicey years of his existence after she'd left where he'd had to scrape and crawl his way up from the gutter to survive at all.

Instead, he let himself settle back into the present.

This must be how Christmas Eve was supposed to feel, cozy, safe, lazy. Normally, he might get some work done, and maybe he should do that now too. The hotel deal in Dubai needed his attention because he was getting snagged on the land-contract details. He should probably be trying to figure out loopholes or setting up meetings with hoteliers who had been through the same thing. But he didn't want to, content to sit on the couch watching the cartoon about the reindeer and eating the best food of his life with the one person in the world who made even this empty penthouse feel like a home.

Maybe she had a point earlier with bringing up family. Maybe a wife was what he needed in his life, someone to be there who he could talk to, bounce ideas around with.

After he'd gone back to the kitchen for a second helping, he noticed as he bit into a piece of bread that Laura was watching him.

"What?" he asked around the hunk of bread still in his mouth.

She grinned. "Nothing. Just that this is nicer than I thought it would be."

He lifted an eyebrow. "What? You weren't looking forward to spending the biggest holiday of the year with a virtual stranger?"

Laughing, she set her plate on the coffee table and leaned back into the couch, tugging the fleece blanket they were sharing up to her chin. She looked cute as hell and he wondered just how long he could get her to stay, a thought which had him literally, but discreetly, checking his head for a fever. He'd never had a woman stay more than a night and as a rule, he used another hotel room to do it.

"I just miss being at home is all. I haven't really seen my family since I took you on as a client and I was really looking forward to getting away from the city to decompress."

"Before I knew who you were, I was actually hoping to hire you to decorate all my lobbies seasonally. People think that's a thing we should be doing apparently."

Laura's eyes got larger. "You were?"

"Yeah, and when I open new hotels, I was hoping to bring on more designers to work on those interior designs."

"Well, that sounds lovely," she sighed, frowning. "But now that we've slept together it probably isn't a good idea."

He'd expected the argument. "If it makes you feel better, the plan to offer you the contract is in the last administration meeting's minutes. That was way before I even knew who you really were. But even so, no one else is better. I've gotten more comments and buzz around town from what you created in my lobby than any of the other marketing campaigns we've done throughout the year. That's remarkable, Laura."

He nearly lost the battle to put his arm around her as her cheeks stained red. She was a hard-ass still, but she had that soft side that he'd always felt compelled to guard. "I appreciate that. It means a lot to me to do a good job."

"It's a fucking fantastic job, Laura—you could do anything you want with your business now. And if you ever need a sound bite from me to catch a new client, I'm happy to do it."

"Thank you." She smiled. You know, when I was in college I always knew I wanted to be in design because I liked the idea of making a place that was unfriendly friendly. The way we grew up, the idea of a real home was so foreign, like some kind of dream that would never actually ever happen. But then it did for me and I guess I felt like I could do that for someone else too. So I'm really glad that people got a sense of that even in your humongous lobby. It means I'm on the right track."

He gave in, abandoning his empty plate on the side table and putting his arm around her. She hesitated, but then snuggled into the crook of his arm and the intimacy was like a drug, pulling him under into a warm cocoon of contentment. Had he ever done this with a woman? It felt like she was the thing that made him restful. He hadn't put away his ambition for even a minute in years, but the work he should be doing didn't seem important at all right now.

"Maybe on some weird subconscious level, that's why you went into hotels," she said. "You give people a home away from home."

He raised an eyebrow at the fanciful notion so at odds with how he thought about the world in general and specifically his work. "I chose hotels because it was the first job I managed to get," he explained baldly. "I was hungry and everybody knew it. If I'd gotten a job as a garbage man, I'd just be the king of trash right now instead."

Laura laughed and that light sound caught him in the gut again.

"You would never be the king of trash," she maintained, shaking her head.

He shrugged. He never thought about what could have happened to him—that was a scary-as-hell road to go down on the best of days. The only road he ever considered was the one ahead of him and for so long that was all he'd had, the destination, the goal. But now he was there. Even if he lost all his hotels today, he'd still be set for life; that was something he'd made sure to do early on with well-placed investments and real estate, but the fact was that he didn't know that he could stop now even if he wanted to.

"I would have been completely content with a garbage empire," he maintained. "I bet garbage contained in cans is far more palatable than the shit I found during my first years cleaning motels in the city anyway. People are pigs when someone else has to deal with their mess."

Laura's face looked stricken as she made a groaning sound of commiseration. "Please," she begged, holding up a hand, "do not share any of those details."

He grinned. "Well, there was this one time—"

"No!" she protested, jumping up from the couch, the blanket falling fully into his lap. "I won't allow it!"

Then she was heading into the kitchen with both of their dirty plates.

"Don't even think about washing those dishes, Laura," he warned because this was a hotel and she'd already made him dinner.

"Too late," she informed, "but you could be nice and help me make some cookies and our breakfast for tomorrow."

Joining her at the island, he watched as she gathered the dishes from the stove and set them on the wide countertop near the sink. She clearly wasn't listening to his warning so he lifted her up onto the counter, enjoying her squeal of surprise.

"What are you doing?"

"Returning the favor," he murmured against her mouth as he made quick work of her flannel pajama pants, an item of clothing he'd never considered sexy and yet on Laura they seemed like the most erotic thing in the world.

His fingers went straight to her core, feeling the silken folds that were already damp. Lust shot through his body so quickly that he didn't even know how it was happening. With just a touch of her he was as aroused as he'd been when their roles had been reversed earlier in this same kitchen.

Her soft sighs were in his ear as he licked and nuzzled down her neck. He moved a finger gently inside her, loving that she was so ready for him. There was no doubt that she wanted him and the assurance steadied his lust, made him want to keep this going until she was absolutely crazy, but he also wanted to prove a point. That she couldn't resist him and that he was in charge of her body.

So he got to his knees, the scent of her mingling with the sweet scent of sugar and he breathed it all in like a dying man. Then he opened her, looking truly at the heart of her, his own heart pounding in his chest like a jackhammer as he revealed the loveliest flesh he'd ever seen. As he was running his tongue up the outer folds, she sighed in pleasure, her head dropping back and revealing a perfect white neck that he wanted to suck and bite and leave a mark. To finally claim her as his like he should have years ago.

He found the slick nub of her, licking gently at first, but then applying more pressure as his finger dipped inside her again. The taste of her was like magic, salty and honey sweet, slick and smoky and just Laura. He wanted all of her, the messy, the neat and everything in between. Her soft moans echoed in his kitchen, turning him from hard to painfully hard, but he wasn't going to take them further. He was only going to return this favor and then maybe pick things up again tonight in bed.

Making Laura crazy was like watching a symphony and being part of it at the same time, playing her but enjoying the sounds, as well. She wrapped her legs around his head, her hands tunneling force-fully into his hair, pulling and urging him on. He slid two fingers inside her, his gaze going to the timer on his phone, knowing he was literally on the clock. Crooking his fingers to find that rough spot inside her right as his teeth grazed her clit and he felt and tasted her come apart under him.

It was glorious as her entire body vibrated against him as he licked her gently to come down from the high. Reaching up to caress her thighs as he gave her one last slow lick.

"Next time maybe you'll listen to me," he said with a grin as he pulled away.

Brushing back the hair from her eyes, he struggled against wanting to say more, to express in words the emotions he was already feeling for her. It would be dangerous for him to say anything, though, because he knew better than anyone that feelings never lasted. But in the meantime, he was going to enjoy their time together.

CHAPTER NINE

CHRISTMAS MORNING ARRIVED and Laura woke up to Will's dark bedroom feeling blissfully sated and lazy. Sex with Will was drugging in a way it'd never been for her. One orgasm from Will and the entire world just felt infinitely better. Things that would have been problems were barely given second thoughts under the umbrella of pleasure she was currently below. Her eyes drifted closed again and she was ready to surrender once more to sleep, but a warm body snuggled in closer to her backside and Will began dropping kisses down her neck and across her shoulder, making her shiver at the anticipatory goose bumps rising up along the her arms.

"Merry Christmas," Will murmured, his voice gravelly and rough. She could feel the long locks of his hair drag silkily along her skin as he traveled back up to her neck.

"Merry Christmas to you too," she murmured, leaning into him, pressing against his warm, naked body. He was hard against her, the thick length of him nudging into her back and she knew she was becoming addicted to his touch.

Will gently brushed her hair aside as he slid featherlight kisses down her spine and a whimper of helpless pleasure escaped her. Her entire body felt weak, as if he could operate her arms and legs like a marionette. Unlike past relationships, she completely trusted Will. His hands caressed over her breasts, light and leisurely because they had all the time in the world, drawing random patterns across the mounded curves, his calloused fingertips pressing ever so slightly against the nipples. She crooked her leg, rubbing her foot along the coarse hair of his calf, exploring and teasing just as he was, reaching down to put her hand over his to caress her together.

His warm mouth plucked at her earlobe, teeth gently scoring the flesh sending more steady waves of slow-rising heat to her core. His other hand glided down her back, then dipped into the slit of her ass, playing there, toying with her. Anxious, she scooted against him and he chuckled low in his throat. "I'm trying to go slow here, Laura, not fast-forward."

But then he poised himself at her entrance and she lifted her leg up on top of his to give him more room. "It would be so fucking easy to slide inside you right now," he murmured low in her ear, his hot breath beading her nipples to an unbearable degree. "Bare and raw and us, I want to feel you all over me, Laura, more than anything."

He gave a single almost imperceptible thrust that

had her head falling back onto his shoulder with a moan of need. "I know I'm clean," she told him, "but we shouldn't."

"I am too, but there's no way in hell I would ever put you at risk," he growled, pulling away from her which had her nearly sobbing in frustration when his fingers served as a poor replacement. "But one day soon and I'll be so fucking close to you, feeling every inch of your skin, every sweet wet centimeter of heat. You'd like that?"

"Yes," she breathed, her hips bucking against his fingers.

"Look down," he directed, showing her that he was using three fingers to enter her, gently pressing them inside her, stretching and exploring and generally driving her mad. Her hips rocked against him and he bit her neck, the bit of pain eliciting a moan of true surrender. She needed more; more contact and more of him.

She reached down to stroke herself, so close to getting exactly what she wanted, but he caught her hand, pulling it above her head and locked it against the headboard with his. "You always were greedy, weren't you?" he murmured against her neck.

But she had no words for him; her body was already a maelstrom of want, liquid and loose, as his fingers made space for him inside her. His thumb brushed over her clit and she bucked, yelping at the loaded sensation. Then he pulled out of her, adding the final fourth finger and pressing back in. The pressure was exquisite, the fullness of him too intense to comprehend as her hips rocked against him on their own volition, seeking more of what he was providing. He let go of her hand, giving it a final squeeze in warning so that she wouldn't move it, then let his fingers drift down the underside of her arm, lighting cold goose bumps under her skin. Eventually, he returned to her breasts, his fingers still inside her, just there to remind her he was presently in control of her body, which her body had absolutely no issue with.

A hand covered her entire breast and she stared at the contrast of his large tanned hair-dusted hand, locked over her delicate skin, pale under the golden lamplight, her veins visible beneath the surface. He squeezed, then applied an increasing pressure to her nipple, his thumb and forefinger twisting as they pressed in.

"More," she breathed, surprising herself, but also feeling more like herself than ever in bed with him.

"Not until I feel like it," was his arrogant response as he continued to play her body like it was a cello and he was a world-renowned cellist with nothing more to do than practice all the ways to manipulate her strings.

That sweet bite on her nipple again, the difficult push as he buried his fingers deeper inside her. "You like the edge, don't you, Laura?"

When she nodded, he sucked the skin of her neck into his mouth, biting just the slightest bit too hard.

"Me too," he said, his voice so low and dark she stopped breathing to hear him. "We always played on the edge together, didn't we? One way or another we were always going to end up here, grasping at every little scrap of life we could get."

He grabbed the hand he'd pinned and brought it down to his length so show her that sometime when she'd been moaning his name in pleasure, he'd slid on a condom.

"Never let some asshole like me take you un-gloved, Laura," he growled.

She wanted to roll her eyes at the obvious advice, but then he was slowly removing his fingers from her, the suction as they left catching her attention and leaving her feeling so empty and bereft that she whimpered again, rocking back against him reck-lessly, wanting him back inside her, wanting him to take her over, to be the only person she'd ever trust to do so.

But he was hell-bent on taking his time so she took charge, wrapping a hand around him and posi-tioning it at her entrance. Thwarting her efforts, he instead rose to his knees and lifted her up to hers, her head still in the pillows, but she didn't care, she just wanted him inside her again, would give nearly anything to feel it.

And when he was, the thick slide of him against her abraded insides, it was like a conflagration, a deep yearning and sensation she'd never quite felt before. With his hands firmly gripping her hips, she felt taken over, leaving everything behind for Will Walker, the boy who had promised her the world and then still gone ahead and gotten it for himself even though she'd left him.

His first entrance wasn't easy; he went in hard, taking her breath away, but his thumb stroked gently over her skin reminding her of his care, reminding her that she was the one truly in control here, but she didn't need a reminder and didn't need to be coddled. She was a grown-ass woman who liked what she liked and wasn't ashamed of any of it. So when his hand came up to grip her hair as he rode her in a filthy fire of wetness and heat and sweat, she loved it, wanted every piece of sensation good or bad that they could experience together.

"More," she breathed again, bucking her hips against him insistently, not at all pleased that he was holding back with her. She knew, she fucking knew, he was dirty and keeping it from her.

Her command had the opposite effect, however, because he immediately pulled out of her and his entire body, along with his warmth, left her. She lifted her head to see what was going on, and saw him lie on his back beneath her, drawing her hips down onto his head.

She cried out in mindless pleasure as his tongue entered where his cock had been, his nose nudging at her engorged bud. He ate her like he was a dying man, almost as if the pleasure he was giving out was a punishment for her demands because no matter how good this was, all she wanted was him inside her, needed that connection, the power; every one of her cells was dying for it. Her body was strung out, searing veins pistoning lust throughout her entire body.

"Will," she choked, climax hovering dangerously close. But he ignored her, doubling down, dragging his tongue over her clit, licking and sucking and nibbling until a wave of numbing pleasure dragged through her body. Crying out her release she came slowly down expecting him to slowly bring her out of it like usual, but instead found her hips being pulled back up and his hard shaft slamming back into her.

Her clit was still pulsing in pleasure and her inner tissues felt chafed and raw from his fingers, but it only intensified the pleasure. He'd lost all control and will power now, shuttling into her with abandon, his long fingers digging into her hips. She didn't need to see his face to know he was close, his hips grinding into her ass, his hair rough on her tender skin. Damn, she needed him.

He slowed the slightest bit to press a thumb to her clit, not moving in the slightest, just there as a reminder of who was in charge as he slowly began moving in her again. She bore down on him, her inner muscles clenching with force to keep him in, to touch him somehow and have that connection.

And then finally, his hand gripping in her hair, he pulled at her and with a harsh breath he stilled inside her, sending his thumb over her just enough to take her over the edge one more time.

They stayed locked together after they went over, and Laura wasn't sure she ever wanted to be separate. She was already falling in love with him. He was Will and he was hers, and yet, he refused to belong to anyone. And she knew it was because everyone always left him, but she would never leave him again.

But for now, her body didn't care about the future because languid and lovely waves of contentment were rolling over her like a heady dream.

Will was on top of her, still inside her, but he was propped up on his arms not giving her his weight, watching out for her as always.

Finally, when the sweat on her body started to cool, he left a string of kisses down her back as he slid out of her and dropped down onto the mattress beside her. "That was the best fucking Christmas present I've ever gotten."

Her head nestled into his soft pillow, her eyes were already drifting closed.

"Me too."

When she woke again hours later, the bed was empty. She got up and took a shower then stopped by her bedroom on the way to the living area to get the gifts she'd gotten for Will. They weren't really anything complicated, just some things she'd picked up at her apartment during her Christmas shopping spree on her first day at Will's.

Before she left her room she made a quick call to

her parents and it was such a bummer still to have missed the holidays with them, but they sounded cheerful as always and her sister and brother were there as well so they weren't alone.

She made her way out into the living room, decked in pair of red flannel pajamas with Christmas trees on them because no matter the X-rated nature of what they'd done in the bedroom just hours ago, it was still Christmas. Expecting to find Will watching television or doing work on his laptop like he'd done a couple of days ago, it was a surprise to find him flipping pancakes on the stovetop while a half dozen or so wrapped gifts sat under the tree.

"What are you doing?" she asked, drinking in the sight of him in a worn slate sweatshirt and black jogging pants.

"Making breakfast," he informed, his hot gaze sliding over her appreciatively. Good lord, she was going to be lucky to make it through breakfast without jumping him.

She met his eyes after his little perusal with a bland smile. "Yes, I can see that, but you knew I was going to do it."

He raised a dark eyebrow. "Well, I was hungry and you were sleeping, so I decided not to listen to you."

Her lips pursed, but they both knew she wasn't actually annoyed and she had bigger issues to confront presently anyway. Picking up a strawberry from the bowl of fruit he'd set out, she nodded toward the tree. "And do you care to explain that?"

"You put up the tree yourself—are you looking for me to extrapolate a theme or something?" he asked, being willfully obtuse. The ass.

"And the presents? Is there a theme I'm supposed to extrapolate from those?"

A corner of his mouth lifted. "It's Christmas— what was I supposed to do?"

She wanted to go back in time and spend every Christmas with him. Knowing that he'd never let her all the way in now because she'd already betrayed him was weighing on her mind. To a person who had trouble believing her worth, to know that he would never believe in her enough to stay with her was tragic.

But they had this. They had now. So she held up her own presents and stuck them under the tree alongside the others before returning to sit at the island. Grabbing some of the berries from the bowl, she chewed as she watched him with the pancakes.

"Are there chocolate chips in those?"

He scooted the bag of chips over to her and she took a few of those as well, realizing just how easy it was to be with him.

"You've made me these before, you know?" she said, watching as he effortlessly flipped over the four silver-dollar-sized pancakes.

He nodded, his eyes still on the pancakes.

"For my sixteenth birthday you tried to get a cake

mix, but the gas station was out of them so you got a box of pancake mix and chocolate chips and made me a whole stack with a candle on top."

She was able to smile at the memory because no matter how shitty their life had been he'd always been able to make things okay.

"It was a great birthday," she told him when he still wouldn't look at her.

"Yeah," he said, finally meeting her eyes. "It was. But I always wished I could have gotten you a real cake."

She shrugged. "I prefer pancakes anyway." At least ones made by Will in his pajamas.

Nodding to the stack of white plates in front of her, he served up the perfectly golden circles onto one of them and handed it to her. "Well, I don't want to eat while you're still cooking," she balked, refusing the plate.

"By the time you're finished getting yours ready these will be done," he said, his tone brooking no argument. "Eat."

She crinkled her nose at him, but swiped some butter over the stack along with some maple syrup. "You warmed it up even?"

"No one likes cold maple syrup."

"You're so fancy now," she grinned, forking off a bite, happiness bubbling up inside her like a geyser. She met his eyes as she took the first bite, the flavor of maple and crispy cake making her mouth extremely happy. "And a good cook."

His eyes darkened as he watched her chew and she felt the response in between her own legs. This was on the books as the dirtiest Christmas she'd ever had.

"Thanks," he told her, the hot look under control. "It was the least I could do after the lasagna last night."

She just shook her head because that was a remnant from childhood too; she'd always been in his debt, but never the other way around. Will always wanted the scales to be balanced. But he'd been right, by the time she was finished with her first pancake, the rest were done cooking and they sat side by side at the island in another comfortable silence as they ate.

Stuffing her face with the last couple of bites, she sat back in her chair and watched as he did the same, only he'd drenched his plate with enough syrup to give a person diabetes.

"Are those really all for me?" she asked, eyeing the stack of perfectly wrapped gifts under the tree. Shiny gold, silver and red boxes with professionally tied bows all sat there pretty as a picture.

"Yep. Don't get too excited—I only had two hours to shop while you got ready yesterday," he said.

"I'm ashamed that I only have a few gifts for you," she told him, taking his empty plate and sticking it into the dishwasher.

Will took her hand, pulling her into him and her entire body relaxed against his just as if it belonged there. "Hey," he said, his voice serious, "anything is perfect and we're both just trying to make the best out of an unexpected situation."

The words had her eyebrows slamming together, but he immediately rolled his eyes. "You know that's not what I mean."

She relaxed again and he walked them to the couch, flipping on the television to a channel with an old Christmas-movie marathon. He'd really learned a lot in the short time she'd invaded his home.

"You want to open them now?" he asked.

"Yeah, what else are we doing? It's Christmas," she pointed out.

"A whole bunch of nothing, I hope," he threw back, setting his coffee mug on the coffee table. At his words she smiled. In just the last few days he'd seemed to chill out and relax. The man she met in the lobby by the tree that day would never entertain a day of doing nothing. Hell, he'd been dragging them all over town in a blizzard just to do work. And yet here he was, finally, maybe, letting his guard down a little. Maybe letting her in a little.

He handed her a pile of presents and her heart tugged that he'd done this for her on such short notice.

"This is so exciting," she teased, giving him a goofy smile as she opened the first gift, a small box with gold wrapping and green fabric ribbon. "It's such a pretty gift I don't want to tear the paper and ruin it."

Will rolled his eyes, barely paying attention to

her, his eyes focused on the television screen. She wondered how often he gave presents to women and if these ones were just the standard parting gifts in his arsenal.

Inside was a box that she opened to reveal a delicate etched-glass ornament the color of an opal. It was lovely and she was definitely going to cry by the end of the gift exchange. "It's beautiful," she told him, holding the bulb up to the sun shining in from the windows. She let it spin so the light could hit all the colors. "Thank you so much. It'll go on my tree always from now on."

He handed her a few more, some of which were more ornaments and pretty cookie tins she could use for gifts, that considering their time together were appreciated and thoughtful. And further proof that he paid attention to her.

She made him open one of hers, which was just a bag of insanely expensive coffee from the coffee shop near her brownstone, probably the best in the city, but he had a big smile on his face so she hoped he enjoyed it. Living in a hotel, he probably had the same stuff all the time and the coffee press was the only thing in the kitchen she'd actually seen him use before today.

But it was her next gift to him that was throwing her into fits of anxiety. Once he actually opened the package and was staring down at the contents as if he had no idea what it was, she thought she might die or fall apart at the seams.

Then, after what was an interminable period of time, like at least fifty years, he met her eyes, his expression studied and blank as he said, "You kept this?"

"Of course I did."

He ran his thumb over the oak frame of the picture. "But I don't want this back—I wanted you to have it."

She knew he'd say that but she'd wanted him to know how much he'd meant to her.

"I always thought you'd end up being an artist," she said, changing the subject as she peered over at the drawing he'd done of her all those years ago. It was a simple pencil sketch, but the details were undeniably her. A shy smile on her face, the kind from a person who was too afraid to smile because once she did, life always seemed to go directly into the toilet. That had just been a fact of her life then.

He laughed. "I have too much hustle to be an artist."

"Well, you could have been," she pressed, undeterred. "But you can keep that—it's just a copy. I'd never give up the original, though I do wish you'd sign it now."

He rolled his eyes and picked up the last gift. She'd wrapped all his gifts in black paper with red-and-silver ribbon because that seemed like his vibe. After opening the rectangular cardboard box inside, he pulled out another picture, this one in a newer and sleeker black onyx frame to match everything else in his decor.

Meeting her eyes, his expression was unreadable. "I didn't know this even existed."

"It did," she told him. "We got one of those disposable cameras one time, remember? But never had the money to get it developed. I took it with me when I left and eventually got the film developed and this one was in there. I have other ones of us, but this was my favorite so I made you a copy."

It wasn't a posed photograph or anything that a photographer would be proud of; it was just them in the abandoned park across the street from their apartment building, sitting on a pair of swings, but he'd thrown his arm around her as he reached up to take the picture, so they were off center and their heads were turned to each other. She wore an old yellow hoodie and he a black canvas coat she remembered he'd saved up for months to buy, working at the gas station down the street, which was how they'd ended up eating for most of her last year there. As soon as Will had been able to work, he'd done it, mostly so they could eat, she knew.

His dark hair fell over his forehead in the picture just as it did now, only the expertly faded sides were salon-cut now whereas he'd let it grow out when they were young.

"I thought this place could use a little personalizing, some pictures of people you know so future visitors don't think you're a serial killer."

He continued to stare at the picture, silent, until she thought she'd screwed up. "I wish I'd had a picture of you," he finally said, his voice so low she could barely hear him. "I was afraid I'd forget what you looked like, but then when I saw you in the hotel I knew how stupid that worry had been. I could never forget."

Tears threatened, so she reached out and pulled him into a hug. "I'd never forget either, but it was nice to have you around all these years too."

He wrapped a single arm around her, giving a nearly imperceptible squeeze.

"Thank you."

The first tear started down her face and she wiped it away before she pulled back to set her lips to his.

"This hasn't been a terrible Christmas," she said, pulling back to give him a teasing smile.

"It's been my best one," Will admitted.

The unemotional statement of fact had her tearing up again because she was very afraid that it was her best one too.

CHAPTER TEN

WILL HAD TALKED LAURA into coming to a business lunch at Palmetto's, the restaurant he usually used for those types of meetings. He'd needed some space after their cozy Christmas day because he was mad as hell. The interminably long lunch over, where he'd gotten no further on his expansion plans, he led her out from under the green awning of the restaurant's entrance, knowing he'd done a shitty job of hiding his anger too.

"So I don't know what happened in there, but you seemed pissed off," Laura said, confirming his suspicions.

Will glanced down at her, looking lovely, and lied to her face because the truth would hurt her feelings and probably start a fight. "That guy I was talking to in there was a dick. He's a local New Jersey guy who thinks he can hose big-city guys on the price of land as if we're not living in the age of information where I can find out how much a piece of property is worth in seconds."

As Christmas day had gone on, he'd gone from surprise, to happiness, and then finally low-grade rage at her Christmas gifts. That Laura had tangible memories of their time together and he'd had fuck all over the years. It just brought back the day she'd left, the panic he'd felt and the eventual hardening of his heart, her betrayal the final piece in what was now an impenetrable wall. He thought he was over his anger toward her, but one look at his drawing had brought it all back.

Over the years when he'd thought about being in relationships, he'd known he was too screwed up for anything like that. When he'd been young and dumb and with Laura, someone who understood all too well what it was like to be passed around and over-looked at every single turn, it could have worked. But now, he'd never trust anyone enough to not head out at the first sign of difficulty—and he'd make it difficult, he knew that. If he'd been poor still, it might have been easier, too, he'd know people stayed because of him instead of his money, but it was too late for that, as well.

He'd been destined to be alone from the moment Laura had walked out the apartment building doors all those years ago. He'd known it then and he still knew it now.

So he buried his anger for her once again because it wasn't her fault and it also helped nothing. Instead he focused on the fact that he felt good with her. He didn't trust her not to run out on him again, but he still wanted to be around her.

"You want to open up a hotel in New Jersey?" she asked, reaching out to hold his hand, but he saw it coming and plucked his phone from his pocket to avoid her.

"I want to open a hotel everywhere," he told her, pretending to type something, but really just tapping out some nonsense and then leaving his phone in his hand so she wouldn't get any ideas.

She laughed at his statement. "You were always ambitious."

Will pulled open the door to his car waiting at the curb and helped her into the back.

They'd been driving a few moments when he saw her hesitate to speak and knew something bad was coming.

"When you asked me to go to dinner with you tonight, is it meant to be a date or is it another business thing?" she asked carefully, referring to the other distraction he'd proposed because he couldn't do another cozy night like yesterday. After her tenants could get out of the city and go home, he needed to move on from whatever this thing was between them. Time with her, having a taste of what his life could have been, was eating at his peace of mind.

He turned, meeting her eyes, making sure his expression stayed neutral. "If you'd like it to be a date, then yes. No formal business will be conducted."

Laura pursed her lips at the nonanswer. "I do want

it to be a date," she declared, her chin jutting out. And he wasn't unaffected by her admission. He loved Laura, more than anyone in his life and while he wanted to give her everything she needed, he also knew that he hadn't forgiven her since any reminder of her leaving sent him into a depressed spiral. "I don't know what this week has been for you, but it hasn't been just about sex for me," she continued.

He didn't respond immediately because of course what they had wasn't just about sex but it couldn't be about anything else either.

Then she added with a quick grin, "Though that has been pretty legendary."

"You want to date me?" he asked, ignoring her attempt at a joke. Apparently he wasn't able to let go of her admission, which he kicked himself for. He shouldn't lead her on, that was fake and cruel, but if he told her the truth, she'd leave.

"Yeah, is that weird?"

"Are you asking me?" he clarified.

Laura shrugged. "I can ask you if you'd like, but it was more just a statement of labeling what we're already kind of doing anyway. I mean, we're basically living together," she teased with a tentatively hopeful smile that had her eyes twinkling. She was lovely and kind and it made him feel like an ass for what he was going to do, but he knew he was going to do it anyway.

"I don't date like that, Laura," he told her, trying to be honest but also not a dick because he still felt a need to take care of her. "I'm not really a dependable guy."

This statement had her eyebrows raised.

"I'm not looking for a dog walker, Will. And you were literally the only person I could depend on for a long time. You can't tell me that has changed much."

He shook his head. "I have changed, Laura. I'd do anything for you, you know that, but a relationship is not one of those things."

Laura held his eyes, considering his words. It wasn't as if he hadn't been honest about things from the beginning so he didn't know what could be going on in her head.

"Maisey's family flew out early this morning for Florida. You could stay with me for a few days. The weather is calling for another snowstorm this afternoon so we could extend our slumber party."

He wanted it so badly, to see her home, to be with her more. It was reckless, it was foolish, he knew it would effectively be leading her on, but even with his anger the idea of her leaving today and not seeing her brought on instant panic.

"Yeah," he finally said, "let's park the car at my place, get our stuff and then I'll have a driver take us there."

It was difficult for Laura to be angry at Will's evasiveness as he followed her into her half of a brownstone because it was basically her favorite place on earth. On one of the quieter streets in the West Village, it was just the place she always wanted in the city, where singles and families alike lived on tree-lined streets and sat on their stoops on Halloween to pass out candy. It was still the city, but it felt like her own little corner.

Lots of people completely upgraded their interiors with shiny marble countertops and chrome finishes, but that had never appealed to Laura. She liked the classic cherry moldings and hardwood floors in her place. Everything was solid and well made and she'd been able to paint the walls fun colors to update the look.

"The bedroom is upstairs," she told him, "if you want to drop your stuff off."

Now that the tables were turned and Will was in her space, she was feeling strangely self-conscious. All this time, she'd been focused on Will and her own absolution but she hadn't considered what would happen if he didn't forgive her. The moment she'd waited for him to agree to come to her place had been interminable and she'd expected him to take the opportunity to pull back, especially after his no-relationship declaration.

But he'd surprised her and now that he was here she was anxious that he stay, that maybe after all these years she'd found the love of her life. Maybe this had been their destiny all along. Finally, she'd found someone who could love her, scars and all.

Once they were in the bedroom, which he barely glanced at even though it was her favorite place in the world, he was on her. His lips took hers in an urgent kiss, reminding her that they were explosive together because every cell in her body perked up and sighed with a singular, *yes, please* as his tongue slid into her mouth.

Her arms went around his neck but he pulled back a moment to meet her eyes, his own dark and intense as if he'd been counting down the moments until this one. He reached into his pocket and pulled out his phone, scrolling to something before he turned the screen to her. "I'm clean and I trust you."

Laura read what appeared to be a lab report from a doctor with an address close to his hotel, which seemed like a good indication that it was legitimate. Not that she thought Will would lie to her, but she wasn't born yesterday and she only had one body and all that.

"There's still pregnancy," she pointed out.

Instead of his being alarmed his eyes actually darkened more, which literally had her heart imploding.

"I've still got condoms," he said, the timbre of his voice low and determined still. "It's no big deal. Either way, I've got you."

Then he was guiding her back onto her bed, the backs of her legs hitting the soft dove-gray duvet. She gained purchase and slid back to the middle of the bed, pulling him with her. "I've got you too." She smiled, giving him a firm kiss before meeting his eyes. "I'm on the pill. I was just kidding."

His nostrils flared as he crawled over her on the bed. "You're really getting it now, Laura," he warned, pulling off one black leather bootie at a time and throwing them somewhere on her bedroom floor. "It's so fun to tease me, isn't it?" He unbuttoned her jeans and tugged them off in one deft flourish, tossing them off to the side, as well.

All signals were a go in her body, alarm bells sounding that a train was coming straight for her core as he leaned down and drew her underwear off with his teeth, lifting her ass clear off the bed with one broad hand. She swallowed against the onslaught of lust that seemed to be attacking even her brain because if someone had asked her something as simple as her name, as she watched him lick his way back up her leg she would have just stared at them dumbly.

Then he flipped her over, and during the past couple of days, she'd come to realize that this was his favorite position. While she had no complaints, she was almost positive it was because he didn't want to look at her when they were having sex because, like her, he might have to admit that this was much more than sex.

But after his speech outside the restaurant, she knew those were words he wasn't ready to hear, and as he inserted two blunt fingers inside her, she wasn't really in much of a confrontational mood. He dropped hot kisses down her spine, sending goose bumps up her back all the way to her scalp. As he was keeping up the rhythm inside her, her hips began to move until he added another finger and she whimpered with pleasure, needing more of him.

When she'd had enough, she flipped over and pushed him down onto the bed against her mountain of pillows. There was no way he was going inside her bare for the first time and not looking at her directly in the eyes so he knew exactly who it was that was taking him. No damned way in hell she was letting him get away with that bit of cowardice.

But God, she had not been prepared for how it would feel. Not just the physical, but his bare self notched at her entrance as she hovered over him. She'd never had anyone else like this and that it was Will was opening something inside her she hadn't expected. The boy who'd kept her safe, who'd been willing to risk everything to get them out, he was hers now for real and she just knew she wouldn't be able to give him up. Not again and not ever.

So she did it, slid onto him, feeling him stretch her, making her his even if he wasn't ready. Her eyes closed as she took him fully in; resting on his hips she heard him audibly inhale and felt the moment crystallize in her head. This was different, they were different, he was different.

"I've never done this with someone before," she admitted, her voice coming out as a broken whisper as she stretched over him.

He gripped her hips in his hands, his fingertips digging into her flesh. "Me neither."

Her eyes flew open to meet his head-on and she

felt her heart just open up and expand in ways she hadn't understood before now. For so many years she'd been looking for the person who fit her life, dating men who looked good on paper, but could never possibly understand her baggage. Will was a loner malcontent and just as lost as he ever was, but that didn't matter to her. She'd looked for uncomplicated men who would be strong enough to overlook her past, but Will was probably the most complicated person she'd ever met, which meant he was the only one who could understand her.

She began to move her hips, their eyes locked even though it felt so good she wanted to shut them and sink into the feeling completely. Her skin was on fire; prickling tingles of heat drew along each inch urging her to move faster over him, to press in, make more contact. But she didn't want it to end, was mildly alarmed when he licked his thumb and pressed it gently on the heart of her because she wasn't going to last at all; he was the sexiest man she'd ever seen, all dark hair and eyes and the heated looks he gave her at the most innocuous of times. He watched their joining now as she moved over him, and imagining what he was seeing was erotic for her and she felt herself getting wetter as she rode him.

"Why don't you touch those gorgeous tits, Laura," Will instructed, his voice deep and serious.

"Why don't you do it," she shot back, "I'm a little busy here."

She saw that he bit the inside of his cheek to keep

from laughing. "I thought you wanted to be in control, but if you're saying you don't, I'm happy to take over."

"That's what you're trying to do by telling me to touch myself," she argued, her voice catching as she thrust over him and a bolt of electricity tore through her.

"You're right. My apologies," he grunted, leaning up to take one of her nipples into his mouth without so much as a warning. Then he began moving her hips over him, faster than she'd been doing before, basically taking the control she'd wanted. But it seemed bad form to protest when she was having such a good time. Her head fell back as he bit and twisted her nipple in his mouth, sending darts of liquid to her core.

Then before she could even enjoy it, he was flipping her onto her back.

"What are you doing?" she demanded, breathing heavily and trying to gain some semblance of balance even though her head was just a little off.

He leaned down for a kiss, the muscles in his arms bulging out with the effort,; his tongue danced with her for just a second before he drew back. "I'm sorry, but you're going too slow and I need you, Laura. I need it more than anything in the world right now. I think I'm literally blind from wanting you to come over my dick like this, bare and raw and I can feel everything. I can feel you," he growled, sliding into her in one decisive thrust that had them both gasping in pleasure.

"Fine," she said, gasping for breath as he expertly hit the rough patch inside her, "But you better make it good."

The directive amused him, but the next thrust wasn't a laughing matter and Laura sucked in as a wave of pleasure consumed her. She was getting close to falling apart and could barely take the pressure anymore as he pounded into her, his hips jackhammering as if he were a machine, his arms strained on either side of her, the dark veins popping out as he leveraged himself into her, each thrust sending both of them into her wooden headboard.

But she didn't care; she wanted every single bit of him she could get. She gripped his hair in one hand to pull him down for another kiss, needing the connection, biting on his lip when he tried to end it, licking and sucking when he relented. It was messy; it was unbridled and inelegant, but she'd never felt so wanted in her life. When he reached down and laid his thumb on her center again, the ultrasensitive nub shouting for attention, she thought she was done for. But then he left her mouth to bear down on a nipple and that was it; she came like a shower of fireworks, twinkling brightly above the earth with not a care in the world.

Her breathy moans echoed in her bedroom and it got her going again to watch him as he got closer, unreserved and without his cultivated urbane mask of emotionlessness. Sweat dripped down his chest, catching in the patch of hair high on it; his teeth were clenched, the corded lines of his throat pronounced and sexy as hell. Straight white teeth were bared as he shuttled into her, stopping every so often to savor the feeling of it, to seemingly catalog just how she felt against his skin, the silky texture of her wetness, the velvet softness of her insides.

"Fuck," he growled, then stilled above her, his body shuddering a mere second before he got himself under control again.

God, she wanted to rattle him out of the man who thought he had to be a statue, wanted him vocal and moaning and as lost to desire as she was. He'd literally taken them to the next level and still wouldn't let himself fully enjoy it.

Their breathing as they came down from the high was the only thing audible in the darkened room. He hadn't collapsed directly on top of her, but their chests were nearly touching before he rolled to his back, bringing her into his crook. She felt vulnerable and a little scared at what they'd done and how much it meant to her. After tonight, she couldn't imagine sleeping with anyone else, not in a million years.

Not being able to help herself, she licked a bead of sweat from his pec and he peered down at her.

"Thanks?" he asked, unsure, but also definitely still a little winded from his outstanding physical performance in the new show called *Sex With Will, The Best Laura Ever Had.*

She licked another bead and he dropped a kiss

on her forehead. "Fuck, Laura," he said. "That was unreal."

"I kind of feel like we should definitely keep having sex that way."

Drawing a hand over her hair, he laughed. "Hell, yeah."

She wasn't quite sure what else to say to him when she had, in fact, a lot of things to say but was too chicken to say them. Eventually, silence fell between them as she drew a finger lazily over his chest and he twirled a piece of her hair between his fingers. It was commonplace but special and she never wanted it to end.

It was a mistake, falling into a relationship with an emotionally unavailable man who had specifically said he didn't want to be in a relationship, but if Will Walker wasn't the man she could take a chance on, then she wasn't sure she'd ever find one who was.

CHAPTER ELEVEN

THE SNOW FINALLY STOPPED. Which meant that the roads were also clear, and Will had foolishly agreed to accompany Laura to her parents' house. Mostly because he hadn't wanted her to drive three hours by herself, but he also needed to spend more time with her. However, as the drive went on he was unable to stop reliving the last couple of days with her at her place, which made him incredibly agitated. Because he realized he was happy.

And he couldn't deny it.

Just like when they were kids, he lived to make her smile, to make her laugh, to make her irritated with him. He'd give up his hotels if it was guaranteed to keep her in smiles for the rest of her life. He was falling and there was nowhere for him to go but to be crushed on the ground.

He hadn't been able to think of a valid excuse to get out of accompanying her when she'd invited him to meet her family. There'd been a million reasons not to go. In fact, he'd already been putting off the work on the international expansion. If it went forward it would be the culmination of all he'd worked for. But he was here in the car on his way to Tewksbury, New Jersey because he hadn't wanted to say goodbye to her. Couldn't even fucking imagine it after what they'd shared.

"I think you're really going to love it at my parents' place," Laura told him, grinning from the driver's seat. The only way he'd agreed to come was if he could do work as they drove, which meant she was driving. He'd wanted to charter a plane, but she'd balked because she didn't want him paying for a plane for what was her trip, so riding in his Range Rover had been the compromise.

"I'm sure it'll be great," he managed, thinking the exact opposite. It was going to be a complete and utter nightmare from start to finish; he'd never been more sure of anything in his life, but if he'd said no Laura would feel even more pity for him than she already did. And sweet Christ, he hated the pity. He was a goddamn billionaire feared by colleagues and employees alike. The whole damned idea of pity undermined his authority and ambition.

"Okay, well, we're almost there," she told him, as they turned into a residential neighborhood.

It was one like any other suburban enclave, cookie-cutter houses decently spaced apart with clean sidewalks and well-groomed landscaping. Blow-up Christmas decorations littered every other yard fighting for dominance over the more tasteful pine wreaths and red velvet ribbon decor. It was one of those quaint places that made him feel out of place. As if these were the kinds of people who could tell that he wasn't good enough for a real family.

The feeling intensified when Laura pulled into an oversize two-car driveway behind three other mid-size SUVs, thready talons of fear pulling at him. Will experienced the seesawing emotions of suffocation and yearning all at once. He would have killed for this setup as a kid, the run-of-the-mill middle-class home that was probably dysfunctional but not in a truly screwed up kind of way.

So, a bead of sweat running down the back of his neck, he pulled an audible and grabbed at his phone. While pretending to concentrate on something important, he ordered himself a Rideshare car that was luckily just around the corner.

Meeting Laura's eyes, he blew out a disappointed sigh. "Laura, I'm so sorry, but I need to get back to the office. A hang-up with the Dubai land acquisition."

Her face fell and he felt like an asshole, but there was just no way he could walk into that house that looked like everything he'd dreamed of as a kid and pretend he was fine with never having it. Not with Laura and not watching the proof of how happy she'd been without him.

"Oh," she finally said, disappointment clear as her eyes went downcast. "But we're already here."

Will leaned over to give her a kiss, her lips soft

and warm. He hated being the person that put that look on her face and normally he'd have done anything to change it, but not today. Today the ghosts of his past were nipping at his heels and he needed to go back to his present where things made sense and he was in control.

When a white SUV pulled up in front of his Range Rover, he swept a thumb over her cheek. "That's my car," he said. "I promise I'll make it up to you when you get back. Would you want to be my date for the hotel's New Year's gala? There's a black credit card and carte blanche with any designer in it for you."

She gazed at him. "I'll be your date, but I'll buy my own dress."

He gave her another kiss, this one slow and sweet and had him wishing he could be a better man for her. But unfortunately, he could only be the one he was.

"I'll see you in a couple of days," he said, dropping a final brush of his lips on her forehead.

Outside, he pulled both of their suitcases and her bag of gifts out of the trunk and set them on the sidewalk as she exited the car to meet him.

"Enjoy your family Christmas, Laura," he reminded her, giving her hand a squeeze. "I'll be waiting for you in the city when you get back."

"Okay," she said, searching his eyes. He smiled at her and gave her hand another squeeze, not letting on that he knew he was being a shitty friend. But it was too much to ask of him to spend Christmas with the perfect family he'd never have and that she left him for. "Have a safe trip."

As he entered the SUV, he watched out the window as a man about his age appeared on the front stoop of Laura's house. His brown hair cropped close to his scalp and blue eyes smiling as he saw Laura and gave her a huge hug. Will felt a tug of alarm as Laura moved farther away from him, but if this was the first step he needed to take to break the spell between them, then he was going to take it.

Laura refused to look back at Will as his car edged out from the curb and onto the road. She was stupidly devastated that he was leaving. It was the first time in their history that Will had ever not come through for her.

She was also ashamed and mortified that she hadn't considered his feelings before bringing him here. Of course, he wouldn't want to relive another Christmas with the family she'd chosen instead of him.

"Laura, dear!" her mom cooed as she came rushing out of the house. A thick red cardigan sweater was draped over her shoulders like an afterthought and fell off as she embraced Laura as if they were two long-lost lovers after wartime. Laura repeated the process with every family member and three tiny toddlers of similar ages.

"Where's your friend Will?" Nancy Edwards asked, peering over Laura's shoulder to the empty lawn behind her before leading her into the house. "We're all excited to meet him."

Laura pulled her suitcase into the foyer and left it there before falling into the faded floral sofa that her parents could more than afford to replace, but could never agree on. She blew out a breath, despite everything, glad to be home.

"He had a last-minute business thing that pulled him back to the city," she said, trying to make it sound reasonable.

Her dad, Rich, sat back in his black leather recliner. "This a boy you're seeing?"

Laura wanted to laugh at the idea of anyone mistaking Will Walker for a boy and that he would ever allow the label of seeing each other to apply to what they were doing.

"I'm not really seeing him, Dad," she explained, "but he's an old friend."

"I hope you didn't drive through that snow all on your own," Rich grumbled, his voice gruff with concern.

"No, I didn't," Laura confirmed, allaying his fear. "Will drove with me and left when we got here."

Her parents shared a look she could probably interpret as questioning what kind of man drove three hours and didn't even come in and say hello. A scared one, probably, Laura assumed. One who knew what a visit to parents meant and hadn't wanted to go there with her. That was probably part of it, but the other part, that Laura knew she was throwing her happy family in his face, was the bigger reason for his sudden departure.

"Well, come," Nancy said briskly, ushering everyone into the kitchen, "you must be hungry after the trip and we have some leftover ham for sandwiches."

The spread on the kitchen island was impressive and the rest of Laura's siblings filed in, everyone making a grab from the stack of holiday-themed paper plates that had been set out for the informal lunch.

Tyler, her brother who'd met her at the door, placed a sliced potato roll on his plate. "So this Will was a foster kid too?" he asked Laura.

"Yeah," she informed, forking out a couple of pieces of ham from a red ceramic platter with white snowflakes on the edges. Laura looked between Tyler and her sister, Sarah. "He never found a good home, though."

"Sounds like he ended up good, though," Tyler said, shoving his sandwich in his mouth.

"Yeah, I researched him and he's, like, a billionaire," Sarah pointed out.

"Yeah, he is, but that doesn't mean he's happy," Laura admitted, thinking of how relaxed he'd been once he'd let her in. Different and more like the boy she'd known, quicker to smile, easier to touch. "We're the ones who got very, very lucky." She put an arm around her mom and gave her a quick kiss.

"We sure did." Tyler grinned, getting in on the hug and rubbing his mom's head.

Nancy swatted Tyler away. "Don't you go thanking me again," she scolded, but the pride and love on her face told another story. "You three made our lives better in every way and I'm so glad you're all finally here now so we can celebrate Christmas properly."

Watching her family chitchat about nothing in particular, Laura understood just how painful this might be to someone like Will. She'd found a better life here, amongst other foster kids with whom she probably formed an even stronger bond than him. It would have left him feeling even more alone. She'd been so focused on spending more time and having a perfect Christmas with him finally after all these years, she hadn't truly considered what that might mean for him. She was kicking herself for being so selfish. She'd apologize later, but she knew an apology would do nothing because it would require him to acknowledge that he wanted any of those things in the first place, which he never would. It was the first lesson of being abandoned; your wishes were never realized so it was best to not even bother.

Sarah opened a can of sparkling water and met Laura's eyes. Sarah's clear blue eyes and brown hair were a striking combination. "Mom wouldn't let us open any gifts until you got here."

"Of course, I did not," Nancy declared proudly. "It wouldn't be right and you two are pitiful siblings for trying to suggest otherwise."

Sarah rolled her eyes.

"But I want to hear more about the billionaire

Laura is shacking up with," Sarah said, after swallowing a bite of her sandwich. When Laura shook her head, Sarah continued. "I might have traded in the two of you for a billion dollars," she said, looking between Tyler and Laura meaningfully.

Tyler rolled his eyes. "You would just spend it on food dehydrators and more goats."

Sarah worked as a physician's assistant as a day job, but made most of her money from raising goats and making soap. She was well-known and one bar of soap sold for something crazy like twenty dollars. Tyler, too, was successful, having taken over Rich's fast-food-restaurant franchise in town and then increasing business exponentially in the three years he'd been running it on his own, opening up two other branches just this year. Laura was immensely proud of them both.

"It's not like he's talking about his money with me," Laura returned.

"And he shouldn't have to," Nancy agreed.

"But he does have a talking toilet," Laura snuck in, grinning, thankful to be home again.

"Well," Sarah said "the last guy you chose was rich too, but you didn't like him either."

Nancy was silent in the conversation, but had come around the island to pull Laura into her arms and give her a smacking kiss on the cheek. "Laura is just discerning, that's all. And his hair was stupid anyway." She grimaced, making an upward fanning gesture near her forehead with her hand to indicate a spiky hairdo. That her mom felt like her spotty dating history was cause for coddling said enough.

"Jacob was an idiot," Rich yelled from the living room, clearly having heard all of the conversation, but choosing to remain in his chair. "And so were Matt and Chad and all the other ones you kicked to the curb."

"Okay," she said, holding her hands up to stop the barrage on her past mistakes, "I think I get the picture."

"Apparently not," Sarah pointed out, "if you're just dating some billionaire loser who punks out of a family event."

"He's not a loser—he's just complicated," Laura hedged, plucking at the chips on her plate. "We were best friends and neighbors when we were foster kids together. I left without saying goodbye and he didn't have an easy life afterward. I was overstepping by making him see how happy I was while he was on the streets struggling to survive. I should have been more mindful of his feelings."

Sarah and Tyler met her eyes, both knowing what it was like to be in foster care, the bone-deep feelings of worthlessness and helplessness. Adjusting to their new life hadn't been easy, but they'd done it eventually.

Finally, her mom took her hand and gave it a squeeze, locking eyes with her.

"If you want to be there for him, Laura, take it from someone who knows. You need to make sure he knows how you feel about him because he's not going give his love or trust up easily. You all know how scary that is."

Laura nodded because she knew just how difficult it would be to get Will to trust her not to leave and then even more so to trust her with his heart. She didn't know how she'd ever get him to do it, but one thing was certain as she ate the rest of her ham sandwich and joked and teased with the family she loved: she felt Will's distance keenly. She hated that he'd run out on her today instead of being honest about his feelings, but she got it. But it also made the forgiveness she thought she was working toward seem that much further away.

Getting Will was going to be a lot of work and she wasn't sure she had the emotional reserves herself to convince him he was worthy of love because there were still days when she had to remind her own self of it.

"Don't give up, dear," her mom advised quietly as Sarah and Tyler fought over the last sugar cookie. "He needs you."

CHAPTER TWELVE

AT HIS OWN New Year's party, a crush with so many people packed into his hotel that he could barely breathe, the only thought Will had was that he wanted to redo his ballroom.

The person he wanted to do it was in his arms too. He wanted Laura not to leave his hotel at all but to move in and be with him, redesign his spaces, make his penthouse into a home, do whatever she wanted, frankly. Yet, he knew he wasn't going to ask that, so a business arrangement with a legally binding contract that she remain in his life seemed like a more secure idea.

The three days she'd been at her parents' house had felt like a lifetime, but had given him enough space to think of a plan. A relationship wouldn't work, but he still wasn't ready for the alternative— her leaving for good.

She was warm in his arms as they swayed along to the live big band playing "What a Wonderful World" as if they were in a movie about falling in love in

New York City. It was a more romantic story than the real one, which was that he'd fallen in love in a dirty, rat-infested tenement with no money, no education and no real future.

"Are you having a good time?" he asked her. She hadn't been acting like herself since they'd gotten to the party. After over a week holed up with her either in his place or her place, he knew her moods and this was one he hadn't encountered before. She'd been strangely taciturn all night as they'd been greeted by guest after guest without much time in between. He wanted to apologize, but like the brunches and dinners he'd dragged her to this was his real life, although he'd been less in demand at those events. For this one, he'd barely had enough time to compliment her dress before being overtaken by the city's bold and beautiful.

"Of course," she said, but the words fell flat. "This is beautiful. This room is beautiful too. I know I've said it before, but you've built something really special, Will. I hope you know that."

He gave a cursory glance to the white marble walls and black onyx floor, glittering chandeliers hung in an elegant line all the way down the center of the rectangular room while crisp white linen tablecloths draped over circular tables with black, indigo, peach and white flower arrangements and gleaming gold flatware. He and Laura were in a far corner near the windows that overlooked the bright lights of Times Square.

Usually he loved the energy of New Year's Eve; surrounded by people and possibility, he couldn't get enough, thrived on the competition. But right now he just wanted to leave it all behind, drag Laura back to his penthouse, curl up on the couch again and ask her for real what was actually wrong.

"I was thinking maybe this room needed a redo," he divulged, seeing if he could figure her out in a roundabout way.

"I'm not an interior designer, if that's what you're trying to get at."

He shrugged. "You're telling me you have no ideas for how you might re-envision this room?"

Laura met his eyes, hers wary. "You know I don't want to work for you that way, Will."

His heart sped up and he felt his fingers flexing on her waist before he realized what he was doing. Fear, that was this feeling crawling up his back like a pair of cold, wizened hands.

"You wouldn't really be working for me—I'd just contract you out like I did for the lobbies."

A light eyebrow quirked. "Is that so? Is that how you want me in your life?"

"Well, my business life anyway," he hedged, leaning down to drop a kiss on her hair that no one around them could possibly see. "What's on your mind, Laura?"

He suspected her change in mood was because early on in the evening he'd derailed the apology she'd tried to make about taking him to her parents' house. As if he couldn't have handled it if he'd wanted to. That she felt needed to coddle his feelings when he'd been the one to be shitty to her was untenable to him.

She shrugged. "Nothing. I guess I'm just coming down from the high of the holidays."

"Do you have a job lined up for the New Year?"

"I'm booked solid until October. Your hotel press really put things into high gear for me. I'm going to have to hire another assistant right away instead of waiting until summer like I originally planned."

"I'm glad—you deserve it," he told her, meaning it, an ache in his chest over how proud he was of her.

"You do too," she said, meeting his eyes, hers warm and brown and like he was falling into a safe space when he hadn't moved at all. But then her eyes darted across the room, "Black and white will always be in style," she continued. "I don't know that I would do anything differently unless you want to have a Christmas ball."

His eyebrows climbed his forehead. "Maybe we can roll a gala into your new contract for next year."

"Is that all we're doing next year, working together?" she asked, pressing him again. He wanted to say no, that he wanted her in his life permanently. In his penthouse or her brownstone, he wasn't picky as long as she was there. He wanted to wake up to her every day, go to sleep with her in his arms every night, have dinners out, dinners in, walks in the park; he imagined and yearned for it all with her.

But those words weren't leaving his mouth.

"You want to—" he started to ask her seriously if she wanted to date him because that seemed, in itself, something so out of the ordinary as cows being undercover unicorns, but that he might hear yes as the answer was urging him on.

But he realized that the band had stopped playing and they were pretty much the only ones left on the dance floor, save a few lovebirds still in each others' arms. So instead he led her off the wooden dance floor onto the black carpet.

As he was about to do what had previously been unthinkable and ask her to be his girlfriend, an old hookup, Lila, appeared before him. Her delicate hand fell on his arm and his whole body wanted to recoil.

"Will, darling," she cooed, hooking onto his hip as Laura stepped back to give him space. He wanted to pull her back but everything was happening so fast. "It's so good to see you. I wanted to thank you for inviting me."

"It's not a problem, Lila," he managed, not at all certain he'd invited her in the first place. A tall, blond, blue-eyed model, Lila was the type of girl he usually went for. She was sophisticated, in demand, and most important, transient in his life. They had a good time every now and then when they ran into each other but that was where it ended.

"Can I get you anything?" he asked when her arm curled around his waist. He stepped back before she could get any purchase, not wanting to glance at Laura because he could only imagine what she thought about it. If he'd wanted, he could end this whole thing right now, but part of him needed Laura to see his real life. And that included women. If she couldn't deal with it, then she wasn't ready to be his girlfriend.

"I was hoping you'd find me later," Lila purred, running a purple-tipped finger down the middle of his chest. "I've missed you, baby."

Will wanted to groan; this was going to be a disaster.

Still refusing to look at Laura's face, he knew it'd gone too far. He gently removed Lila's hand from his chest, "Lila, I'm here with someone."

"Who?" she asked, glancing back to where Laura had been, revealing an empty space.

Fuck.

"I have to go," he told her, leaving her gaping at his rude exit as he navigated his way out of the ballroom.

It took him over an hour of shaking hands with more of the city's richest men and women, socialites who drove business to his hotel, and acquaintances he'd made over the years before he made it out of the ballroom. Through it all, he didn't see a single glimpse of Laura, not her soft strawberry blond hair or the strapless cornflower-blue dress he'd remember on his dying day.

By the time he got to the penthouse it was nearly midnight, the energy in the hotel and outside on the street vibrating through his veins. All he wanted to do was start the year with her.

The elevator doors opened and he saw her outside, the fire on the terrace roaring in the grate along with the standing heater. One of the thick fleece blankets from his couch draped over her bare shoulders as she stared out over the skyline, her pale skin luminous beneath the lights of the city.

Laura knew the moment Will arrived in the penthouse behind her; she felt it in the air. She wasn't jealous of the woman who'd glommed onto him as if Laura wasn't even there, but it had brought home the fact that she'd been living in a fantasy world where Will was still her friend and protector like he'd been when they were kids. But he wasn't.

Will Walker was a billionaire hotel magnate who could crook his finger and have anyone or anything in this city. That she'd thought all he needed was her love was so heartbreakingly naive of her. He was so far beyond her dream of a normal life and family that she felt embarrassed that she ever thought he needed her.

It was clear from him punking out on her family and all the work events he'd dragged her to that Will didn't want a lifestyle change. He'd given no indication that he needed her in his life in any real or meaningful way. And she wasn't going to beg. She hadn't begged for a family when she was a kid and she wasn't going to do it now, so it was time for her to accept that he didn't want to be in her life like that.

Will came to stand by her at the all-glass railing, watching her for a moment.

"She's just an old friend," he finally said, his voice low but audible over the steady roar of the crowd forty floors below them on the street.

"I believe you," she allowed, drawing the blanket farther around her shoulders. The fire and the heater did a lot to keep it warm, but it was still the dead of winter.

"Why'd you leave then?" he asked, his forearm coming to rest on the glass railing as he regarded her, his fingers so close to hers and his eyes searching. "I was hoping for another dance."

"I'd just had enough of the crowd, I guess," she lied. "If you didn't want to come to the gala, I would have skipped it too," he said, surprising her. But then she didn't actually believe him. He wanted to do whatever he could for her, but every event he'd dragged her to had been a way to push her away, to make sure she didn't get too close to him. She knew every trick in the book, had used them all on her boyfriends past.

"I didn't want you to feel like you needed to babysit me when you had stuff to do."

She saw his tongue bury itself into his cheek like it did when he was trying to work something out. "I never consider spending time with you babysitting. I liked having you there. These two weeks have been the first time these kinds of things haven't been a complete pain in my ass and that's because of you."

Laura smiled, having a hard time not touching him. He was so close, she could reach out and run a finger down his silky black lapel, like she'd wanted to do while they were dancing, but the time for that had passed. He was out of jeans and a leather jacket and in a bespoke Tom Ford tux that had been delivered to his penthouse from the designer this morning. Every bit of the tux was black, from the tailored pants to the fitted jacket and shirt to the onyx cuff links and buttons. The lapels were shiny silk, but that and his tie were the only variation in color. He looked as handsome as ever, but mostly she just wanted to rip it off him.

So she drew him to her, reaching out to pull off his bow tie, then letting it drop to the ground.

Shouting started in the street, the crowd already roaring in anticipation of the ball dropping. Slowly, her eyes on his, she unbuttoned his shirt.

His eyes were burning through her clothes. He'd never be easygoing, but watching him watch her undress him was painfully erotic. Even in his hotel where he ruled his own little kingdom, she was in charge and it was everything. All at once, she pushed off his jacket and shirt and leaned forward to drop a kiss on his collarbone. "I liked this even back then," she told him, her voice hushed with reverence as she explored his body for what she knew was the final time. But unlike last time, she intended to show him just how much he meant to her before she had to say goodbye.

"Yeah?" he asked, face still as a statue as she licked across the protruding bone, his skin salty and smelling faintly of musky tobacco and bright vetiver at his pulse, which was beating steadily in his neck.

She nodded her head yes in response, drawing her hands across his shoulders and down the cords of his arms. "These have changed, but I always thought you were the strongest person in the world, even when the muscles might have been a little smaller."

Dropping the blanket because she was already overheated, Laura moved around him, drawing a single fingertip down the sections of his abdomen and around to the muscled planes of his back. She drew kisses down his spine and back up to his shoulders. "I'm sorry I never said goodbye," she told him, finally breaking the seal on their past. "I wanted to."

He stiffened so she knew she'd hurt him. "I should have left with you—I know that. I should have trusted that you could take care of us."

"You would have been an idiot to do that," he rasped, and she could see his throat working.

"I thought about it all the time," she admitted, resting her forehead on his shoulders. "I missed you so much, Will. And I wanted to go with you and I'm sorry you were alone." Tears fell to her cheeks as she imagined for the thousandth time Will completely and totally on his own in the world after she left.

"You were my only friend in the world and I left you alone and I didn't ever expect you to forgive me."

Taking a deep breath, she reached around and undid the button of his pants, pulling them down to the ground as she came to stand in front of him, his strong legs splayed powerfully apart, his hands fisted at his sides. "What do you want, Laura?" he got out, his eyes burning holes into her.

"You," she told him truthfully. She went to her knees then, took off his shoes and socks, pushed them aside and glided her hands up his legs; her trail stopped at his knees to run her thumb over an old, now faded scar. She remembered he'd gotten jabbed by a barbed-wire fence he'd been climbing to get her backpack that some bullies had thrown over to torment her.

She leaned over to kiss the pale slash, the tears coming in earnest now and she didn't stop them. They were for now and for then and for what they could have been, then and now.

Standing, she faced him and he remained stock still, his cock jutting out and throbbing for her. He reached out, his thumb brushing away the tears on her face, eventually kissing them away. She wrapped her arms around his neck, finally giving in and kissing him. "I'm sorry," she breathed against his lips, wanting the absolution he had never once tried to give her in the weeks they'd been together. And she knew why, but just hadn't wanted to accept it.

She kissed him, blindly, her lips and tongue sliding over his with little finesse, only feeling and desire and hopeless desperation to be his and to be forgiven and to be loved unconditionally by him like she'd once been. The two of them against the world.

The barely there sound of her zipper lowering drifted through the air around them as her dress slid into an iridescent silken puddle on the ground. Lifting her bodily out of the pool of fabric, he held her in his arms, his hardness throbbing against her stomach, the strong bands of his arms encasing her just a little too hard as he fought against the avalanche of their inevitable end.

His fingers found her center, testing and coming away wet because she wanted him more than anything she'd ever wanted.

"Laura," he gritted, leaning his head on her forehead, his breath warm and wine scented on her cheek. "I want—"

But she didn't want anything other than what she wanted, which was everything, so she met his lips with hers swallowing the words that would inevitably fall short.

He picked her up, carried her and the blanket to the chaise lounge in front of the fire, kissing his way down her chest, taking a nipple hardened by cold air in his mouth and then sucking softly, the gentle movement incongruous with the shouting going on below and around them as the world prepared to ring in the New Year. A pop star she recognized performed a block away, the pulsing bass beat reaching them even as high up as they were.

He placed himself at her entrance, already stretching her through what felt like molten-liquid heat between her thighs. Everywhere he touched, from her hand, to her fingertips, to where the hair of his legs subtly abraded the smooth skin of her legs was electric.

"Laura," he choked out, as he pushed his way inside her.

The crowd below began to count down just as he started to speed up, his pace and hers a frenzy of limbs, clutching nails and seeking mouths. She needed more of him, pulling him tightly to her as she ground up against him, their groans lost to the night.

"Fuck," he growled as she pulled his hair back so she could bite into his neck, all of her bottled feelings and resentment that he just wouldn't forgive her coalescing as she used a little more force than necessary.

He levered higher over her, breaking the contact as he pounded into her, his hip bone hitting her clit so hard that she saw stars, her whole body flooding with sublime pleasure. She lay there, stroking him as he hammered into her as if he could change everything, change the fact that they still meant everything to each other but they were too terrified to admit it. The rigid length of him stretched her, the shuttling wet channel clasping against him as she shuddered her release, screaming it into the countdown as they and the city met the New Year together.

One more thrust and he went completely still inside her, shuddering against her before lowering himself beside her on the chaise, panting with exertion.

Shouting, screaming and joyful music floated up from the street below, but she barely noticed the countdown to one or the ball dropping or any of the raucous revelry. She had everything she wanted and she still had to let him go again.

Thirty seconds in and it was already shaping up to be her worst year yet.

CHAPTER THIRTEEN

WILL'S OFFICIAL NEW YEAR started by waking up in his pitch-black bedroom with a heavy sense of dread pushing on his chest. His hand reached out to the other side of the bed for Laura but as he'd feared, she wasn't there. The handful of cold thousand-thread-count cotton confirmed his worst nightmare. Fear but then rage, hot and icy and sweet, scalded through his veins.

She had left him again.

He was just about to throw the covers off when he heard shuffling across the room. After waiting for his eyes to adjust to the darkness, he saw her lurking around the room, probably trying to collect her things before he woke up so she could head out and continue living her perfect life without him.

"What are you doing?" he asked, his voice ripping through the quiet like a glass breaking. He watched as she halted abruptly by his dresser, caught.

"Sorry," came her hushed voice. "I was trying to be quiet."

"Are you leaving?"

He knew where she lived so it wasn't as if she was going to disappear, but if last night was goodbye then he was going to make her say it to his face. Make her explain why exactly she couldn't be bothered to entertain what was obviously a relationship already just because he hadn't said the words?

Christ, did she think he let people stay at his penthouse? Let alone for nearly an entire week? Or make dinner together or show up to multiple events with the same woman on his arm? Because he did none of that.

"I have a lot of work to do tomorrow, so I thought sleeping at my place would save me time in the morning."

"Is that so?" he asked, his anger, along with dread that she was leaving, rose in his veins in a slow, but insistent burn. That she was running out on him again hurt him beyond measure. There was no measurement for complete and total emotional devastation, it just was. Rationally he knew he was overreacting, but just those few moments when he thought he'd never see her again had locked the air in his chest as fear coursed frantically through him.

"Yeah," she said, her body straightening as his eyes further adjusted to the darkness. Her blue evening dress was dangling in her hands.

"You have clients on New Year's Day?" He was baiting her, but he was so tired of pretending he didn't have feelings for her. When they'd been kids he'd been trying to protect her, keep her alive and fed and safe, so he'd accepted that someone else, like an actual adult, could do that better for her. But for her to walk out of his life now after they'd finally reconnected, he couldn't handle it.

"Well, no," she hedged, "I was just planning on doing work on their jobs."

"At," he glanced at the digital face on his watch, "four o'clock in the morning?"

"I wasn't going to work on it now," she explained in a falsely reasonable tone as she pulled the dress on, "but I thought if I spent the rest of the night at home I'd be able to get up early and get an early start on work. If I stayed here I'd have to do a walk of shame back to my apartment, shower, etc.—you know how it goes."

"Yeah, I do know how walks of shame go. It seems like that's the problem," he said.

"No, I'd just like to be home, that's all," she managed, her tone unconvincing.

"I never pretended I didn't have a past, Laura. I've slept with Lila a total of three times in my life. Sometimes she's in town and we do and sometimes she's in town and we don't. I don't know what her middle name is, I don't know where she's from, where she lives now, who her friends are, if she likes movies or the kind of music she listens so. I know literally nothing about her."

Laura's face went from mildly annoyed that he was keeping her from leaving to full-on glare by the end of his explanation. "You are cracked if you think that somehow makes me feel better."

Will regarded Laura, not knowing quite how to fix this situation and not knowing even if he could try. He had his own anger to contend with that in the face of hers was only gaining ground. She'd talked up her perfect, well-adjusted family life just to throw him off, to make him believe that he was the one with intimacy problems, and he definitely had them, but not for one second should he have believed her charade. Laura had scars just as deep as his.

"Why would I be trying to make you feel better?" he shot back. "You're trying to cut out of this before it even begins."

"I am not cutting out, Will."

He threw the covers back and stood, knowing he was completely naked and not giving a single shit. "Tell me the truth now, Laura. Did you have any intention of coming back here after you left tonight?"

"What are you talking about?"

He crossed his arms over his chest, digging in. "You know exactly what."

She started shaking her head, twisting her body so she could zip up the back of her dress, finally getting it with a vicious tug as she glared at him. "You have no idea what you're talking about."

"Maybe not, but it seems to me like you're sneaking out of my place in the middle of the night right after things got the slightest bit bumpy between us."

"There is no us!" she suddenly shouted, swinging to face him. "You have made that quite clear."

He grabbed his robe from the back of the bathroom door and yanked it on.

"I've made that clear how?" he asked her, amazed at how steady his voice was considering how out of control he felt. "By housing you and celebrating a holiday I've only ever hated? Maybe by buying you gifts and sleeping at your place even when I live in one where people bring me whatever I need in under a minute?"

"You know exactly what I mean," Laura said, not buying it. "Just like tonight, you have gone out of your way to let me know that this isn't a relationship. I left the gala for nearly two hours before you finally followed me. But now that I'm leaving and you're not the one in control, you've decided to have this little hissy fit."

That she could be so flippant about his feelings hurt. Her leaving wasn't him having a hissy fit, it was him breaking apart again.

"Well," he bit off, stalking to the bedroom door and pulling it open with an angry flourish. "Don't let my hissy fit change your mind. By all means, you can get out."

Her eyes widened, but he just didn't care. All of the angst of his entire life seemed to be bubbling up in his chest like a medieval cauldron of the disgusting dregs of his early life and he couldn't stop from boiling over if he tried.

"Were you even planning on telling me this time that you weren't coming back?"

"I live in the same city, Will—it's not like you can't find me. This isn't goodbye."

"Felt like it."

"I'm not in charge of your feelings, Will," she told him, still not budging toward the open door.

The words cut more than she knew because he'd loved her so much, like a sister, like a girlfriend, like a friend; she'd been everything and one day she had literally just disappeared from his life as if she'd never been there at all. What did he have to do to get her to stay with him just once? Rip open his veins and bleed for her?

"I can't change my past, Laura—I've been with women."

"I don't want you to change your past."

"Then why are you leaving right now?"

"I'm not leaving!" she shouted, agitated again, but he knew it was because he was right. And because she *knew* exactly how deep things were between them. There was no going back if they went forward. It was too real for her to deal with, to accept that he loved her. But damned if he wasn't going to make her deal with it just like he was.

"You're scared," he challenged.

Laura stomped over to him, fire in her eyes. "Yeah, because even if you allowed yourself to have a relationship with me, which is still doubtful, you have no idea how to be a real boyfriend," she exclaimed. "You don't care about anything but your hotels. The entire time we've been together, you've never even asked me about my own past relationships. You haven't asked about my life with my new family, my friends, my work, nothing. All these weeks have been is sex, you putting me on your arm for work events so I could see just how high you've climbed and me forcing you to do Christmas things."

Her description of the best two weeks of his life was like a knife in his heart. "If you're telling me that I'm emotionally unavailable, no shit."

"Yeah, and that's a problem," she told him.

"Oh, because you're so open?" he shot back, feeling raw and exposed. "You, who have a perfect Christmas story and make Christmas perfect for everyone else, but fuck the person she left to have it?"

"Will," she breathed, her eyes haunted. "I thought we'd been over this."

"No, *you've* been over it!" he yelled, finally breaking. "You've explained and apologized and made excuses and glossed over all of it, but *we* have not been over this at all."

In point of fact, he shut the bedroom door because they were finally going to have this out. "You talk about how much better your life got after you left and I'm happy for you, Laura, I am. All I ever wanted was for you to be happy and safe. Period. I don't ever want you to think that for a moment I would have rather you stayed with that fucked-up family than leave. But you did leave me, too, Laura. Without a

word, a letter, a note, a sign, anything. And it wasn't
as if you couldn't have found me later—you knew
where the hell I lived, knew my name. Christ, the
internet exists, you can literally find *anyone* now.
But you didn't. Not even when we were in the same
city. Do you know how much that hurt? How much
it still hurts."

She opened her mouth to respond but he held up a
hand to stop her. He couldn't bear to hear any more
excuses.

"For weeks after you left I searched everywhere,
wondering if you'd gone into hideout because you
were scared that asshole would hit you. Then I wondered if they'd taken you back to the group home
because you threatened to tell the caseworker about
the abuse. I made a list of places you might have run
away to start over. You name it, I thought it. I asked
the secretary at school if you'd withdrawn, but they
couldn't tell me anything. You left *me*, Laura."

"I told you I didn't have time to tell you," she said,
her voice weak, her hands at her sides as the fight
went out of her because she knew he was right. "I
said I was sorry."

"For what, Laura?" he asked. "Exactly what are
you sorry for?"

He held his breath because he just needed her
to understand the magnitude of what her leaving
had done to him and realize on some level what that
meant. She'd changed the trajectory of his entire life.
That was how important she was to him, that he

hadn't been interested in sharing his life with anyone else because the only person he'd ever tried to do it with left without so much as a second thought.

"I should have told you," she finally said. "And I should have found you afterward. I was scared of how upset you'd be, and then once enough time passed I was scared that you'd forgotten me completely."

He met her eyes then, locking with them so she wouldn't misunderstand his next words or their significance. "I wasn't upset that you left. I was upset that you didn't tell me or even let me know afterward that you were alive. You wanted your whole life erased, Laura, and I get that I was a part of it."

Tears slid down her face. "I sent you letters, Will—they were returned. I promise I didn't want to erase you."

"Yes, you did," he insisted because it was the truth. He hadn't gotten any letters from her. "You didn't want me to be a part of your new perfect life."

"It isn't true," she insisted.

"Yes, it is. You saw your shot at a better life and didn't want to remember your old shitty one. Even now, you're leaving me in the middle of the night because despite all that love and security that your perfect foster family gave you, you still don't know how to accept love from me because I love the broken, broke and old Laura just as much as the new shiny one who creates picture perfect Christmases because her life is so magical now."

"You talk a big game, Will," she said, her eyes narrowing. "You accuse me of leaving you, of not contacting you, of writing you out of my life like it was the easiest thing in the world, but that isn't the whole story, is it?"

She took two steps forward until they were nearly toe to toe. "I loved you more than anything when we were kids. Like you said, you were my best friend, my brother, my dad, the person I wanted to be my first boyfriend, but you never did anything to let me know how you felt then or now. Sure, you let me stay here because I was homeless and allowed me to keep staying because you like me around and the regular sex. You can pretend that all of those things meant something so that you didn't have to say out loud that you cared, but I'm not buying it. You've never told me how you feel because you're just as scared."

"I think I've been pretty clear about my feelings," he argued.

"Do you mean that you're in love with me?"

He stared at her because he'd already said the words, he wasn't going to put them on the table again when his hand was already showing.

"Yes, I was in love with you then and now," he said, saying fuck it because if this was the end, then she was going to walk away with everything even if she took a literal piece of him with her.

"Oh, really? Great, then, let's try it," she said, her voice high. "Let's be in a real relationship, me and you."

His brow furrowed at her quick turnabout. "What are you getting at?"

She started to unzip her dress again. "Just what I said. I'll stay here tonight and then tomorrow we'll go to brunch and then probably have amazing sex again and then in three weeks when I do something you don't like, you won't tell me *for fifteen years*!" The last she shouted after her voice had steadily risen throughout her speech.

He opened his mouth to speak, but she cut him off again, standing naked in front of him like he had done for her before.

"No! It's my turn. You don't let anyone in! I have no idea what you're thinking, ever, Will. You've just told me you loved me and I have been over here, living the same life as you and I had literally no clue at all. Because you live your life without thinking about anyone else. And that's how you had to be—I get it, but like you said, my scars are just as deep as yours and I need the reassurance, Will. I need to know what you're thinking, how you're feeling, that you're going to stay, that I won't run into women you slept with *in your hotel* at any moment. That's what I need to feel secure in a relationship and you can't give me any of that."

She was breathing hard, tears running down her face. "But I love you so much," she whispered, choking on the words. "I've loved you all my life and I should have told you I was leaving, and then I should have found you afterward but I didn't think you'd care and that would have broken me. I needed you to love me so much then and I couldn't have dealt with it if I found out that you hadn't."

Reaching behind her, she pulled on his drawer and put on a pair of his too-big sweats and T-shirt, letting her tears run unrestrained. He wanted to take her into his arms, but her red light was up and he didn't know how to get to green.

"I thought for so long how dumb I was because how could I have possibly found my soulmate when I was sixteen years old and miserable? But no matter how great the guy I was dating was, I knew it was wrong, knew I'd never trust anyone with my heart but you."

She opened the door then, meeting his eyes, his heart aching to be able to wipe away the tears that were dripping off her chin now.

"Then you were right under my nose the last five years," she said, her voice cracking as she gestured to the building at large. "And I thought it was fate that we finally met again. That the universe was trying to tell me I'd been right to wait."

"I want to be with you, Laura," Will pleaded, reaching for her finally because he couldn't stand watching her in pain.

But she stepped into the hallway beyond his bedroom, out of reach. "You don't know how to love, Will. I'm not sure I know either, but I know that love shouldn't feel this way, like one person owing the other something. You haven't forgiven me for leaving and I won't start a relationship being in your debt."

She turned and ran down the hall; his mouth opened to tell her to stay but the words wouldn't come. He stood there in a daze, barely hearing the front door shut, his eyes on her forgotten gown on the floor at his feet.

Laura had done it. She'd left him again. And for a person who loved to be alone, for the first time since she'd left the first time, he didn't like it at all.

CHAPTER FOURTEEN

LAURA WAS STILL angry at Will the day after she left him in his penthouse tower. She was still angry a week after that. And after two weeks, the rage she felt might have diminished the slightest bit, but it still made her edgy. All of her designs for a client's fiftieth wedding anniversary, a famous singer, nonetheless, were in a moody black. She cut out pictures of black candles, black roses, and only changed her mind when she realized that it was Will's signature color.

It was silly, it was ridiculous, all of it was just so pathetic she wanted to crawl into her bed and not come out until she could forget every bit of it. But she wasn't going to give Will Walker the satisfaction. So here she was diving back into work so she could forget everything else in her life.

"Um, do you want something for lunch?" Maisey asked, briefly interrupting her bleak inner dialogue. "I'm going out."

Laura shook her head. "No, thanks. Have fun."

And then maybe she saw Maisey later when she came back, maybe she didn't. The days and nights bled into each other.

Inside her apartment, Laura shoved a plate full of Thai leftovers into the microwave and poured herself a glass of too-expensive white wine, then leaned back against her kitchen counter getting lost in the past again.

After sitting down at her table with her dinner, she opened her laptop, not quite sure what she was doing when she typed Will's name into the browser.

So many articles popped up on him and pictures that Maisey had brought up during their research, but that Laura had never had the time to look at. Will Walker had been Will Serhant when she'd known him. He'd been a punk kid whose mom had literally dropped him off at a group home when he was six, telling him that he was just going to a school to play with kids, and then never returned.

But fate had led them together then and now. Scrolling through the photos of him, starting from over five years ago, she yearned to have the time they'd lost back. The decision to leave had been right, but she should have left the note she'd written. Not the ones she'd written later, the ones that had been returned, but the one she'd written the day she'd left when she knew she'd never see him again and had literally poured her heart out on the page. But chickened out at the last minute because she'd been too scared to let anyone know how she felt back then.

After rising from the table, she went upstairs to her bedroom and pulled out the old, battered shoe-box every girl had to have full of flotsam-and-jetsam memories she'd kept over the years. She hadn't left him anything of hers but she had taken something of his. Moving aside yellowed birthday cards from her parents, she found the old ring Will used to wear. It was just a simple black band, but they'd seen it at the mall once and he'd loved it. It had taken a lot of midnight shifts at the gas station, sacrifice and grit to buy that ring, but he'd done it. That's who Will was. He didn't give up.

And she'd taken the ring from him too because she was a total and complete shitty person who felt just as unlovable as he did, but could never take the leap and trust him enough to move forward. Lila or whoever didn't matter to her; he was all that mattered and she knew it.

He'd definitely been right about that part.

She slid the ring on her thumb because it was far too large for her own ring finger. The ring was important but it wasn't actually what she was looking for. Pulling out the letter she'd written him but never left, she knew it wouldn't do her any good to give it to him now but he should have it regardless.

So she put the unopened George Washington High School envelope she'd poached from school that day into a larger envelope, addressed it and then put it by her purse to send the next day. She stuck her plate and glass into the dishwasher and was about to call it a change-into-pajamas kind of night when the phone rang, her mom's face appearing on the screen.

"Hi, honey," her mom said after Laura answered, slumping down into her carefully curated blue velvet couch. Tears were already in her eyes at the sound of her mom's dear voice. "We haven't heard from you so I wanted to check in. Your brother thinks you've just been shacking up, as he put it, with Will, but I wanted to make sure everything was okay."

Laura forced out a laugh she didn't feel. "No, I've just been busy," she lied.

"Oh, okay," her mom said, her voice a little too high as she read into Laura's answer. "Well, what have you been up to? How's Will?"

Laura had to cough to cover up the sound of her own choked voice as she tried to respond to her mom. "He's good. I think he's in Dubai right now. He's in the middle of taking his company international so I haven't seen him much since the holidays ended."

This was information she'd obtained from several sources, but mainly the director of operations for Will Walker Enterprises with whom she was currently working to sort out the final details for her work on the next Christmas display for the hotels. She'd thought about passing on the job, but regardless of what happened she wanted Will to remain in her life even if they were just friends or friendly acquaintances. He was her family just as much as the one she'd found in his place. Even if it took a while for them to get there.

"Oh, well, that's exciting for him," Nancy cooed, pride in her voice for a man she didn't know. But then, that's how Nancy was. From the moment Laura had arrived in the county office to meet her new foster family, they'd made her feel like they truly cared about her. Unlike the family she'd left, they hadn't needed the money that came with it, they were just a couple of people who'd tried to have children but couldn't. Laura, after being passed around for over seven years, had been extremely jaded, but Nancy had proved her wrong. Over the first couple of months of regular meals, constant encouragement and even stern rules, Laura had begun to trust that she was in a home for good. Her brother and sister had come only months before her and while wary of each other, they were all so secretly eager to feel like they were really part of a family.

"Yeah, I think he's excited," Laura parroted. She honestly had no idea if Will was excited about opening up his hotels in other countries. His ambition was clear, but she didn't know if the money and power satisfied him.

"The truth is that we're not seeing each other anymore," Laura told her because whatever her faults, she wasn't a liar.

Nancy sighed on the other end of the line. "Oh, honey, I hate hearing you sound like that. What happened?"

And that's when it all came tumbling out of her mouth. From the time she left him to how she'd refused to accept his offer of love because it was begrudgingly given. She let it all go with a rush of shame so hot she thought it would consume her.

"Laura," Nancy soothed, her voice a touch of scolding mixed with sympathy. "You're a grown woman who I know has been through it, but you've also healed and know it's an ongoing struggle. Will knows people make mistakes so if you want him in your future, you can't wait for him. Tell him how you feel and accept his love."

"I did tell him how I feel and I do accept that he loves me," she protested, wiping tears from her face as the ache in her chest finally started to dissipate. "But he won't tell me he forgives me and I know he's still angry at me."

Nancy took a deep breath and Laura could see her slightly exasperated but loving expression over the miles that separated them. "I think the first thing you need to do to get Will back in your life, sweetheart, is forgive yourself and accept that you deserve his forgiveness."

Despite being the owner of a hotel chain, the very place designed specifically for travelers, Will wasn't actually a huge fan of traveling. He'd much rather be working in his hotel office where everything made sense and he was in his own domain. Traveling here and there just made him feel like he was constantly starting over again, like he had as a kid. He liked the stable and predictable life he'd built for himself. He had a reputation as being some kind of bad boy, but it couldn't be further from the truth.

As he headed into a seventy-story office complex in the heart of Dubai with his entourage of employees who could barely contain their excitement, all he wanted to do was be back in his penthouse making cookies with Laura. It was the most embarrassing thing to admit because this land purchase was of paramount importance. With luck, they could break ground before the end of the year and by next year he'd have done it, grown his business to a degree that even he hadn't thought possible. It was mostly everything he'd ever dreamed about having all very much within his grasp.

Unfortunately, as he toured the site and signed the final papers, the satisfaction he expected to feel never came. He celebrated with his staff, bought everyone the meal of their lives and opened up a tab at the bar for them. After a few drinks, though, he returned to a neighboring hotel, leaving them to their celebrating. The hotel wasn't as nice as his own, but what was, really, and it was over three thousand dollars a night so he couldn't complain. He drank another whiskey on the rocks as he flipped aimlessly through the television channels.

It'd been nearly a month since his fight with Laura and he'd been through every emotion since that night. Anger first, certainly, had held on for the longest time, but now that the heat of it had passed, he was just left with sadness and regret. And the knowledge that she was right, he hadn't forgiven her. It was why he hadn't gone after her then or now even though the pain and emptiness in his chest grew daily the longer he was without her. He was listless, depressed and just plain at a loss for what to do next.

There hadn't been a situation in his life up to now that he hadn't been prepared for. From the moment he'd known he was in charge of his own destiny, he'd planned, schemed, worked, maneuvered until he got exactly what he wanted. But every time he tried to pick up the phone to call or text her, he remembered how awful it had been when she'd left. He didn't know if he could let that pain go; it, along with the general abandonment by his mom and the calamity of horrors that made up the rest of his childhood, had been the driving force in his life. He'd been working so hard for so long just trying to outrun the past, to show anyone and everyone that he, Will Walker, was *something*, that he didn't know who he was without that anger.

He threw back another whiskey and tried going to bed, but as with most nights, the only thing he saw when he shut his eyes was the memory of Laura's tear-streaked face as she'd left him in his bedroom. Drawing in a ragged breath, he brought out his phone, his fingers hovering over the small keyboard nearly typing out some inane greeting, like, *how's it going?* But everything seemed wrong and he wasn't ready.

In his heart, he'd forgiven her a million times over, but the sadness and fear remained.

Shoving his phone back on the nightstand, he got out of bed. There was no way he was going to fall asleep so he pulled out the travel office he always brought along on trips. It was basically an extra large suitcase, but one that expanded when he opened it and had his laptop inside. He took the stack of mail from one of the folders and flipped through the opened envelopes, noting the dates his assistant had written on the outside. Mail wasn't a huge thing these days so it wasn't as if he had a lot to sort through, mostly contracts he needed to sign. But the next piece he opened had another envelope inside.

Puzzling over why he'd be receiving mail from his old high school, his hands got a little clammy as he opened the second envelope up. The paper was faded to a dull yellow and the glue had given up, leaving the flap rigid, undone and open.

Hands shaking because he knew, before he even registered his name written across the front in curvy girly handwriting he would have recognized anywhere, what was inside.

The torn notebook paper was still well-preserved along with the ink rippling hastily across the page as if she'd been in a hurry, which of course, he knew she had been because the day scrawled across the top was December 22, the day she left.

Hands shaking, he read the words on the page, barely believing it was happening. He scanned the pages, drinking in every word she'd written, wondering and yet understanding why she'd never actually given him this letter. The three lined sheets were filled with love and affection, the secrets of her soul poured out on the pages as if he should have always known it. How could he not have known it, except that she'd left him without a word? But reading this now, he knew why she had. This was a declaration that couldn't have gone unanswered.

And she'd had to go.

He'd been prepared to support her, but once she'd left he had one semester to get himself into college and really the rest was history as he built his empire. If he'd had a sixteen-year-old girlfriend to care for and had to immediately go to work full-time until she finished school, his life would look completely different now. He doubted highly that he would have had the freedom to build his dream.

Leaning back in the black office chair, he let his head fall back and as he stared at the ceiling, the letter still gripped in his hand as his mind raced, images of his life and Laura assaulting him at all angles. He imagined her writing this letter thinking he might find it. The fear she might have felt to have him read her deepest secrets and how it felt for her *not* to leave it for him. For the first time in years, he let the tears fall. Let everything go, for once, because they'd just been kids. They hadn't known a goddamn thing about anything except maybe how to stay safe and take care of themselves on their own because no one else was going to.

That's exactly what Laura had done. She'd taken care of herself *and him*. And the truth was that he loved her more for it. Loved her for being strong enough to leave so they both might have a better life, because the truth was that he never would have left her on his own. He'd needed her too much.

He shut his briefcase and took the letter back with him into his bedroom, then read it several more times as he contemplated just what to do next. He didn't come to any conclusions, but after a while he fell asleep, and for the first time since she'd left, he slept through the night.

CHAPTER FIFTEEN

LAURA WAS NOT looking forward to the meeting at WW Hotel today. It was the first time she'd been there in a month and a half. She still hadn't heard a peep from Will since she'd sent the letter. Not a text with a stupid thumbs-up, not a phone call, not a confirmation email—nothing. But she was fine; if he needed more time before they could communicate as acquaintances and colleagues again, then that was all right. She'd deal with it. More or less. Yes, it felt like she was dying inside, a slow but steady inexorable slide into death, but *she was fine.*

She'd dressed in a favorite gray suit, which felt like armor against whatever happened today. Will probably wouldn't be at the meeting, but she'd be in what was basically his house and it wasn't going to be easy. Every moment she didn't take the elevator up to his penthouse would be the hardest battle of her life.

Stepping out onto her sidewalk, she noticed the black town car waiting at the curb and the driver get out when he saw her.

"Ms. Edwards," he said, wearing a black uniform with the WW Hotels gray logo on the pocket. "Mr. Walker has requested that I drive you to your meeting."

She nodded, then ducked her head into the car, nerves jangling up and down her skin. Did this mean he was going to be at the meeting? He hadn't been in the meetings she'd taken with his director of operations so she had no reason to believe he needed to be there today. But God, how her heart was beating crazily inside her chest. How in the hell was she supposed to get through an entire hour with him with nearly everything unsaid between them and mountains of things *to say*.

Breathing deeply, she looked through her drawings and folders full of ideas in preparation, but after about fifteen minutes she realized they were heading into the tunnel and not to the hotel.

"Um, sir," she called, knocking lightly on the glass between the front and back of the car. "This isn't the way to the hotel."

"My information is that the meeting has moved off-site, miss."

Then he shut the glass.

Mildly alarmed, she texted Jeannie, her main WW Hotels contact who confirmed that the meeting had been moved off-site, which was the reason for the car.

Satisfied that she wasn't being taken to be murdered and subsequently dumped into the Hudson

River, she leaned back again into the plush leather seat of Will's car. But as more time went on, an hour to be precise, and they still hadn't arrived at the destination, she became increasingly confused. Traveling into the depths of New Jersey, she watched helplessly as they passed wooded suburban enclaves, bustling downtowns and eventually country roads before getting back to a city she could never forget.

She hadn't been back here since she'd left the first time and things hadn't changed too much. The downtown area where they'd lived was still a hodgepodge of industrial plants and smaller office-based businesses and local restaurants with neon signs. New buildings had popped up and as they headed into the not-as-nice area that had been her home, she understood what was happening.

But as she got closer to where their dilapidated old brick apartment building had been, the car kept going. Past the corner gas station that had served as their grocery store, past their old high school that looked basically the same with the addition of some sad-looking bushes in the front and new basketball nets, and eventually into a small, quaint neighborhood that she would have given anything to live in back then.

The car stopped in front of a three-story brick house with big white columns in a cul-de-sac at the end of a street lined with centuries-old maple trees whose limbs were so long they created a loose canopy over the newly paved street. She went to open the car door, but it swung wide before her hand reached the handle, the driver standing at the ready to help her out into the *porte cochère*.

"Thank you," she told him, noticing that there were no other cars in the driveway, but that the big white double front doors were open.

"I'll be here when you're finished, miss," he assured her, settling back into the car.

Laura walked slowly up the shoveled walkway, bordered by black pebbles barely visible under the tufts of snow, up the wide staircase that led to a spacious wraparound porch. Her heart was racing as she pushed the cracked front door the rest of the way open to reveal a roomy foyer with shiny white marble floors and a glittering crystal chandelier. No one was around, but as she walked toward the back of the house, a figure appeared at the top of a towering red-carpeted stairway, the railing curling up to the second floor.

Will stopped on the landing, his eyes finding her at the bottom of the stairs. He looked the same, dressed in a black sweater and jeans. Slowly, he descended the steps until they were a few feet apart.

"I wasn't sure you'd come," he said, shoving his hands into his pockets.

She tried to get her pulse under control, breathe through the nerves, but seeing him again was so lovely that she was barely holding herself back from throwing herself into his arms and begging for forgiveness.

"Well, I didn't have much of a choice unless I wanted to jump out of a moving vehicle."

He raised a dark eyebrow. "It's not the Mafia, Laura—if you'd told the driver to take you home he would have."

She gave him a half shrug. "If you say so," she said, cracking as much of a smile as she could, which under the circumstances wasn't much. Though she was super happy to just lay eyes on him even though he looked tired, probably the same as she did. Although, she'd caked on the concealer this morning so she probably just looked like an unnaturally alert raccoon.

"What is this place?" she asked.

"It's a house," he said, stating the obvious. "I missed you a lot, Laura."

The words stilled every cell and muscle in her body.

When she didn't respond immediately, he continued, "And not just the past month. I've been missing you since you left the first time. I don't know that I ever really recovered from it because I loved you so much then. You were the only person who ever stayed and then you were gone."

Christ, she was going to cry again and there was just nothing she could do about it. Goodbye, concealer, after all.

"I'm sorry I yelled at you that night you were leaving. I was so caught up in my own feelings, I didn't want to hear yours. And you were right, I hadn't forgiven you yet. I mean, not all the way, not really."

"I'm sorry," she whispered, feeling it deep in her gut. She'd forgiven herself, but it was still difficult to hear him talk about it.

His hands came out of his pockets and started to reach for her, but he pulled them back. "You have nothing to be sorry for," he said. "You did the right thing and I would have told you at the time to go. I just missed you, Laura, that's it. It's life and it's nobody's fault."

Tears fell down her face and she took several deep breaths. "Thank you for that," she managed, rummaging in her purse and eventually dragging out a tissue to wipe her face off. Not that it did any good since she'd basically turned into a vessel for tears.

"I should have said it a long time ago," he told her. "But I'm kind of asshole, which is something that I'm working on, but that you should know."

Her eyes slid closed as she laughed. "I'm aware of the condition."

A corner of his mouth lifted. "That's good."

"Are you ever going to tell me what this place is?" she asked again, wanting to get to the bottom of why she was here and what all of this was about.

"Soon," he said. "First, I want to say that I got your letter and I felt the same. Then and now, Laura. I was in love with the girl I knew and now I'm in love with the woman I've met. I don't know how I ever found you again but whatever good I did to bring you back into my life, I'm taking seriously."

"I love you too," she said, wishing he'd touch her, but then she realized she didn't have to wait, pulled him into her arms and pressed her wet lips onto his.

They ended the kiss on her sigh, her heart shocked, but no longer racing. Instead, a sense of calm was drifting over her like those precious lucid moments right before sleep where everything in the world drifted away. He gave her a last kiss, dropping another whisper of one on her cheek before setting his forehead to hers. "I love you so much, Laura. I don't know how to be anyone's family but I know I want you to be mine if you'll have me."

He was literally wrecking her, the sobs racking her body as she squeezed him against her. She was never letting this man go again.

"You've always been my family, Will," she said, pulling back to meet his eyes, wiping a bit of wet-ness off his cheek.

Taking a small step back, she showed him her hand. "I have this," she told him, taking his ring off her thumb. "I've been wearing it because I missed you, but you should probably have it back."

Laura held his hand in hers, pushing the ring onto his pinky finger since it no longer fit on his ring finger.

He stared at it, spellbound. "You had this the whole time?" he asked, still staring at it on his finger.

"Yeah, I took it. I'm sorry."

He met her eyes, his dark ones glittering. "I thought I'd lost it."

"I thought you'd know I took it. I wanted to have something of yours. And now," she said, pulling him back into her arms, his strong, warm body feeling perfect against hers, "it means you're mine and we're together and we're family. For keeps."

He kissed her then, hard, desperate, the years of being alone giving way to the warmth of living life with someone by his side. She understood because she felt the same way.

"Now," she told him, gripping the front of his sweater and giving him a playful shake, "are you going to tell me what we're doing here?"

He blew out a loaded breath and looked up the stairs before meeting her eyes once again.

"I used to pass this house all the time when we lived in town. It was my favorite one in the whole city and when I knew we needed to get you out I always thought that this was the kind of house I'd want us to have. When I got that job at the gas station and life was a living hell, I kept thinking about us living in this house instead."

She opened her mouth to say something, but he continued. "So I bought it."

At her probably horrified expression, he laughed. "No, we are not going to live here," he assured. "I'm not that masochistic. I still don't want anything to do with this town—trust me."

He brushed a piece of hair out of her eyes, then pushed it behind her ear, his eyes searching hers. "But I wanted to make something good out of our shitty childhoods. So I bought this house and I'm going to turn it into a group home, but a nice one. Not some industrial, dirty, ill-staffed one like we had, but a real one. I talked to your folks and they've agreed to oversee it and make sure the children here have the happiest possible experience."

"That's really lovely of you, Will, and it'll be nice for my parents to be closer to me and my siblings."

"No more Christmases apart," he said brushing his thumb over her cheek, every touch so clearly cherishing her that she was pretty certain she was going to melt into a puddle of blubbering emotions at his feet.

"I think it's a perfect idea." She sniffed, looking at all the open space for kids to run around both outside and inside. She would have loved to be in a place that was actually a home with people who were well paid and happy instead of overworked staff members who barely cared enough to throw a hot dog on a tray for dinner. That was the worst part about it all, knowing that no one cared enough to do even the slightest extra. Because wasn't that what being loved meant, that you could make mistakes and ask for more and have it be okay?

"And I brought you out here today because the decor is a little austere and since you basically made all my hotels, not to mention my penthouse, feel more

like a home than any home I've ever been in, I was
hoping you'd do the same to this house."

He pulled her against him then, seeing that she
was clearly in no condition to have an actual speaking conversation about this at the moment.

"Also," he continued, really going in for the kill,
"I was hoping you'd be cool with me moving into
your place until we find something that's both of
ours. I'm tired of living at my job and your place
is nicer."

"It's our home," she croaked out, gripping the
back of his shirt as she tried to get herself together.

"For now," he warned. "Eventually, we'll need
a bigger one as our family grows. Though I can't
guarantee that I'll ever be a suburbs kind of guy."

She sniffed against his shirt. "I hate driving anyway."

"Is this ring you put on my finger an engagement
ring or am I going to have to do more of the heavy
lifting in this relationship?"

Laughing, she swatted him on the shoulder. "I'll
get down on one knee if you'd like, but I also hope
your taste in jewelry has changed since you were
eighteen."

He looked down at the black clothes that basically
served as his uniform. "I don't know that it has."

Instead of arguing with him, she started to sink
down, but he pulled her back up.

"No," he said against her lips. "I trust that you're
going to stick around without a ring for now."

"I love you," she said, spreading kisses all over his face, their whole wonderful life together ahead of them rolling out before them like so much joy.

* * * * *

DIRTY SECRETS

REGINA KYLE

MILLS & BOON

To everyone who works too hard.

Like Ferris says, life moves fast.

Don't forget to stop and look around or you'll miss it.

CHAPTER ONE

Brie

I OWN WAY too much shit.

I'm pretty sure my driver wanted to kill me when he saw how many bags I had. If I hadn't threatened him with a one-star review—and promised him a hefty tip that I can't really afford—I'm betting he would have left me at the curb.

Now the trunk of his Honda Civic is full, and I'm crammed in one corner of the back seat, hugging my knees to my chest, surrounded by suitcases. I thought about sitting in the front for a hot second, but then I saw the discarded fast food wrappers, cigarettes, and empty Red Bull cans. It may be less comfortable back here, but it's a hell of a lot cleaner.

I knew I should have ordered a bigger, better car service, but, sadly, money is an object, at least until I get my first check for the Netflix series. Fortunately, I won't have to stay curled up like a pretzel for long. Connor's apartment is only a few blocks away.

My gut twists when I think about where I'm going and what I'm about to do. I've known my brother's best friend practically my whole life, but showing up on his doorstep, unannounced and uninvited, and asking if I can move in with him, is gutsy, even for me. Maybe that's why I brought along all my worldly possessions instead of going back for them later. It'll be a lot harder for him to toss me out on the street with all this crap in tow.

I hope.

The fact that I'm willing to pull this stunt shows just how desperate I am. But losing out on yet another apartment—my fourth in as many weeks, the New York City real estate market is brutal and my credit history isn't exactly the best—was the last straw. I can't keep squatting at Jake and Ainsley's. Especially now that I'm going to be staying in the city for the foreseeable future. Or at least until the series gets cancelled.

Don't get me wrong. My brother and his fiancée have been more than hospitable. But being a third wheel to their storybook romance is uncomfortable as hell. The lovey-dovey looks. The constant smooching. The wall-banging sex.

And that's not a euphemism. I can literally hear the headboard of their California king slamming against the drywall. Every. Freaking. Night. And it's not like my room is next to theirs. I'm down the damn hall.

Their late-night gymnastics have been totally

messing with my sleep schedule. When the first A.D—that's assistant director for those not familiar with TV production lingo—made a half-serious, half-snide remark to the makeup artist about needing to cover the dark circles under my eyes, I knew it was time to find new digs. I worked my ass off for this gig. Beat out hundreds of other girls. I'm not blowing it because my brother and his blushing almost-bride can't keep their hands—and other body parts I don't even want to think about because ew, my brother—off each other.

Hence my somewhat—okay, totally—impulsive decision to spring myself on Connor. He's the only other person I know in this city, other than my brother, of course, who has an apartment big enough to house a freaking marching band. With any luck, he won't even know I'm there. Once he says yes to me crashing with him, that is.

Plus, Jake let it slip the other night that Connor broke up with his live-in girlfriend a few weeks ago. Hopefully he'll appreciate an extra hand around the house. I'm good at vacuuming. I actually like folding laundry. And I make a mean vegan coconut chickpea curry.

My car pulls to the curb in front of Connor's luxury high-rise, and the driver picks up his phone and swipes right to end the ride.

"Nice building." He turns around and surveys the piles of bags and boxes taking up most of the back seat. "I suppose you want me to help you bring all this crap inside."

"Only as far as the lobby. I can handle it from there." Fingers crossed. My plan is to get the door-man to take pity on me and watch my stuff as I bring it up to Connor's penthouse apartment in stages. Then, when it's all stacked up strategically outside his door for maximum you-can't-turn-me-and-literally-everything-I-own-away effect, I'll ring the bell and pray. "There's a tip in it for you, remem-ber? And a five-star rating."

"Forty bucks." He holds out his hand, palm up. "Paid in advance."

That's about twice what I want to shell out. But he's got me over a barrel. There's no way I can get everything inside in one trip, and I'm sure as hell not leaving anything out on the sidewalk for any Tom, Dick, or Harriet to walk off with. So I pull out my wallet, fish out two twenties, and fork them over. "Here."

It takes a good ten minutes, but we finally get ev-erything out of the cab and into the lobby. I thank the driver, promising again to leave him a glowing review. Then I work my magic on the doorman—he's prickly at first but he changes his tune when I show him my driver's license and he realizes I'm "Mr. Lawson's" sister—and he agrees to keep an eye on my things while I bring the first batch of stuff up to "Mr. Dow's" apartment on the seventh floor.

The "Mr." thing cracks me up. I mean, intellectually I know Connor and my brother are big-shots. Top Shelf—the club they own—is one of the hottest night spots in the city. They've been on Forbes 30 under 30 and countless lists of Manhattan's most eligible bachelors. But to me, they're still my annoying big brother and his constant, geeky sidekick who liked to play Tomb Raider and Magic: The Gathering and—even worse—wouldn't let me, five years their junior, join in on the fun.

Five trips later, and it's go time. All my crap is piled in the narrow hallway between the elevator and Connor's door. The only thing left for me to do is ring the damn bell.

It takes a few minutes and more than a couple of rings before the door swings open and—gah. Connor's so—naked.

Okay, so he's not exactly naked. But he might as well be for how little those tiny gym shorts are covering. What is this, the seventies?

Not that I'm exactly complaining. What's not covered looks damn good. Why have I never noticed how yummy he is before? He's gone from geek to Greek god. The slight sheen of sweat makes his muscular arms and torso glisten like an Olympian in ancient times, all oiled up for competition. And when did he get a tattoo on his ribcage? It makes his six pack look even sexier. If that's possible.

"Brie." He runs a hand through his dark, damp hair, messier than usual. "What are you doing here?"

Crap. He sounds pissed. What if I've come at a

bad time? What if he was sleeping? Or even worse, still in bed but, um, otherwise occupied? I know he just broke up with his girlfriend, but maybe he's got some rebound chick in there. That would explain the mussed hair, the sweat, the almost total lack of clothing.

I swallow hard and force a smile. "I, uh, hope I'm not interrupting anything important."

He reaches one hand up to grab the door frame, making all those glorious, shiny muscles ripple. My mouth goes dry and I wipe my clammy palms on my jeans. I'm going to have to figure out how to keep my stupid hormones in check if we're going to be sharing space. Even if that space is the size of a ski lodge.

"I was in the middle of a workout," he says, shifting his weight and drawing my attention to his cross trainers.

Okay. Better than morning sex. But still not exactly getting off on the right foot.

"Sorry. I'd come back later but—"

I wave a hand at the stacks of stuff behind me and he blinks as if noticing them for the first time. Which maybe he is.

"What the hell is all this?" I start to answer, but he holds up an hand to stop me. "Wait. Let me guess. You want to hold a garage sale in my apartment. Or Jake finally kicked you out."

What does he mean, finally? Has my brother said something to him about wanting me gone? No, that's not Jake's style. If he had an issue with me, he'd tell me to my face. He always has before. Damn Connor for making me doubt him.

"Neither. But it was time for me to move on. My brother and his fiancée need their space."

And I need my sleep. Not that I'm about to discuss my brother's sex life with his best friend. I glance over Connor's shoulder into his palatial digs. There's lots of neutral tones and clean lines. Very upscale. Very masculine.

"Can we take this discussion inside? I'm assuming my things will be safe out here for a few minutes, seeing as you're the only one on this floor."

"Do I really have a choice?" He steps back, opening the door wider and waving me inside. "I can't exactly slam the door in my best friend's sister's face. Which I'm sure you were counting on when you came over here."

"Thanks." I breeze past him, ignoring the jab—because, well, it's true—and trying my hardest not to accidentally-on-purpose brush against him as I walk by. "I know this is your place and all, but would you mind, uh, putting on a shirt. All that bare flesh is very…distracting."

He closes the door and follows me into the apartment. "Let me make sure I've got this right. You barge into my personal space and complain that I'm underdressed?"

I shrug. "That pretty much sums it up."

"I've got to give you credit. You've got balls of steel, Blabby."

I wince at the childhood nickname. Okay, so I have trouble keeping my mouth shut. And Gabby rhymes with Blabby. Hence why I started going by Brie—also short for Gabrielle—when I started high school.

"The last time I checked, I didn't have balls."

"I was speaking metaphorically."

He grabs a T-shirt from the back of a chair and covers up. While he's occupied with that, I do a quick survey of my surroundings.

Sweet Caroline. I thought my brother's place was swank. This makes his digs look like the Super 8.

"So." Connor arches a brow at me. "What brings you—and all your crap—here before ten on a Saturday?"

I plop myself down on one of his neutral-toned, clean-lined arm chairs and cross my legs, preemptively making myself at home. It's like that old saying. Dress for the job you want, not the job you have. Or, in this case, the apartment you want. "Aren't you going to offer me a glass of water? Cup of coffee? Maybe a light snack?"

"I'm all out." He folds his arms across his chest, pulling his shirt tight over his pecs. Damn thing is doing nothing to kill my dirty sex fantasies.

"Of what?"

"Everything."

"Even water?" I manage to croak past dry lips. The more I study the way his shirt molds to his torso, the more I'm desperate for a damn drink.

"Just spit it out," he says with a sexy smirk that adds even more fuel to the aforementioned fantasies. "The suspense is killing me."

"I was hoping I could stay here for a little while. Only until I can find a place of my own." I add the last bit hastily, before he can say no.

But it doesn't stop him from turning on the heel of his Reeboks and running from the room like I asked him to be my baby daddy.

CHAPTER TWO

Connor

SHE WANTS TO WHAT?

I fling open the door of my stainless steel fridge with way more cubic feet than any one person could possibly need and grab an IPA from one of my favorite local craft breweries. Okay, so it's not even 10:00 a.m., but I'll make an exception to my strict no-alcohol-before-noon policy for this.

My best friend and business partner's little sister wants to move in with me. Which you wouldn't think would be a problem. I mean, we've known each other since we were kids. I should want to help her out, right?

Right. Except for one tiny—or not so tiny—thing. Namely my dick, which is already doing a happy dance at the thought of having Brie sleeping in the next bedroom.

Have I mentioned that she's my best friend's sister? His little sister? And that I've had the hots for her since I was old enough to figure out girls were good for more than just teasing?

But it's against the bro code to mess around with your buddy's sister, especially when you and said buddy are in business together. I've managed to do a pretty damn good job of keeping my distance from Brie for years now. But having her take up residence in my luxury loft, no matter how spacious, is going to make that—not to mention my aforementioned dick—awfully hard.

I pop the top on my beer and slug it down. I'm going to have go back out there soon. I can't hide in my goddamn kitchen forever, like the coward that I am. But I need some liquid courage first. I'm not a ladies' man like Jake. Or, God forbid, my father. I can get a little tongue-tied around women. Especially ones I'm attracted to.

Until I get them in bed. Then something goes off in me, like a switch, and I'm the king of dirty talk. And it's not only me who says so. I've had more than one woman praise my linguistic skills in the bedroom.

But I digress. The point is, I'm not great at chatting up chicks I'm into unless we're between the sheets. Add in the fact that I have a hard time saying "no"—to anyone, for anything—and it's clear why my current situation is a recipe for disaster.

"Everything all right in there?" Brie's voice floats in from the other room.

"Uh, yeah. Be right out. Want a beer?"

See what I mean? Instead of tossing her sexy ass out the door, I'm offering her drinks. Idiot.

"At ten in the morning?" she scoffs.

"Hey, it's five o'clock somewhere." Just not here.

I toss back the rest of my IPA, rinse out the bottle, and put it in the recycling. Okay, so I'm a neat freak. And eco-friendly. Sue me.

When I finally work up the nerve to go back into my own damn living room, Brie's in front of my bookcase, studying the array of family photos. Ironically, there are more pictures of her family than mine. Not surprising given that I spent more time at their house growing up than my own.

She bends over and picks up one photo to examine it more closely, and my heart and my dick simultaneously twitch at the sight of her ass on full display. She's got a booty like Beyonce, ripe and round, tempting me to—

Stop. This is exactly why Brie and I can't be roomies. My mind may be willing to keep her in the strictly platonic box, but my flesh is definitely weak.

I clear my throat, and she turns around, picture still in hand. It's one of the few I have of my family in happier times. Before my mom's ALS kicked into high gear and my dad went off the deep end and started screwing everything in sight.

"Your mom was really beautiful," she says, a little choked up. "Like Grace Kelly in that movie with Cary Grant."

I'm surprised at the emotion in her voice. It's not

like she knew my mother all that well. Our families didn't move in the same circles. My father wouldn't have allowed that. Hell, he barely tolerated my friendship with Jake. I think the only reason he let us hang out was because he thought it might make me more jock than geek, like some of Jake's natural athleticism would rub off on me if we spent enough time together.

Spoiler alert: It didn't. Sure, Jake introduced me to the gym, which eventually helped me go from scrawny to brawny. But I'm still shit at sports, and I still prefer a well-played round of chess to anything with touchdowns, baskets, or home runs.

Much to my father's disappointment.

"*To Catch A Thief*," I supply, taking the picture from her and glancing at it before carefully putting it back into place. She's right. My mom was beautiful. And classy. And kind. Everything a mom should be.

Great. Now I'm starting to get choked up.

"That's the one. I always mix it up with *North By Northwest*." Brie eyes another photo, this one of me and Jake at our high school graduation. We're a study in contrasts, him the big, burly four-sport letterman and me the shorter, slighter computer nerd.

She looks at me, then back at the picture, then at me again. "What's your secret?"

"Secret to what?" I ask, grateful to be talking about something other than my mom.

The question isn't really necessary. I've got a

pretty good idea where Brie's going with this. But some vain part of me wants her to say it. Wants the satisfaction of knowing all my hard work in the weight room has paid off. But even more, of knowing that she's seeing me, really seeing me, like I've been seeing her all these years.

"You've looked at yourself, right? I mean, you must have a mirror somewhere in this mausoleum." She turns her attention from the photos on my shelves to the books, her question obviously rhetorical since she clearly doesn't expect an answer. Not that it matters, because I already have mine. She's seeing me, all right.

Which, I suddenly realize, makes it all the more imperative that I get her and all her crap the hell out of here, stat. Yeah, it's gratifying knowing she likes what she sees. But it'll be even harder to resist jumping her bones now that I know the attraction isn't one-sided.

"Have you read all of these?" She runs a finger down the shelf, reciting the titles as she goes. "*The Great Gatsby, A Moveable Feast, How to Win Friends and Influence People.* That's some pretty heavy stuff."

That's right, part of me wants to scream. *Brains and brawn, baby. The perfect package.*

But the other part—the smart part—says it's time to stop screwing around and get down to business. The business being growing a pair and telling Brie she has to go.

"Why me?" I ask. "You've never lacked for friends. You must have someone else you can crash with."

"All my friends are struggling actors, like me. Which means they've already got a roommate or two. Or if not, their apartments are the size of postage stamps, and I'd be sleeping on an uncomfortable pull-out couch." Her gaze flits around my cavernous condo. "Seems kind of silly when you've got—what, two extra bedrooms?"

"Three," I mumble. Seems excessive, I know. I bought this place with the idea of settling down some day. Wife. Two point five kids. A couple of cats—I don't care what anyone says, they're way less maintenance than dogs. The whole deal, save the picket fence. I know some people think bringing up kids in the Big Apple is a recipe for disaster. But I can't think of any better place than Manhattan to raise a family. Great schools. Plenty of parks to run and play. Top-notch entertainment and a wide variety of cultural activities.

I've already got the cats—Mirri and Ajani, after characters in the role-playing game Jake and I were obsessed with as kids. Two of the laziest felines on the planet, but they're good company most of the time.

And I thought I'd found the first part of the equation—a wife—in Giselle. We dated for almost two years before she moved in with me. That lasted all of two months. Turns out no matter how long you've been in a relationship with someone, it doesn't always prepare you to share living space with them.

Even if that living space has three spare bedrooms and just as many baths.

Brie's talking again, and I realize that thanks to my mental sojourn, I have no idea what she's saying. From the death glare she gives me, I can tell she realizes it, too. I swear, this girl could wilt a cactus with that look.

"You haven't heard one word I've said, have you?"

I flop down onto the couch, prop my feet up on the coffee table—something I never do—and grab my phone from the cushion next to me and start scrolling, feigning indifference to her. "I assume you were doing your best to convince me to let you stay. Which isn't happening."

She shoots me another death glare, and I can almost feel my balls shrinking. "You're seriously going to toss me out on the street?"

I shrug and keep scrolling. "You can always go back to your brother."

"That's a big hell to the no." She shudders and sits sideways in one of my overstuffed chairs, her long legs, in skin tight jeans, dangling seductively over the arm. She hesitates a moment, running a hand through her dark curls, and when she starts speaking again, her tone is different. Desperate. "Please, Connor. You're my only hope. Don't make me go back there."

"Points for the *Star Wars* reference. But it can't be that bad at Jake's."

"It's worse. You've been around them. You know what they're like. All sickly sweet. And all over each other. It's nausea inducing. Now imagine that 24/7. And when I say 24/7, I'm talking day and night. Emphasis on the night, if you know what I mean."

I do. And okay, she's got a point. Jake and Ainsley are pretty sickening sometimes. Make that most of the time. I sympathize with her situation. But that doesn't change the fact that she can't stay here. Not if I want to keep my hands off her. And my friendship with Jake.

"I promise, you'll barely know I'm here." She's flat out begging now, her hands pressed together like she's praying. "I start shooting a new Netflix series next week. My schedule's going to be crazy. I'll basically be using this place as a crash pad to shower and sleep."

Great. Now I'm picturing her in the shower. And damn, it's a pretty picture. She's naked, naturally, eyes closed, her head thrown back as the water cascades over her perfect breasts and down to—

Nope. Not going there. I will myself to focus on something else. Like her Netflix deal. That's safe territory.

"Jake told me you booked a series. Based on the Mortal Misfits comics, right? That's huge. Congrats."

"It's a recurring role with the potential to become a series regular in season two if we get picked up," she says, excitement lightening her hazel eyes from reddish brown to golden amber. "So it's important that I be at the top of my game. Which I won't be if my brother and his fiancée are keeping me up all night. Or if I'm sleeping one someone's sofa."

She swings her legs over the arm of the chair and sits up, fixing those amber eyes on me. "Please, Connor. This job could be my big break. And it's only until I find a place of my own. Or a half-way acceptable roommate."

Shit. How am I supposed to say no to that? This is her career she's talking about. The one she's wanted since she was Little Red Riding Hood in the third grade class play. I'd have to be a first-rate asshole to let her walk out that door and risk messing that up.

And I'm not. So I guess I'm going to have a new roomie for a few weeks.

But she doesn't know that yet. She takes my silence for indecision and launches back into her pitch, ticking off the reasons I should say yes to her proposal on her fingers as she goes. "Not only will I hardly be here, when I am I'll be quiet as those Blue Man Group guys. I don't mind cleaning, and I'm a pretty decent cook. I promise not to cramp your style if you want to, uh, entertain at night, if you get my drift. And it's not like I expect to stay here for free. I'll pay you—"

I toss my phone back on the cushion next to me and stand. I doubt I'll be having any nighttime visitors anytime in the near future. Especially not ones of the female persuasion. Not when the female I really want—but absolutely cannot have—in my bed is sleeping just down the hall.

Besides, Giselle's barely moved out. In fact, she texted me this morning about picking up some stuff she left behind. Seeing her name on the screen left me feeling a little raw. The last thing I need is to get involved with someone else right now. "We can work out the details later."

A broad smile breaks across her face and she jumps up from her chair. I try not to notice the way the sudden movement makes her breasts jiggle in her tight T-shirt. Is she even wearing a bra? "Does that mean I can stay?"

"I can't very well kick you to the curb and have you jeopardize your career, can I? I don't want that on my conscience."

"Oh my God, thank you so much."

With a squeal, she launches herself at me, and my arms instinctively go around her. I'm immediately reminded why this is a bad idea. She fits perfectly against me, her head coming just under my chin, my already stiffening dick nestled against her thigh. I can smell her shampoo—sort of minty and summery at the same time—and it's driving me fucking crazy.

Yeah, this is going to be even harder than I thought. Way harder.

I give myself a second to savor the sensation, then step back, releasing her. "I've got to get to the club. I'll call the doorman to help you bring your stuff in. And I'll get you a key made while I'm out."

"Thanks." She stands on tiptoe to kiss my cheek. The innocent gesture turns me on more than an hour-long make-out sesh. "You won't regret this. I swear."

She bounds off in the direction of the door, leaving me shaking my head as I watch her sexy ass sashay away.

Won't regret this?

Hell, I already do.

CHAPTER THREE

Connor

I'M IN MY office all of five minutes, sitting at my desk booting up my computer, when Jake strolls in, looking like his dog died. Note that I said his dog, not his parents' dog. He and his fiancée, Ainsley, met when Brie hired her to help take care of Roscoe, their parents' gigantic, slobbery Irish wolfhound, while the elder Lawsons were on a world cruise. They've been back for months, but Roscoe's still living with Jake—and now Ainsley.

I'm half convinced the whole thing was an elaborate set-up. Mrs. Lawson has wanted grandbabies for ages, and Jake, as the eldest child, would be the most the logical target for her motherly machinations. I wouldn't put it past her to get a dog for the sole purpose of foisting it off on Jake in the hopes that it would help him meet the right woman. I mean, dogs are supposed to be chick magnets, right?

Jake slumps into one of my guest chairs, a piece

of paper clutched in one hand and a cardboard cup with a familiar green logo in the other.

"You're in early." I'm the morning person. Jake usually strolls around noon, especially now that he's got Ainsley keeping him busy at home, but that's okay with me. He's at the Top Shelf until the wee hours most nights, long after I'm tucked in bed. The set-up works for us. Jake the pretty-boy front man, mixing and mingling with the customers on the floor of the club and keeping everyone happy. Me quietly toiling away in the background, crunching numbers and making sure we stay profitable.

He doesn't say anything, just scowls at me over the rim of his cup.

My stomach goes instantly into freefall. Shit. Does he know about me and Brie?

Wait, that sounds wrong. There is no me and Brie. And there won't be, no matter what my damned dick says. There's me, and there's Brie, and there's my more-than-enough-room-for-two-people apartment, where we just happen to be platonically cohabiting for the time being. Still, I was hoping I'd get the chance to explain all that to Jake before he jumped to the wrong conclusion.

"Who pissed in your coffee?" I ask, playing it cool and crossing my fingers he's still in the dark about my new roommate. "Is there a problem with the renovations?"

We're in the process of adding more VIP seating and a state-of-the-art screening room where we can live stream concerts and show first-run movies. Jake's taken point on dealing with the contractors. Is it wrong that I'm half hoping another delay or over-run is the reason for his shitty mood?

He waves the piece of paper in his hand. "Brie moved out. She left a note and was gone before Ainsley and I woke up this morning."

Okay, so no overruns. I didn't think my stomach could fall any further. But it does. "Did she say where she went?"

"No." Jake glares at the note, like he's trying to intimidate it into giving up his sister's location.

A little bit of the air creeps back into my lungs. "I'd think you'd be glad. Now you and Ainsley can do whatever the hell it is you guys do when you're alone. Walk around naked. Netflix and chill. Pee with the door open."

That gets a slight smile out of him, but it disappears as quickly as it came. "Don't get me wrong. It's great to have the place to ourselves. But I'm worried about Brie. You know how she can be. She's not exactly the most responsible person on the planet."

My skin tingles with the irrational need to defend her. "Brie's a big girl. She's perfectly capable of taking care of herself."

"Really? Then why didn't she bother to tell my parents where she's at? I made the mistake of calling them, thinking they'd know where she was. And now they're freaking out."

"Give her a break," I hedge, still not ready to

admit she's staying with me. If she hasn't told them yet, I'm not sure she'd want me to. "It's only been a few hours. She's probably waiting until she's settled in."

His phone buzzes, and he pulls it out of his back pocket to check the screen. "That's my mom. Again. Brie's not responding to her texts or calls, so yours truly is left holding the bag. As usual. She wants to call the cops. She's convinced Brie's dead in a ditch somewhere. Or floating in the Hudson."

"She watches way too much of those true crime shows," I mumble.

"I told her to lay off the *Forensic Files*. I swear, she sees serial killers around every corner. She's driving me crazy."

His phone buzzes again, proving his point. He reads the message, sighs, and stuffs the phone back in his pocket, rising from his chair. "I've got to go deal with this before she tries to get the FBI involved."

"Wait." This may be a huge mistake, but I can't let him—and his parents—suffer any longer. "I know where Brie is."

His brows draw together into a dark, confused line. "You do?"

I briefly debate standing and crossing to him but decide to stay seated behind my desk. I'm not exactly sure how he's going to react to what I'm about to tell him, and having a thousand-pound hunk of mahogany between us suddenly seems like a good idea. "She's at my place."

His confused frown deepens and he drops back down into my guest chair. "Your place?"

I can't tell whether he's pissed or relieved.

"She showed up this morning with all her stuff stacked in the hall outside my door. I couldn't very well turn her away. It's only temporary," I add hastily. "Until she finds another place."

The bastard takes what seems like forever to answer, sipping his coffee like he's the fucking king of England and our friendship isn't hanging in the balance. The entire time my heart's pounding so loud I swear he must be able to hear it across the desk.

"Thanks," he says, finally. "I owe you one."

My heart rate slows down a hair. "So, you're okay with her moving in with me?"

"Why wouldn't I be? It's not like she's your type. Or you're hers."

Now it's my turn to scowl. "What's that supposed to mean?"

He shrugs. "You know Brie. She's reckless. Impulsive. She usually goes for the dangerous, live-in-the-moment, bad-boy type. And you're not exactly Mr. Spontaneous. Hell, you color code your underwear drawer."

"I do not." Any more. Of course, my closet is still organized by hue.

"You know what I mean. You and Brie are nothing alike. It's not like I'm worried you'll be getting jiggy with it."

I want to argue with him. But that would be a huge red flag. Plus, a huge part of me is afraid he's right. Brie and I are polar opposites, personality wise. She's shiny and sparkly, built for the spotlight. I'm more of a behind-the-scenes kind of guy. That's another reason I haven't acted on my obvious physical attraction. As if her being my best friend's sister wasn't enough.

"Getting jiggy with it? What are you, thirteen?"

"Truth be told, I'm glad she's at your place. At least there I know she'll be safe." He stands, pulling his phone out of his pocket again. "I'd better let me parents know. And read my sister the riot act for scaring the hell out of them. And me."

The second he's gone, I grab my cell and call Brie. The least I can do is tip her off about the shit storm that's coming her way.

I don't have her cell number yet—I make a mental note to exchange digits with her now that we're roommates—so I try my land line. Yeah, I'm one of the ten people in the five boroughs who still has a land line. What can I say? I like to err on the side of caution. You never know when you might need a backup.

Fuck. Jake is right. I am so not Brie's type.

I'm still mulling that depressing thought over when she picks up the phone, breathless.

"Hello?"

One word. That's all it takes for my body to respond. But it's not my fault. Or my dick's fault. It's her voice. So fucking sexy. She sounds husky and breathy, like she's been running around unpacking boxes—which she probably has.

Great. Now I'm picturing her all sweaty, stray strands of hair clinging to her cheeks and her damp T-shirt hugging her curves.

I brush off that mental image and adjust my fly. "Hey, Brie. It's Connor."

"Oh, thank God. I wasn't sure if I should answer the phone or not. Didn't want to scare away any potential conquests."

"Conquests?"

"Yeah. You know. Women."

Right. This girl is totally not thinking of me as a fuck buddy if she's ready to be my wingman. Or wingwoman.

That's enough to deflate my dick. I grab a pen from my desk blotter and start clicking away, a nervous habit I picked up in high school and haven't been able to shake completely.

"How's the moving going?" I ask, hoping that starting off with an innocuous question will soften the blow of telling her that her family is on the warpath.

"Slow, but good. Ernie helped me move my stuff into one of the spare bedrooms."

"Ernie?"

"Your doorman. He's the sweetest guy. Did you

know he was in Saigon when it fell? He was a Marine, stationed at the U.S. Embassy. He met his wife there, helped evacuate her and other Vietnamese before the NVA took control of the city."

No, I didn't. But leave it to Brie to get the guy's life story within ten minutes of meeting him.

"I took the room across from yours," she went on. "I hope that's okay."

"Uh, yeah. Of course." Really, what difference does it make what room she's in? I'm going to be hyperaware of her no matter where she sleeps. "Listen, before you finish unpacking, there's something I have to tell you."

"Let me guess. You're kicking me out already."

"No, nothing like that," I assure her. "I saw Jake this morning."

"Wow, he's in early. Usually he and Ainsley aren't vertical until after nine."

TMI. I do not want to be talking about my best friend's sex life with his little sister. "Yeah, well, he got your note."

"Good."

"No, not good. You neglected to mention where you were going."

"I wasn't sure you'd let me stay. I'll text him now. If I can find my phone in this mess."

"Too late. He already knows."

"You told him?" she asks, he voice rising an octave.

"I didn't have much choice." I throw the pen back

down. The constant clicking used to drive my teachers crazy, and it's even bothering me now. "He's worried about you. Your parents, too."

"Jake's worried about my parents?"

"No, your parents are worried about you. Jake called them looking for you. They've been trying to reach you."

"Oh. Crap. I didn't mean to scare anyone."

"I know. Just do yourself a favor and call your family before your mother alerts the authorities."

"She really needs to stop watching *Forensic Files*."

I chuckle despite myself. "Your brother said the same thing."

"I'll call her. Jake, too. Thanks for the heads-up."

I lean back in my chair and stare out the window at the street below. A bike messenger whizzes past, darting around the rush hour traffic. "You're not mad at me?"

"Why would I be? You did what you had to do to keep my family from going into full-on *Dateline* mode." I hear the dull thud of a box hitting the floor, followed by the sound of cardboard against cardboard. "Unless it's for the shocking lack of food in your refrigerator. I didn't realize man could exist on avocados and almond butter alone."

Damn. I'm embarrassed. My fridge is usually better stocked than that. I'm not some stereotypical bachelor, subsisting on take-out and frozen pizza. I care about what I put into my body. But I've had a crazy busy week. And it's not like I knew I was going to have a roommate until, oh, say, three hours or so ago.

"I'll stop at Whole Foods on the way home."

"No worries. Before Ainsley, Jake and I used to use a delivery service. I'll call them and get some stuff sent over. Maybe even make dinner for you tonight."

I thought picturing her in the shower was bad, but that's got nothing on the images swimming in my brain now. Brie hovering over a pot on the stove. In a frilly apron. And nothing else. It's disturbingly both domestic and erotic at the same time. Weird. "You don't have to do that."

"I know I don't. But I want to. I told you, I'm a good cook. I make a mean vegetarian lasagna."

"You're vegetarian?" I ask, surprised. I swore off animal flesh after I watched that documentary on how the meat industry is killing the planet. But I'm pretty sure I saw Brie with a burger in her hand at the Lawson's annual Fourth of July picnic last summer.

"No. But you are."

Wow. She remembered. I'm surprised. And strangely flattered.

"I usually don't get home until after ten," I lie. I'm not sure why. Maybe because this is getting uncomfortably personal. I'll never be able to keep her at arm's length if she's playing happy homemaker, cooking me dinner and catering to my personal preferences.

"No worries. That's the beauty of lasagna. Easy to reheat. Just text when you're on your way and I'll have it ready for you."

"Don't you have to work?" I ask, suddenly remembering the new job that's supposedly the reason for her change of address. Or, at least, the reason she gave to sucker me into taking her in.

"I'm not on the call sheet until Thursday. That's why I picked today to move. Gives me a couple of days to get settled before I have to be on set."

I hear a crash, then a long, plaintive meow and a muffled curse. "Get out of there, Mirri. And Ajani, don't let him give you any ideas. I'm watching you, too."

"He's a she. They both are." Their names are on their ID tags. But not their gender.

"Oops. Sorry about that, ladies."

Brie giggles, and the sound shoots straight to my stupid cock, which I will to stand down. Otherwise I'll wind up with a tent in my pants the size of Barnum and Bailey's, and I'm fairly certain jerking off in the executive washroom is against company policy.

"I should have warned you that I had pets." Which I would have, if I hadn't been in such a damn rush to get out of there. "I hope you're not allergic."

"Nah, I'm cool with cats. Just not messing with my stuff when I'm trying to unpack."

"Yeah, they love to go where they don't belong. Especially if there's boxes involved. And don't let them try to convince you they're hungry. I topped off their automatic feeder this morning."

"Will do. I mean, won't do." Another crash, and more meows and mumbled swearing. "I'd better go finish putting this stuff away before they destroy everything I own. Don't forget to text me when you're heading home so I can heat up the lasagna."

"I told you, you don't have to—"

But it's useless. She's hung up, and I'm left preaching to a three-person choir.

Me, myself, and I.

CHAPTER FOUR

Brie

I MAY HAVE exaggerated my culinary skills.

Okay, so I've never made vegetarian lasagna. I've never made any lasagna. Except the kind that comes out of a box that you just stick in the oven. And even then, the first time I made it I didn't realize you had to put a baking sheet under it and it leaked all over the place.

But I can read. And like my mom always says, if you can read, you can cook.

Let's hope she's right.

I grab the hand towels I'm using as oven mitts since I couldn't find any anywhere in the restaurant-quality kitchen I doubt Connor's ever used and gingerly open the oven door. It smells great. Tangy and spicy and tomato-y—if that's a word—like a lasagna should. I think. That's a good sign, isn't it?

I grab the edges of the baking sheet—I'm not making that mistake twice—pull it out of the oven, and set it carefully on the stove top, hip-checking the door closed. My lasagna looks a little, um, crunchier around the edges than the one in the picture next to the recipe I found on the internet, but I chalk that up to the few extra minutes I let it cook after the timer went off. I'd rather have crispy edges than lasagna soup.

I'm about cut into it and do a taste test when I hear a lock click and the front door swing slowly open. I run to the entryway, knife still in hand, not sure what I'm going to do with it or who I'm going to find there. It's not even eight. Way too early for it to be Connor.

But it is. His eyes go wide behind the frames of his dark-rimmed glasses and he drops his briefcase to put his hands up in an I-surrender gesture when he sees the knife I'm brandishing at him.

"Am I going to get this welcome home every night?" he asks, eyeing the knife warily. "Because if I am, I take back my invitation."

I lower the knife. "In my defense, I thought you were a burglar. You told me you weren't going to be home until after ten."

"I, uh, left early." He looks everywhere but at me, and I'm starting to think he was less than truthful about his working hours. "Figured it was the least I could do if you were making the effort to cook for me."

"Well, you're timing is perfect. I was just about to dig in."

"Great." He reaches down to pet one of the cats, who's come out of hiding and is winding around his legs. I think it's Ajani. Or maybe it's Mirri. Their coloring is similar, and I can't read her name tag from here. "Give me a few minutes to take a quick shower, and I'll join you."

He disappears down the hall, Ajani—or Mirri—following at his heels, and I retreat to the kitchen. I've barely had time to plate two generous portions of lasagna when he returns, sans cat. He's in grey sweats and an Avengers T-shirt that clings to his damp pecs, his feet bare and his hair, wet from the shower, curling around his ears.

I've seen guys in way less. Actors doing quick changes in the wings. Movie stars in their skivvies on the backlot. Hell, just last week I shot a commercial with a half-naked NHL hottie who I can't name because I signed a non-disclosure agreement. But none of them made my pulse pound or my palms itch like they're doing now.

Maybe it's the gray sweats. They're a thirst phenomenon, amiright? Just tight enough and light enough that you can see the outline of a guy's package. And from what I can tell, what Connor's sporting under there is pretty damned impressive.

He runs his hand through his slick hair, blissfully unaware that I'm checking him out and inhales. "Smells great."

Hopefully it'll taste as good as it smells. His earlier-than-expected arrival means I didn't have time to sample the goods before deciding whether to serve the damn thing or throw it in the trash and call for take-out.

He pulls out a high-backed stool at the marble-topped kitchen island and sits. I mentally cross my fingers and slide a plate across to him. Then I hold my breath as he cuts into the square of lasagna with the side of his fork and lifts it to his mouth.

"Not bad," he says finally, after what seems like an eternity of thoughtful chewing. "Do I detect a hint of basil?"

"Yes. And oregano. Neither of which you had in your sad excuse for a spice rack, so I ordered some with the groceries."

"Sorry. My cooking's kind of basic. Salt and pepper are pretty much the only seasonings I use on the regular."

He takes another bite, and I'm transfixed by the way his jaw muscles work. I've never found chewing a turn on before. But I swear, I'm getting hot and bothered by watching him eat. It's like now that my brother's best friend who I've known almost since I was in diapers has suddenly registered on my sexual radar, I'm finding every damn thing he does suggestive. Even something as mundane and normally borderline disgusting as chewing.

He swallows—yes, that's sexy, too, dammit, the way his Adam's apple slowly bobs in the strong column of his tanned throat—and licks his lips. And before you ask, that's fucking sexy as hell, too. Maybe

even the sexiest thing he's done yet. It's got me thinking about what I want to do with those lips. And
what I want them to do to me. Damn, at this rate
I'm going to need an ice bath before I even get to
the main course.

"I take it back." He tips his head back, closes his
eyes, and moans, like he's entered nirvana. "This is
better than not bad. It's fantastic. I can't tell you the
last time someone cooked for me."

"What about what's-her-name? Your fiancée?" I
dole salad into two wooden bowls and pass one to
him, along with a bottle of Italian dressing. "She
didn't cook?"

He spears a cherry tomato and pops it into his
mouth. "Number one, her name is Giselle. Number
two, she was my girlfriend, not my fiancée. And
number three, hell, no. She was more comfortable
in the classroom than the kitchen."

I pour us each a glass of wine—an expensive looking merlot I found in the fancy floor-to-ceiling wine
rack—sit opposite him, and dig into my lasagna. "The
classroom?"

"She's a professor. Teaches at philosophy at Columbia. That's where we met. She was working on
her dissertation when I was finishing up my master's." He puts his fork down and sips his wine. "Why
are we talking about my ex?"

"Isn't that what roommates do? Dish about their
love lives over dinner?"

"I don't hear you dishing about yours."

"We'll get to me." Not. "But right now we're talking about you."

I don't know why I'm so interested in his extracurricular activities. Strike that. I do. We're going to be living together. I'm entitled to know whether I should expect overnight guests. The last thing I want is to walk in on one of his, uh, conquests in the bathroom. It's definitely that and not because I want to know if he's seeing anyone so I can check out the competition.

He shrugs and takes another sip of his wine. "There's not much to talk about."

"What do you mean?" He's a total catch. Smart. Rich. Hotter than the ever-loving sun. He must have women falling all over themselves to get with him.

He shrugs and sips again. "I just got out of a long-term relationship. The last thing I'm looking for is to get involved with someone else."

"Who said anything about getting involved?" I ask through a mouthful of pasta. It's like I'm trying my hardest to be unappealing. But dammit, I'm hungry. My stomach is reminding me that I was too busy unpacking to eat anything all day. "I'm talking about some between the sheets action. A little bow-chika-wow-wow. S-E-X."

With me.

He almost chokes on his lasagna and reaches for his wine glass, chugging what's left to wash it down.

Shit. Did I say that last part out loud? I really need to learn how to keep my inner monologue on the inside.

"I'm not in the market for a fuck buddy at the moment, either."

My heart rate slows down a hair. If I said the last bit out loud, and if he heard me, he's not acknowledging it. Which suits me just fine. Two can play the avoidance game.

"Why not?" I press. Just because I dodged a bullet doesn't mean I'm abandoning the subject. I just have to be more careful about what comes out of my mouth. I push away my half-full wine glass and hop off my stool to get some water from the dispenser on the refrigerator door. Can't be too cautious.

He cuts himself another healthy-sized square of lasagna and refills his wine glass, apparently not as concerned with committing an alcohol-induced slip of the lip as I am. "Are we seriously talking about this?"

"It'll be quicker and far less painful if you answer and get it over with. Like ripping off a bandaid."

He shoots me a skeptical look over the rim of his glass but answers anyway. "Would you believe me if I said I prefer to get to know a girl before sleeping with her?"

"So go out. Get to know one." Or two. Or ten. Who am I to judge what he's into?

Then again, he could always stay in and get to know the one who's sleeping in the next bedroom...

I give myself a mental bitch slap. I promised him I'd be Blue-Man-Group level quiet. Unobtrusive. Practically invisible. Not some creepy stalker who wants to play hide the cannoli.

Connor stares longingly at his lasagna. "You make it sound so easy."

He says it so low I almost don't hear him. And even though I did—each word, soft but distinct— I'm having a hard time believing what I think he's saying. "Are you telling me you have trouble meeting women?"

"Not trouble, exactly. I just find the whole dating scene—distasteful. All the women at the club see is my money. And status. The whole on line thing is ridiculous. Nobody is who or what they say they are. And don't even get me started on apps like Tinder and Bumble. They're a whole new level of cringeworthy. I'm not some sex-obsessed swinger like my—"

He cuts himself off, but it doesn't take a mind reader to know where he's going. I might have only been in elementary school at the time, but I remember overhearing my parents speaking in hushed tones after they thought Jake and I were asleep, whispering about "that douchebag Vincent Dow"—my father's words—and how he was "screwing around on his sick wife" with a woman barely ten years older than his twelve-year-old son.

That relationship didn't last—big surprise— but from the pictures I've seen of Connor's dad in gossip mags—he's some big-shot mystery/thriller writer, but I'm a happily-ever-after kind of gal so that suspense-y stuff is totally not my jam—his appetite for pretty young things hasn't diminished over the years.

"How did you meet Giselle, then?" I ask, sensing Connor needs to be jolted out of his melancholy introspection.

He reaches for his wine glass, and I don't blame him for needing a little liquid courage to deal with the shit that thinking of his dad must stir up. "Like I said, we were at Columbia together. But truth be told, I probably never would have gotten up the nerve to speak to her in the first place if it wasn't for Jake."

I arch a brow at him. "Do I want to hear this story? Or is it going to gross me out? Remember, that's my flesh and blood you're talking about. I don't want to know if you were dating his sloppy seconds."

"Give me a little credit. I'm not that desperate." He takes one last bite of lasagna and pushes the half-eaten square away. "Jake convinced me to go to this frat party with him. Giselle was there. He saw me gawking at her, dragged me over, and forced me to introduce myself."

"Now I get it. Jake's your Angelica Schuyler. Or he was, until he and Ainsley got together." With my brother off the market and spending every free second with Ainsley, Connor's lost his wingman. He needs someone to help bring him out of his sexy shell.

"My what?"

I gape at him incredulously. "Don't tell me you haven't seen *Hamilton*."

"Who's got the time? Or an in to get tickets. Aren't they sold out for months?"

"I've got a friend in the ensemble. I could hook you up with house seats." They're pricey, but he can afford them.

"Will that help me understand why Jake's my— what's her name?"

"Angelica Schuyler. She's the one who fixed her sister Eliza up with Hamilton, her eventual husband." At great personal sacrifice, I might add. If you believe the musical, and the book it's based on, Angelica had the hots for good old Alexander herself. But she stepped aside to ensure her sister's happiness, even knowing it meant she'd never be satisfied.

Kind of like I'm about to do now. Because as much as I'd like to keep my brother's super smexy best friend all to myself, I know that's a recipe for disaster. And not only because of the whole brother's-best-friend-and-business-partner thing. I've got a pretty good feeling we'd be combustible in the bedroom, but out of it, we're like oil and water. He's serious. I'm silly. He's into health food. I'm a junk food junkie. He's firmly planted in the Big Apple. I'm a rolling stone, going wherever my work takes me.

See what I'm talking about? Oil and water. And that's just the tip of the iceberg. We're pretty much polar opposites in every conceivable way.

He slips a piece of pasta to one the cats who's planted herself at his feet, staring up at him hungrily. Another way we're different. I'm so not a cat person. Don't get me wrong. They're okay. But given the choice, I'm #teamdog all the way.

"I told you," he says, shaking his head. At first, I think the head shake is for me, but then I realize he's staring down the cat, who's begging for more food. "I'm not looking for a relationship."

"And I told you, this isn't about jumping into another relationship. It's about putting yourself out there. Meeting people. Having a little fun." I take a deep breath and go there. Once I start down this road, there's no turning back. "And I'm going to help you make that happen."

"Oh? And how exactly are you going to do that?"

The corners of his mouth turn up in a sexy half-smile that has me reconsidering my decision not to barricade us in this apartment and ride him like a Kawasaki. For a hot second. But I quickly snap back to my senses and return to my original, plan.

"By taking my brother's place. I'm going to be your Angelica Schuyler."

CHAPTER FIVE

Connor

FOR THE SECOND time in twenty-four hours, I'm asking myself the same question.

She wants to what?

I guess my earlier deduction was right. She's volunteering to be my wingman, er, wingwoman. Which means she's put me firmly in the friend zone.

I should be relieved. Hooking up with my best friend's baby sister would be a bad idea on so many levels. So why do I feel this acute sense of loss and disappointment? I'm like a kid who's just been told Christmas isn't coming this year.

"Hello, McFly? Earth to Connor." Brie reaches across the counter and raps me on the back of my hand. "What do you say? You. Me. Taking on the singles scene."

"That's a big hell to the no. I don't need a wingm—" I stop myself and go for a more gender-neutral term. "Wingperson."

"I beg to differ. Man cannot exist alone. We're social creatures. We're meant to have company. Not live like hermits."

"I can." It's not that I'm anti-social. I enjoy a night out with friends as much as the next guy. But I also value my private time. Me and my thoughts, maybe the latest Neil Gaiman book on my e-reader, an HBO documentary on my flat screen, or a game of online chess with one of my internet buddies.

I abruptly push back my stool, and Mirri, who's still parked at my feet hoping I'll cave and pass her another treat, mews loudly and skitters away. "Look, I appreciate your offer, but I'm doing just fine on my own."

"Have it your way." She stacks our plates and brings them over to the sink. "But if you change your mind—"

"I won't."

"—don't be afraid to let me know."

I take the dishes from her. "You cooked. I'll clean. Go finish unpacking."

I set the plates down on the counter and give her a gentle nudge toward the door. Big mistake. The skin on her bare shoulder—she's wearing a strappy little tank top that ends an inch or so above the waistband of her denim cutoffs—is soft and warm, and now I'm wondering if she's as soft and warm everywhere. My guess is the answer is yes.

Please, God, let her take my not-so-subtle hint and make like a tree and get out of here. I desperately need some space between us, or I might be tempted to test my theory.

She and shoots me a grateful smile that has my stomach and my dick doing cartwheels. "Thanks. I'm pretty much settled in—or as settled as I'm going to get, since I'm leaving the stuff I don't use on a daily basis in boxes. But our showrunner changed my schedule, and now I have to be on set tomorrow at six. So I should probably get some z's."

"Six?" I open the dishwasher and slide a plate between the tines. Maybe if I'm otherwise occupied I'll stop fantasizing about feeling her up. "In the morning?"

She nods. "The van is coming to pick me up at five."

"Damn, that's early."

"We're on location at a restaurant in Brooklyn, and we have to be out before the staff comes in to set up for the dinner service." She yawns and stretches, her already short shirt lifting even higher to reveal more of her toned, tanned stomach. So much for squelching those fantasies. "I guess I'll see you in the morning, then."

The look on my face must say no way am I waking up that early because she laughs and rolls her eyes. "Or not."

She starts to go, but at the last minute I remember the keys I had made for her on my way home. Since there's no chance in hell I'll be awake at zero dark thirty to give them to her before she leaves, I have no choice but to stop her.

"Hang on." I brush past her, being careful to avoid touching her again, and grab my briefcase from the couch, where I dropped it when I came in. "Here."

I fish the keys out and toss them to her, and she snags them in a sweet, one-handed catch. I let out a low, appreciative whistle. "Nice move."

"I learned from the best. Who do you think tossed the ball around with Jake when Dad was busy and you were at chess club? Or debate practice?"

"I wasn't on the debate team. It was the academic decathlon."

"Wow. You really were a nerd, weren't you?" She flashes me another smile—this one more of a cheeky grin—that takes away any sting in her words.

"Were being the operative word," I quip back. I might have been the king of the nerds back then, but I'm anything but now. At least, not on the outside. And from the way Brie's eyes drank in my muscled pecs and washboard abs when I opened the door this morning—neither of which I had back in high school—she knows it, too.

"Fine. You're hot. But I bet you're still a geek deep down. You probably still play Dungeons and Dragons."

Damn. I can't hide anything from this girl.

"So does Joe Manganiello," I say defensively. "And *People* magazine named him one of the sexiest men alive."

"You read *People* magazine?" Her cheeky grin

gets impossibly cheekier. "I pegged you as more of a *Smithsonian* kind of guy. Or maybe *Wired*."

"Only in the supermarket checkout line. They don't carry *Wired* or *Smithsonian* there."

With a smoky, past-her-bedtime laugh that shoots laser beams of lust right to my groin, she says goodnight—again—and heads down the hall to her bedroom. I take care of the rest of the dishes, put the leftover lasagna in the fridge, and head to my own room to take a cold shower, watch an episode of *Mindhunter* on Netflix, and read one of the short stories in Ted Chiang's *Exhalation* until I finally pass out myself.

I'm not sure how many hours—or minutes—I'm out before I'm awakened by the sound of someone in the hallway outside my bedroom door, then banging around in my kitchen. It takes me a second to remember that I've got a house guest, but when I do I move the cats off my chest, throw on a pair of boxers and a T-shirt—yeah, I sleep in the buff—and go check on her. Brie's making a hell of a lot of noise. Which means she's either the clumsiest sleepwalker on the planet or she's looking for something. Either way, I can't leave her to fend for herself.

But when I find her, I'm starting to think I should have stayed in bed. She's wearing even less than she was the last time I saw her—some kind of frilly sleep shorts and yet another tank top, this one in an almost see-through pale pink with "Let Me Sleep" emblazoned across her perky tits. The shorts are short enough on their own, but they're made even shorter by the fact that she's on her tiptoes, reaching for something on the top shelf of one of my ridiculously priced, hand-painted custom cabinets, making the shorts slide further up her smooth, shapely thighs.

I clear my throat to subtly let her know she's not alone. She jumps anyway, almost dropping the glass she's barely managed to snag from the cabinet.

"Holy crap." She puts her free hand over her heart. "You scared me half to death."

"I'm sorry. That wasn't my intention."

"Then what did you intend, sneaking up on a girl in the middle of the night?"

"One, I wasn't sneaking. Hence the throat clearing. Two, you were making enough noise to wake the dead. It sounded like you were trashing the place. I had to protect my investment."

She holds up the glass. "If you kept your glassware on the bottom shelf, where normal-sized people could reach without practically killing themselves, I wouldn't have to wake the dead to get a damn drink of water."

"I'm normal sized." I'm tall, but it's not like I'm Andre the Giant.

"For a guy, maybe. But I'm a vertically challenged chick."

She looks average height to me, but I'm not going to argue with a pissed off woman in the middle of the night. "Feel free to rearrange things so you can reach them."

"I was planning on it." She sets the glass down on the counter and starts right in on the rearranging, swapping a few of the glasses on the top shelf for some of the mugs on the bottom one, leaving both shelves with a few of each. "What did your ex do when she had dry mouth at two a.m.? Suffer? Drink out of a coffee cup?"

I don't have a clue. And I don't want to talk about Giselle. Not with temptation staring me in the face in the form of my best friend's off-limits little sister, wearing next to goddamn nothing. She's clearly not going anywhere, so it's up to me to put some space between us before I do something I'll regret in the morning. Or not regret. I'm not sure which would be worse.

"Is there anything else you need?" I ask even as I'm already backing away.

"I think I can handle it from here."

She goes on tiptoe to move another mug to the top shelf, but just as I think she's got it up there safely, it slips from her grasp and falls to the tile floor, shattering into a tiny shards that scatter all around her pretty, pink-tipped toes.

"Shit," she squeaks, the word coming out on a kind of high-pitched bark, like a fox.

She bends to start picking up the pieces, but I hold out a hand, stopping her. "Don't move. I'll be right back."

"Where are you going?"

"I figure at least one of us should have some shoes on."

She looks down at her exposed, bare feet, then at mine, then drags her gaze up to my face. "Good point."

I grab a pair of deck shoes from my closet and slip on some shorts for good measure. Wearing shoes without pants is just—wrong.

I'm back in the kitchen in seconds. Shockingly, Brie's followed my gruff command and is right where I left her. I cross to her, slivers of porcelain crunching under the soles of my Sperrys, and scoop her up fireman-style.

"What do you think you're doing?" Her hands alternate between pounding on my back and clutching my T-shirt.

"What does it look like I'm doing? I'm carrying you to safety."

"You realize you could have just brought me a pair of shoes, don't you?"

Honestly, I hadn't thought of that. Not that I'm going to admit that to her. "This way's more dramatic."

"Well, I'm pretty sure it's safe to put me down now, Lancelot."

I look around, and she's not wrong. I've carried her all the way out of the kitchen into the living/dining room area, well past the danger zone.

"Right." I lower her down, her body sliding slowly, agonizingly against mine until her feet touch the floor. For some reason, even though she's safely back on terra firma, my arms stay banded around her waist. Hers don't move, either. They're wrapped around my neck, her fingers flirting with the ends of my hair.

"I think I'm good," she whispers against my ear. "You can let go."

"So can you."

I don't, and neither does she. The air around us seems superheated, charged with sexual energy. All my nerve endings are on fire. Especially the ones between my legs.

"What are we doing?" Brie asks, her voice wavering. And is it my imagination, or are her eyes locked on my lips?

My tongue instinctively darts out to moisten them. "I don't know. But I don't want to stop."

She looks up at me with those doe eyes, her freckled cheeks flushed and her barely covered breasts rising and falling with each shuddering breath. "Then don't."

It's an invitation even a monk would have a hard time refusing. And I'm no damn monk. Which means my odds of resisting are somewhere between zip and zilch.

I bring my head down to hers and our mouths meet. It's a kiss that's been years in the making— at least for me. Given that much of a buildup, it shouldn't live up to expectations. And it doesn't. It surpasses them.

Her lips are sweet and tart, like raspberries. Her body is soft and pliant as it melts into mine. And she smells like coconut, sunshine, and salt water, a combination that's downright intoxicating. In my arms, she's not Jake's little sister. She's all woman. And from the sound of her moans, high-pitched and urgent, she's mine for the taking.

I'm not sure how we get there, but the next thing I know I've got her against the wall. I nudge a knee between her legs, my hard thigh nestling right where she wants it if the way she grinds against me is anything to go on. This kiss has gone from a tentative exploration to too hot for network television in the space of a heartbeat. Not that I'm complaining. I'm as fucking far gone as she is.

Until I'm not. Something cold and wet brushes against my ankles, yanking me out of the moment and back to reality. Half reluctant, half relieved, I slide my lips from Brie's and look down.

"Dammit, Ajani." I don't know what she's gotten into, but her fur's damp and matted and the it-wasn't-me expression on her furry face is as guilty as hell. Probably drinking from the toilet and fell in. Again.

"Something wrong?"

Brie's husky, sexy drawl almost sucks me back in, but I fight the urge to pin her against the wall and show her exactly how much I want her. Instead, I do the polar opposite, releasing her and pulling away, leaving her with a confused frown that's like a punch to my gut.

"Yes. No. It's just—I need to go check on Mirri."
If one of them was in the damn toilet, odds are the
other one wasn't far behind. And Mirri's not anywhere near as good at climbing back out again as
Ajani. Besides, I'm taking this as a sign. My cats are
either the world's greatest cock blockers, or they're
saving me from making a huge-ass mistake. And I
have to clean up some broken glass.

"All righty, then." Her husky, sexy drawl is a thing
of the past. Now her voice is flat, clipped. "I'll just
grab my water and go back to bed."

She breezes past me and heads for the kitchen,
calling over her shoulder as she goes. "Nighty night,
Lancelot. Sweet dreams."

I can't stop my eyes from watching her ass do
that sexy swivel as she walks away. Little vixen.
She knows exactly what—or who—I'll be dreaming about tonight. And it sure as hell won't be sweet.

More like X-rated.

CHAPTER SIX

Brie

"CAN I INTEREST you in a caviar and crème fraîche tartlet?"

They sound disgusting to me. I mean, fish eggs? Blech. But what do I know about what one-percenters like to eat? I've got simple tastes. I'm a pigs-in-a-blanket kind of girl, through and through.

The tuxedoed gentleman shakes his head, and I continue circulating through the crowd of similarly clad men and their elegantly dressed companions. I feel vastly underdressed in my standard issue polyester pants—black, of course—and white button-down shirt.

I'm not even sure what this fancy fundraiser is for. All I know is that when my friend and fellow actress Tiffany called and told me the catering company we occasionally work for was looking for wait staff on one of my few free nights, I jumped on it.

Some people might call me an idiot for cling-

ing to this gig. But I disagree. I think I'd be an idiot
not to. I may be a working actress today, but who
knows about next month or even next week. Too
many things could go wrong. The show might not get
picked up for a second season. My character could
get written off. They could decide to replace me with
someone younger, thinner, more athletic.

If any of that happens, I need something to fall
back on so I can pay my student loans. And the in-
crease in rent I hope to have soon for my own place.
Because ever since that kiss—that earth-shaking,
soul-shattering, mind-melting kiss—living with
Connor has been, well, awkward.

It's not like he's done anything overt to make me
feel uncomfortable. Hell, I've barely seen him in
the last week. That's the awkward part. It's like he's
dancing around me, afraid of a repeat performance.
Which is too damn bad, because I wouldn't object
to an encore. But apparently the whole best-friend's-
sister thing is too much for him to handle.

Oh, well. You win some, you lose some. Although
it would be nice to rack up some wins.

Unfortunately, I haven't had any wins in the finding new digs department, either. Everything affordable is too far from midtown, and everything within
a reasonable commuting distance is out of my price
range, even with a roommate or two. I'm going to
have to either adjust my budget or my definition of
what's a reasonable commuting distance.

My tray is empty, so I head to the kitchen for

some more tartlets, or whatever equally nauseating, hoity-toity treat they load me up with. This time it's open-faced cucumber sandwiches, with some sort of fancy, flavored cream cheese and slivers of red onion. I make the bold decision to taste one.

Yep. Nauseating. I don't understand why they don't serve normal stuff like at these things. Like bacon wrapped scallops. I mean, everything's better with bacon, amiright? Or buffalo wings. People love that shit. And it's gotta be cheaper than the crap we're peddling tonight, meaning more money for whatever charity this shindig is supposed to be raising money for.

I hike up my now fully laden tray and brave the grand ballroom, scanning the crowd for familiar faces. There's nothing worse than working an industry function, handing out cocktails or canapés to producers and casting directors I've auditioned for in the past and hope to again in the future.

There's only one familiar face I see tonight, though. And it's not anyone in the entertainment business. It's the face of the guy whose apartment I'm squatting in. The one who's been avoiding me like the plague.

I hang back in the corner, studying him from the shadows like some creepy stalker. Connor in casual dress—his usual jeans or khakis and a button down or polo, or even workout gear—is hella fine, but Connor in a formal wear? Damn. He looks like a younger, hotter James Bond—sorry, Daniel Craig—with his expertly styled hair and his strong jaw highlighted by his neatly trimmed beard and his perfectly pressed tux molded to his hard body.

I'm still shamelessly staring, drinking in the sight of him like a dying man in a desert, when he's joined by possibly the most stunning woman I've ever seen. Seriously, she looks like she stepped straight off the pages of *Vogue* magazine, blond and statuesque in a skintight, floor-length gown and sky-high sling-backs, both designer, I'm sure.

She puts a possessive, manicured hand on his arm and leans in to whisper something in his ear that puts a smile on his usually serious face. I flinch like I've been slapped, almost dropping my tray.

I recognize the feeling clawing at my gut, but that doesn't mean I like it. My mother always said that jealousy was a disease. One that eats you away from the inside, leaving you hollow, angry, and discontented.

Besides, what right do I have to be jealous? It's not like Connor and I are in a committed relationship. Or any kind of relationship. We kissed. Once. Big deal. And he's made it perfectly clear ever since that he wants nothing to do with me.

"Lawson." The catering manager's bark makes me startle and I almost drop the tray for the second time in as many minutes. "What are you doing hiding in the goddamn corner?"

"I was just, uh—" *Ogling my roommate? Suffering from a bout of irrational jealousy? Trying to remember your name? Lloyd, I think Tiffany said it was.*

Possibly Lloyd cuts me off with a sharp wave of his hand. "Whatever your excuse is, I don't want to hear it. Just get back to work. You're not getting paid to lollygag around."

Lollygag? Who even uses words like that anymore? Except my eighty-two-year-old grandmother.

"Yes, sir."

I'd give him a mock salute, but my hands are occupied with the tray. So I settle for a crisp nod before heading into the throng of hungry socialites.

As hard as I try, I can't stop my eyes from searching the room for Connor and his—companion. I don't find them anywhere. Which fires my green-eyed monster up again. I'm imagining all sorts of Showtime-After-Dark scenarios. Like them going at it in the linen closet. Or the ladies' room. Or the—

"Excuse me, ladies and gentleman."

A voice over the speakers cuts off my runaway pornographic thoughts. I look across the ballroom to the stage that's been set up for this evening's festivities, and lo and behold, there she is, microphone in hand. Connor's—friend. And there he is, too, standing slightly behind her off to her left, looking equal parts sexy and self-conscious.

Oh, well. They may be together, but at least they're not in the linen closet. I suppose that's some small consolation.

"For those who don't know me, I'm Elizabeth

Ashby, and I'm the chairperson of this year's Fight For Hope."

Great. Now I can put a name to the too-perfect face. Elizabeth. She strikes me as the type who demands to be called by her full name. No Liz. Or Lizzie. Or Beth.

I move closer to the stage, handing out sandwiches as I go.

"I want to thank everyone for coming tonight," call-me-by-my-full-name Elizabeth continues. "And for opening your pocketbooks for a worthy cause. With your help, there's hope that someday we'll win the fight against ALS. And no one's more invested in that fight than the man up on stage with me tonight, Connor Dow."

She motions for him to join her, and he does.

"Connor lost his mother to ALS, and over the years he's continued to donate to the search for a cure. Personally, he's given over a million dollars. And later this year, he's allowing us to use his nightclub, Top Shelf, for our biggest, most ambitious fundraiser yet. So tonight, we'd like to present him with this plaque that commemorates his long-standing commitment to ALS research."

She hands the plaque to Connor, then the microphone. He clears his throat and starts to speak.

"Thank you, Elizabeth, and thank you to all the members of Fight For Hope's board of directors for giving me this honor. But it's really the health care workers and researchers on the front lines, treating patients and working toward a cure, who deserve to be up here tonight. I accept this award on their behalf and in memory of my mother and everyone who has battled this progressive, debilitating disease."

Okay, now I feel like a total asshat. Me and my dirty mind. He's getting an award for philanthropy—trying to help cure the disorder that killed his mother, for fuck's sake—not sneaking around for a quick hookup.

The audience applauds, and Connor hands the microphone back to Elizabeth. Then he looks out over the crowd. His eyes skate past me then flick back, confused. I can tell the moment the pieces click into place and recognition sets in.

He says something to Elizabeth before descending the stairs at the center of the stage, heading straight for me. My palms itch and the hair at back of my neck stands on end. Now he wants to talk? When I'm at work? With the crème de la crème of New York society listening in?

No. Freaking. Way.

My tray's empty again, so I decide to retreat to the kitchen for another refill. I get about halfway there when the Lloyd—that's definitely his name, I remember now—stops me. "Code Red. I need you on champagne cocktails. One of the other servers had to leave. Family emergency."

He says the last two words like they're causing him actual, physical pain. And just like that, I see my my escape-to-the-kitchen plan fading before my eyes.

"What about Tiffany? Can't she do cocktails?"

"Tiffany's not standing in front of me with an empty tray. You are. So head over to Derrick—" He points to a bartender at one of the stations ringing the room. "—and have him stock you up so you can make the rounds."

I glance over my shoulder. Connor's gaining on me. I need to end this conversation. Stat. Maybe I can lose him on my way to the bar.

"Right. I'm on it."

I make it over to Derrick and he's almost got my tray all loaded before Connor catches up to me. Probably because people keep stopping him to congratulate him on his award. He's like a rock star to this crowd. Not that I blame them. A million dollars is pretty damn impressive. At some point, I'll tell him as much. When I'm not pissed off at him for choosing here and now to end his self-imposed radio silence.

"Brie," he says, leaning on the bar rail next to me. "I didn't expect to see you here."

I don't look at him, keeping my attention on Derrick as he adds another glass of champagne to my tray. "We're roommates, not BFFs. We don't have to tell each other where we're going or what we're doing."

I keep my voice light so he doesn't suspect how much the awkwardness between us has been bothering me. Because yeah, it's bugged me. No woman wants to be kissed by a man like he means it, then ignored like she's yesterday's leftovers.

"But—I'm confused." He pushes his sexy-but-shouldn't-be thick-framed glasses up the bridge of his nose. "I thought you were an actress, filming a TV show. And you're here. Working as a waitress."

"Not that it's any of your business, but I am an actress. And a waitress. The two aren't mutually exclusive."

"I realize that. It's just that Jake said—"

Of course. Jake. It always comes back to my big brother, doesn't it? He's like an omnipresent shadow, looming between us.

I grab my tray and glare at Connor over the rims of the champagne flutes. "Whatever he had to say about my career path, I don't particularly care. Now, if you don't mind, I have to get back to my job. The waitressing one, that is."

In my rush to end this uncomfortable conversation in the quickest way possible, I make a rookie mistake—turning around without looking first, full tray in hand. Until I run smack dab into a distinguished looking older gentleman, and it goes crashing to the floor, the sound of breaking glass almost deafening.

Heat rushes to my face as I bend down to start cleaning up the mess I've made. I'm not normally so careless. Or so clumsy.

"Why don't you look where you're going?" the older man, who's mopping champagne from his lapel with a napkin—or trying to—snaps. "See what

you've done? This tuxedo is a Tom Ford. It will need
to be dry cleaned. And you're paying for it."

I don't bother pointing out to the pompous asshole
that it was an accident. Or that I'm just as soaked as he
is, and you don't see me bitching and moaning about it.
Or that if he can afford a Tom Ford tuxedo, he's clearly
got more money to spend on dry cleaning than I do.

"I'll take care of it," Connor insists, kneeling beside me and gingerly picking up slivers of glass,
which he adds to the pile I've already started on my
now wet, empty tray. "It was my fault. I shouldn't
have distracted her."

"You didn't," I lie. "And I don't need you riding
to my rescue."

Again. First the kitchen, now this. It's humiliat-
ing, how I can't seem to hold on to cups or glasses
when Connor's around.

"What's going on here?"

Lloyd is back. Yippee. Just when I thought things
couldn't get any worse. He's the last person I need to
see right now. I was hoping I'd have all this cleaned
up and be back on the floor before he heard about
what happened.

If he even heard about what happened.

"This server—" The pompous asshole waves his
damp napkin at me. "—dumped an entire tray of
drinks on my designer tuxedo."

"Which I've already offered to have dry cleaned."
Connor stands, wiping his hands on his tux pants
like he doesn't care if he has to get them cleaned,

too. He's got at least four inches on the pompous asshole, who subtly takes a step back but refuses to completely back down.

"That doesn't change the fact that I have to spend the rest of the evening in a wet formal wear."

Lloyd puts a hand on his shoulder. "I'm sorry for the inconvenience. Why don't you come with me? I'm sure the staff can find some towels to help you dry off."

He looks down at me, still crouched on the sticky-sweet carpet surrounded by glass shards, and the expression on his face tells me I'm screwed even before the words leave his mouth. "Hand in your tray and go. And don't forget to clock out."

"Are you firing me?" My stomach drops to my sensible, flat-soled shoes. There goes my safety net.

"That's above my pay grade. But I will be filing a report with the corporate office. Someone should be in touch with you shortly. And the cost of the glasses you broke will be deducted from your pay."

Great. There goes a huge chunk of tonight's pay. I leave my tray on the floor and scramble to my feet, glass crunching under the soles of my afore-mentioned sensible shoes. The rest of the mess will have to wait. "But—"

"It wasn't her fault," Connor pipes up, interrupt-ing me. "I'm the one who distracted her by striking up conversation."

"Fraternizing with the guests. I'll add that to my report." Lloyd steers the pompous asshole toward the huge mahogany double doors that lead into and out of the ballroom. "Come on, let's get you those towels. You'll feel better once you're dry."

Connor starts to go after them, but I step in his path, blocking his way. "Haven't you done enough already?"

"If you just let me talk to him I can—"

"Can what?" My hands ball into fists on my hips, my go-to power stance. "Give him another reason to fire me?"

He doesn't answer, but at least he has the good sense to look embarrassed.

"Don't worry about me," I continue. "I'm like your cats. I always manage to land on my feet."

It's a bit of bravado, but there's an element of truth to it, too. The life of an actor isn't an easy one. You have to learn how to roll with the punches and come up swinging.

He starts to say something, but full-name Elizabeth materializes out of nowhere, like she apparated from Hogwarts. She sidles up to Connor, digging her blood-red claws—sorry-not-sorry, nails—into his forearm. "There you are, darling. I wondered where you'd run off to. Some of the board members would like to speak with you."

Her use of the endearment stirs up all my earlier suspicions. Maybe they are more than donor/donee. And maybe it's none of my damn business, and I'm an idiot for caring.

"Go mingle with your adoring public. I'll see you

at home." I throw in the last bit just to see the stunned look on Elizabeth's face, and she doesn't disappoint. Watching her features fall is like witnessing an avalanche. Fast and furious.

But my perverse satisfaction in seeing her reaction is short lived. Because I know what she doesn't. That while we might share the same address for the time being, the chances of Connor and me having any intimate, late-night chats—or even being in the same damn room for more than a few seconds—are about as slim as being struck by lightning.

CHAPTER SEVEN

Connor

WHEN I GET HOME—about three hours later than I'd like, because I can't exactly skip out on a reception in my honor—my apartment's dark and the only ones stirring are the cats. I shed my tux jacket, loosen my bowtie, and undo the first couple of buttons on my shirt as I walk through the apartment, calling out Brie's name. No response. I even knock on her bedroom door and crack it open to peek inside when no one answers—but she's not there.

Worry starts to creep in, but I shove it down. It's like I told Jake. Brie's a big girl. She can take care of herself. She's probably out with friends, drowning her sorrows in Fireball and fried food.

I cringe at the memory of Brie, kneeling on the floor on a bed of glass. The anger and shock in her eyes when her boss told her she was done for the night. And maybe for good. All because I had to open my big mouth. I couldn't wait until after she was done working to talk to her.

Stupid. Selfish. Douchebag. Just like my god-damn father.

That last thought completely guts me. It's bad enough I share DNA with him. He's the last person in the world I want to emulate. In my defense, I wasn't trying to be a jerk like my dad. It's just that I was totally taken off guard when I saw her at the fundraiser. And I was afraid if I didn't take advantage of the opportunity to talk to her, I might never get another chance.

It seems counterintuitive, I know, because, duh, we're living together. I should have plenty of chances to talk to Brie. But we might as well be on different planets for the amount of times we've been in shouting distance of each other in the past seven days. Ever since that kiss. That epic, thrilling, terrifying kiss.

I don't know if she's making herself scarce on purpose or if our schedules just don't mesh. She did warn me—or promise me—that she wouldn't be around much. But one way or another, I'm going to find out.

I grab my e-reader, pour myself a shot of Johnnie Walker Platinum 18, and settle into my favorite armchair, which just happens to have a birds-eye view of my front door. I'm only a couple of chapters into my book and halfway finished with my scotch when I hear a key in the lock and the door swings open.

The room is in semi-darkness, the only light from the table lamp next to me and my e-reader, so it takes a second for Brie to register that I'm sitting there. When she does, her displeasure is clearly readable even in the half-light, etched across her face and in every rigid inch of her posture.

"I thought you'd still be out, celebrating with your fan club."

I set my e-reader aside and shake my head. "I haven't got the time or patience for a fan club. I donate because it's the right thing to do, not to have my ass kissed by strangers and sycophants."

She drops her purse on the couch and takes another step toward. "I dunno. You seemed to enjoy having that Elizabeth chick fawn all over you."

I lean forward, resting my forearms on my knees. "Jealous?"

She snorts. "Of what?"

"Elizabeth is a friend. That's all."

"You should tell her that."

"I have." I reach for my scotch, swirling the amber liquid around in my glass. "But I didn't wait up for you so we could talk about Elizabeth."

"Then why did you wait up for me?"

"So I could apologize for tonight."

"Just for tonight?"

She crosses her arms over her chest and stares me down. Way down, because she's standing and I'm in my comfy chair, swilling scotch.

The power dynamic isn't lost on me, and I'd be lying if I said I didn't find it a turn-on. One I try my damndest to ignore. My goal is to have a conversation, not a quickie. Although in my fantasies, which are plentiful and pornographic, sex with Brie is anything but quick. She's the kind of woman you take your time with. Exploring every curve and crevice. Figuring out what makes her moan and writhe and call out my name.

I sip my scotch, not sure where this is going. "Is there something else I should be apologizing for?"

"Hmm, let me think." She huffs a stray lock of red-brown hair off her forehead. "First, you kiss me. Then you pretend I don't exist."

"I thought you were steering clear of me," I counter. "Or busy filming."

She shoves her purse over and sits on the sofa, and a huge, invisible weight is lifted off my chest. Sitting means staying, and staying means she's willing to listen to what I have to say.

"Well, my schedule has been crazy." She slips off her no-nonsense waitressing shoes—which she somehow manages to make look as sexy as a pair of six-inch stilettos—and tucks her feet underneath her. "You really haven't been avoiding me?"

"Really."

"And I haven't been avoiding you. So you're telling me this has all been a giant misunderstanding?"

I shrug and polish off my scotch, setting my empty glass back on the side table. "I guess so."

"And what about that kiss?"

Right about here is where I should remember that Brie is my best friend's sister and shut things down.

But it's awfully hard to think about Jake with her sitting across from me, looking like everything I've ever wanted.

"What about it?" I ask.

"Was that a misunderstanding, too?"

She bites her lip and looks at me with huge, hungry hazel eyes. Her openness, mixed with a hint of uncertainty, shreds any resolve I have left. Fuck it. I'm done resisting this woman. Yeah, she's my best friend's sister. And yeah, we're all wrong for each other. But I want this. So fucking badly. And from the way those hazel eyes are undressing me, so does she.

Suddenly, being across the room from her feels like we're a million miles apart. I need to be with her. Really with her.

I move faster than I've moved in my entire life, and that's counting the time I miraculously managed not to come in dead last in the fourth grade fifty-yard dash. In a nanosecond, I've tossed her purse on the floor and I'm next to her on the couch.

"I wanted to kiss you. Then and now."

"What's stopping you?"

I move closer to her on the couch, taking her head in my hands. Her cheeks are soft and warm under my palms. "Because if I kiss you again, it won't stop there."

"And that's a problem—why, exactly?"

"Right now, I can't think of one damn good reason."

I lower my mouth to hers. She parts her lips as my head descends, so that when our mouths meet I can taste her breath, sweet and cinnamony from the Fireball I correctly guessed she'd been drinking. She always loved that stuff.

And now I love it, too. Her taste is intoxicating, taunting me to go in for more. I coax her tongue out to touch mine, and it's like I've been zapped by a live wire. I groan into her mouth and slide my hands to the back of her neck, threading my fingers through her thick, chestnut curls.

If I thought our first kiss was explosive, this one takes things to a whole new earth-shattering level. Maybe because we're both on the same page. We know where things are going this time. And it won't end with a kiss.

She's responding to me now with equal fervor, her groans matching mine, the sexy sounds she makes sending my hormones into hyperdrive. Our mouths fit perfectly together and the way she uses her tongue—fuck, that's hot. She's breathing hard—we both are—and that's before her hands get in on the action.

They're everywhere. Working their way up my forearms to my biceps. Digging her nails into my shoulders through the thin cotton of my dress shirt. Raking through my hair, pulling me tighter to her.

And still it's not enough. She must agree, because the next thing I know she's in my lap, straddling me.

My semi-hard cock springs to attention, straining against the zipper of my tux pants.

"Is that a cucumber in your pocket, or are you just happy to see me?"

I chuckle as my hands drift down to cup her ass. "A cucumber?"

She smiles back and rocks against the firm ridge of my erection. "Well, you are a vegetarian."

"I'm flattered. And overjoyed."

"That makes two of us."

She initiates the kiss this time, but I have her gasping in seconds, teasing her with lazy flicks of my tongue. She tastes so damn good and she's so fucking responsive. With her on top of me, I can feel every little twitch and quiver. It's the biggest turn-on going, and my cock feels like about to split my zipper and burst out of my pants.

I leave her mouth to trace a wet trail across her jawline, down her slender, elegant neck, to her collarbone. I can feel her pulse hammering at the base of her throat, another telltale sign that she's as into this as I am. That and the way she lets her head fall back, giving me free rein to continue my exploration.

I undo the top button of her shirt and travel lower, toward the soft swell of her breasts. Again, it's not enough. I slip another button from its hole and nudge her shirt apart with my nose. She smells downright decadent. Her familiar scents of coconut and salt water mixed with something new.

Desire.

"Need this off," I grumble, freeing a third button. "Now."

"You first."

Her hands fist in my shirt and she yanks it out of my pants. We fumble furiously with each other's buttons, eventually succeeding, our shirts falling to the floor in a heap.

She's wearing a pale peach satin bra that covers all her curves but is still as provocative as fuck. I thumb her nipple through the shiny fabric, loving the way it pebbles almost immediately under my touch. Like I said. So. Fucking. Responsive. "Do you realize how sexy you are?"

"Do you?" She runs her hands over my chest and abs, lingering on the ridges and valleys of the six-pack I've worked hard to maintain. "I suppose I should thank Jake for introducing you to the gym."

Her brother's name—my best friend's name—is like a bucket of ice water over my libido, and I pull my hand back.

But Brie's having none of that. She grabs my hand and replaces it on her breast, covering it with hers to keep it there. "Oh no, you don't. In case you haven't noticed, I'm all grown-up."

"Oh, I've noticed, all right." I can't help myself. Her satin-covered tit is full and firm under my fingers. A perfect handful, begging to be squeezed. So I do.

She rewards me with a low, husky purr that shoots straight to my already aching groin. "Good. Then you'll understand that, as a consenting adult, who I choose to sleep with is nobody's business but my own. Especially not my brother's."

"Point taken." I nuzzle the sweet spot between her breasts again, the temptation of silky smooth satin and equally silky smooth skin too much to fight. "But it would help if we could maybe not talk about him anymore. At least when we're half-naked. Or completely naked, for that matter."

"Are you saying you want to get completely naked?" She trembles when I move my mouth to her nipple, gently sucking it through her bra.

I respond without lifting my head, the words vibrating against her like a tuning fork. "I'm not opposed to the idea."

Without warning, she pushes my head away from her chest and climbs off me. I'm confused and disappointed and more than a little frustrated, but only for a second. Then she treats me to the most erotic strip tease I've ever experienced, removing first her pants, then her bra, then her matching peach panties, revealing a neatly landscaped patch of hair above the juncture of her thighs.

When she's naked, she turns around, giving me a full view of her ripe, round backside, and heads for the hallway that leads to the bedrooms.

"Where are you going?" I croak, frankly surprised that I have any ability left to string words together into a coherent sentence. The way her hips sway when she walks is hypnotizing.

"You tell me." She stops, popping a hip and looking flirtatiously at me over her shoulder. "Your bed or mine?"

CHAPTER EIGHT

Brie

IT OCCURS TO ME, as I'm standing butt naked in the middle of Connor's living room, posing like a 50s pinup girl sans the vintage two-piece, that I may have made a critical error in judgment.

I mean, I thought Connor was on board with where this was going. He sure seemed like it a few minutes ago when I was riding his lap. The evidence of his arousal was obvious. And impressive.

But now he's just sitting there. Staring at me. Unmoving.

I'm hoping it's because he's stunned speechless in a good way, and not because he's repulsed.

I drop the pose and turn to face him.

"You realize there's no wrong answer here, right?" I tease, trying to hide the fact that with every passing second I'm increasingly conscious of the fact that I'm in my birthday suit and he's still half dressed. "Sure, your bed's bigger. But I'm pretty sure mine will work just as well."

"Mine."

He stands and stalks toward me, looking like he's going to go all caveman again and toss me over his shoulder. Except this time nothing is broken and I don't need rescuing.

"Down, boy." I say, taking a step back. "I appreciate the romantic gesture, but I'm perfectly capable of making it to your bedroom under my own power."

His eyes run me over from head to toe, sending a flash of heat to my lady bits. "What if I don't want to wait that long to hold you?"

Damn. How can a girl say no to that? I sure can't.

I spread my arms wide in invitation, my self-consciousness a thing of the past. He clearly likes what he sees. And the feeling is entirely mutual, even if I'm not seeing as much as I'd like.

Yet.

"Go for it, Lancelot."

He does, but this time it's no rough-and-tumble, over-the-shoulder fireman's carry. Instead, he lifts me gently, effortlessly, with one arm around my back and the other under my knees, cradling me to his smooth, strong chest.

Swoon.

I bury my face in the sprinkle of dark, fine hair between his pecs, inhaling his clean, soapy scent as he carts me off to his inner sanctum. I've only gotten glimpses of the master bedroom in passing through his partially open door. All I've been able to see are dark wood and earth tones.

The full view doesn't disappoint. Like the rest of Connor's flat, it's a study in upscale, masculine chic. There's a wall of windows with a specular view of the Manhattan skyline. And I was right when I guessed that his bed was huge. It's big enough for him, me, and the Knicks starting back court.

But I'm not interested in gawking at his magazine-worthy bedroom or the most famous skyline in the world right now. There's another view I'm jonesing for. If you ask me, it's high time I'm not the only one in this scenario who's wearing nothing but a smile.

Connor lays me on his massive bed, kissing down my neck, between my breasts, circling my nipples. I lose myself in the sweet sensations created by his lips and tongue until I remember that he's still got his damn pants on, and I reach for his belt.

He covers my hand with his, stopping me. "Not yet."

"How the hell is that fair?" I groan.

"Nobody said this was going to be fair."

He pauses to remove his glasses, folding them carefully and setting them on the nightstand. I want to scream. How can he be so calm, cool, and collected when I'm about to spontaneously combust?

"But trust me, I'll make it up to you."

And boy, does he. Connor Dow is nothing if not a man of his word. He slides down my body, inching my thighs apart with his hands and settling between my legs, his mouth centimeters from my core. He plants wet, sucking kisses on my inner thigh, teasing his way up to the spot where I really want him.

When he gets there—finally—the damn teasing doesn't stop. Instead of sucking on my clit like I want him to, he licks everywhere but. His rhythm is slow, steady, and deliberate, like he's determined to drive me crazy before letting me come.

I moan and close my eyes, fisting my hands into his comforter. If he keeps this up much longer, I might pass out from pure pleasure.

"That's it," he murmurs against my pussy. "Just lie back and let me make you feel good."

I twist the comforter tighter in my fists. "I don't think I can feel much better."

"Sure about that?"

He takes my clit into his mouth and bites down. Not hard, just enough to shoot sensuous tingles to every pore in my body.

My eyes fly open and my hips piston off the bed. "Did you just bite me?"

He looks up at me with a "Who, me?" grin. "And what if I did?"

I'd like to wipe his smug, sex-god smile right off his face. Except he's got every reason to be smug. The guy's seriously good at this. Like expert level good.

Sex-god level good.

I lift my head to eye him right back, not afraid to tell him what I want. No, this is beyond want. We're into need territory. "Then I'd ask you to do it again."

He gives me another nibble then adds a finger to the action, pushing it slowly inside me. I can feel myself start to tighten, and I know I'm not going to last long, especially when he starts moving his finger in and out, angling it so it finds my g-spot.

All the while he's still licking and sucking. The trifecta of lips, tongue, and finger is too much to take, and it's not long before my muscles clench and I'm spasming around him.

He lets me ride out my climax on his lips. When I'm done—after what seems like an eternity, I don't think I've ever come that long or that hard—he withdraws his finger and brings it to his mouth. He runs it along his lower lip then sucks it in, tasting me.

Holy hell, that's hot. Sure, he's had it directly from the source. But there's something so decadent about watching him lick it from his finger. Like he doesn't want a drop to go to waste.

When he's done, he trails his wet finger down my abdomen, leaving a row of goosebumps in its wake. "Was I right?"

"Huh?" What did he just say? I prop myself up on my elbows and stare at him through glassy, post-orgasmic eyes. My fuzzy brain has no clue what he's talking about.

"Was I right?" he repeats, emphasizing each word.

Okay, still clueless. I don't whether he's being deliberately coy or whether I'm so blissed out I can't even comprehend a simple question. "About what?"

The corners of his mouth twitch, like he's fighting a laugh. "Making it up to you for not losing my pants."

"Hell, yes." I'm not afraid to admit when I'm wrong. Especially when I've just had the best orgasm of my life. Hopefully the first of many tonight. "That was incredible. Now do I get to see you naked?"

"Greedy girl."

"Guilty as charged." I hold my arms out and cross them at the wrists. "Lock me up and throw away the key."

"If I had known you were into that kind of stuff, I would have borrowed a pair of handcuffs from the security guard downstairs."

He kisses my stomach just above the landing strip that leads to my sex and crawls up the bed until he's lying next to me. When his waistband is in reach, I go for his belt buckle, unfastening it then the button at the top of his fly.

I stop at his zipper, taking a moment to appreciate the obvious bulge underneath. I run my hand down it, squeeze it in my fingers. It pulses in my palm, hard and hot even through his trousers.

"Thought you wanted me naked," he growls.

"You had your turn," I tell him. "Shut up and let me have mine."

"Bossy."

I give his dick another squeeze, and it throbs harder. "Don't pretend like you don't love it."

He doesn't have a snappy comeback for that one. Or maybe he does, but it gets swallowed up in his groan when I slide down his zipper and slip my hand under the waistband of his boxer briefs. I elicit another groan when I circle his length with my fingers and stroke.

Not waiting anymore for me to undress him, he lifts his hips and shoves his pants and briefs down to his knees in one quick jerk. I release him long enough to help get them off completely, along with his shoes and socks. Then all my attention is back on his cock.

"I could fucking die right here a happy man," he says as I resume stroking him. "So goddamn happy."

"Dying isn't exactly the reaction I'm going for." I continue to fondle his dick as I worm my way down his magnificent body. He's got those vees where his hips and abs meet. You know, the ones that point to the promised land and make women stupid. Even his calves are ripped, every inch of him a new revelation. And who has sexy feet? Seriously, there's not a thing about him that doesn't rev my engine.

I keep moving south until my it's my lips that are inches from his naughty parts. Returning the favor. Or is it turnabout is fair play? Maybe a bit of both. "I was thinking more seeing stars."

"If you put your mouth on me, I'll be seeing entire constellations. Planets. Comets shooting through the night sky."

I move closer, my warm breath teasing the tip of his cock. "Then prepare to go into orbit."

I take a second to admire him before going down on him. I'm still not convinced he won't regret defiling his best friend's baby sister in the morning. This may be the only chance I get to experience the wonder that is Connor Dow, sex god. I want every second, every image burned into my memory bank.

I've never thought of a guy's junk as beautiful, but his is. It's standing loud, long, and proud, the thick, spongy crown a shade darker than the rigid shaft. A clear bead of liquid pearls at the slit, shining like a beacon, begging me to lap it up.

"Remember what I said about dying? That's a real possibility if you don't put that pretty mouth on my dick in the next ten seconds. Either that or I'm going to flip you over and bury myself inside you."

Seems like a win/win situation to me. I go for door number one, figuring door number two is always on the table for later. My hand works the base of his cock while my mouth concentrates on the head. He hisses when I flick the slit with my tongue, then swirl it around the tip, teasing his frenulum.

The hisses turn to full-on moans when the teasing stops and I suck him deep, taking him as far into my mouth as I can. He's smooth and stiff and pulsing and tastes as good as I imagined. Like skin and soap, with a hint of musky sweetness.

I slide my lips over his length, up and down, over and over, encouraged by his ragged breathing and his husky sex sounds and the way his hands sink into my hair, not directing or controlling my movements but just guiding them. After what could be two minutes or twenty—hard to keep track of time when you're focused on rocking a guy's world—he tugs on my hair, easing my mouth away from him.

"Did I do something wrong?" I ask, knowing full well that I didn't.

"No. You did something very, very right. So right that if you keep doing it I'm going to come."

"Isn't that the objective?"

"Not until I'm inside you."

Oh, goody. Door number two. "Please tell me you have condoms stashed somewhere in this palace."

He rolls away from me and opens the nightstand drawer. After a few seconds of fumbling, he pulls out a foil packet and rips it open. I skootch back up the bed and let myself enjoy the show as he suits up.

And it's a hell of a show. He rolls it on without missing a beat, one handed. It's quick and confident and strangely sexy. Worthy of a Pornhub video. Except this one's for my viewing pleasure only.

He cocks an eyebrow at me. "Like what you see?"

"You're very good at that."

"That's not all I'm good at."

He rejoins me on the bed, stretching his big body out next to mine.

"Spread your legs."

The rough command surprises me, not that that stops me from complying. And then he's on top of me, his mouth on mine as his cock slides through the slick heat between my legs, prodding at my entrance but not penetrating.

Tease.

I arch my hips, silently begging him to do it already. When that doesn't have the desired effect, I reach around and grab his ass, pulling him into me. Finally—finally—he rolls his hips and plunges into me, filling me so fully, stretching me so completely, that I gasp at the sensation and wrap my legs around him, locking my ankles behind his back.

"Oh, yeah." He's panting as he thrusts and withdraws, thrusts and withdraws, hard and fast, quick and dirty. He looks like a dark conquering hero looming above me, braced on his corded forearms, his sex-mussed hair flopping over his forehead with each new invasion. "Just like that. Take me deeper."

The heat and friction between us build quickly, and I feel another orgasm rising within me. As it hits, my calves clamp on his ass and my muscles clamp around his cock. A wave of pleasure ripples through my body, starting at my toes, rolling over my legs and chest, tingling its way to my fingertips and the ends of my hair.

Connor calls out my name and pushes into me one last time. I see his climax break across his handsome face at the same time I feel him pulse inside me as he comes.

"Fuck," he grunts out.

His eyes lock with mine, dark and demanding, not letting me look away even if I wanted to. Which

I don't. Because Connor mid-orgasm is seriously one of the most stunning sights I've ever seen. His strong jaw slack with lust, lips parted, chest heaving with exertion.

When we're both spent, he collapses on top of me, his face buried in the crook of my neck and his dick still hard inside me. I loop my arms around his shoulders, holding tight to him, and we stay that way for a few minutes, happy and sated, our breathing evening out, until he rolls to one side and flops onto his back. My pussy practically screams in protest when he pulls out.

As much as I hate to, I sit up and swing my legs over the side of the bed. Reality is creeping back in, and along with it the realization that I just had possibly the best sex of my relatively young life with my brother's best friend. Who might not be so thrilled that he shagged his BFF's little sister now that the sexual endorphins are beginning to wear off.

"Where are you going?" he asks.

"I'm dying of thirst. I could use a glass of water."

He sits up next to me. "Oh, no, you don't. Remember what happened last time?"

"You hauled me over your shoulder like a Cro-Magnon man and kissed me." Not a bad outcome, in my not-so-humble opinion.

"Before that. I like my coffee mugs. I don't want to lose another one." He drops a kiss between my shoulder blades. "Stay here. I'll get the water."

Okay, so I guess remorse hasn't set in. At least

not yet. Maybe those endorphins are stronger than I thought, and he's still on a post-coital high. Like me.

He disappears into the master bath—presumably to dispose of the condom—then heads for the kitchen. He comes back with two glasses of ice water, hands one to me, and sits down on the bed. We both sip silently, the awkwardness I expected starting to set in.

"About Jake—" I say finally, broaching the elephant in the room.

Connor chokes mid-sip on his water and lowers his glass. "I thought we agreed not to talk about your brother while we were naked."

"I was only going to say that I don't see any reason for him to know about this."

"Agreed."

"And if he doesn't need to know what just happened, I don't see any reason why he needs to know if it should, maybe, happen again—" I let my voice trail off, leaving my implication hanging in the air, like the last notes of a Stephen Sondheim song.

He takes my almost empty water—I wasn't kidding when I said I was thirsty—and sets both glasses down on the nightstand. "Are you propositioning me?"

I tilt my head to one side and look up at him seductively from under my lashes. "If I were, what would you say?"

"Does this answer your question?" He lowers me

to the bed, his cock stiff and throbbing against my thigh.

"Already?"

"For you, always."

His mouth captures mine as one hand slips between us to cup my breast. Then he spends the rest of the night proving his point.

CHAPTER NINE

Connor

"HONEY, I'M HOME." It's half joke, half wishful thinking. As in I wish Brie and I were more than fuck buddies. That our living arrangement was one of commitment, not convenience.

Stupid? Probably. Brie and I aren't who anyone would pick as the perfect couple. Not only because of the best friend's sister thing. It's like Jake said. Brie and I are nothing alike. She craves attention. I might as well be allergic to it.

It's like we're circling in two different orbits. I should be happy they happened to overlap for however long whatever we're doing lasts.

Shouldn't I?

"I'm in here," she calls from somewhere in the recesses of our—my—apartment.

I drop my briefcase just inside the door and follow the sound of her voice. It's one of her rare days off. Which is why I cut my time at the club short and raced home. It's been over two weeks since the night of the black-tie benefit. And thanks to our crazy, conflicting schedules, I can count on one hand the number of times we've managed a repeat performance.

That ends tonight.

I find her curled up on the couch flanked by my traitorous cats. She's concentrating on something on her laptop screen, a pencil between her teeth.

I hang back and let myself study her, unobserved. She's gorgeous, even in baggy sweats and a faded T-shirt, her hair in a messy bun, her face free of makeup. Especially in baggy sweats and a faded T-shirt, her hair in a messy bun, her face free of makeup.

Without taking her eyes off the screen, she takes the pencil from her mouth and jots something down on a pad beside her. "Are you going to come over here and kiss me, or are you planning to stand there staring at me all day?"

Tough choice. I come up behind her and press a soft kiss on her exposed neck. As I do, I catch a glimpse of what she's looking at on her computer, and my stomach tightens.

"What's that?" I ask, knowing full well what it is. We haven't talked about her moving out since we started sleeping together. But it shouldn't surprise me that she's still looking for a new place. She said from the start that this was temporary. The fact that we're fucking doesn't change that.

So why do I feel like someone's shoved a knife in my gut? A rusty one, with a serrated edge.

"Apartment hunting." She sounds almost giddy. The knife twists deeper. "This one actually looks promising. Within my price range, not too far from the 6 train, and the guy I'd be rooming with seems halfway decent. At least he doesn't expect me to share the place with his collection of taxidermy foxes, like the last one."

Guy? I lean in to take a closer look at the listing on the screen. What I see only ratchets up my frustration.

My hands ball into tight fists. It's a good thing I'm still behind the couch and she can't see them.

"You are not moving there." *With another guy.* "It's not safe. They have one of the highest murder rates in the five boroughs. And instead of a Starbucks, there's a methadone clinic on every corner."

"Good. I'll finally be able to kick the habit."

My teeth clench and a muscle in my jaw tics. Not two minutes ago, I walked through the door in such high spirits. How did things go so far downhill so fast? "Not funny."

She slams her laptop shut and stands. "Neither is you trying to dictate where I can and cannot live."

The cats, sensing trouble, leap from the couch and flee the room. Can't say I blame them. I wish I could escape, too.

Instead, I man up and come around the sofa so I'm standing in front of her. I'm not having this discussion with a three-hundred-fifty-pound piece of furniture between us. "I'm not dictating where you live—"

"You are not moving there," she says in a lilting, sing-song voice, mocking me.

"I did not sound like that."

"Did too."

"I'm concerned about you. Is that a crime?"

She plants her hands on her hips, which has the bonus effect of thrusting her breasts forward. "I already have a big brother. I don't need another one."

Is it wrong that we're in the middle of an argument and I want to strip her clothes off and screw her senseless? I swear, she's even hotter when she's pissed off. There's an almost primal sexuality about her.

"My feelings for you are anything but brotherly."

"You know what I mean."

"All I'm saying is that there's no rush for you to leave. Take the time to find a place that's more than just affordable and near a subway line. Preferably one in a better neighborhood. With a roommate who wears bras instead of boxers."

The last part slips out before I can stop it. And of course, it's what she latches right onto.

"So is it the location you object to? Or the fact that I'd be living with a guy?"

I try to look sheepish. "Would you be mad at me if I said both?"

"Look who's jealous now." Her hands are still on

her hips, but her tone is gentler, her eyes softer. "But I can't mooch off you indefinitely."

I step in to her, taking her hands from her hips and putting them around my neck. Then I wrap my arms around her waist. "You're not mooching. You're an important part of this household."

Her fingers tunnel in my hair and her lips curve into a sarcastic smile. "Having sex with the master of the house doesn't count."

"You did the grocery shopping," I say. We're so close my voice is almost a whisper, and I lean in to rest my forehead on hers. "Made lasagna. Rearranged my kitchen cabinets. And that was in your first twenty-four hours here. Do you want me to go on?"

"I don't want to overstay my welcome," she whispers back.

There's something in her eyes—a hint of doubt or hesitation—that guts me. "Trust me, that is not going to happen."

I cover her mouth with mine. It's not a gentle kiss. It's fast and firm, designed to wipe out any uncertainly about whether and for how long I want her here. I suck her bottom lip between my teeth and tug, making her gasp. That gives me an opening, and I take advantage, snaking my tongue inside to find hers. Tasting. Exploring.

Somehow, we wind up on the couch, her laptop pushed to the floor, her body sprawled across mine. Our sex is like my kiss. Frantic. Furious. Neither one of us wants to take the time to fully undress—it's a damn miracle I remember I've got a condom in my wallet—and I enter her with our shirts on and our pants around our ankles. I come in minutes, something that would normally be embarrassing as hell except that except that she's right there with me, her heady moans filling the room as she tumbles over the edge.

As great as it is, I know the sex doesn't solve anything. The question of when—or if—Brie will be packing her bags and hitting the road still looms. But it's forgotten for now. Obscured in a haze of hormones and sheer physical exhaustion. And I'm scoring that in the win column.

Later, after we shower together to clean up—which of course only gets us dirty again—we order take out from the Thai place around the corner and end up back on the couch for an evening of Netflix and chilling.

I'm struck with the strange thought that, in the eight weeks we lived together, not once did Giselle and I do this. Spend a quiet night at home watching television. We were always either out at some function or another or, when we were home together, working in separate rooms.

Now that I think about it, it says a lot about why our relationship crashed and burned. Neither one of us was willing to make the effort required to have a true partnership. It makes me wonder if I'm more like my father than I want to admit. Incapable of real intimacy.

But then Brie snuggles into me, her head nudging into the crook of my shoulder, her already familiar coconut scent wafting over me—it's her shampoo, I've learned—and I'm flooded with a supreme sense contentment I never felt with Giselle. Maybe the problem isn't me. Maybe the problem is that I was with the wrong woman.

"If you're not going to pick something for us to watch, I am," Brie says, trying to snag the remote out of my hand.

I hold it out of her reach, point it at my flat screen, and start scrolling through the options. I'm done dwelling on the past. Time to concentrate on the here and now. And the woman next to me instead of the one who walked out without a backward glance. "How about an oldie but goodie? Like *High Fidelity*. Or *The Princess Bride*."

She stares at me, open-mouthed. "You'd watch *The Princess Bride* with me?"

"Why not? I love that movie."

"Jake hates it. He says the only good part is the sword fighting."

"Inconceivable."

"Wow." She lets loose with a low, appreciative whistle. "You weren't kidding when you said you love it. But I had something else in mind."

"Oh?" I trail a finger down her side, letting my hand come to rest on her hip, just inside the waistband of her yoga pants. I never realized how sexy those things are. Or maybe it's that Brie is sexy in whatever she wears. She could be in one of those shapeless 1950s housedresses and my dick would stand up and salute. "Is it a *Fifty Shades* sort of something else?"

Not my usual cinematic fare. But with Brie, it might be fun to watch. And I wouldn't mind if it led to a little Christian Grey/Anastasia Steele role play.

Yeah, I know the characters' names. I even read a couple of chapters of the book—the first one—to see what all the fuss was about. I still don't get it. But women sure do.

Brie gives my hand a playful smack, hard enough to sting a little but not to swat it away. "Has anyone ever told you that you have a one-track mind?"

"Yeah, but I'm pretty sure they meant it as a compliment."

"Only a guy would think that."

I stretch my legs out in front of me, settling in for the next few hours of whatever the heck it is we're going to watch. Don't get me wrong. I don't particularly care what it is. As long as I'm watching it with her. "So no *Princess Bride* and no *Fifty Shades*. What do you suggest?"

Before she can answer, my phone dings with an incoming text. I grab it from the table next to me and check the screen, making sure it's not an emergency at the club. Like the time Jake got himself knocked on his ass playing knight in shining armor for Ainsley.

R u home? Is my sister there? Ainsley's been trying 2 reach her. Something about going dress shopping 4 the wedding.

"Everything okay?" Brie asks.

"It's your brother. He says your future sister-in-law is trying to get in touch with you. She wants to you to go wedding dress shopping with her."

She scrunches up her nose. It's fucking adorable. "I left my cell in my bedroom. Can you tell him I'll call her back tomorrow?"

I type out a quick response and put my phone back on the table. "Now, about that movie—"

"I was kind of hoping we could watch *Captain America*."

"Which one? There's three, you know."

"The first one."

"Let me guess," I say, half teasing, half serious. "You've got a thing for Chris Evans."

"Who doesn't? Objectively, he's one damn fine-looking specimen. But that's not why I picked that movie."

She twists sideways and puts her legs in my lap. As sexy as her yoga pants are, I almost resent them now. Without them, I'd be able to run my hand down her bare skin, feel the goosebumps rise wherever I touch.

"Then why?"

"We've finished shooting my origin story and we're moving into the superhero scenes. I have a stunt double for the tough stuff, but I figure a little kick-butt inspiration couldn't hurt."

"If you really want to be inspired, you need an education in kick-ass female superheroes. Like Wonder Woman. Or Captain Marvel."

"You're the one who had a stash of comic books under your bed as a kid. You choose."

"You knew about that?" I saved my allowance to buy them then hid them from my father, who hated anything related to nerd culture.

"My brother has a big mouth." Brie hops off my lap. "I'll get us some snacks while you decide."

She goes to the kitchen to pop some microwave popcorn, and I queue up *Captain Marvel*. Yes, she's not as well known as Wonder Woman. But unlike mythical Amazon warrior Diana Prince—aka Wonder Woman—Carol Danvers, Captain Marvel's alter ego, is an actual human being, with human flaws and strengths in addition to her superpowers. For Brie, it makes her character more well-rounded and relatable. Ergo, inspirational.

The opening credits are starting to roll when my phone chimes with another text. I pause the movie and curse Jake out under my breath for interrupting us again. But when I check my phone, it's not Jake who's texting this time. It's my father.

I'll be in town on Friday to meet with my publisher. I'd like to see you. Dinner at the Polo Bar. 8:00.

It's a demand, not a request. Typical Vincent Dow.

Brie plops back down next to me, a huge bowl of popcorn in her arms. She tosses a piece in the air and catches it in her mouth. "If that's my brother again, tell him to focus on his future wife and leave me alone."

"It's my father."

The words leave my mouth before I can stop them. I don't like talking about my father or our joke of a relationship. To anyone.

But something about Brie makes me feel like I can confide in her. Like she'll listen without judgment. Offer sympathy—and maybe even some sound advice—without platitudes. Besides, unlike most people, she already knows some of my dysfunctional family history. She was there. She saw it first-hand.

"What does he want?" she snaps, her body stiffening beside me. I love how she's immediately defensive on my behalf. It gives me the courage to keep going instead of doing what I usually do when it comes to my father—shut down.

"He invited me to dinner on Friday. No, invited is the wrong word. More like ordered."

"What are you going to tell him?"

"I'm going to tell him to fuck off."

She holds the bowl of popcorn out to me, and I reach in and grab a handful. "While I understand and fully support the sentiment, you might want to soften it a little. Be the better man."

See what I mean about the sound advice? "No

four-letter words. But don't expect me to be polite. I don't have the energy to pretend to be civil."

I shove the popcorn into my mouth and type out my response. It doesn't take long. Two words. Nine letters. I don't even bother to use punctuation.

Can't sorry.

I go to turn the phone off, but before my finger can find the button those three familiar dots start dancing, and my father's answer flashes on the screen a couple of seconds later.

Sunday then. I have a box of your mother's things for you. Fiona found them in the attic.

Fiona. His latest conquest. Bleached blonde hair, big boobs, and not a day over thirty. Just like her predecessor. And the one before her. And the one before her. My father's nothing if not consistent. And predictable.

"What did he say?" Brie asks.

I hand her the phone. She studies it thoughtfully for a minute then hands it back. "Well, you have to go now."

"Do I?"

"Don't you want to know what's in the box?"

"If there even is a box." I wouldn't put it past my father to lie just to get me there so he can spend the entire meal telling me what a disappointment I am.

"Are you willing to take that chance?"

Leave it to Brie to get right to the heart of the matter. It's a good question. And the short answer is no. I don't have anything of my mom's. I was only seventeen when she died, and then a few months later I was off at college. If there really is a box, it may have some photos. Or letters. Something I can take out and look at every once and a while.

"Fine. I'll go. But I'm doing this on my terms, not his." Lunch, not dinner. Easier to make some excuse and cut things short when they invariably go south. And no stuffy Polo Club.

"I can come with you if you want," Brie offers, setting the popcorn bowl on the coffee table and pressing her palm on my thigh. "If you think it would help."

"Don't you have to work?"

"We never shoot on Sundays. And I haven't had a catering gig in weeks, so—"

I grimace. "Don't remind me."

"It's okay. Tiffany said has Lloyd a short memory, and she can probably get me back on the roster by the time we wrap this season." She moves her hand from my thigh and links our fingers together. "So, what do you say? Do you want some company for your dinner with Dad?"

Suddenly, the prospect of seeing my father is a lot less stomach-turning.

"Lunch." I lift her legs into my lap and lean in to kiss her. "And it's a date."

CHAPTER TEN

Brie

"ARE YOU SURE you're ready for this?"

Connor runs his hands through his hair, smooths it down, then shoves them in the pockets of his khakis. It's like he doesn't know what to do with them. With his whole body, really. His eyes are darting all over the place and one foot taps restlessly on the sidewalk.

I put a hand on his forearm, feeling the tension in his tight muscles, and squeeze. "Are you?"

We're standing outside Boqueria, the tapas bar in midtown Connor and his father finally agreed on for lunch after much negotiation. We're a few minutes early for our reservation, but Connor's been this way since he got out of bed this morning. I've never seen him so keyed up.

"No," he admits with a heavy sigh. "But the sooner we go in, the sooner we get this over with."

I hate that he views lunch with his father as some sort of a chore. An obligation to be endured until he can come up with some reason to escape. As annoying as they can be sometimes, my family is practically the Brady Bunch, and it breaks my heart that Connor doesn't have that kind of support system.

I guess that's why I offered to come with him today. He deserves someone in his corner.

He opens the door and ushers me into the restaurant. The hostess sits us in a booth at the back of the room, out of the flow of traffic and away from most of the other diners. Smart move. It's almost like she knows things might get uncomfortable.

Connor's dad isn't there yet, so we order drinks to get us started—sangria for me, a house Bloody Mary for Connor with guindilla pepper and gin instead of vodka. Alcohol and family reunions can be a dangerous combination. But Connor's not one to overindulge. And I'm hoping some liquid courage will loosen him up a little before his father shows up.

"Sláinte." I raise my glass to clink with his.

He touches his glass to mine. "I didn't know you spoke Gaelic."

"That's the extent of my comprehension."

That coaxes a smile from him. I'm momentarily reassured, but then there's some sort of commotion in the bar, and his smile fades as quickly as it appeared.

I twist around, craning my neck. From my vantage point, I can't see what all the fuss is about, no matter how much I twist and crane. But I can hear the collective cheer that rises up, and the applause that follows.

I turn back to Connor. He's sitting across from me, looking like he wants to crawl under the table and die. "What do you suppose that is?"

"That would be my father," he says, his voice flat and resigned. "The reigning master of American crime fiction. If you don't believe me, ask the *New York Times Book Review*."

He takes a huge hit of his Bloody Mary. "He likes to make an entrance. Brace yourself."

I follow his example—to a degree—and sip my sangria. "How bad could it be?"

"You're about to find out."

He gestures behind me. I swivel around and see a man approaching us from the bar area. It doesn't take a rocket scientist to figure out he's Connor's dad. He's the spitting image of his son, albeit about thirty years older with a distinguished touch of gray in the dark hair at his temples and the beginnings of crow's feet around his eyes.

He's dressed in dark brown dress pants, a crisp white button down, and a tweed jacket, complete with patches on the elbows. If he threw on a bow tie, he could pass for Indiana Jones. Or Matt Smith's Dr. Who. Which I only know because Jake forced me to watch all forty of his episodes when we were snowed in one weekend last year.

"Sorry I'm late." Vincent Dow's words say one thing, but his flippant, I-don't-give-a-shit-about-anyone-but-myself attitude says something completely different. He slides into the seat opposite

Connor, not even bothering to shake his son's hand or, God forbid, hug him. "You know how it is. Everyone wants an autograph. Can't disappoint the fans."

Connor sets his glass down on the table with a hollow thunk. "But disappointing your family is okay."

Vincent ignores his son's dig and snaps his fingers to signal for a waitress, like King Tut summoning one of his servants. Then his gaze shifts to me, like he's noticing for the first time that he and Connor aren't alone at the table. "You didn't tell me you were bringing a friend."

"You remember Brie Lawson." Connor puts a protective—or is it possessive?—arm around my shoulder. "Jake's little sister."

Vincent's eyes drift down to my breasts, lingering long enough there make me feel a little icky before going back to my face. "Not so little anymore."

I'm pretty sure the waitress's timely arrival is the only thing that stops Connor from leaping across the table and strangling his father. She takes Vincent's drink order—bourbon, neat—and goes off giggling with his autograph on a napkin in her pocket.

"Still like them young, I see." Connor mutters.

I dig my nails into his thigh and give him a warning glare. We talked about this on the way over.

"Be the bigger man," I grind out through gritted teeth, reminding him of our conversation.

"How's Fiona?" he asks, prying my hand off his thigh. Oops. Guess I dug in deeper than I thought.

"She's fine. Sends her regards from the Hamptons." Vincent's drink arrives, and he takes it from the still giddy waitress with a flirtatious wink that makes her blush and me squirm.

Connor runs a finger around the rim of his glass. "She didn't come with you? I'm surprised she didn't jump at the chance to spend some of your money on Fifth Avenue."

"Bigger man," I grumble again.

But Vincent only shrugs. He's either completely clueless or so self-absorbed that insults bounce off him like rubber bullets.

"She stayed at the cottage. She had a tennis tournament or a garden club meeting or some other event she couldn't bear to miss."

Cottage, my ass. I'll bet my entire life savings—meager as it is, it's a lot to me—that what he calls a cottage is bigger than the White House.

"So, what should we order?" I ask, opening my menu. "I hear the huevos con chorizo is out of this world."

It's a cheap diversionary tactic, but it's the best I can come up with on the spot. Anything to cut down on the obvious father-son tension. Well, obvious to me. And Connor. Like I said, I think Vincent is oblivious.

It works for a while. We settle on an array of brunch and lunch dishes to share. The waitress comes back to take our order—cue another round of uncomfortable flirting—and then she's gone and the tension creeps back in.

"How often do you get into the city, Mr. Dow?"

"Why the hell did you ask to meet me today, Dad?"

Connor and I speak at the same time, but his father ignores both of our questions, opting for one of his own.

"I didn't know Connor was seeing anyone. How long have you two been dating?"

"We're not—"

"A few months," Connor blurts, cutting me off. "Which you'd know if you cared enough to be a real part of my life."

His arm tightens around my shoulders. If it wasn't possessive before, it is now. He gives me a side-eyed look that silently begs me to go along with him.

I squeeze his leg under the table to let him know that whatever he needs, I'm game. I came here to support him, and that's what I'm going to do. Even if I don't fully understand how pretending we're more than friends with benefits is going to improve his relationship with his father.

I move my hand from his thigh to his forearm, resting on the table. An open and obvious display of affection. "We're not really advertising it. But yes, we're together."

Connor punctuates my statement by leaning in and kissing me. It starts firm and forceful, like an exclamation point, but morphs into more of a semicolon, softer and sweeter, hinting of something yet to come.

As the kiss shifts, so does the world around me. Suddenly, the pretending feels all too real. Like there's actually a chance this undefined thing we're doing can evolve and grow into an actual, honest-to-goodness relationship.

A discrete cough forces Connor to lift his head. At first, I assume it came from his father, but the wait-ress is there with the first of our tapas plates, so it could have been her. Either way, whatever spell I'm under is broken. She sets the dishes down, promis-ing to return with the rest of our order and a fresh round of drinks.

Goodie. More alcohol. I can't decide if that's going to help or hurt.

Connor spoons some pan con tomato con jamón onto his plate—bread rubbed with tomato, garlic and olive oil, topped with Serrano ham, Manchego cheese and olives—then passes it to me so I can do the same. "Now that we've nailed down my relation-ship status, maybe you can tell me what we're doing here. I believe you mentioned something about find-ing a box of Mom's stuff."

"It's right here."

Vincent picks up a plastic container about the size of a shoebox from the seat next to him and hands it across the table to Connor. Did he have that when he came in? Obviously, he must have. But I swear, I didn't see it. Probably because I was too focused on how much he looks like his son.

Connor runs a hand over the top of the box, like he's thinking about cracking it open, then sets it down on the bench seat between us. "I've got to admit, I'm surprised. I assumed the whole box-from-mom thing was a bullshit excuse you used to lure me here."

Vincent pushes his glasses up his nose. Something else he has in common with his son, although Vincent wears thin, gold wire rims where Connor's frames are dark and heavy. "Well, there is something I wanted to tell you in person."

"Called it." The waitress drops off our drinks, and Connor immediately knocks back a good third of his Bloody Mary. "Let me guess. You and Fiona are getting divorced and you're moving on to wife number—what is it? Four? Five?"

A group of eager autograph seekers chooses that inopportune moment to approach our table. Vincent spends the next ten minutes soaking up their adulation and signing anything and everything put in front of him—napkins, take-out menus, even one woman's breast. Connor and I are left to sit in stunned silence watching the spectacle unfold, our presence—hell, our existence—seemingly forgotten.

"I'm sorry," Vincent says when his fan club finally leaves, even though it's clear from the way he's basking in the afterglow of their attention that he's not. "It's been this way ever since the studio announced that they're making a Dax Russell movie. All the publicity. I can't go anywhere without being recognized."

"Yeah, I'm sure you hate that," Connor mutters.

I frown over a forkful of daitles con beicon—dates stuffed with blue cheese and almonds and wrapped in bacon. They're proof that whoever coined the phrase "everything's better with bacon" is a freaking genius. "Dax Russell?"

"His alter ego," Connor explains. "The hero of all his novels."

"You haven't read any of my books?" Vincent asks. "*Try Dying*? *Grab And Smash*? *Drop Dead Fed*?"

From his tone, you'd think he was asking whether I'd ever heard of the Beatles. Or indoor plumbing. I shake my head. "Most of my reading is plays or scripts, with an occasional romance novel thrown in for pure pleasure."

"There's a bookstore on the next block. I could sign one for you when where done here."

"We have plans after lunch," Connor lies, spearing a bacon-wrapped date with his fork and popping it into his mouth. "What's so important you couldn't tell me over the phone?"

"Fiona is pregnant." Vincent leans back and sips his bourbon, looking like the poster child for masculine pride. I wouldn't be surprised if the next words out of his mouth were to brag about his super swimmers. "You're going to have a little brother."

"Half-brother," Connor corrects him.

Vincent lowers his glass. "You could at least congratulate me."

"Congratulations. I hope you'll be a better parent this time. Maybe start by not cheating on his mother."

Vincent's jaw twitches and his eyes narrow into angry slits. If I didn't understand the expression if looks could kill before, I do now. "I hope he'll be a better son instead of a complete disappointment."

Oh. No. He. Didn't.

Connor's fork clatters to the floor and he grips the edge of the table so hard I can see the whites of his knuckles. I shove my plate away, my appetite gone even for food made better by bacon.

"A disappointment? Are you kidding me?" I'm loud enough that even from our booth in the back people can hear me, and I can sense that they're starting to stare. But I'm past caring. Connor may be too polite to cause a scene, but I'm not.

"You have no idea of the kind of man your son is, do you? He's smart and funny and thoughtful and kind." I count them off on my fingers as I go. "He's been a good friend to my brother for over twenty years. He let me stay with him when I had nowhere else to go. Plus, he's a hugely successful businessman. I think you'd at least respect that. Did you know his club is one of the most sought-after hot spots in New York City? And they're in the middle of a major renovation, adding another VIP section and a screening room for first-run movies and live-streamed concerts. When that's done, it will be even harder to get into."

I stop to catch my breath and get a glimpse of Connor out of the corner of my eye. He's released his white-knuckle grip on the table and the grim set of his mouth is gone, replaced by a bemused smile.

He stands, grabbing my hand and pulling me to my feet. Then he throws a wad of bills down in front of his father. "That should more than cover lunch. Tell Fiona I'll send something for the baby."

Without giving his father a chance to respond, he heads for the exit, dragging me along with him. We're almost out the door before I remember something.

"Wait." I stop, forcing him to stop with me. "Stay here. I'll be right back."

His brows knotted. "Did you forget something?"

"No, but you did."

I race back to our table. Vincent is still there, knocking back what's left of his bourbon. So is the box of stuff that belonged to Connor's mom, right where he left it under his chair.

"Did you come back to lecture me some more?" Vincent asks.

"No. I think I made my point. I came back for this." I bend down and scoop up the box.

He raises his empty glass to let a passing waiter know he's ready for round number three. Two too many, in my not-so-humble opinion. "Connor was always a bit of a mama's boy."

Mama's boy? Vincent Dow may be Connor's father, but he really has no clue who his son is. "Maybe that's because she didn't see him as a—what was it? Oh, yes. Complete disappointment."

"I thought you were done lecturing me."

Oh, I'm done, all right. I've had enough of this asshat and his monster ego to last ten lifetimes. I tuck the box under my arm and make my escape, tossing one last jab over my shoulder as I go.

"I guess I had a little left in me after all."

CHAPTER ELEVEN

Connor

"PLEASE TELL ME you went back there and kneed my father in the nuts," I say to Brie when she catches up to me outside the restaurant. "No, wait. Don't tell me. Because if you did and I missed it, I'll never forgive myself."

"Don't worry, you didn't miss anything. Nothing physical, anyway. Although I admit, I was tempted to throw a drink in his face. Lucky for him, the waitress already cleared the table."

She produces something from behind her back. It takes me a second to realize it's the box with my mom's things. "You left this behind. I figured you'd want it once you calmed down."

My heart stops for a second, then thumps harder. This woman never ceases to amaze me. All I wanted was to get the fuck away from my father as fast as humanly possible. In that moment, nothing else mattered. Not even what might be my one and only chance to have mementos of my mother.

Trust Brie to have my back.

She hands me the box, and I stick it under one arm so I can use the other hand to tip her chin and kiss her. "Thank you."

"Your father's even worse than I remembered. I'm sorry I made you made you do this."

"First, you didn't make me do anything. And second, I'm not sorry we came."

"Because you got your mom's stuff?"

"That. And because if we hadn't come, I wouldn't have had the pleasure of watching you take down the great Vincent Dow." I push her hair off her face and kiss her again. "That was the hottest thing I've ever seen."

She grins up at me. "So me going off on your father turns you on?"

"Honestly, pretty much anything you do turns me on." I step in closer to her so our bodies are touching. Barely, but touching. It has the double benefit of making it easier to hear me when I lower my voice and let her feel the physical evidence of my arousal. "But I've never wanted to fuck you more than I do right now."

My phone buzzes—thanks for the fabulous timing, universe—with a notification that the Lyft I called while Brie was not throwing a drink at my father is here. I spot a black Volvo XC90 pulling up to the curb and quickly confirm that the make, model, and license plate match the information in the app.

"This is our ride," I say, leading Brie over to the car and opening the door.

She slides into the back seat. "I thought you said we had plans after lunch."

"We do." I take a second to appreciate the flash of upper thigh as she adjusts her short skirt then climb in after her, pulling the door closed behind me and setting the box down at my feet. "They involve you and me getting naked as soon as possible."

Our Lyft driver, a silver-haired, middle-aged woman who the app says is named Linda, turns around and glares at us. "Not in my car, you don't."

Brie meets her glare with a smile designed to charm the surliest of rideshare operators. "It's okay. I'm sure I can hold him off until we get home."

"You'd better," Linda snaps, unmoved. "Because I won't hesitate to kick your bare asses out in the middle of 7th Avenue. And there's a hundred-and-fifty-dollar surcharge for cleaning up bodily fluids."

I nod. "Duly noted."

Apparently satisfied we're not going to hump like jackrabbits in the back of her car, she turns around and pulls away from the curb. The sudden motion puts Brie off balance, jostling her against me. I sling my arm around her and gather her in.

"Did I tell you how hot you were standing up to my father?" I whisper the words in her ear, not willing to incur the wrath of Linda and risk getting tossed out of the car in the middle of Sunday matinee traffic. I bet she wouldn't even bother to slow down.

"You did." Brie's purse slips down her arm, and she lets it fall to the seat beside her. "But I don't mind hearing it again."

"And that no one's done that for me in a long time? I think the last person was your brother, back in high school. And he wasn't anywhere near as sexy as you."

Brie lets out a snort that would be unladylike in other circumstances but she somehow makes endearing. "I'd be worried if you thought he was."

She takes my head in her hands and pulls me down to her, planting the mother of all kisses on my lips. You know that final kiss in *The Princess Bride*? The one that left the five most passionate, most pure kisses behind? This kiss makes that one look like a peck on the cheek.

Linda shoots us a warning glance in the rear-view mirror but keeps driving. We reluctantly pull apart, managing to keep it PG—okay, PG-13—for the rest of the fortunately short ride.

But the second the doors of the elevator to my penthouse apartment close behind us, all bets are off. With the box in one hand, I'm at a slight disadvantage. But I do the best I can with the one I've got free, fisting her blouse and yanking it from her waistband.

She bats my hand away. "I am not getting naked in this elevator."

I advance on her, backing her up against the wall

of the elevator, my palm flat on the glass above her head. "How about half naked?"

"We'll be in your apartment in like thirty seconds."

"That's thirty damn seconds too long."

I lower my head to kiss her, but the elevator dings and the doors slide open.

"Saved by the bell." She ducks out from under my arm and strolls through the doors into the hallway. "Literally."

"Not for long," I say, my eyes tracking the sexy back and forth of her ass as I follow her out of the elevator. "As soon as we're inside that apartment, you're mine."

She steps to the side so I can put my key in the lock. "I'm counting on it."

The lock clicks, and I push the door open. She breezes past me, dropping her purse then her denim jacket then unzipping and stepping out of her skirt. Like Gretl leaving a trail of breadcrumbs.

I dump the box on the kitchen island and follow the trail to down the hall to my bedroom. She's reclining on the bed, her long, bare legs stretched out in front of her, her candy apple red five-inch heels that scream "fuck me" still on her feet. As I cross toward her, she kicks the shoes off and starts to unbutton her shirt.

"Stop."

"Why?" She undoes another button, and her shirt falls open. "I thought you wanted me naked."

She's wearing a lacy lavender bra that matches

her panties and makes her tits look fantastic, and for a split second I consider joining her on the bed. But I have other plans for her. "I do. But not there."

"Then where?"

"Stand up. Shirt off." My eyes flick to her do-me heels, discarded on the floor. "And put the shoes back on."

She follows my instructions, a damn goddess in her lacy lingerie and sexy stilettos. I lead her to the wall of windows overlooking the street below and the Hudson River beyond.

Her eyes widen to greenish-gold saucers. "Here?"

The corners of my mouth twitch. "Worried someone will see us?"

"Are you?" she asks, one delicately arched brow lifting.

"We're on the twelfth floor. The chance of any pedestrians looking up here is slim."

She bites her lip and stares out the windows, her gaze going left then right. "What about the people in the building across the street?"

"It's only seven stories, so we're a little higher than they are. But I suppose someone could still see us." I press my hand gently into her lower back, urging her toward the glass. "Does that bother you? Or excite you?"

"A bit of both, I guess." My hand slides down, settling on the sweet curve of her ass, and she shivers. "Isn't that what makes it so hot? The sense of urgency. The risk of getting caught."

Fuck, this woman. She makes me want things—
do things—that are totally out of my comfort zone.
Things I've never contemplated—much less done—
with any other woman. Like semi-public window sex.

If I think too much about the psychology of it,
it'll freak me out. Me, Connor Dow, abhorrer of attention, shunner of the spotlight, fornicating in plain
view of all of lower Manhattan.

So I don't think about it. And I don't answer her
question. Not with words, anyway. Instead, I let my
hands do the talking. One grabs her wrists and pins
her arms above her head, palms flat against the glass.
The other slips under the edge of her panties, my
index finger grazing her clit.

"Jesus Christ, you're wet," I growl. "You weren't
kidding when you said the thought of getting caught
excites you."

"I never kid about sex." She arches her back, begging me without words to penetrate her. "Or what
makes me feel good."

"Does this make you feel good?"

I push my finger inside her, and she moans. Her
hot breath forms a steamy circle on the window, and
I can feel sweat beading at my brow even though
my thermostat is permanently set to a comfortably
chilly sixty-two.

"How about this?"

I add a second finger and bend down to nip her
shoulder. She sucks in a ragged breath and closes her
eyes, resting her forehead on the glass.

"I'll take that as a yes."

She moans again, and that's all the encouragement I need to go further. I kick at her feet in those fuck-me pumps, nudging them apart.

"Open your eyes," I demand.

"What if I don't want to?" she asks, eyes still closed.

I withdraw my fingers. "Then I won't let you come."

"Bastard," she hisses. But her eyes open and she lifts her head off the window.

"That's better." I grab the thin lace of her tiny panties and tear them off in one quick move, the sound of ripping fabric echoing in my cavernous bedroom.

"Hey," she protests even as her breathing quickens and she widens her stance. "I liked those."

"So did I."

"You could have asked me to take them off."

"I could have. But I didn't want to wait that long." She sighs as my hand returns between her legs, my fingers pushing into her again. "I'll buy you a new pair. Hell, I'll buy you a hundred new pairs."

"What do I need a hundred pairs of underwear for? Unless you're going to keep tearing them off me."

"Better make it two hundred."

"They're not cheap, you know. I have expensive taste in lingerie. It's my one indulgence."

"Then it's a good thing I'm filthy rich." I suck her earlobe between my teeth and bite down. Not hard, just enough to draw out a sexy little gasp from her pouty lips. "Now stop complaining so I can make you come."

She wiggles her ass, pushing back against me, fucking my fingers. I can see her seductive smile reflected in the glass, and her next words make my answering grin even broader and my dick impossibly harder.

"As you wish."

CHAPTER TWELVE

Brie

WHO IS THIS GUY?

I know who he is, obviously. I'm not in the habit of having sex with strangers. But the man pinning me to the window, torturing me with his fingers as Manhattan continues to go about its daily business below us, is not the man I've been living with for the past month.

Sure, that guy likes to take charge in the bedroom. And his dirty talk is off the charts. But this? This is next level alpha male. He's bold. Daring. Reckless.

And if he doesn't quit dicking around and make me come soon, I'm going to end him.

"Quit teasing me. What happened to making me come?"

I grind against his fingers, desperate for release. He, of course, pulls them out ever so slightly, enough that he's no longer hitting my g-spot.

Fucking tease.

"I'm getting there," he says, his fingers withdrawing even further, belying his words.

"Get there faster." I press my palms against the window, using it for leverage as I continue my bump and grind, trying to force his fingers back inside me. If he's not going to fuck me, dammit, then I'm going to fuck him.

A low, sexy noise comes from deep in his throat, and he ducks his head to nip my shoulder. "The build-up is half the fun. The sexual tension. The delayed gratification. The anticipation."

"Says the person doing the teasing. It's agony for the one being teased."

He nips me again, right at the hollow where my shoulder meets my neck. What's with him and the biting? Not that I'm complaining. It's hot AF.

"Trust me. It'll be worth it."

Trust him. It scares me, but I do. I trust him enough to fuck him where anyone could see. To relinquish control of my orgasm to his talented fingers.

To be careful with my heart and not break it.

Wait, what? Where did that thought come from? My heart has nothing to with this. This is about scratching an itch. Friends with benefits. Not happily ever after.

Right?

I groan and let my head drop to my chest. My eyelids flutter shut and my forehead bangs against the glass. "You'd better not leave any marks. I have to

be on set tomorrow, and I'll never hear the end of it
from the makeup artist who has to cover them up."

His free hand, which was around my waist, comes
up to tug on my hair, jerking my head back. "Eyes
open, remember?"

Damn him.

I force my lids open and turn my head to look
at him over my shoulder. His shirt is unbuttoned—
when did that happen?—his face is flushed, and his
whiskey-brown eyes are clouded over with passion.
A thin line of sweat dampens his brow, and if I'm
not mistaken, his dick is about to bust through the
zipper of his jeans.

"Please." I'm barely able to breathe, so the word
comes out as a whisper.

His fingers start moving again, going deeper this
time as his thumb dances across my clit. He strums
me like a master, finding all my hot buttons and applying the perfect amount of pressure, bringing me closer
and closer to the edge with every stroke, every thrust.

"Look down," he murmurs, his breath fanning
the hair at my temple. "Do you want them to see
you come?"

My only response is a groan, my mouth no longer
able to form coherent speech. He kisses my shoulder,
my neck, the sensitive spot behind my ear. When his
lips part and he and sinks his teeth into my skin, a
shiver rolls through me. It travels down my spine,
swirls around my hips, and settles between my legs,
making me jolt back into him.

My orgasm slams into me like a tsunami, my body shaking and my hands smacking the glass. When it's over, I'm left gasping for air, trapped between the heat of Connor's ripped body and the cool, smooth window. The contrast is both electrifying and unnerving.

"You okay?" he asks.

I can feel his smile against the nape of my neck. Arrogant jerk. He knows damned well he wrecked me.

"You killed me," I admit between hoarse, shallow gasps. "I'm dead."

"The French don't call it *la petite mort* for nothing."

He takes me by the shoulders, turning me around to face him, and I study him through lust-glazed eyes.

"This is starting to become a pattern."

He frowns down at me. "What is?"

"Me naked—or almost naked—and you still clothed."

His already self-satisfied smile gets even more smug. "Feel free to do something about that."

He releases my shoulders and takes a step back, spreading his arms wide as if to say "have at me." I wobble a little, still feeling the aftereffects of the orgasm to end all orgasms, before recovering and going straight for his zipper.

I palm him through his pants, deciding to let him suffer a little before freeing him. He's heavy and long and mouthwatering. Christ, I'm practically salivating. It's not fair, dammit. I'm suffering as much as he is.

Not able to hold off any longer, I slip the button at his waistband through its hole and sink to my knees, taking his zipper down with me. His pants and boxer briefs go next. It's a joint effort. I push them over his trim hips and down his muscular legs. He kicks them off along with his shoes and socks.

Holy. Hot. Damn. Yeah, I've seen his dick before. But that doesn't stop it from having its usual effect on me. He's already erect, undulating proudly in a way that's almost hypnotizing. A bead of pre-cum hangs from the tip, seemingly defying gravity.

"Come to mama," I murmur, taking his impressive length in my hand and trying—but failing—to wrap my fingers around it.

There's no closing my eyes this time as I guide him to my mouth. I tease the head with my thumb before taking him inside. I'm afraid I'll never get enough of this. The taste of his warm, clean flesh. The naughty things he whispers as I take him deep into the back of my throat.

"Fuck, yes." His head falls back, eyes closed.

I run my tongue down his length before releasing him with a soft pop.

"Eyes open, remember?" I say, taunting him with his own words.

He grumbles but complies. I put my mouth on him again, and he looks down through sinfully long lashes that any woman would kill for, watching his cock as it slides in and out, again and again. One hand tangles itself in my hair, anchoring me. Or maybe it's him he's trying to keep steady.

I concentrate on taking him as deep as my throat will allow. My jaw aches and my eyes water, but none of that matters. My mind has one track, and right now it's fixed on making this the best fucking blow job Connor's ever had. Something he'll remember long after this thing between us has run its course and we've gone our separate ways.

His body tenses and his breathing gets increasingly erratic, signaling that he's about to come. When he does, it's explosive, and I swallow every drop, continuing to suck on him even as his cock softens and his grip on my hair loosens. Eventually, he drags me off him, groaning when my tongue comes out to lick my lips.

"Holy fuck." He rakes a shaky hand through his sweat-slicked hair. "That was—"

"Hot as hell," I finish for him, sitting back on my heels.

His head turns slowly toward the glass wall, like he's just remembering where we are. That anyone can see us. Then he reaches down and hauls me to my feet, pulling me away from the windows.

"I think lower Manhattan's had enough of a show." He tilts my face up so our eyes meet. I expect to see desire there, but instead there's something deeper. More profound. And infinitely more frightening. "I want this next part to be just between us."

I release my lip—which I wasn't even aware I was biting—from between my teeth and exhale. "Next part?"

"You didn't think we were done, did you?" He grabs me by the waist and lifts me up like I weigh next to nothing. "We're just getting started."

He deposits me on the bed, taking a foil packet from the nightstand drawer and tossing it onto the comforter before joining me. His dick is already starting to get hard again—he really does have the most amazing restorative powers—and it pulses against my hip.

I grin and spread my arms over my head, knowing from experience how incredible it's going to feel when he's inside me. Filling me. Stretching me.

He props himself up on his elbow, smiling back at me, flashing that damn dimple, the one that never fails to make my heart go pitter-patter. "Give me ten minutes, and I'll be good to go."

But it doesn't take ten minutes. It doesn't even take five once he starts moving against me, rubbing his cock on my thigh in slow, tantalizing strokes.

"I like this." He fingers the delicate strap of my bra then slides it over my shoulder, following its path down my arm with his finger.

A familiar tingling sensation builds between my legs. Because he ran his finger down my forearm. But who am I kidding? He looks at me sideways and I'm turned on.

"If I say I like it too, are you going to rip it off?

Because I'm warning you, my bras are even more pricey than my panties."

"I'm pretty sure I can afford to replace it." He reaches underneath me to unhook the clasp. "But don't worry. I'll take it off the conventional way. This time."

He does, and we're both finally, blissfully, totally naked. One hand cups my breast as the other reaches around for the condom he dropped on the bed earlier. He finds it and is tearing it open when I put a hand on his forearm, stopping him.

"It's okay if you don't want to. I'm on the pill. I'm clean. And I trust you."

If I didn't already realize the import of my words, the expression on his face would be a huge tip-off. His smile is slow and dreamy, and his eyes go all soft and gooey, like chocolate ice cream left out in the sun.

"Are you sure?"

I nod. We've never had sex without a condom. Truth be told, I've never let anyone fuck me bareback. But this isn't anyone. This is Connor.

He chucks the condom onto the nightstand and glides into me, nice and easy, inch by inch. I plant my feet on the bed and arch into him, willing him to go deeper, faster, harder.

But he doesn't take the bait. It's clear he wants to take his time. Savor every touch, every kiss, every sweet slide of his thick cock into my wet heat.

"Is this what you wanted?" he asks, sinking deeper

until his firm, flat stomach is resting on my softer, rounder one. His eyes are inches from mine, his nose practically touching my own and our breath commingling in the small space between us.

"Yes." Without a condom, each sensation is a little warmer, a little more intense. And a lot more pleasurable. Which is really saying something, because it was pretty damn pleasurable before. "You feel fantastic."

He nuzzles my ear. "So do you."

His twines his fingers with mine, securing them over my head. Then he starts to move, rolling his hips, grinding us together then pulling us apart.

Our breathing and the rhythmic slapping of our bodies coming together, backed by the distant rumble of traffic twelve stories below, are the only sounds in the room until we both cry out, clinging to each other as hard shudders wrack through us. When the spasms pass, we stay locked together, his dick still buried inside me, our heartbeats slowing in tandem.

It's intimate and tender and emotionally vulnerable, and I understand why Connor didn't want anyone else to see it. Because what just happened—that wasn't fucking.

That was making love.

CHAPTER THIRTEEN

Brie

"WHY DID I let you convince me to take this class?" I grumble to Ainsley as we climb off our stationary bikes. Her more gracefully than me. She looks like she stepped straight out of the pages of *Women's Health*. Her hair is still securely fastened in a tight ponytail, and if she's sweating at all, it's more of a healthy glow than a full-on drenching. What's that old saying? A lady doesn't sweat, she perspires.

I, in contrast, am clearly no lady. I feel like I'm about to drown. Rivers of sweat are running down my face, my T-shirt is plastered to my skin, and there's not a muscle in my body that doesn't ache. I don't dare look in any of the full-length mirrors we pass on our way to the locker room, but I'm pretty sure if I did, I'd see something that looks more like the Creature from the Black Lagoon than a fitness model.

Ainsley takes the towel from around her neck and dabs at a non-existent pool of perspiration at her throat. "Because we haven't seen each other in weeks, and you miss me."

She's right. We haven't. And I do miss her. She may be my brother's fiancée, but she was my friend first.

We reach the locker room, and I pull the door open. All the muscles from my wrist to my shoulder scream in protest. "I hate this instructor. I swear, he's Satan. Who uses dumbbells in a spin class?"

"Are you kidding? Karl is one of the most popular instructors here. His classes are always full. We were lucky to get in."

"You call it luck. I call it masochism." I used to be a regular at RPM—Ainsley and I met in a spin class—but my schedule's been so swamped I haven't been to the studio in weeks. Jumping back in with one of Karl's torture sessions was definitely not one of my smartest decisions. "Couldn't we have met for coffee or something? Drinks at Tammany Hall?"

Since Ainsley and her friend Mia introduced me to it, the tacky, unassuming dive bar in the heart of Greenwich Village has become one of my favorite places to grab a drink or watch a ballgame. Not that I've had time to do much of either since I started filming.

"We could head over there now," she suggests. We're at our lockers. She spins the dial on her combination lock, opens the door, and takes a sip from her water bottle before putting it inside. "It's still happy hour for another hour and a half. Unless you've got someone to run home to."

I swat her with the towel I've just taken from my locker. "Shut up. You know I'm living with Connor."

"My point exactly. Wasn't that supposed to be temporary? It's been—what? Three months?"

"Two," I correct her.

"Still sounds more than temporary to me."

"It's hard to find affordable housing in this town."

Even harder when you've all but stopped looking. It's not something Connor and I actually discussed. It just sort of happened. He hasn't said anything about me leaving. And it's not like I'm in any hurry to go anywhere. Not with him in my bed every night. Or me in his.

The only problem is that the longer we do whatever it is we're doing, the more I'm falling for him. He's not just my brother's super sexy best friend any more. He's the guy who brings me coffee in the morning, or sets up the Keurig for me the night before when I have an early call time. Texts me funny memes and cat videos. Lets me control the remote when we're Netflix and chilling.

Ainsley closes her locker door with a metallic clang that jolts my thoughts away from my roommate/bedmate/boyfriend and back to present company. "If money's the issue, I'm sure Jake would help you out. All you have to do is ask."

"I'm sure he would, too." I sit down on the long wooden bench and strip off my sweaty T-shirt, leaving me in my equally sweaty sports bra. "But I'm not asking. This is something I need to handle myself."

"Have it your way," she says, sitting down beside me. "But I wouldn't blame you if you wanted to drag things out a little."

"Why would I want to do that?" I ask, feigning innocence.

"Hello, McFly. Have you looked at your room-mate? He's an eleven on a scale of one to ten. Maybe a twelve."

I make a face at her. "Have you forgotten that you're engaged to my brother?"

"I may be engaged, but I'm not blind. And nei-ther are you. You can't seriously expect me to be-lieve that you haven't tried to sneak a peek when he's in the shower."

"Um, no. That's super stalker-y. And totally inap-propriate. Besides, we're more like two ships pass-ing," I lie. "Connor's place is so big, we could go weeks without seeing each other."

We could. But we don't. Not that I'm admitting that to Ainsley.

At some point, we'll have to come clean with her and Jake. Maybe. But today is not that point. I'm not having that discussion with her until I've had one with Connor.

I toss my T-shirt over my shoulder and stand. "If we want to make happy hour, we'd better quit yak-king and hit the showers."

She stands with me, pulling out her ponytail and shaking out her shoulder-length blond hair. "Fine. But don't think I'm done grilling you about Connor."

I roll my eyes and slam my locker shut. "Heaven forbid."

We shower, change, and make it to the bar in time to order a round before happy hour ends. Ainsley goes for something fruity and frothy with a cherry on top and one of those paper drink umbrellas. I stick to one of the craft beers on tap. No cherry. No umbrella.

We find a table in the corner, under the watchful gaze of a taxidermy deer head—Ainsley likes to describe this place as a cross between a bordello and a hunting cabin—and I slide into the red-velvet-covered booth. Ainsley slides in across from me.

"Jake and I have a bet." She takes the umbrella from her drink and twirls it between her fingers.

"What kind of bet?" I ask, even though I'm pretty sure I don't want to know.

"He thinks you and Connor are at each other's throats. And I say you're in each other's pants."

It takes every ounce of self-control I've got not to pluck the stupid umbrella right out of her hand and stab her with it. "We are done talking about me and Connor."

"Ah ha." Ainsley jabs the pointy end of the umbrella at me. I knew I should have taken it from her when I had the chance. The girl is lethal with sharp objects. "So you're admitting there's a you and Connor."

"I admit nothing."

I'm at least temporarily spared from Ainsley's version of the Spanish Inquisition by my phone, which chimes from somewhere deep inside my purse. I'm expecting a text with my call time for tomorrow, so I fish it out and check the screen.

Unfortunately, it's not from Drew, the second A.D who's responsible for doing the call sheet. It's an alert from my credit card company, reminding me that my payment is due.

I delete the message and leave the phone face up on the table, where I can see it when Drew finally texts. If my call time is before eight, I'm going to have to cut this short. I don't want to show up on set late, or even worse, hung over.

"All right, if Connor's off limits, how about we talk about my wedding?" Ainsley puts the umbrella down and takes a sip of her drink. "I've been trying to get you to go dress shopping with me for weeks."

"I know. I'm sorry. I've just been so busy filming." *And totally tapping your fiancé's—my brother's—best friend.* "But I promise, my next day off I'm all yours."

My phone chimes again, but this time it's a call, not a text. And it's not from Drew, it's from Connor. His name flashes across the screen, along with the photo I saved as his contact picture. A selfie I took of us snuggling on the couch, watching yet another one of the Marvel movies in my quest to get into butt-kicking character.

At the time, it seemed harmless. Innocent. But looking at it now, it screams intimacy. The way my head is resting on his shoulder. His arm around me, hand casually brushing the curve of my breast.

Shit shit shit shit shit.

I scramble to silence my phone and flip it over so it's face down on the table, but not before Ainsley sees the picture and snorts.

"Two ships passing, huh?" She sits back smugly and crosses her arms. "You two sure seem pretty cozy to me."

"It's not what it looks like," I hedge.

But Ainsley's not buying it for a second. She points a finger at me. Bet she wishes she was still holding that stupid umbrella. "Don't bullshit a bullshitter. I know two people in love when I see it."

I almost choke on my beer. "Who said anything about love?"

"Lust then." She digs her phone out of her purse, swipes the screen, and starts tapping away.

"What are you doing?"

"Texting Jake. I won the bet. He owes me fifty bucks."

"Wait," I shout so loud the people at the next table turn and stare at us. I shoot them a mind-your-own-business glare, lower my voice, and lean in, resting my elbows on the table. "Please."

Ainsley's finger freezes, and she raises her gaze from her phone to study me. "Are you telling me I didn't win the bet? Because if you are, I call BS."

I slowly sip my beer, stalling for time while I debate what to say next. Do I keep lying to her? Or drop the performance, which apparently isn't winning any Academy Awards—so much for my acting skills—and admit that Connor's putting his wand in my chamber of secrets on a regular basis?

She tilts her head and smirks at me, her finger hovering over the screen of her phone. "You've got ten seconds before I hit send."

I set my beer down on the table with more force than necessary. Amber liquid sloshes out of the glass and onto my hand, but that's the least of my concerns. My best friend is about to tell my brother that I'm messing around with his best friend and business partner. It's like an episode of *Empire*.

"What happened to sisters before misters? Chicks before dicks? Besties before testes?"

"Nine, eight, seven—"

"I don't want my brother to find out like this," I blurt out, the tacit admission the quickest way I can think of to stop her from tapping the little blue arrow that sends her text through cyberspace to Jake. "It should be me that tells him. Or Connor."

She hesitates for a second, then swipes the screen and puts the phone back in her purse. "Fair enough."

I breathe a sigh of relief. That was close. Too close. "I can't believe you'd out us to my brother. I know you're marrying him, but I met you first. And you wouldn't even be with him if I hadn't hired you to help take care of Roscoe."

She gets a dreamy look in her eyes and her lips quirk into a wistful smile. "For which I'm eternally grateful to you and that big, lovable doofus. The dog, I mean. Not your brother. I don't know what I would have done if your parents hadn't decided to leave him with us after the cruise."

"If you're so grateful, how could you threaten to tell Jake I'm sleeping with his best friend?" I ask.

The dreamy look vanishes as quickly as it appeared, replaced by cool, clear calculation. "That's just it. I threatened. I never really intended to go through with it. I knew you'd fold like an ironing board."

"Who even uses an ironing board anymore?" I grumble.

"My grandmother," she answers quickly. "And my mother. Not that you'll catch me using one. That's what dry cleaners are for. But you're missing the point."

"Which is?"

"I threatened. You caved and confessed in a desperate attempt to stop me from spilling the beans to Jake. Just like I knew you would."

Dammit, she's right. I shake my head at her. "You're diabolical, you know that? The CIA should use you as an alternative to waterboarding."

"Thank you," she says, spreading her arms wide and doing a little mock bow.

"That wasn't supposed to be a compliment."

"Sounded like one to me."

I shrug and reach for my beer. "Have it your way."

My phone dings for a third time, diverting my

hand from my glass. I guess the third time really is the charm because it's Drew—finally—with my ass-crack-of-dawn call time.

I throw the phone into my purse, toss back the rest of my beer, and stand. "I hate to cut this short, but I've got to run. Early call time tomorrow. I'll text you with my schedule and we can figure out the dress shopping thing."

"Sounds like a plan." She stands and hugs me. "For what it's worth, I'm happy for you guys. I think you're a great couple, no matter what Jake says."

I'm torn. Half of me wants to scream that we're not officially a couple. The other half is ready to do battle with my brother over his objections, whatever they are, even though he's miles away. He takes the whole overprotective thing to a new level.

"What does Jake say?" I ask, option for a neutral approach.

Ainsley bites her lip, clearly regretting having brought the subject up in the first place. "I'm sure he'll make his feelings known when you tell him the big news. But one of you better do it soon. Because you know how hard it is for me to keep my mouth shut."

My stomach drops. I thought I'd bought us a little more time. "Don't worry. We'll take care of it."

"Good. I'd hate to let something accidentally slip when Jake and I are—"

I hold up a hand. "Stop. I beg you."

She raises an eyebrow. "I was going to say when we're playing Scrabble."

I roll my eyes. "Sure you were."

We laugh as we say our goodbyes, but inside I'm a mess. Because having to tell Jake means I have to let Connor know that our secret's not a secret anymore.

And the truth is, I'm not exactly sure how he's going to react.

CHAPTER FOURTEEN

Connor

"What are you still doing here?"

I look up from my computer to see Jake lounging in the doorway of my office. My eyes flick to the clock on my screen, then back to him. "What are you talking about? It's barely seven. That's not late."

"For the old, Connor, yes. The one who lived at the office until well past dinnertime. But not the new Connor, the one who's been hightailing it out of here before the sun sets for the past few weeks."

Fuck. I thought I'd been pretty stealth, sneaking off to spend nights with Brie when she's not working. Tonight, she's having some girl time with Ainsley, so I figured I might as well stay at the office and get some work done. Now I wish I had stuck to my original plan and gone home, even if it was to an empty apartment.

Funny, it never used to feel empty, even before Giselle moved in with me. I'm the kind of guy who

has always valued what my mom called "alone time."
I like my own company. All I need is a good book
on my e-reader or a half-way decent documentary
on TV, and I'm good to go.

Or I was. But now, the thought of spending the
night in my monstrosity of an apartment without
my roommate seems worse than having a root canal
without Novocain.

"Ainsley thinks it's because you've got a new girlfriend," my annoyingly persistent best friend continues, pushing off the door frame, plopping his ass in
a guest chair, and propping his feet up on my desk.

*Got it in one. Question is, she does have any theo-
ries on who the lady in question might be? And has
she shared them with Jake?*

I loosen my tie and undo the first couple of buttons on my dress shirt. When did it go so damn hot
in here? I'm suffocating. "Ainsley needs to mind her
own business."

"If you can get her to do that, do me a favor and
tell me how." His toothy grin takes the sting out of
his words. The guy is completely whipped. And loving it. "My fiancée is very strong-willed."

"You can say that again." I push his feet off my
desk and shut down my computer. No use pretending like I can concentrate on work now. Not when
Jake may or may not suspect that I'm fooling around
with his baby sister.

"So is it true?" He leans forward, elbows on his

knees. "Are you seeing someone? How long has it been going on? Have you slept with her yet?"

"What are we, teenage girls? Are we going to do each other's hair and paint our nails next?"

"We're evolved men, comfortable discussing our thoughts and feelings." He waggles his eyebrows suggestively. "And our women."

Uh, yeah. Pretty sure you don't want the deets on all the ways and places I've screwed your sister.

"Does this look like the locker room at the Y?"

I gesture around my tastefully decorated office, worthy of a spread in *Architectural Digest*. My eyes land on a framed photo of my mom and me on the bookshelf.

It's a new addition. One of the ones in the box Brie rescued from my father. I'm about seven or eight and we're at the beach, probably someplace in the Hamptons, splashing in the surf wearing matching swimsuits and broad smiles. Similar to the grin splitting my face now at the memory of how Brie surprised me by framing the photo and sneaking it into my briefcase one morning before I left for work.

Jake leans over my desk, lifts one of the silver balls on my Newton's cradle, and lets it fall, starting the chain of balls in motion. "Dunno. Haven't been to the Y in years. Not since I installed my home gym."

I grab the Newton's cradle and stop it, the rhythmic click-clicking already driving me crazy. "You know what I mean. I'm not giving you a blow-by-blow of my sex life."

"No one asked for a blow-by-blow. I'd settle for who's the girl and when did it start."

"You're not getting that, either."

"Since when? We've shared that kind of stuff since we were in middle school."

Since the who is your sister and the when is when hell freezes over, as in I'll answer your questions when hell freezes over.

I snag my mug off the desk blotter and drain the cold dregs of my afternoon coffee. "You did. I didn't even date until tenth grade. And it's not like there was all that much for me to talk about."

He shrugs and stands. "Be that way. But I'm warning you. Ainsley's a woman on a mission. And she has a way of making people talk."

"Thanks for tipping me off."

Jake leaves, and I lean back in my chair, tipping my head back to stare contemplatively at the ceiling. I'd be lying if I said I wasn't more than a little unsettled by our conversation. I'm tired of hiding. Tired of sneaking around. I want to man up and tell Jake about my relationship with his sister. We're two consenting adults. There's absolutely nothing wrong with us having a little fun together.

And maybe more than a little fun. Yeah, we've only been together for a couple of months. And no, our differences haven't magically disappeared. She's still the glittery, sparkly star attraction. I'm content waiting in the wings. But despite those differences, being with her feels right. It feels good. There's window-rattling, mind-blowing, off-the-charts sex, sure. But there's also easy laughter and casual touches and a comfortable, uncomplicated friendship I haven't had with any other woman I've been intimate with.

Before I spill my guts about any of this to Jake, I need to talk to Brie. I'm not going public unless she's fully on board. And it would be nice to know if she—like me—wants more than a short and steamy fling.

I sit up straight and grab my cell phone off my desk. I go to my recent calls and find her number—near the top, of course—but I stop myself before I hit send, remembering that she's still with Ainsley, doing whatever it is women do when they get together. I don't want to interrupt their female bonding time. What I have to say to Brie can wait a few hours.

I'm about to stash my cell in my back pocket and pack up my things to head home when it rings. A quick look at the screen tells me it's Brie. Guess I won't have to wait to talk to her after all. Although the more I think about it, the less I'm sure this is a discussion we should be having over the phone.

"Houston, we have a problem," she says when I pick up.

I drop the file I've been working on into my briefcase and sit back down in my desk chair, spinning it around so I'm looking out the window at midtown. I love this time of day, when the sun has set and the city lights are coming to life.

"You and Ainsley get yourselves in trouble? Do I need to bring bail money?"

"Not me and Ainsley. She left a few minutes ago. I'm taking about me and you."

I spin my chair back toward my desk. "What's wrong?"

She drops her voice to a whisper so I have to strain to hear her. "Ainsley knows."

The hairs on the back of my neck stand on end. "Knows what?"

"About us."

"How?"

There's a long pause, then she lets out a long sigh that reverberates across the phone line. "I told her."

I close my eyes and pinch the bridge of my nose with my free hand. "You what?"

"I had to. She saw our picture on my phone. I tried to convince her it was nothing, but she wasn't buying it. She was going to tell Jake. Apparently, they had some sort of stupid bet on whether we were going to hook up."

I pick up a pen and start nervously clicking it. "He was in here a few minutes ago sniffing around. Asked me if I had a new girlfriend."

"What did you say?"

"Nothing. I stalled him." I throw the pen down on the blotter. "Do think Ainsley told him and that's why he was asking questions?"

"No. She promised me she wouldn't, at least until we've had a chance to tell him ourselves, and I trust her. But one of us has to. Soon. She won't hold off forever."

"I'll do it."

"Are you sure?"

"Yeah." I rest my elbows on the desk. "Truth is, I wanted to say something when he came in here tonight. Only I couldn't do that without talking to you first."

"You did? Really?"

She sounds surprised and maybe a little hopeful. Now I regret even more that we're having this conversation over the phone and not face-to-face so I could read her expressions and body language.

"Really. Why are we being so damn furtive? We're not doing anything wrong."

"You're right. We're not." She hesitates, and I can picture her twisting a lock of her hair around her finger like she does when she's deep in thought. "But I'm not sure Jake will see it that way."

"I'll make him see it that way," I say with more confidence than I feel. I push back from my desk and stand. "I'll call you when we're done."

"Wait." Her voice has gone from surprised to panicked. "You're going to tell him now?"

"Why not? You said it had to be soon, right? And what's sooner than the present?"

"Do you want me to come over there? I could hop on the subway and be there in twenty."

"No." I shake my head, even though she can't see it. "This is something I have to do on my own."

"Let me guess. The bro code."

"What do you know about the bro code?"

"I've seen *The Hangover*." She pauses again, and I can hear traffic noises in the background. "So what are you going to tell him? That we're—hooking up?"

Hooking up. The words sound wrong coming out of her mouth. Cheap. Dirty.

I perch my ass on the corner of my desk and rub the back of my neck with my free hand. "Is that what we're doing?"

"You tell me."

I want to, but I also don't want to scare her off. So I go for the soft sell. "I hope it's a little bit more than that. It is for me. But we don't have to define it, or put a label to it, if you're not ready."

"Is that what you're going to tell Jake? That we're not putting a label on it?"

"If that's what you want."

"He might not like it. You might wind up with a black eye. Or worse."

"That's a chance I'm willing to take."

For you.

"I'm not sure I am. I'd hate to see that pretty face all banged up."

My hand moves from my neck to scrub across my jaw. The end-of-day stubble scratches my palm. "You think my face is pretty?"

"Don't be an ass," she says, laughing. "You've got a mirror. You know you're good-looking."

"Doesn't mean I don't like hearing it once in a while."

"Just call me when the dust has settled and you're

on your way home. That way I can make sure I've got an ice pack and some ibuprofen handy."

"Will do." I push myself off the desk and start toward the door. "But I won't need them. Jake's been my best friend for over twenty years. He might be surprised at first, maybe even pissed, but he'll get over it."

He has to. Because I'm not backing down. I'm not going to let some stupid unwritten bro code stop me from seeing where this thing with Brie is going.

I end the call and head down the hall to Jake's office. I don't bother knocking—he never does—and waltz in, unannounced. He's standing with his back to the door at the mini bar, pouring himself what looks like a scotch.

"Drinking on duty?" I ask.

He turns to me and lifts his glass. "You know the club has a strict no-alcohol-while-on-the-clock policy. This is iced tea. Want some?"

I hold my hand up. "I'm good, thanks. Have you got a second, or are you heading down to the floor?"

"Too early for that. I don't usually go downstairs until after ten. That's when things start hopping." He gestures to one of his guest chairs. "Sit."

"I'll stand. This won't take long." I hope.

He shrugs and sits on the corner of his desk. "Suit yourself. What's up? Did the booze distributer screw up our order again?"

"No, nothing like that." I change my mind and decide to take a seat. It's either that or start pacing the room, which would only make me more on edge than I already am. "You asked me earlier if I was seeing anyone."

"Yeah. And you skillfully avoided answering me."

"That's because the person I'm seeing is someone you know."

His forehead creases in a frown. "Don't tell me you're back together with Giselle."

I frown right back at him. "It's not Giselle."

"Thank God. You dodged a bullet with that one. I never liked her. She's way too high maintenance. Even her name screams pampered princess."

"You're the one who practically forced me to ask her out."

"That was before I got to know her."

"You could have told me you felt that way earlier. Like maybe before I asked her to move in with me."

"Would you have listened?" He quirks a brow at me as he sips his iced tea.

I chuckle. "Probably not."

"If it's not Giselle, then who is it?"

"I'm not sure you're going to approve of her any more than my ex."

"Why? Is she a demanding diva, too?"

"Not exactly." Damn, I wish that was scotch he'd offered me. To hell with the no-alcohol-on-the-job policy, I could really use a stiff drink right now. I take a deep breath and plunge on. "It's your sister."

He chokes on his iced tea, spewing it all over the paperwork messily strewn his across his desk. If I'm a tad on the OCD side, Jake is a certified slob. I don't know how he finds anything in this mess.

"You're shitting me," he says, grabbing a napkin from one of his desk drawers and trying unsuccessfully to blot up the dark stains seeping into his papers.

I rake a hand through my hair. "This isn't something I'd joke about."

He crumples up the napkin and tosses it in the trash. "Fuck. I owe Ainsley fifty bucks. She bet me you two were more than roommates."

"That's what you're worried about?" I say, disbelieving. "Losing a bet? You're not mad at me for dating your sister behind your back?"

"The behind my back part stings a little. I don't get why you felt like you had to hide it from me."

"I don't know. I guess I was worried you'd think it was weird. Or that I'd wind up breaking her heart."

"I'm more concerned she's going to break yours."

That has my defense mechanisms on full alert. I tense up and my pulse kicks into high gear. "What do you mean?"

"Your life is here, in New York. And Brie's career takes her all over the place. What's going to happen when she gets a job that's shooting in Los Angeles? Or Toronto? Or a role in a play at some regional theater in who knows where?"

Good question. One I'd like to know the answer to as well. But, sadly, I'm not a fortune teller. Jake's guess is as good as mine.

I will myself to relax, starting with my shoulders and working my way down. "Lots of people are in long-distance relationships. They make it work."

"Yeah, but is that what you want? Once this Netflix thing starts streaming, Brie's whole world is going to change. I'm talking red carpet premieres, fancy charity galas, big-time award ceremonies. Remember how much you hated that kind of stuff with your dad?"

Yeah, I do. After my mom died, my dad dragged me to a ton of his PR events. Book signings. Readings. Lectures. All those people, crowding around him, demanding his attention. Especially the women, once word got out that he was single, under fifty, and more than reasonably attractive.

My dad, being the world's biggest narcissist, ate it all up, of course. Half the time he forgot I was even there, unless he needed to use me as some sort of publicity prop. Look at me, Vincent Dow, father of the freaking year.

But for me, it was the seventh circle of hell. Having all those eyes focused on me made me squeamish. All I wanted to do was read or play hand-held video games in a quiet corner, away from the chaos and commotion. Eventually, as I got older, I put my foot down, and he agreed to let me stay with the Lawsons when he was on book tour as long as I let him parade me around like a show pony at one or two of his bigger events each year.

I keep telling myself that Brie's not my dad. That

things will be different with her. She may enjoy the spotlight, but she doesn't crave it like he does. At least, I don't think she does. And she's not a user, either. She'd never treat me like arm candy, there to make her look good.

Jake raps his knuckles on the desk, making me flinch. "Earth to Connor. You still with me?"

"You're not saying anything I don't already know," I admit. "But we're talking about Brie, not my dad."

"I realize that. But she's going to have certain obligations, and she'll want the man in her life at her side. How are you going to deal with all that public scrutiny? Hell, you don't even like making appearances at your own club."

I can't argue with him. So I don't. "That's your only objection? That I can't handle being Brie's plus one?"

He finishes his iced tea and nods, punctuating it by setting his glass down on the desk with a decisive thunk. "That's a simplistic way of putting it, but yeah."

"And aside from that, you're totally okay with me dating your sister?"

He stares at me for a moment, then nods again.

"Then let me worry about me. I'm a big boy. I can take care of myself."

There's a long pause, then he stands and rounds his desk, holding a hand out to me.

"Deal. Just promise me one thing."

I rise so we're on eye level but keep my hand at my side for now, waiting to hear the catch before I agree to his terms. "What's that?"

He gives me a wry half-smile. "Don't hate me when I say I told you so."

CHAPTER FIFTEEN

Connor

I LOOK AROUND at the throng of elaborately dressed cosplayers streaming into the Javits Center, then down at my nondescript khakis and classic white polo shirt, and wonder if maybe Jake was right after all. Maybe I don't belong in Brie's world.

Or maybe I just don't belong at Comic Con. I thought I was into geek culture. But these people make me look like a rank amateur.

I finger the VIP pass hanging from a *Walking Dead* lanyard around my neck. I'm still not sure why Brie wants me here so badly. I'm sure she'll have plenty of fans lined up to meet her and the rest of the Mortal Misfits.

But the bottom line is that she asked me to be here, so I'm here. I didn't have the heart—or the desire—to say no to her. It's like Jake said. If I'm her man—and goddamn it that's what I want to be—I should be at her side. No matter how damn uncomfortable being in the public eye makes me.

Plus, a little—okay, big—part of me wants to prove Jake wrong. To show him—and me—that I can stand up to the scrutiny. That although Brie and I are polar opposites in some respects, those differences won't drive us apart.

With renewed resolve, I fall in line between a frighteningly accurate Night King from *Game of Thrones* and what I think is supposed to a steampunk Princess Leia and make my way into the convention center. When I get to the attendant manning the gate, I flash my badge, and she hands me a program and a map.

"Welcome to Comic Con," she says in a monotone, probably sick and tired of repeating the same thing over and over to the thousands of conventioneers streaming past her. "The line for the Jensen Ackles signing is to the left. Artists alley, panels, and screenings are to the right. The show floor is two levels up, escalators are straight ahead."

Jensen Ackles? I don't even know who the hell that is. I might as well turn in my nerd card right now.

"Thanks, but I'm looking for—"

I don't bother finishing my sentence seeing as I'm already two feet inside the gate, well past the attendant, pushed forward by the momentum of the crowd. I manage to maneuver myself out of the flow of traffic into a corner so I can check the map and schedule.

I'm fumbling with the map, trying to open it with

one hand while holding onto the thick program with the other, when someone taps me on the shoulder.

"Need some help?" It's steampunk Princess Leia, the woman who was ahead of me in line coming into the convention center.

I hold up the partially unfolded map with a sheepish smile. "I look that lost and out of place, huh?"

She returns my smile with a mega-watt grin that lights up her face. She's the type of girl I normally go for. Petite. Curvy. Cute, if maybe a tad too perky. In different circumstances, I might have worked up the courage to ask her out. But that was before another petite, curvy, cute-if-maybe-a-tad-too-perky girl bullied her way into my apartment, upended my world, and dragged me into the craziness that is Comic Con.

"Not lost and out of place," steampunk Leia reassures me. "Just new and confused. Where do you want to go?"

"The Mortal Misfits panel. It starts in—" I turn my wrist over to check my Ulysse Nardin tourbillon watch. It's the one and only thing I have in common with my douchebag dad. A fondness for high-tech, designer timepieces. "Ten minutes."

"That's where I'm headed, too. I'm meeting some friends there. We can walk together."

"That would be great." I fold the map back up and stick it in the program. Thanks."

We head down a long passageway to Exhibit Hall 1A, where Leia tells me all the panels and screenings are taking place.

"So, you're a fellow Mortal Misfits fan?" she asks.

I dodge a couple dressed as Dr. Who and the Tardis, meaning I have to hustle to catch up to my escort before I answer. "You could say that."

"Are you meeting someone at the panel, too? Or are you here alone?" The side-eyed look she gives me lets me know which answer she's rooting for.

"I'm meeting someone," I say. "My girlfriend."

Girlfriend. As good as it feels to say it out loud, the word also feels small. Unsatisfactory. Inadequate to express the breadth and depth of my feelings for Brie.

"Oh." To Leia's credit, her smile only falters for a moment. Then she recovers and launches into an enthusiastic discussion about the panel we're about to see. "I've read all the Mortal Misfits comics. I was super stoked when they announced that they were making a series based on them. Although I'm not sure about some of the casting."

My fingers curl into tight fists at my sides. If what she's implying involves Brie, I don't like it one damn bit.

"What's wrong with the casting?" I ask, trying to keep my voice light and breezy, like I'm not seething internally at the thought of anyone being less than pleased that Brie's part of this series.

"Don't you follow that chat boards?"

"Chat boards?" I echo dully.

"It's all over the forums. Comic Book Realm. CGC Comics. Comic Book Resources Community. People are upset that they basically went with a bunch of unknowns. There was some excitement at first when everyone thought Brie Larson was going to play Sage. But turns out it's another actress with a similar name."

"Brie Lawson," I mumble.

"Yeah, that's it. Lawson." We're outside the exhibit hall, and she grabs my wrist, pulling me inside. "So you do follow the forums after all."

"Not really. I heard it on *Entertainment Tonight*," I lie, gently shaking her hand off.

"My friends are over there," she says, pointing to a group of steampunk *Star Wars* characters. There's steampunk Luke, steampunk Han Solo, even steampunk Darth Vader. "Do you see your girlfriend anywhere?"

I scan the room. The stage is still empty but the audience is jam-packed, barely a free seat to be found. For the first time the enormity of how much Brie's life is about to change really hits me. Of how much my life is going to change if I'm with her.

Jake's warning rings in my ears, but I ignore it. I'm determined to prove him wrong and shove his stupid I-told-you-so down his throat. He may be my best friend, but that doesn't mean I can't want to make him eat his words.

"Wanna join us?" Leia prods since I haven't answered her initial question. "With your girlfriend, of course, when you find her. It looks like my friends have a couple of extra seats saved."

My phone buzzes, and I pull it out of my pocket. It's a text from Jake with a question about our liquor permit, which I renewed last week. But Leia doesn't know that.

"Thanks, but that was her," I lie again. "She's got seats for us up closer to the stage."

"Well, enjoy the panel. Maybe I'll see you around later."

I thank her again for helping me find my way, and we part company. I snag a seat about halfway down the center aisle, between the ice princess from that Disney movie and the Mad Hatter, and thumb a quick response to Jake assuring him that the license is all taken care of before stuffing my phone back in my pocket.

As I leaf through the program waiting for the panel to take the stage, I can't help but wonder whether Brie's heard the casting bullshit Leia was referring to. If she has, she hasn't let on. I guess the keyboard warriors are an occupational hazard. She's probably learned to ignore them. But that doesn't lessen my irrational desire to track them down and defend her artistic honor.

"Hello, everyone." A microphone squeals, and I look up to see a tall African American woman center stage. She lowers the mic, waits a few seconds—presumably for the sound tech to deal with the feedback issue—then brings it back to her mouth. "Sorry about that. I'm Lynette Bell from Geek Girls

Rule, and I'll be your moderator for today's Mortal Misfits panel. Are you read to meet the misfits?"

A cheer rises up from the crowd, and Lynette motions with her hand toward stage right. Five waving, smiling individuals emerge—three men, two women—and take the five director's chairs lined up behind her. My brain briefly registers that they're all in costume before it zeroes in on one particular misfit in one particularly eye-catching costume that has my dick doing the Macarena.

It's not eye-catching in the sense that it's revealing. To the contrary, there's no gratuitous skin showing. Unlike so many female superhero getups—Dagger from *Cloak & Dagger* and Sue Storm from the *Fantastic Four* come to mind—Brie's—or Sage's—costume doesn't have any unnecessary cutouts. She's wearing combat boots, not stilettos, and a one-piece bodysuit instead of a glorified swimsuit or a skirt too short for any self-respecting superhero to chase bad guys in.

But damn if that bodysuit doesn't hug her curves like a Formula 1 race car. The black and gray-green spandex/leather combo is a cross between body armor and a sleek, utilitarian space suit. Functional, but hot as fuck. Sexy, but not sexist. She looks ready to kick ass and save the world without breaking a sweat.

I shift in my seat, subtly adjusting the crotch of my suddenly too tight pants. As I do, I realize I'm not the only one who's impressed with Brie's crime-fighting couture. Next to me, the Mad Hatter is not-so-discretely elbowing his friend—dressed, naturally, as the White Rabbit—and pointing at Brie.

"Get a load of Sage," he stage whispers to Bunny Boy.

"Sweet," his friend agrees. "I hope she acts as good as she looks."

"Who cares?" Mad Hatter says with a disgustingly creepy waggle of his fake orange eyebrows. "As long she's wearing that."

"Think she'll be at the signing after?" Bunny Boy asks.

Mad Hatter glances at his program. "Schedule says she will. Let's go. I want a chance to see her up close and get very personal."

He waggles those stupid eyebrows again, and I press my lips into a thin, harsh line. I'm not a violent man. I've always battled with my wits, not my fists. But right now I'd like to punch the Mad Hatter right in his unnaturally white face.

Fortunately for him—and me—Lynette's back on the mic introducing the five cast members, and the panel discussion gets rolling. Hatter and his buddy wisely shut up and listen, giving me time to cool off. The last thing Brie needs is her jealous boyfriend starting a brawl. Obnoxious fanboys are just another thing I'll have to learn to live with.

Once I've calmed down enough to pay attention, the panel's actually pretty interesting. Brie's fairly tight-lipped about her work—she's under a lot of NDAs—and I don't like to pry. But on stage, at an event arranged and organized by the production company, she's every inch the star she was born to be. Charming. Articulate. Unassuming.

But also genuine, honest, and vulnerable. It's clear she's not pretending up there. She's letting the audience see all her messy, fragile parts, and she's got everyone—me included—in the palm of her hand.

And that's when I know. The realization crashes into me, like a two-ton tractor trailer.

I am so far gone for this girl, it's fucking ridiculous. Inside-out, head-over-heels, ready-to-beat-the-crap-out of-any-man who-looks-at-her-sideways gone.

The rest of the panel passes in kind of a blur. My mind is somewhere else as I exit with the crowd. On the conversation I need to have with Brie. Preferably later and in private, not surrounded by costumed characters.

But first, she's got this signing thing, which, if the line that's forming at the Mortal Misfits booth in autograph alley is any indication, is going to take a while. And as her ever loyal, always devoted boyfriend, I'll be there by her side for every long, excruciating minute. Or as close to her side as I can get in this mess. Making sure she knows I'm with her one hundred percent.

And guys like Mad Hatter know she's one hundred percent mine.

CHAPTER SIXTEEN

Brie

MY BACK ACHES, my eyes are starting to blur, and my hand is cramping from signing my name so many times—on everything from to fan art to body parts. And I've never been happier.

It's happening. After years of waiting tables, eating ramen noodles, and pounding the pavement from audition to audition, it's finally, actually, unbelievingly happening. I'm in a series that everyone's talking about. The producers just announced that it's been picked up for a second season. And my character is being bumped from recurring to principal. Meaning more screen time, more money, and hopefully some movie roles when we're on hiatus.

The only fly in the ointment is Connor. Not that he's done anything wrong. He's been a perfect angel. I just wish he was sitting next to me instead of stuck standing in the corner, being chatted up by a guy dressed as Geralt from *The Witcher*. I know this must be agony for him. Connor, I mean. Not Geralt.

Yet there he is, sipping a bottle of water that probably cost five dollars—not that he can't afford it, but it's still highway robbery—and letting Geralt chew his ear off about God knows what. Every so often I catch him sneak a glance at me and our eyes meet for the briefest of seconds before I have to divert my attention to the person who is standing in front of me, shoving a program or photograph or comic book at me to sign.

It's almost embarrassing how that flare of connection makes my insides feel all warm and fuzzy. I've had my share of relationships—more than I can count on one hand, less than I can count on two—but no guy has given me the warm fuzzies like Connor does. It should freak me out. Two and a half months. Ten short weeks. That's all it took for me to fall hard and fast for my roommate. My brother's best friend. The guy who's known me since I was in pigtails and braces.

But it doesn't. Our personalities may contrast, but Connor is exactly what I need. He's the salt to my pepper, the light to my dark, the calm to my storm.

The only thing that's got me a little on edge is that I have no clue whether he feels the same way about me as I do about him. Okay, so there are some clues. Like the fact that he's here, surrounded by crazed comic fans in the middle of autograph alley, the last place on earth he'd choose to be voluntarily.

For all I know, that could be his way of thanking

me for last night's blow job. It doesn't necessarily mean he's ready for any kind of commitment. He's still fresh off his break up with Giselle. Then there's his parent's train wreck of a marriage. There's no way that hasn't messed him up. Maybe he's sworn off serious relationships altogether.

But that doesn't seem like the Connor I've been living and sleeping with. The one who gives me foot rubs and leaves little notes for me everywhere and lets me pick the movie for our Netflix and chill nights.

Although that last one's probably not such a hardship. The guy seems to enjoy chick flicks as much as I do.

When the line of autograph seekers finally thins out, he chucks his empty water bottle into a recycling bin and makes his way over to me.

"Hey," he says, his eyes flashing as they drift down to my chest then back to meet mine. "Nice outfit."

My heart does somersaults in my rib cage. I can't help it when he looks at me like that. He's got the whole Tyra Banks smizing thing down pat, even though I'd bet my grandmother's false teeth he's never seen an episode of *America's Next Top Model*. Chick flicks: yes. Reality TV: no, unless it's some sort of educational program, like the stuff they show on Nat Geo or the History Channel.

"You, too." I take in his crisp white polo and

neatly pressed khakis. "Who are you supposed to be? Jake from State Farm?"

"His shirt is red." His tone is mildly accusing, but any bite is undercut by the smizing. "No one told me I was supposed to dress up."

"Not everyone's in costume. I didn't think that would be your scene."

He bends down, bracing his hands on the table, and lowers his voice. "It's not. I'm just messing with you."

I raise myself up slightly and lean in so we're almost nose to nose. Not quite kissing, but close enough that I can feel the heat of his breath on my cheek. "I know."

"Is this guy bothering you?" Steve, one of the volunteers assigned to our table, asks from over my shoulder.

Way not to read the room, buddy.

I lower myself back into my chair and give the clueless volunteer a reassuring smile.

"No, he's not. This is my boyfriend, Connor." *Boyfriend.* My heart flip-flops again. "Is it okay if he waits back here with me while I sign these last few autographs?"

Steve shrugs. "Fine by me. As long as he's not in the way."

He ushers Connor into the booth, and I make some quick introductions to my cast mates and the production assistant who's been shepherding us around all day. Steve rustles up a stool from somewhere, and

Connor sits quietly in the back of the booth playing a game on his phone until I'm done signing.

"Ready to head out?" I ask, stooping to drag the duffel bag with my street clothes out from under the table. So much for the glamorous life of an almost famous actress.

He hops off the stool and stuffs his phone in his back pocket. "Would you hate me if I said I've been ready since I got here?"

"No. Because you stayed anyway. For me."

I go up on tiptoe to give him a quick kiss, earning me a dirty look from Steve. I'm not sure what his problem is. Probably has tickets to one of the big after parties, and our PDA is holding him up.

Sorry, not sorry Steverino. I'm not apologizing for kissing the man I'm 99.9 percent certain I love.

"Yeah, I stayed for you." Connor tugs on a stray curl that has escaped from my ponytail. "And for the five-dollar water."

I playfully smack his hand away and hoist my duffel bag onto my shoulder. "I have to change. Then we can go."

"Damn." He snakes his arms around me and pulls me close so he can whisper low and sexy in my ear. "I was hoping they'd let you keep the costume for the night."

Steve's really glaring at us now, but he'll have to wait. It won't kill him.

I reach up and pat Connor's cheek. "Dirty boy."

"Are you complaining?" he asks, a teasing smile lifting the corners of his mouth.

"Hell, no. But this thing costs like three times my salary. There's no way production is letting it out of their sight. That's why he's here."

I gesture to the PA, who taps his watch. Time to quit fooling around. Steve is one thing. I don't want to piss off the people signing my paychecks.

I sigh and wriggle out of Connor's embrace. With my fellow actors, I follow the PA to a suite that's been reserved for us to use as a changing room. When I'm back in my civilian clothes and my costume is safe with the PA, I meet Connor back at the booth, and we make our way out of the Javits Center and into a cab.

"Where are you going, my friends" the cabbie asks in a lilting Jamaican accent as I slide into the back seat.

Connor shoots me a questioning look as he slides in next to me and closes the door. "Do you want to get some dinner? I could try to get us a table at Rezdôra?"

I shake my head and give the cabbie Connor's address. Our address. The last place I want to be tonight is one of Manhattan's most popular, most crowded restaurants. "Can we order take-out? I'm fried. If I have to talk to one more person today, I going to lose my shit. Except for you, of course."

"Of course." He whips out his phone and opens GrubHub. "Thai?"

"Perfect."

I don't even have to tell him what to order. He knows. Chicken satay and drunken noodles for me. Fried tofu and vegetarian pad Thai for him.

The delivery guy gets there just as our cab is pulling up to the curb. Connor pays the cabbie, I grab the food and tip the delivery guy, and we head upstairs, greeting Ernie at the doorman's desk on our way through the lobby to the elevator.

Connor takes the food from me as soon as we're inside the apartment. "You must be exhausted. Why don't you take a hot shower and relax while I set the table and pour us some Riesling?"

I drop my duffle bag by the door, wait for him to set the food down on the kitchen island, then make my move, backing him up against the marble counter top and undoing a button on his polo shirt so I can press a palm to his skin just below his breastbone. "Sure you don't want to join me? Thai food is great reheated in the microwave."

His eyes narrow, his lips hovering millimeters from mine. For a hot second, I think he's going to kiss me. Then his hands span my hips, and he lifts me up like a china doll and sets me aside.

"We'll have plenty of time for that later." He rains little love bites down my neck, his fingers massaging my waist through my shirt. "Let me pamper you first."

Is this guy for real? A hot shower, Thai food, and Riesling, with a little—who am I kidding, a lot of—sex thrown in as an after-dinner treat? He's seriously too good to be true. I take some of the skin on my forearm between my thumb and index finger and squeeze.

He raises his head. "What are you doing?"

"Pinching myself to make sure I'm not dreaming."

"No dream, babe. This is your new reality. Or it can be, if you let it."

I want to press him further, ask for details. Is he talking about what I think—hope—he's talking about? Does he want to make our living arrangement permanent? Or does he have something even more official in mind?

But my brain has apparently gone AWOL. It's wandering down a path strewn with images of happily-ever-after. Before I can reel it in and formulate an intelligent, grammatically correct follow-up question, his hands move up to my shoulders and he turns me around so I'm facing the opposite direction, toward the bedrooms.

"Go." He swats my ass, nudging me down the hall. "Do whatever it is women do when they spend hours in the bathroom. The food and I will be waiting."

I shoot him a grateful glance over my shoulder. "Can I use your shower?"

The master bath has this amazing rain shower with a million different settings, including a rain curtain, head and body sprays, colored lights, and a fragrance mist. It's like bathing in a tropical paradise, without the water bugs and poisonous snakes. Heaven in twenty square feet.

Connor grins, showing off that dimple that always turns my girly parts to goo. "Mi shower es su shower."

"Gracias."

I take his advice and spend an extra long time under the warm, relaxing spray, washing away the stress and strain of being "on" all day. Then I wrap myself in my favorite silky, kimono-style robe, give myself a hydrating face mask, and blow dry my hair until it's only slightly damp and slightly more manageable.

When I finally feel human again, I pad barefoot into the kitchen, stopping on the way to pet Mirri and Ajani, who have apparently been fed and are making their way to Connor's bed for yet another cat nap. He's standing in front of the open refrigerator, pulling out a chilled bottle of Riesling.

Two place settings are laid out next to each other on the island, with cloth napkins, real plates, and silverware that's not plastic. He's got the forks and knives mixed up—forks go on the left, knives on the right—but the scented candles burning around the room give it a soft, romantic feel and more than make up for the lapse in etiquette.

The overall effect is imperfectly perfect. Just like the man responsible for it.

He closes the refrigerator door and turns, bottle in hand. When he sees me, his eyes darken and he

lets out a low whistle. "I think I might like this outfit even better than the last one."

"My 'Hang On Let Me Overthink This' T-shirt
and ratty jeans?" I tease, knowing full well he's not
talking about the clothes I wore home from the convention.

"No, the black and green catsuit. Although if I'm
honest, I wanted to fuck you in the T-shirt and jeans,
too."

"It's not a catsuit, it's body armor. And you
couldn't have wanted me that much if turned down
my shower invitation."

"Like I said." His voice lowers to a sexy purr.
"Later. Delayed gratification heightens the pleasure."

His words send a shiver through me. "Is that a
threat or a promise?"

"Can't it be both?"

He motions for me to sit and pours us each a glass
of wine. Then he joins me, opening up the contain-
ers of Thai food and passing the satay and drunken
noodles my way.

"You know what I love about vegetarians?" I ask
as I pick up a skewer of chicken and dip it into the
peanut sauce. "No asking to switch meals. And no
sharing."

He laughs and spears a piece of tofu with his fork.
"I hope that's not the only thing you like about me."

"It's one of your many good qualities." I take a
bite of chicken and dunk the skewer back into the
peanut sauce. Double dipping. Another perk of dat-

ing a vegetarian. "But right now, it's the most important one."

He seems to accept that explanation. We eat and
drink and talk like usual. This isn't the first meal
we've eaten together. It's not even the second or
the third. We've shared plenty of meals in our two
months as roommates-turned-lovers.

But there's something different about this one.
And it's not the food, or the wine, or the place settings that would have Emily Post rolling over in her
grave. It's not even the candles, which, admittedly,
are a new touch.

But they aren't what's making tonight feel special. Important. Like we're on the verge of something monumental. The air between us sizzles with
more than sexual attraction. It takes me a minute to
figure out what it is.

Possibilities. For him. For me. For us. For the future.

It's scary and exciting and more than a little bit
nerve wracking. We're playing a game of chicken,
each waiting for the other to make the first move.

Dinner ends in a stalemate, neither one of us
brave enough to take that first step. I collect our
plates, intending to load them into the dishwasher.
Connor pries them from my hands and puts them
in the sink.

"Leave it. We'll deal with the cleanup—"

"Let me guess." I lean against the counter next to
him, watching his strong, slender fingers as he pol-

ishes off his wine and adds our glasses to the pile of dirty dishes. "Later?"

"Right." His arm comes around me, hand resting, fingers splayed, on my ass. "Later."

He leads me to his bedroom—ours, really, since I've been spending most of my nights there—but instead of taking my clothes off or stripping himself, he shoos the cats onto the floor and reclines on the bed, pulling me down to lay next to him. He props himself up on one elbow and reaches his free hand out to trace a path from my temple to my cheek. "Have I told you how amazing you were today? That whole room fell in love with you."

How about you? I want to scream. *Did you fall in love with me?*

Instead, I sling a leg across his hips, bringing my naughty bits dangerously close to his junk. Not surprisingly, it's already half hard, just like I'm already damp. We seem to have that effect on each other.

I pull his shirt from his waistband and slide my hand underneath so I can feel his heartbeat. Its rapid, excited thumping matches mine. "You were the amazing one. I know it couldn't have been much fun, standing around watching me sign my name thousands of times. Being forced to make small talk with strangers all day."

"I confess to wanting to punch out a guy dressed as the Mad Hatter." He chuckles, the sound reverberating beneath my palm. "But other than that, everyone was pretty cool."

"Well, I'm glad you didn't get your ass thrown in jail. It meant a lot to me that you were there."

His eyes are heavy-lidded, his breathing erratic, his voice husky. "Where else would I be?"

"To be honest, I wasn't sure you'd come. I remember how miserable you'd get when your dad made you go to signings and stuff with him."

"One, you didn't make me do anything." Connor swipes a stray curl out of my face and tucks it behind my ear "And two, you're way prettier than my dad. Nicer, too. The way you took the time to talk to everyone what wanted your autograph—my dad never does that. Unless it's an attractive woman under thirty, with or without a wedding ring."

My robe falls open a bit—or maybe his wandering fingers have something to do with it—and he cups my breast, rolling my nipple between his thumb and forefinger. It's a slow, calculated seduction, and it's making it harder and harder for me to concentrate.

"Does that mean you'll go to another event with me?" I manage to ask. Now it's my voice that's breathy and husky. "Because the Soho Independent Film Festival is coming up in a few weeks, and I'm scheduled to present one of the awards."

"Do I get to break out my tux?" He moves against me, gliding his cock up and down between my legs, hitting every nerve from my clit to my asshole. "Because I look awesome in formal wear."

"I know," I moan, practically floating off the bed

when he ducks his head to suck my nipple into his mouth. "I saw you at the fundraiser, remember? And you can wear a tux if you want, but you don't have to."

"Count me in." He loosens the tie on my robe so it opens completely, exposing my bare breasts and neatly trimmed pussy to his hungry gaze. "All the way."

Then he strips his clothes off and we make long, slow love well into the night, communicating with our bodies what we can't quite say with words.

CHAPTER SEVENTEEN

Connor

"MISS LAWSON, OVER HERE!"

"Brie, look this way!"

"Who designed the dress you're wearing, Brie?"

"Miss Lawson, who's your escort tonight?"

The questions and camera flashes come fast and furious as we inch our way down the red carpet. I thought being on book tour with my father was wild, but this is like that on steroids. I stick my hands in the pockets of my tux pants, trying to look cool, but inside I'm freaking out. All those eyes on us. It's unnerving.

Not Brie. She's poised and confident and so damn beautiful in the purple sequined Valentino gown she and Ainsley picked out together, smiling and waving, stopping every so often to speak to a reporter from E! News or TMZ or Entertainment Tonight.

She snakes her arm through mine and drags me over to one of them, a baby-faced reporter with a bowl haircut and a microphone.

"Don't worry." She gives my bicep a reassuring squeeze. "I've known Doug since college. He's one of the good ones."

"He doesn't look old enough to shave, much less go to college," I mutter.

"Graduated top of my class at Pace," Doug says, wrapping Brie in a one-armed hug. "Right, Brie?"

"And yet here you are, one step above muckraking. What happened to winning a Pulitzer?"

"Guy's gotta start somewhere. I'm working my way up from the arts and entertainment beat." Doug turns his watchful reporter's gaze to me, sizing me up like I'm his next victim. Or his competition. "Who's your friend?"

"This is Connor Dow." Her grip on my bicep tightens, and she smiles up at me, telegraphing our relationship status and making my heart lurch. "My date."

"Date?" Doug puts hand to his heart and staggers back like he's been wounded. "Does this mean I'm out of the running?"

She smacks his shoulder with her purple sequined clutch, another new purchase courtesy of her shopping spree with Ainsley. "As if you were ever in the running."

"Well, it's nice to meet the lucky man who gets to be on your arm." Doug sticks out his hand for me to shake. When I take it, he pulls me in and lowers his voice to a conspiratorial whisper.

"Word to the wise—watch everything you say

on the red carpet. I'm not the only reporter with big ears. And next time it might not be something as harmless as a crack about my youthful appearance."

Crap. I'm not usually so careless. Or such a jerk. Chalk it up to nervousness. "Thanks for the heads up. And, uh, sorry about the dig."

He releases my hand and slaps me on the back. "No worries. I get it all the time. You can make it up to me by giving me an interview. Maybe even an exclusive on the new man in Brie's life."

"See, I told you he's one of the good guys," Brie chimes in. "But Connor's not giving interviews today. I, on the other hand, am happy to talk to you. And I promise, as soon as we're ready, we'll give you first dibs at the whole, sordid story of how we got together."

"Fair enough."

Doug motions to his cameraman to start filming, and Brie gives a short interview, gushing about how excited she is to be here and how lucky she is to be part of the Mortal Misfits. After the camera stops rolling, we say our goodbyes and thank-yous and start back down the red carpet, but we don't get two feet before our path is blocked by a woman who looks like a low-rent version of Rita Skeeter from the Harry Potter movies, cat-eye glasses and all.

"Brie Lawson. I'm Irene Fisher from *Celebrity Intel*."

"Of course." Brie smiles through clenched teeth. "Lovely to see you, Irene."

"And who's the handsome hunk with you?"

Brie warned me about this. Not the objectification. Although she warned me of that, too. Of getting hit with variations of the same question, over and over.

And this particular question isn't exactly surprising. It's my first "official" appearance with Brie, and it's only natural that people are going to wonder about our relationship. I've got no problem setting the record straight.

"Connor Dow." I'm not sure whether it's proper protocol to shake hands with a reporter your date didn't go to college with, so I avoid the issue by sticking them back in my pockets. "Brie's significant other."

Irene tilts her head and squints at me behind her glasses. "You look familiar to me. Have we met before?"

"Connor owns Top Shelf," Brie says, jumping in. "The nightclub in Chelsea. Maybe you've seen him there."

Not likely, seeing as I spend most of my time at the club upstairs, out of sight. But it's a shot.

Irene taps a finger thoughtfully on her cheek. "I don't think so. But I'm sure I know you from somewhere."

"I'm sorry, Irene." Brie looks past the reporter, down the red carpet, and up the stairs leading to the main entrance of the Academy of Visual Arts, the venue for tonight's event. "You'll have to excuse us.

The ceremony is starting soon, and we have to get inside."

I lift the cuff of my dress shirt and casually check my watch. We've got plenty of time to find our seats. I'm guessing Brie knows that. And Irene, too.

But if she's aware that Brie's bullshitting, the reporter doesn't call her on it. Instead, she pastes on a smile as fake a Brie's and reluctantly steps aside. "I'll remember eventually. I always do. I never forget a face."

"That woman gives me the creeps," Brie mumbles when we're inside and out of earshot of the press corps.

"That makes two of us." I put an arm around her as we follow the crowd up the split staircase to the second floor, where the theater is located. "I'm glad that's over."

"If only it were. I'm sure we'll see her at the after party. And if I know Irene—and I do, unfortunately—she's frantically Googling you on her smart phone as we speak, trying to figure out where she's seen you."

I don't like the way that sounds. The thought of that Rita Skeeter wanna-be searching the internet for dirt on me makes my skin crawl, even though, aside from the fact that I'm the son of the literary world's most notorious playboy, there's not much to find.

"This is us," Brie says when we reach our seats. Down front, on the aisle so she's got a straight shot to the stage when it's time for her to present the award for best actor in a narrative feature film, whatever that means.

The ceremony itself is kind of dull except when Brie takes the stage. Which, unfortunately, gives my mind plenty of time to dwell on Irene and her smart phone. What if she's already connected me to Vincent Dow, king of the modern mystery/thriller? Hell, what if she's already posted her scoop on line, and it's gone viral?

I can see the headline: *Rising TV Star Seen With Son Of Renowned Author And Philanderer.*

I've run far and fast from my past, and for good reason. I didn't want my success—or failure—to hinge on my parentage. I've worked hard to build a business with my best friend on nothing but sweat and determination. I knew dating Brie would put my personal life under a microscope, but until tonight I never fully considered what that might mean for Top Shelf.

"What's wrong?" Brie asks three too-long hours later, when we're in a cab on the way to the rooftop after party.

"Nothing. Just tired, I guess." I mentally smack myself for the lame-ass excuse.

"We don't have to stay long. Just enough to make the rounds and touch base with Miriam."

"Miriam?"

"My agent. She wasn't able to make the ceremony, but she's meeting me at the party. Fair warning, I've told her all about you, and she'll probably grill you even worse than the vultures on the red carpet."

"If you've told her everything, what's left for her to grill me about?"

Brie looks up at me through long, dark lashes, a flirtatious grin parting her lips. "Well, maybe not everything."

"Don't look at me like that," I growl. "Or I won't be able to stop myself from taking you right here in the back of the cab."

"Is that supposed to be a deterrent? Because it sounds pretty good to me. Too bad this cab ride will be over in a few minutes."

She's not kidding. We probably could have walked to the damn party if Brie wasn't in heels higher than the Empire State Building. In less than ten minutes, we're in the middle a rooftop garden, surrounded by some of the most beautiful flora and fauna—and people—in Manhattan.

The night is chilly, even for late October, but the space heaters strategically placed around the terrace keep it nice and toasty. I snag a couple of champagne flutes from a passing waiter and hand one to Brie.

"Thanks." She raises her glass and clinks it with mine. "It's funny. The last time I was at a shindig this fancy, I was the one passing out drinks, and you were the guest of honor."

I wrap an arm around her waist and sip my champagne. "I'm happy to supply you with alcohol and bask in your reflective glory."

Before she can respond, Brie's agent, an older, heavyset woman with sleekly styled gray hair wearing a dress that could double as a circus tent, sweeps in and steals her away to meet the director of some indie film she thinks Brie would be perfect for. I finish my champagne and make my way to the bar for something stronger.

"Scotch," I say, sliding a twenty-dollar bill to the bartender. "The best you've got. Neat."

"I'd offer to pay," a voice over my shoulder says. "But I'm guessing Vincent Dow's son can afford to buy his own drinks."

I turn to see Irene, a smug look on her overly made up face. She's got a photographer in tow, and he snaps off a string of quick pics.

"Can you tell him to put that away?" I ask.

Her arched eyebrows disappear under her bangs. "Why would I do that?"

"I'm not the story tonight. It's Brie you should be talking to."

"The story is what I say it is." The smug look is gone, replaced by a cold, calculating glare. "And tonight, I say it's the reappearance of Vincent Dow's estranged son."

"I never disappeared. I've been here all along. And who says my father and I are estranged?" I take my scotch from the bartender and move away to make room for others at the bar, hoping she won't follow.

"So the rumors aren't true?" She trails after me, dragging the hapless photographer along with her.

Against my better judgment, I give in to temptation and wheel around to confront her. "What rumors?"

She whips her smart phone out of her oversized pocketbook, taps on the screen a few times, then holds the end with the microphone up to her mouth. "Word on the street is that your father left your dying mother to have multiple affairs, and that you two haven't spoken in years. Do you have any comment?"

She shoves the phone in my face, expecting some sort of response. The one I'd like to give involves smashing the damn thing into a million pieces. Or sticking it where the sun don't shine.

I scan the room, looking for Brie. I'm not skilled in dealing with the press like she is. If she were here, she'd know how to shut this down.

I spot her across the room, in what looks to be an intense conversation with her agent and a hipster-looking guy in a tan suit and matching fedora— seriously, a fedora—who I assume is the director Miriam wanted her to meet. Looks like it's up to me to handle Irene.

I stare her down and calmly sip my scotch. "Word on the street is notoriously unreliable."

"Your father and stepmother recently announced that they're expecting." She pauses, presumably to give me a chance to express my surprise. Or outrage. Or whatever emotion she thinks I should be feeling. When I don't, she continues, undaunted. "What about your half-sibling? Do you plan on being a part of his or her life?"

Okay, now she's treading on dangerous territory. It's one thing to talk shit about me or my father. We're big boys. We can take it. I'm not letting her drag my innocent, unborn brother or sister into this.

"No comment."

She sticks her phone right under my nose, like she's coming in for the kill. "Is that because you're not even sure this baby is your half-sibling?"

My fingers tighten around my glass, the condensation making it cool and slippery. "What part of 'no comment' don't you understand?"

"A source tells me your stepmother was seen coming out of The Pierre with her tennis instructor while your father was in California meeting with studio execs about his screenplay for the Dax Russell movie. Isn't it true that she's been having an affair, and this baby is a bastard?"

My arm coils back to toss my drink in her face, but I'm too late. Irene is already drenched, dark, jagged lines of mascara running down her cheeks, tendrils of wet hair clinging to her neck.

"You crossed the line, Irene." Brie stands next to me, an empty glass in her hand and a determined glint in her eyes.

"I'd say you're the one who overstepped." Someone hands Irene a cocktail napkin and she dabs at her face, smearing the mascara even more. It makes her look like a creepy circus clown. "I could sue you.

Or better yet, call the police. Have you arrested for assault."

Brie doesn't back down. "I'm sure New York City's finest have better things to do than referee a catfight."

Irene crumples up the now soaked cocktail napkin. Her photographer hands her another, and she shoves the used one at him. "I hope you got pictures. I can have this up on the blog in ten minutes. The headline practically writes itself. *Mortal Misfit Attacks Reporter.* Your career will be over before it starts."

The room's gone quiet, and I realize it's because everyone is focused on us. Irene does an overly dramatic flip of her straggly, damp hair and turns on her heel.

"Come on, Paul. We've got work to do."

Miriam appears at Brie's side, her forehead creased with concern. "What the hell just happened here?"

I step in, drawing her attention from Brie like I'm a human lightning rod. This whole mess is my fault. It's my job to fix it as best I can. If I can. "Let me explain—"

She waves a hand, cutting me off. "I've changed my mind. Not here. Not with all these people listening. We need to leave. Now."

Miriam marches off like a general leading her troops into battle, and we follow her like good little soldiers, stopping briefly at the coat check to grab

Miriam's oversized fur jacket—faux, she assures us—and Brie's cashmere cape.

The elevator ride down to the lobby is awkward and silent. Once we're downstairs, Miriam finds a grouping of uncomfortable looking high-backed chairs in a quiet corner and sits us down.

"All right. Spill. And don't leave anything out, or I won't be able to do damage control."

I give her every last, gory detail. Brie chimes in at the end, taking the credit—or the blame—for throwing her glass of sauvignon blanc at Irene. Miriam taps notes into her smart phone, only looking up when we're done.

"You." She points at me. "You should have walked away when you had the chance. And you."

She points at Brie. "You know Irene likes to stir up trouble. It's how she and that gossip rag she works for stay in business. You can't let her get to you. Especially in a room full of industry power players."

"I know." Brie's eyes are downcast. "And I'm sorry. But she—"

Miriam waves her hand again. "No buts. I swear, I have half a mind to drop your sorry ass. I have plenty of clients. I don't need to be dealing with this shit at 11:00 on a Saturday night."

The color drains from Brie's face. "Please. I—"

"Don't worry," Miriam says, her tone softening slightly. "I'm not going to drop you. Yet. But you have to promise to do exactly what I say, or you can kiss your budding career goodbye."

"I promise," Brie answers solemnly.

"Me, too," I throw in for good measure. I feel as responsible for this shit show as Brie. More. Her agent is right. I had the chance to stop things before they started, and I didn't.

Miriam stands, tossing her phone into her bag and shrugging into her coat. "I'm going to make some phone calls. Try to head this thing off before it gets out of control. Keep your cell handy. I need to be able to reach you any time, day or night."

Brie nods, and Miriam reaches down to pat her hand reassuringly. "Don't worry. I've dealt with a lot worse in my day. Handled correctly, this stuff will blow over. But it can't happen again. Once is a mistake. The public will forgive you. Twice becomes a habit that gets you anger management counseling and a spot on every producer's blacklist."

"Understood."

Brie rises to hug Miriam, who returns the embrace then breezes through the lobby and out the door into the chilly New York night. Brie excuses herself to use the restroom—which I'm almost positive is a cover story so she can have a few minutes to herself—and I call an Uber, figuring it will be easier than flagging down a cab at this hour.

She's unnaturally quiet on the ride back to the loft, and so am I. Miriam's words keep ringing in my head.

It can't happen again.

Twice becomes a habit.

A spot on every producer's blacklist.

If I stay with Brie, odds are it will happen again. Some other bottom-dwelling blogger will bring up my background. And Brie, being Brie, will leap to my defense.

I love her too much to let her throw away the career she's worked so hard for and enjoys so much and is so good at. The thought is simultaneously breathtaking and bittersweet.

I love her. And I have to let her go.

"Well, that sucked," she says when we're finally inside the apartment. "But next time will be different. We'll be prepared for their questions. I'll see if Miriam or the studio's PR person can work with you."

"I can't." The words stick in my throat. It takes all my inner strength to push them out.

"Can't what?" She brushes past me into the living room, blissfully unaware of the turmoil twisting my insides into knots the size of golf balls, and takes off her cape, tossing it over the back of a chair. "Meet with them? I'm sure we can find a time that works with your schedule."

I follow her, each step heavier than the next with the weight of what I'm about to do. "No, I can't be with you."

"You mean you don't want to accompany me to any more events?" She kicks off her high heels and lifts one foot to massage her toes, painted a deep, rich purple to match her dress. "I can't say I'm not a little disappointed. But I guess I could live with that."

"You shouldn't have to live with it. You should be with a guy who's willing to support you one hundred and ten percent. Who's proud to be by your side every step of the way. And I'm sorry, but that guy's not me."

Tears are welling up in her eyes, each one a tiny knife to my heart. "Look, I know tonight didn't go well. But we can find a way to make it work."

"What if I don't want to find a way?"

I mentally cross my fingers behind my back for the lie. But if I tell her the truth—that I'm doing this for her—I'm afraid she won't let me walk away. That she'll choose me over her career and grow to resent that choice later. And that's a chance I'm not willing to take.

She flinches as if I've physically struck her. "Please tell me you're not saying what I think you're saying."

"I did this once with my father. I can't do it again. I'm not cut out for the limelight."

"If that's what you really want…"

Her voice trails off, giving me one last chance to change my mind.

I don't. I can't.

"You can stay here for as long as you need. But I think it would be best if you started looking for a new place as soon as possible."

I turn and head for the sanctuary of my bedroom. No stopping. No looking back, not even when I hear her soft sobs.

Because if I do, it will be me who won't be able to walk away.

CHAPTER EIGHTEEN

Brie

I HESITATE BEFORE inserting the key I haven't had the heart to return to Connor into the lock on the door of what, for a brief time, I considered our apartment. Emotion clogs my throat, and it takes a few tries for me to speak.

"Are you sure he's not going to be here?"

Ainsley nods. "Positive. He and Jake have a ten o'clock meeting with the contractor overseeing the renovations at the club. There's no way they'll be done before lunchtime."

"Good." Sneaking in to grab the rest of my stuff when he's not home may be a chickenshit move, but I don't care. I'm not anywhere near ready to face him.

I let us into the loft. When I walk through the door, a sad sense of familiarity overwhelms me, and I suck in a breath and try to collect myself, not wanting my friend to see how much being here is affecting me.

I didn't think it would be this hard. It's been almost a month since I moved out the morning after the film festival. Even that's not enough time to erase the pain of our epic, messy breakup.

Ainsley puts a hand on my shoulder. "You okay?"

I let out the breath I've been holding. So much for not letting her see me break down.

"No," I admit. "But I will be. Eventually."

Maybe if I keep telling myself that, it will become a self-fulfilling prophesy.

Mirri and Ajani come padding out from who knows where to greet me. I kneel down to pet their furry little heads, tears threatening the backs of my eyelids.

Ainsley lets her ever-present messenger bag slide off her shoulder to the floor and squats next to me, reaching out to scratch Ajani between the ears. "I still think you're making a mistake."

I drop my bag next to hers and swipe a traitorous tear from the corner of my eye. She's wrong, but she means well. And as much as I hated having to run back to her and Jake with my tail tucked between my legs, I'm grateful they took me in. Again.

"I'm not sure what you expect me to do. It's not like Connor gave me much choice."

"Did you try telling him how you feel about him?"

I don't bother denying that I'm in love with him. Actions speak louder than words, and she's seen me mooning around like a teenage girl for the past four weeks, eating chocolate chip cookie dough straight from the package and binge-watching *Tiger King*.

"It doesn't matter because he doesn't feel the same way about me. At least not strongly enough to make up for having to live under the glare of the paparazzi." I give Mirri one last belly rub and hoist myself up, taking my bag with me. "Come on, let's get this over with. The sooner I grab the rest of my things and get out of here, the better."

I lead the way to the spare bedroom I occupied when I first moved in. I cleared most of my stuff out the day I left, but there are still a few things I couldn't manage to grab in my rush to escape. Connor might have offered to let me stay as long as I needed, but that wasn't happening. Being that close to him and not being with him, not being able to touch him or taste him, would have been torture.

"Where do you want me to start?" Ainsley asks, taking her coat off and flopping down on the bed.

"Not there." I pull an empty garbage bag out from my oversized purse and toss it to her. It lands on the pillow above her head. "There's some stuff hanging in the closet. Just throw it in the bag. I'll sort it out later."

"Hangers, too?"

"All of it." I strip my jacket off and hang it the bedpost. Then I fish my phone out of my purse and open my favorite Spotify playlist, hoping a little music will cheer me up. And keep Ainsley from continuing to grill me about Connor. "Mind if I put on some tunes?"

She shrugs and pushes herself upright, taking the garbage bag with her. "Knock yourself out."

I press play, and Harry Styles' "Watermelon Sugar" fills the room. Ainsley gets working on the closet, and I take an empty box from under the bed into the adjoining bathroom to make sure there's nothing of mine left in there.

We work in companionable silence until everything is in bags or boxes. It takes longer than I thought—I totally underestimated the amount of stuff I left behind—and it's almost noon by the time we're done.

Ainsley tosses my Vans checkerboard slip-ons into a bag and slumps down onto the floor, her back resting against the wall. "Has anyone ever told you you own way too many shoes?"

"My brother. At least once a week the entire time I've lived with him." I slump down next to her. "Thanks for helping me pack. And for letting me come back and crash with you guys on such short notice. I'll be out of your hair soon."

"As if we would turn you away." She slings an arm around my shoulders, and I lean against her, happy to let her take some of my burden. "You're family. We'll always be here for you. Just promise you'll be back from Toronto in time for the wedding."

"Are you kidding?" I scoff. "There's no way I'm missing that. Besides, production says I'll be done shooting in a few weeks. That gives me plenty of wiggle room to get back here in time for all the festivities."

Including the bachelorette party her best friend Mia and I are planning for her at Top Shelf. But she doesn't know about that. Not yet. It's a surprise. Even Jake is sworn to secrecy.

"I'm so stoked for you." She gives my shoulder an affectionate squeeze. "Your first big feature film role. I want a front row seat at the premiere."

"I don't know about big. It's only a supporting role in a indie movie."

A nice, juicy one, though. I'll be playing a sexual assault victim who sues her attacker, the son of a prominent politician and champion of the #MeToo movement, after the justice system lets him off with a slap on the wrist. It's dark and edgy and the exact opposite of my role in the Mortal Misfits. And I'm working with one of the hottest indie directors out there.

I still can't believe he hired me after all the shit that went down at the film festival. Irene's article went viral the next day, as expected. But Miriam worked her magic. Got me on a few daytime talk shows, gave me a chance to explain my side of the story. And she was right. After a few days of seemingly nonstop coverage, the whole thing died down, and the tabloids moved on to the next celebrity scandal.

"Remember what I told you when you booked that

ensemble role in *Les Mis*?" Ainsley nudges my knee with hers. "There's no small parts—"

"I know, I know. Only small actors." I stand, brushing my hands off on my jeans. My stomach grumbles, reminding me that I skipped breakfast. I grab my jacket from the bedpost and stick my arms through the sleeves. "It's almost lunchtime. We should probably get this stuff out of here. And maybe grab some sushi at Shoji."

Translation: I'm starving, and I don't want to risk Connor showing up after his meeting and finding me here.

"Sounds good to me."

She gets to her feet, put her coat on, and hoists one of the now full garbage bags over her shoulder. I grab a box and follow her out of the bedroom.

It takes a few trips to get everything down to the lobby, where my doorman buddy Ernie has agreed to watch it until it's all out of the apartment and we're ready to go. We're finishing up our last run, about halfway down the hall on our way back to the living room, when the ominous click of a lock echoes through the quiet apartment.

Ainsley stops in her tracks, and I almost plow into her, clutching the box I'm carrying to my chest to avoid dropping it.

"Shit," she hisses, hitching the garbage bag in her hands higher on her shoulder. "Connor's home."

"Maybe it's his cleaning lady," I say, knowing deep down that it can't possibly be that easy. Not the way my love life—or lack thereof—has been going lately.

"I'm sorry," Ainsley whispers. "I should have asked Jake to text me when their meeting was over."

"It's not your fault. He's my brother's best friend. I'm going to have to face him at some point."

Although I was really, really hoping that point didn't have to be today.

I hear the door open, and there's no time to formulate any sort of game plan before the man who ripped my heart into a million tiny, painful pieces is standing in front of me. For a split second, his face registers shock and something that looks like remorse. But it's gone as quickly as it appears, replaced by a blank stoicism.

"Hey," I croak, my eyes drinking him in even as my head is telling me to proceed with caution. Is it my imagination—or maybe wishful thinking—or are those dark circles under his eyes? And his skin is pale and drawn, like he's been getting as little sleep as I have.

"Hey," he echoes, nervously rubbing the back of his neck.

"I used my key to get the rest of my stuff." I jerk my head at the box in my hands. "I hope that's okay."

"Of course."

There's a beat of awkward silence, then Ainsley pipes up. "I'll bring this down to the lobby and call an Uber."

She lowers her voice to a loud whisper and not-so-subtly elbows me in the ribs. "Tell him how you feel. You'll regret it if you don't. Trust me."

"Traitor," I mutter as she brushes past me.

"Bye, Connor." She stops to kiss his cheek. He may have broken my heart, but he's still practically family. I don't expect her or Jake to cut them out of their lives on my behalf. Which makes this all that much harder. "Don't be a stranger."

"I won't," he mumbles, shuffling his feet. It's obvious he's as uncomfortable with this situation as I am.

Ainsley turns back to me with a look in her eyes that makes my stomach sink. I know that look. It usually means she's got something up her sleeve. An I'm-not-going-to-like-it kind of something.

"I'll see you downstairs," she says. "But don't rush on my account. I'm sure you two have a lot to talk about."

She takes off down the hall, leaving me and Connor staring after her. A few seconds later, I hear the door to the loft swing open and click shut.

"So." The box is getting heavy. I shift it in my arms. "This is awkward."

"It doesn't have to be." He takes the box from me, ever the gentleman, even in less than ideal circumstances. "Jake told me you booked an independent film in Toronto. Congratulations. When do you leave?"

"Next week. As soon as shooting wraps on the Mortal Misfits."

I can't believe we're having this conversation in the hallway. Or that I'm seriously considering taking Ainsley's advice and spilling my guts to Connor. But she has a point. It's been a month, and my feelings for him haven't waned. I'll always wonder what could have been if I had been brave enough to open my mouth. And my heart.

I take a deep breath, swallow hard, and charge ahead. When the words come out, they come fast and furious, like a dam inside me has broken, releasing a floodgate of emotions. "Connor, I know you don't think we can be together. And I'm not trying to change your mind. But there's something I never told you, and this might be my last chance. I lo—"

"Don't," he says, low and pleading, cutting me off. His jaw is tight, his face hard. "Please."

An ache builds and takes root deep in my soul. "Why?"

"It doesn't change anything." Each syllable he utters is a fresh blow to my already splintered heart. "I still can't be the man you need."

What little hope I'd been clinging to seeps out of me, leaving me feeling like a deflated balloon. That's it then. He knows how I feel, and it doesn't matter.

I snatch the box out of his hands and push my way past him to the door, determined not to let him see me cry this time.

"Is there anything else that needs to go downstairs?" he asks almost apologetically.

"No, this is the last of it." Thank God. I don't think I could survive another encounter with him today.

He goes to open the door for me, but my icy glare stops him short. I shift the box to my hip and use my free hand to dig into my pocket.

"Here." I pull out the key to his apartment, the one he gave me when I first moved in what seems like an eternity ago. "I won't be needing this anymore."

I press the key into his palm, relishing one final brush of his skin against mine, and walk out the door for the last time, leaving my heart behind with him.

CHAPTER NINETEEN

Connor

I LOVE CHRISTMAS in New York. Or at least I used to. But this year, every classic carol, every cheerfully decorated window, every sappy, small-town-girl-goes-to-the-Big-Apple Hallmark movie is a painful reminder that I won't be spending the holidays with the woman I love.

She'll be back from Toronto next week, just in time for Christmas Eve. Not that I'm cyber stalking her or anything. But Jake talks, even when I'd like him to shut up.

He and Ainsley have invited me to join them for Christmas dinner. But I think they both know that's not happening, not with Brie in the picture. That would take painful to a whole new level.

A passing car blares its horn, making me jump and jerking me back to the present. I'm not sure why I thought it would be a good idea to walk the two plus miles from the club to my apartment. At 7:30, it's already dark. And it's cold enough that I can see my breath coming out in frosty white puffs. But despite the darkness and the near-freezing temperature, the long walk is still preferable to rushing home for another lonely night of frozen pizza and online chess.

I cross Broadway and pass a bookstore I must have driven by a thousand times before. But this time, something makes me stop and look inside. Maybe it's the line snaking outside the door. Or maybe it's the poster in the window that catches my eye.

Meet the author!
Vincent Dow signs copies of his holiday thriller,
Jingle Bell Glock.
Thursday, December 19
6:00–8:00 p.m.

Thursday, December 19. That's today. I know because I spent the greater part of my work day writing it on checks for the contractors doing the renovations.

I peer through the store window again, and sure enough, there he is. My father, sitting behind a table piled with copies of his latest release, looking—lost?

I take a second look, then a third, really studying him. This isn't the Vincent Dow I'm used to seeing at book signings. Gone is the charming smile, the flirtatious glint in his eyes, the dramatic flair when he signs his name. Instead, his smile is forced, his eyes humorless, his movements slow and measured.

It's like he's sleepwalking, going through the motions with poorly feigned enthusiasm.

Christ. I turn my back to the window, feeling like a jackass for ignoring the calls and texts he's been sending me all week. I figured he wanted to guilt me into coming out to the Hamptons for the holidays. A fate worse than having my fingernails pulled out one by one.

But maybe there's something deeper going on. My father might be a colossal tool, but that doesn't mean I have to be one, too. The least I can do is go in and talk to him. Make sure everything's okay, or as okay as it ever is with my dad.

Plus, it's warm inside, and it beats going home to my empty apartment.

Almost without thinking, my feet carry me to the end of the line. It's getting shorter—I assume because the signing is scheduled to end in less than half an hour—and I'm inside the bookstore in just a few minutes.

Once I get through the door, though, I start to reconsider my plan. Walking up to the table with a book in hand like some starstruck fanboy seems kind of like an ambush. So I duck out of line and into the nearest book stack, where I can kill time and keep an eye on things.

I'm about ten pages into a biography of a man billed as the FBI's most wanted fugitive—not my usual choice of reading material, but I'm stuck between the true crime section and one on wedding planning—when the last person in line takes a selfie with my father, tucks her signed copy of *Jingle Bell Glock* in her bag, and is on her way. I stick the biography back on the shelf where I found it and make my way over to my father.

"I'm sorry." A woman who I assume is the bookstore manager steps in my path, brandishing a stack of books. "The event is over. Mr. Dow has signed a few extra copies of *Jingle Bell Glock* for us. I was just about to put them out on an endcap in our suspense section. If you're interested, I could hold one for you while you shop."

"He can have this one." My father stands and comes around the table, holding out a book to me. "This is my son, Connor. He owns Top Shelf. It's one of the hottest nightclubs in Manhattan. Or so I've been told."

He sounds almost proud. I don't know how to respond to this new, unfamiliar Vincent Dow, so I take the book with a mumbled "thanks" and stick it in the outside pocket of my briefcase.

The bookstore manager's face flushes an embarrassed pink. "I'm so sorry. I didn't realize your son would be joining you."

"Neither did I." My father puts a hand on my shoulder. "It's a nice surprise."

The manager apologizes again, thanks my father for a successful signing, and goes to shelve her books, leaving my father and I standing awkwardly next to each other.

"I've been trying to reach you," he says after an uncomfortable pause, dropping his hand from my shoulder.

"I know." I scan the bookstore, wall-to-wall with holiday shoppers. This isn't the place for a heart-to-heart. Or a knock-down blowout. I'm still not sure which way this is going. "Do you want to get out of here? Get a drink somewhere? Or is Fiona expecting you back on Long Island?"

Something dark and wistful crosses his face. "I'll make time. We need to talk. Just give me a minute to pack up."

"Where's Pam?" He always has his assistant with him at these things. She's been working for him since what seems like the dawn of time.

"I gave her the night off. It's her husband's office holiday party."

Holy shit. He really is mellowing. The Vincent Dow I grew up with would never have given his assistant time off for something as trivial as an office party. I remember once he made Pam stuff and send out VIP reader boxes on the day of her daughter's high school graduation. She only made it to the ceremony on time because I was home from college for the summer and broke the land speed record to get her there.

My father gathers his things and we hit the first bar we find, an Irish pub. We grab two seats at a table in the back and order a couple of pints of Guinness.

"So." I lean back in my chair, my gaze flicking to

the rugby union game on the TV above the scarred oak bar. "You wanted to talk."

"There's no easy way to say this." He scrubs a hand across his jaw, which I notice up close is dotted with stubble, uncharacteristic for my normally fastidious father. "Fiona lost the baby."

I'm ashamed to admit that my first reaction is relief he won't have the chance to screw up another kid. But it's followed by shame, then sadness. For my father. For Fiona. For me. I was kind of looking forward to having a little brother or sister. Sure, the age gap between us would be huge. But that might not be such a bad thing. I could babysit. Teach the kid how to play video games. Dungeons and Dragons. Chess.

It would be like getting a second chance at some sort of functional family unit.

"I'm sorry," I say finally. And I'm surprised that I really am. Our drinks come, and I wait for the waitress to leave before continuing. "How's Fiona handling it?"

"Not great. She's with her sister tonight. I wanted her to come into the city with me. Even offered to let her run up my Amex Black card at Tiffany. Take her to for dinner at Le Bernardin. But she said she's not up to being out in a crowd yet."

"And you?"

"I'm trying to be strong. For her. But inside—" He breaks off and takes a healthy slug of his beer, like he's searching for some liquid courage.

I follow suit, needing a little courage of my own. "Is there anything I can do?"

"You don't mean that." My father's tone is flat, resigned. I start to disagree with him, but he holds up a hand, stopping me. "And I don't blame you. I was shit for a father. Still am."

It's true, he was—is—but I'm not about to pour salt in the wound. Like Brie said that day we all had lunch together, it's up to me to be the bigger man.

Brie.

My heart stutter-steps over her name. I reach for my beer again. Anything to numb the pain of losing her. Pain that's as fresh and raw today as the day I walked away from her.

It must show in my face because my father is staring at me over the frosty rim of his mug, looking at me like I've got an alien growing out of my head. "What's wrong with you?"

I lift my beer to my lips and sip. "What do you mean?"

"You look even worse than I do. What's got you down? Did something happen between you and your girl?"

"One, she's a woman, not a girl. And two, we're not talking about me now. We're talking about you."

He rests his elbows on the table, cradling his mug in his hands. "If there's trouble between you and your gir—woman, you should fix it. She's a keeper. It's not everyone who can put me in my place."

"We're talking about your life, not mine. Remember?"

"Fine, then learn from my bad example. I had the love of a good woman. And I was too stupid to recognize it."

"You've had the love of a lot of women," I quip.

"This is serious." He takes another, fortifying sip of beer then sets his mug down on the table with a dull thud. "When your mother got sick, I reacted badly. I only thought of myself, not her. Or you. My first book had just hit the New York Times bestseller list. I'd gotten a six-figure advance for my next one."

"I remember. I was twelve, not two."

"All that attention made me arrogant and selfish. And I think, deep down, I was terrified of losing her. I thought it would be less painful if I left her before—"

He breaks off, but I know what he means. Before the disease took her, and Mom left us.

"So I walked away," he continues, staring into his beer as if the amber liquid held the answer to all life's questions. "Maybe not physically. Divorce wasn't an option for a whole host of reasons. But emotionally."

"You think that's what I did with Brie? Walked away?"

His gaze snaps back up to me. "I read the tabloids. Occasionally. Saw the articles about the spat you two had with that reporter from *Celebrity Intel*. I put two and two together."

"And got five?"

"And got that you're afraid reporters will keep bringing up your backstory, and you don't want to jeopardize her career."

Now it's my turn to stare into my beer. I don't know if my father found any answers in his, but there are none in mine. "It's my fault she threw that drink. If I hadn't been there, she would never have been in that position."

"Your reasons for walking away may be more noble than mine. But the result is the same, isn't it? You're alone. And miserable."

"That doesn't change the fact that Brie risked her career to defend me."

"Isn't that her choice to make?" He pushes his beer aside and leans across the table to make his point. "A life without love is pretty empty, no matter how great your career is. Trust me. I know."

Damn. I must be living in the upside down.

My father is giving me relationship guidance. And he's right.

I polish off my beer and pull out my wallet, signaling the waitress for the check. "Thanks for the advice, Dad. I've got this."

"Leaving so soon?" He glances at his still half-full beer. "I was hoping we could talk some more. Next round is on me."

I study the broken man sitting opposite me. It's like losing this baby has forced him to reflect back on all the mistakes he's made. I know we're not going to fix years of dysfunction overnight, but if the guy wants to try, who am I to say no?

I smile, remembering Brie's words again. I'm the bigger man, that's who.

I plunk twenty-five bucks down on the table. That should cover the tab and tip. "Tell you what. How about I come out to the Hamptons Christmas Eve? Spend a couple of days. We can talk all you want then."

He finishes his beer then clears his throat. "I'd like that."

"Good." I push my chair back and stand, shrugging on my coat and grabbing my briefcase. "Now I've got to go see about a girl."

"Woman," my father corrects, grinning. It's the first real smile I've seen on him tonight, and it takes years off his face. "Bring her with you for the holidays. Tell her I'll try not to behave like an ass this time."

He stands, sticks out a hand for me to shake, then changes his mind and pulls me into a hug, chuckling. "And if I do, she can always read me the riot act again."

CHAPTER TWENTY

Brie

"Cut."

The director makes a slashing motion with his hand and I break character, swiping a tear off my cheek. Damn that scene was rough. Richard wasn't kidding when he said he saved the hardest one for last. But he was right. It gave me time to really inhabit my role, making her emotional courtroom confrontation with the man who assaulted her that much more powerful.

"That's it, people. This scene is in the can, and we're done for the day. Which means, sadly, that Brie has finished filming and will be leaving us." Richard hops down off his director's chair and comes over to give me a huge hug. "Beautiful work, love. Really beautiful."

The cast and crew break into applause, and I blink back tears. This has been the absolute best experience, with the most amazing group of people. In the few short weeks that I've been here, they've become like a second family to me.

I've been on enough sets to know how lucky I am. Not every shoot is like this. The only thing that would make it better is if Connor were here with me. Or at least waiting for me when I get home. But with the way we left things, I know that's not going to happen.

"Thanks everyone," I choke out. "I'm going to miss you all so much."

I swallow the lump in my throat and hug Richard back even harder. I owe him for taking a chance on me after the whole award ceremony fiasco. And he's already talking about a possible role for me in his next movie.

Richard releases me to go confer with our second AD about tomorrow's schedule, and Tom, the happily married father of two who plays my rapist, throws an arm around my shoulder. "None of that mushy stuff. Not yet. We've got your wrap party to go to tonight. Rumor has it there's going to be a taco and tequila bar."

"Oh, goodie. I love tacos. And tequila. Not necessarily in that order."

I put on a brave face and let him lead me from the soundstage we're filming on to the back of the building where our dressing rooms are located. We stop outside my door, and he leans against the jamb, crossing his arms.

"Richard wasn't bullshitting, you know. You're seriously talented."

"Thanks. That means a lot coming from you. And him."

"This movie is going to be better because you're in it. That first girl bailing was a blessing in disguise."

"I should send her a fruit basket," I half-joke.

Some actresses might be bothered knowing that they were second fiddle. Not me. I booked *Les Mis* in California when one of the ensemble members left to join the Broadway company. This time it was a big budget feature film that lured the actress who was supposed to play my role away.

Either way, it's me up on that stage or in the final credits. It doesn't matter how I got there. So what if there was a bit of luck involved? It's like one of my acting professors at Pace used to say—luck is when opportunity meets preparation.

Tom laughs. "Or maybe one of those edible arrangement things. But seriously, I hope we get to work together again soon. Maybe on Richard's next film. I just signed on to play the lead. And I know he's looking at you for my wife."

"That would be awesome, as long as it fits with my Mortal Misfits shooting schedule."

"If Richard wants you, he'll make it fit." Tom bends down and kisses my forehead, then gives me a nudge toward the door. "Go. Get ready for your party. I'll see you at the studio cafe."

He heads to his dressing room down the hall. I open the door to mine, looking forward to a few minutes alone to decompress before getting out of costume and wiping off my stage makeup.

Before I even step inside, the fragrance of fresh flowers overwhelms me. Lilies, to be specific.

Once I get through the door, I see why. On my vanity is a tall, cylindrical glass vase overflowing with stargazer lilies, their deep pink and white blossoms unmistakable. I walk over and bury my nose in them, inhaling their sweet scent. They must be from production, congratulating me on a successful shoot. I search through the blooms for a card to confirm my suspicion.

"I almost went with roses, but I didn't want to be cliché. The clerk at the florist said these symbolize prosperity and abundance. I just thought they looked nice. Smell good, too."

The familiar, smoky voice has my heart racing and my nerve endings on edge. I spin around and see Connor lounging on the futon across the room. He's wearing a plaid button down with the cuffs rolled to just below his elbows and those damn Jake from State Farm khakis. And he's never looked so good to me.

"What—?" I sink onto my dressing table chair, not sure how much longer my shaky legs will support me. "How—?"

"I assume you want to know what I'm doing and how I got here." He sits up and leans forward, resting his forearms on his knees. His brandy-brown eyes bore into me, their magnetic effect not diminished by the few feet between us. "That's easy. I'm groveling, and your agent helped me grease the wheels with the movie people so I could surprise you."

"Miriam?"

"Jake tracked down her number for me. It was on one of the comp cards you left at his place. Did you know she's a closet romantic?"

"Deep in the closet, maybe," I mutter. I'm starting to regain my equilibrium. And with it, my senses. I have questions for him. So many questions. But first, I need to hear what he has to say.

I kick off the sensible pumps the costumers put me in for the courtroom scene and cross my legs, smoothing my pencil-thin courtroom skirt over my thighs. "If you came here to grovel, you might as well get started."

He pats the seat next to him. "It would be easier if you were over here."

"No can do. I can't think when you're that close to me." And I need all my synapses firing for this conversation.

"Okay, then I'll get straight to the point so we can kiss and make up." He words are bold and brash, but the sheen of sweat at his temples and the way he keeps nervously licking his lips tell me he's not as confident as he wants me to believe. "I'm an idiot."

I try but can't fight off a slight smile. "That's a good start."

"I thought I was doing you a favor. Bowing out so wouldn't have to choose between me and your career. What I didn't realize was that it wasn't fair for me to make that choice for you."

"I don't understand." I shake my head to clear it. I don't know exactly what I was expecting from him, but this isn't it. "You said you were breaking up with me because you didn't want to be thrust into the spotlight, like you were with your father."

"I was lying," he admits, at least having the decency to look shamefaced. "I'll never be totally comfortable living life in the public eye. But if it means I get to live life with you, I'll learn to deal with all the attention. Because you're worth it. We're worth it."

"I'm not your father, Connor," I reassure him. "I don't act for the applause. And you're more to me than arm candy."

"I know," he says, so earnestly it's impossible not to believe him. "Funny thing is, he's the one who helped me see what an ass I was being. If it wasn't for him, I wouldn't be here."

"Your father?"

"It's a long story. One I'd rather save for another time. Right now, I can think of better things I could be doing with my mouth."

"Really?" My pulse rockets into hyperdrive. "Like what?"

"Come here and I'll show you." He crooks a finger, beckoning me over to him.

I stand and cross to him on legs that are shaky

again, but this time with anticipation instead of shock. He pulls me into his lap and wraps his arms around me. I let my hands wander, reacquainting myself with his chest, his arms, his shoulders, his back.

God, how I missed this. The strong, solid feel of him. He's my anchor, keeping me steady. And I'll be his wings, making sure he remembers to push his boundaries and go outside his comfort zone once in a while.

He lowers his head to kiss me but stops with his lips a fraction of an inch from mine. "Last chance to change your mind and save your career."

"First, our relationship is not a threat to my career. You've seen Miriam in action. She'll make sure that never happens. And second, my career comes second to my man. Always."

I thread my fingers through the hair at the nape of his neck, loving the feel of the thick, silky strands. Another thing I don't have to miss any more. "What about you? Are you sure you can handle the press? Believe it or not, there are reporters even worse than Irene. And don't get me started on the paparazzi."

"If you're trying to scare me off, it's not going to work. I'm in for the long haul. One hundred and ten percent."

"Then we're doing this."

"You bet your ass we're doing this." He kisses one corner of my mouth, then the other. "And a lot more. This is only the beginning. Now shut up so I can kiss you right, Blabby."

He does before I can object to the nickname. And then any objections are forgotten as he coaxes my lips apart with his tongue and we play tonsil hockey like we're teenagers under the bleachers after the big game.

A few minutes or a lifetime later—I tend to lose track of time when Connor's got his tongue in my mouth and his hands under my shirt—my cell phone chimes from somewhere deep in my bag across the room. I reluctantly drag my lips from his. "Crap. That must be Tom."

"Tom?"

He raises a jealous eyebrow. It's cute, but totally unnecessary. Connor is the only guy I've wanted since that day I showed up at his apartment unannounced and he opened the door in those teeny tiny gym shorts.

"Down, boy. Tom is my costar. And he's happily married with two adorable kids he FaceTimes every night. He's probably giving me grief for being late to my own party."

"What party?"

"It's my last day on set, and they're having a wrap party for me at the studio cafe."

He eases me off his already rock-hard erection. "As much as I hate to say this, you'd better give me some space so I can get Little Connor under control, or we'll miss your celebration altogether."

"We?" I ask, skipping over the fact that he calls his dick "Little Connor." That's a subject for another day. "There might be some local press there. If you'd rather skip it, you can wait for me back at the hotel. I can give you my room key."

"I told you, I'm in this one hundred and ten percent. That means wrap parties, red carpets, and anywhere else you want me at your side."

He stands up, taking me with him, and sets me on my feet. Then he kisses me, fiercely and fervently, like he's a thirsty man in a desert taking his first drink of water in days, and gives me a playful swat on the backside. "Now go get yourself ready so you can show me off at this shindig."

And that's exactly what I do. Because Connor might still have a lot to learn about show business.

But when he's right, he's right.

* * * * *

COMING SOON!

We really hope you enjoyed reading this book. If you're looking for more romance, be sure to head to the shops when new books are available on

Thursday 26th November

To see which titles are coming soon, please visit

millsandboon.co.uk/nextmonth

LET'S TALK
Romance

For exclusive extracts, competitions
and special offers, find us online:

f facebook.com/millsandboon

𝕏 @MillsandBoon

◎ @MillsandBoonUK

Get in touch on 01413 063232

MILLS & BOON

THE HEART OF ROMANCE

A ROMANCE FOR EVERY KIND OF READER

MODERN

Prepare to be swept off your feet by sophisticated, sexy and seductive heroes, in some of the world's most glamourous and romantic locations, where power and passion collide.
8 stories per month.

HISTORICAL

Escape with historical heroes from time gone by. Whether your passion is for wicked Regency Rakes, muscled Vikings or rugged Highlanders, awaken the romance of the past.
6 stories per month.

MEDICAL

Set your pulse racing with dedicated, delectable doctors in the high-pressure world of medicine, where emotions run high and passion, comfort and love are the best medicine.
6 stories per month.

True Love

Celebrate true love with tender stories of heartfelt romance, from the rush of falling in love to the joy a new baby can bring, and a focus on the emotional heart of a relationship.
8 stories per month.

Desire

Indulge in secrets and scandal, intense drama and plenty of sizzling hot action with powerful and passionate heroes who have it all: wealth, status, good looks…everything but the right woman.
6 stories per month.

HEROES

Experience all the excitement of a gripping thriller, with an intense romance at its heart. Resourceful, true-to-life women and strong, fearless men face danger and desire - a killer combination!
8 stories per month.

DARE

Sensual love stories featuring smart, sassy heroines you'd want as a best friend, and compelling intense heroes who are worthy of them.
4 stories per month.

To see which titles are coming soon, please visit

millsandboon.co.uk/nextmonth

JOIN US ON SOCIAL MEDIA!

Stay up to date with our latest releases, author
news and gossip, special offers and discounts, and
all the behind-the-scenes action
from Mills & Boon...

 millsandboon

 millsandboonuk

 millsandboon

It might just be true love...